Gill Sims

WHY MUMMY'S SLOSHED

Because the bigger the kids,
the bigger the DRINK!

HarperCollins*Publishers*

HarperCollins*Publishers*
1 London Bridge Street
London SE1 9GF

www.harpercollins.co.uk

HarperCollins*Publishers*
Macken House, 39/40 Mayor Street Upper
Dublin 1, D01 C9W8, Ireland

First published by HarperCollins*Publishers* 2020
This paperback edition published 2021

3 5 7 9 10 8 6 4

A catalogue record of this book is
available from the British Library

ISBN 978-0-00-835856-3

Printed and bound in Great Britain by
CPI Group (UK) Ltd, Croydon

WHY MUMMY'S SLOSHED

To Pauline
I told you it would be fine.

CONTENTS

JANUARY	1
FEBRUARY	33
MARCH	85
APRIL	115
MAY	155
JUNE	219
JULY	241
AUGUST	267
SEPTEMBER	305
DECEMBER	329
ACKNOWLEDGEMENTS	341

JANUARY

Friday, 25 January

I finished my tea and put the cup in the dishwasher. Despite a rather sleepless night, plagued with terrifying dreams of out-of-control clown cars careering towards me at speed, I was quite pleased with how very organised I'd been this morning – up and dressed, dogs walked and fed, and my precious moppets roused from their pits and nutritious breakfasts refused by them. I'd even found time to spend five minutes furtively perusing the *Daily Mail*'s Sidebar of Shame over a second cup of tea, while wondering if I should try 'flaunting my pins' to see if that could get me a new boyfriend, or perhaps I'd be better off 'showcasing my curves', or, better yet, I could give up rotting my brain with such nonsense before I found myself watching *Good Morning Britain* and agreeing with Piers Morgan.

This was the sort of morning I used to dream of when I was trying to shovel Weetabix down recalcitrant toddlers, who were more focused on trying to get Weetabix on the ceiling than in their mouths (do you have any idea how hard it is to try to chip dried-on Weetabix off a ceiling? It's worse than trying to get fucking Artex off). Or the sort of morning that seemed impossible when I was trying to jam shoes onto the feet of a child who had 'forgotten' how to put on their shoes, while arguing with the other child about why, yes, they *did* have to wear trousers to nursery and could not in fact just waltz in there bare-arsed, no matter how much *Rastamouse* they'd been watching.

Of course, my mornings are not usually like this. They usually still involve a fair amount of shouting things like 'I DON'T KNOW WHERE YOUR PE KIT IS, YOU NEED TO FIND IT YOURSELF!' and 'NO, standing in the middle of the room, giving a cursory glance around you and claiming you still can't find it IS NOT ACTUALLY LOOKING FOR IT!' and muttering dark curses as I attempt to log into ParentPay to fork over yet more money.

However, I'd been super organised last night, having made them pack their bags, including finding PE kit and art supplies, because I was determined there would be no stress, no shouting, no aggravation, for all would be calm and serene for Jane's sake, because today was her driving test, so she needed a peaceful environment to enable her to stay focused and able to concentrate. I felt a tiny bit smug at how successful I'd been in creating this.

I gathered up my keys, coat and handbag, said goodbye to the dogs, and called upstairs to Jane that it was time to go.

Twenty minutes later, I was still yelling up the stairs, with no response from Jane. I'd been upstairs and banged on her door and got some kind of muffled snort, I'd issued grave threats about how she needed to be downstairs in ONE MINUTE or I was going without her (somewhat pointless, as why would I go to her driving test without her?), and here I *still* was, now getting slightly hoarse.

'Jane! JANE! Jane, *hurry up*! We're going to be late! Jane, can you hear me? JANE! Are you listening? For Christ's sake, Jane, just get down here now, we need to GO!'

Peter stuck his head out of his bedroom door. 'Mum, can you, like, stop shouting, yeah? I'm on the Xbox and all my friends can hear you? It's like, *really* embarrassing?'

'Well, can you go and tell your sister that we need to leave *now*, please?'

'Not really, Mum, I'm like, totally in the middle of a game here!' said Peter in horror, clamping his headphones on again and retreating back to his room and whatever awful, mind-numbing computer game he was frying his vulnerable teenage synapses with now.

'Peter!' I yelled after him. 'PETER! Get off that computer and get ready for school, you're going to be late. I haven't got time to take you to the bus stop, you'll have to walk! Peter! Did you hear me?'

A grunting sound was emitted from Peter's room, which could mean anything from he was agreeing he'd heard me and would get ready, to being some teenage-boy communication code he was grunting down the internet to his friends, to the grunt being the noise the computer made when he murdered a prostitute. However, given that Peter is now several inches taller than me, I can't physically drag him off the computer, and can only issue dire threats and occasionally change the Wi-Fi password to make him do as he is told.

'JANE!' I bellowed again, wondering how many days, months or indeed years of my life I'd spent at the bottom of the stairs, howling fruitlessly for my beloved offspring to emerge from their lairs and leave the house. It would probably be a really depressing statistic, like the number of weeks you spend on the toilet in a lifetime, though I feel that figure about time on the toilet should not be given as an average, but instead broken down into how much time men spend on the toilet compared with women, because I still cannot comprehend how the male digestive system is so different to a female one that they need to spend approximately fifteen times as long in the loo. I suppose at least I can take comfort from this by assuming that next time I see something that claims we spend 213 days of our life just pooing, that this statistic is vastly skewed and in fact women probably spend about three days of their entire lives having brisk, efficient poos, and men spend eleventy fucking billion years on the bog, having their many multiple and protracted Important Daily Shits.

I was roused from this contemplation by Jane FINALLY slamming her bedroom door and sauntering down the stairs.

'At last!' I said. 'What *have* you been doing all this time?'

'Er, curling my hair, *obvs*,' said Jane scathingly.

'Of course,' I sighed. How foolish of me to think that there was any occasion in life that might take precedence over Jane's all-encompassing devotion to the Grand Altar of GHDs.

'Right, come on, we'll be *late*!' I said again.

'Like, just *chill*, Mum!' said Jane. 'Why are you always so stressy? It's not good for you, you know. You'll end up having a heart attack. And anyway, we've got plenty of time!'

'No, we don't!'

'Well, I'll just drive faster on the way there, it'll be fine.'

'Jane, no, that is not how it works. You can't get done for speeding on the way to your driving test! Apart from anything else, *I'll* get points too for being the responsible driver, and you'll be uninsurable if you've got a speeding ticket on a provisional licence.'

'If you're talking about me getting my own insurance, does that mean you're going to buy me a car if I pass?' demanded Jane.

'What? No! That's not what I said.'

'Well, what does it matter then, if you're not even going to buy me a car? How am I going to get to school if you don't buy me a car?'

'On the bus! Like you have for the last six years,' I pointed out. 'Anyway, this is entirely academic as you haven't *passed* your test yet, and you won't unless we go *now*, because you'll be late!'

Jane finally got into the car with another stroppy toss of beautifully waved hair, and we set off for the test centre, me in the passenger seat, desperately clutching the door handle with white knuckles and trying not to gasp in terror at every junction, nor to stress Jane out too much by screaming 'BRAKE! BRAKE!' every time I saw a car in front or 'INDICATE! For fuck's sake, INDICATE!'

I'm no longer allowed to chant 'Mirror, signal, manoeuvre' at her before she moves off, even though it's the only thing I can remember from my own driving lessons, as we had a rather nasty row about that on the day she pointed out to me that I rarely bother with mirror, signal, manoeuvre myself, which was why I once had a bijou *tête-à-tête* with a neighbour's car ('bijou *tête-à-tête*' is my phrase for it; Jane insists on referring to it as 'When You Crashed the Car Again, MOTHER!').

We finally arrived at the test centre, Jane having only stalled twice at traffic lights on the way. This was actually Jane's second attempt at passing her test. After sailing through her theory test with flying colours, and even nailing the hazard perception section (surprising, given her lack of perception of any hazards when actually driving), she'd insisted on sitting her practical test shortly afterwards, only for it to end in a storm of tears and recriminations and wails of it 'Not being fair' when a trembling examiner returned her to the test centre early, Jane having attempted to go around a roundabout in the wrong direction, something Jane insisted 'could have happened to anyone!'

I still had reservations about Jane really being ready to sit her test, based on the driving skills she'd so far demonstrated while out 'practising' with me (I'd been carefully picking roundabout-free routes), but her instructor apparently thought she was good to go. So who was I to argue, especially since it would save me forking out the GDP of Luxembourg on a weekly basis for lessons, as well as enduring the white-knuckle rides of the practice sessions in my car while I desperately prayed to the God of Gearboxes (if there was such a thing? Maybe it's Edd China, with his lovely big hands) to save my poor gears from their daily grinding. I couldn't help but wonder if it was fear for his own gearbox and a desire to be free of Jane's eyerolls and sarcasm that had led to her instructor's keenness to put her in for the test.

I couldn't even consult Simon, Jane's father and my ex-husband, about his opinion on whether she was ready or not, because during her one and only practice session with him, Jane had done an emergency stop after a mile and got out of the car and walked home, declaring she was never driving *anywhere* with him again because he was such an annoying backseat driver. In fairness to Jane, I'd once done the same, only luckily I'd been able to drive too at the time, so I kicked Simon out and made *him* walk home, because he really *is* a desperately annoying passenger, his right foot constantly pumping the air, as it searches for the non-existent brake, and hissed intakes of breath every thirty seconds at some perceived 'near miss', or his favourite, 'There's a vehicle ahead, Ellen, are you aware of the vehicle ahead, you need to slow down now, Ellen, VEHICLE ahead!' To be honest, sometimes it astounds me that I didn't divorce Simon *years* before I actually did, although at least he eased off on the passenger prickdom after he had to walk four miles home in the rain.

Unfortunately, Jane had the same examiner as on her previous test, and I did notice that the poor man visibly blanched at the sight of her. Nothing daunted Jane, however, and she merrily skipped off with the driving examiner, complete with his clipboard, but sadly lacking the beige anorak and driving gloves I always imagine for them, after overexposure to *Lee and Herring's Fist of Fun* at a formative age (I've had to fight the urge to shout 'Are you a FOOL? Are you a STUPID FOOL! You CAN'T EVEN DRIVE!' at Jane in our practice sessions, as I fear she wouldn't be mollified by my explanation that such things were what passed for comedy in the nineties).

Meanwhile I retired to the steamy café over the road. I mean it was steamy as in the windows, not steamy as in a porn café – do you even get porn cafés? Maybe in Amsterdam, where they're much more relaxed about such things. Here, there would probably have to be lengthy risk assessments completed about the dangers of boiling liquids and naked genitalia, not to mention the hygiene aspects. On reflection, it's probably best if porn cafés aren't a thing anywhere. You do get cat cafés, of course, although I wonder why you don't get dog cafés, given that most cats actually hate people, whereas most dogs (with the exception of my elderly and grumpy Border terrier, Judgy Dog, but I'm pretty sure he's part cat anyway) *love* people and would adore nothing more than a stream of strangers to scritch their ears and give them illicit cake under the table.

Obviously, I was musing to myself about cat/porn cafés (I suppose you could combine the two and just call them pussy cafés) to distract myself from dwelling on how on earth I'm old enough to have a daughter who's on the brink of being able to *drive*, and even more terrifyingly will shortly be old enough to drink alcohol. Well, legally, I mean. In an actual pub. As a result of what I like to think of as my 'liberal' approach to parenting, or what *Daily Mail* readers would probably refer to as 'lax' parenting, I've been permitting Jane to experiment with sensible amounts of not-too-strong drink for a few years. By which I mean I let her take some cider to parties and pretend not to notice when she's hungover to fuck the next day after getting rat-arsed on vodka and Mad Dog 20/20, which is apparently a *thing* among the youth again. Who knew? They have all sorts of exotic flavours now, though, like 'electric melon' instead of just the strawberry or peach that was available in my day. Was it strawberry or peach? Oh God, I can't even remember, it's so lost in the mists of time, now that I'm an ancient crone with a grown-up daughter. Just please, please don't let her get knocked up for at least ten years. I'm so not ready to be Granny Ellen yet. Though my mother might finally keel over at the horrendous thought of being a great-grandmother! … But even that wouldn't be enough to make up for granny-dom before fifty!

The growing up is all happening terribly fast, and it feels rather strange to think that soon, after so many years of the main focus of my life being keeping my children alive and fed, first one and then both of them will no longer be my responsibility. Before Christmas, we had all the stress of filling out UCAS forms and trying to pick courses and universities, when it only seems like about five minutes since I was doing that for myself. Well, I say 'we' had the stress of filling in forms, *I* had the stress of nagging Jane about it, and pleading with her to show it to me, and finally being told she'd sent it off without even letting me see her personal statement. She did eventually, grudgingly, tell me what she'd applied for and where, though. Her first choice is

Edinburgh, which surprised me, as that's where Simon and I went to university, so I thought she'd shun it on principle, but apparently it's good for History and Politics (her current chosen course), and 'It's, like, really far away, Mum, so you couldn't come and visit all the time.'

I got myself a nice cup of tea and a bun (oh God, I *am* practically a granny) and settled down to gnaw my nails and await Jane's return. I wasn't sure what outcome would be preferable, actually. Jane passing her test would mean she could give me a lift to the pub, and I wouldn't have to drive her places, but Jane failing her test would mean that I didn't have to share my car and wouldn't have to lie awake at night imagining her trapped in a tangled heap of metal in a ditch. In truth, my faith in Jane's driving abilities was formed when she was four and a half, and we'd visited my best friend Hannah, who had a little electric jeep for her children Emily and Lucas (who, helpfully, are also my children's best friends) to play in. Peter and Jane had been desperately excited by this, and considered being given a shot in it to be the most thrilling thing that had ever happened to them.

Somehow, Peter managed to get the first go, to my apprehension, as he was only two and a half, but Hannah assured me he wouldn't be able to get it off the drive. He managed splendidly, turning, reversing, and finally parking with a flourish. Then it was Jane's turn.

'I want Emily to come in with me too!' Jane insisted, and so her friend duly hopped in the passenger seat.

'This is so fun, Emily!' squeaked Jane, slamming her foot on the accelerator and flying straight through the hedge as we hurtled into the street after her, Jane still completely oblivious to her *Dukes of Hazzard*-style exit from the driveway.

'Oooh, look, Emily, it's got a phone. Let's pretend to phone Milly!' babbled Jane, veering wildly back and forth across the road as I bellowed, 'JANE! JANE! STOP! STOP!' and attempted to throw myself in front of her, as Jane paid no heed to the road or me whatsoever, as she was 'phoning' Milly, while chattering to Emily, one hand casually on the wheel and her foot still firmly on the accelerator, the brake pedal a mere redundant piece of plastic as far as Jane was concerned.

My final anguished bellow of 'JAAAAAAANE' as she belted towards a very shiny BMW parked a few yards away from her perilous progress finally got through to her, and she turned around to say, 'Yes, Mummy?'

Luckily, in the process of turning around, she took her foot off the accelerator and by dint of basically rugby tackling the fucking electric jeep, I was able to stop it in time before it ploughed into the shiny and doubtless hugely expensive Beamer. I've rarely been so relieved about anything in my life, as Jane crashing a car and causing extensive and expensive amounts of damage at the tender age of four would have given Simon endless ammunition in his 'amusing' remarks about 'women drivers' (this, obviously, was prior to me kicking him out of the car for being a condescending twat!).

I nibbled my bun and sipped my tea as the hour slowly passed. Seventeen years ago, it didn't seem possible that I'd be sitting and waiting to hear if Jane had passed her driving test. What was I doing seventeen years ago? Apart from feeling old and thinking I was already a dried-up husk because I was the ancient and decrepit age of thirty-one, which now, with hindsight, seems utterly ridiculous. I'm forty-eight and look upon women of thirty-one as mere babies! They are but ingénues, so hopeful and young, with not the slightest idea of how much cronedom lies ahead of them, or just how much they yet to have dry up. They're all hash-tagging madly on Instagram about things I don't understand, like 'bulletproof coffee' and kimchi and starting podcasts. Anyway. Seventeen years ago. Baby Music. I used to go to Baby Music on Friday mornings. Every Friday morning, sitting in a circle on a hard, cold, church-hall floor, attempting to pin a furious and writhing Jane on my lap while clapping along with the other smiley-happy mummies to an irritating song about an old brass wagon.

What else was I doing? It's all a bit of a blur, really. I walked a lot. I mean a *lot*. Hours in the park, pushing Jane on the baby swings, feeding the ducks, although of course now you aren't meant to feed ducks bread, which means already I'm finding myself saying things like 'In my day!' like my granny used to, and I'm mildly terrified that the next step is that I'll come out with some awful casual racism, and when I'm (rightly) upbraided for it I'll brush it off by saying something terrible like, 'But everyone said it in *my* day, dear.' And if I do it in public, then someone might overhear and I'll end up in some grim *Daily Mail* article about Political Correctness Gone Mad, and they'll misquote both my age and the value of my house.

There was a lot of pureeing vegetables and carefully freezing them for Jane to reject. I gradually learnt that the more Annabel Bloody Karmel assured me that *all* children *adored* some revolting concoction she'd come up with, the more likely Jane was to point-blank refuse to try it. Finally, one day, after spending an hour coaxing Jane to try the revolting sludge I'd spent the previous two hours peeling, chopping, steaming and pureeing, seasoning it only with my fucking tears, I caught sight of Annabel's beaming face on the cover of the book and something snapped. I hurled the damn book into the garden, then stormed after it and jumped up and down on top of it while screaming obscenities. I felt so much better for doing that, that I did the same to Gina Fucking Ford.

And then there was attempting to go back to work, when Jane was six months old, and feeling terribly guilty that I didn't feel guilty about leaving her at nursery to be Brought Up By Strangers, as my mother put it, as she thought it would be *far* more suitable if I employed a full-time nanny like my sister Jessica did, instead of risking Jane learning Bad Habits from Common Children when she was at a formative age and thus could never be broken of them. My mother was vague on the subject of what Bad Habits she thought Jane was going to adopt, and even vaguer on the subject of how she thought I was going to pay for a full-time nanny. The bliss, though, of stepping through that door and handing Jane over to someone else for a few hours while I went and had adult conversations and used my mind and got to eat a sandwich without someone screaming for a bit and then spitting it over me when I gave them some.

Nothing makes you appreciate even the most socially inept of colleagues like the alternative being the company of small children. Of course, it was a logistical nightmare trying to go back to work, but for me it was worth it, if just to feel slightly like myself again. The judgement on all sides was hideous, of course – the stay-at-home mummies tutted about how could the dreadful working mothers leave their babies, the full-time working mothers tutted that I didn't know how easy it was only working part-time, and the other part-timers all insisted their jobs were the most stressful and no one knew how hard it was juggling everything.

What was Simon doing seventeen years ago? I don't really remember. I've vague recollections of a shadowy figure who required dinners made and complained about being tired a lot, because Jane was a terrible sleeper who was still up through the night until she was nearly eighteen months old. This was despite never being the one who actually got out of his bed and went to see to her, because he had to go to work and be Busy and Important, even once my maternity leave had finished and I was back at work. And when I was pregnant with Peter and so tired I thought I might actually die from it, he apparently found me getting up and down to Jane very disruptive to his night's sleep.

With hindsight, I'm buggered if I know how I even managed to get pregnant with Peter. I don't recall actually ever having the time or inclination for sex, but at some point I must have put out (possibly for Simon's birthday), because there's the evidence in the form of Peter, and although I'd never tell him this, he was in fact something of an accident, because Jane almost broke me. Not only do I not recall any sex, I also don't recall any conversations we had in those days apart from furious games of competitive tiredness, and one night when he walked into the kitchen while I was chopping carrots, when he started complaining about something, I just stared down at the knife and considered plunging it into his heart. I gave serious consideration to how much force I'd have to use. I was even trying to remember which side the heart was on so I could aim correctly, and working out that I needed to remember to aim for *his* left, not mine, when Jane started crying and the moment was lost.

Obviously, it's just as well the moment was lost, as it's unlikely Jane would currently be out there sitting her driving test had I murdered her father and spent the rest of her childhood in prison, and of course, if I'd done that, Peter would not have existed at all. A lack of Peter in the world would definitely be very sad, but it would probably have done wonders for our carbon footprint as a family, given the amount of food he eats, electricity he uses on gaming and methane he produces, as he's farted pretty much constantly from birth and shows no sign of letting up. And then there's the loo roll. We never have any loo roll, so I'm starting to think he eats it. I'm constantly at the shop buying more – I have to rotate which check-out person I go to, in case they think I have some kind of terrible digestive problem.

And we won't even touch on his excessive tissue consumption. Part of me thinks for green reasons I should furnish him with handkerchiefs, but the other part of me thinks the polar bears will just have to take their chances as I cannot actually face the idea of washing the dubious matter out of a teenage boy's handkerchief, assuming of course that he wouldn't just use his sock in the absence of tissues. I wonder what the menfolk did about such things in the olden days before tissues. *Did* they just use their hankies? Or their stockings? Leaves? I'm pretty sure interfering with oneself is not a modern-day phenomenon, but it's not really the sort of thing one can go into a museum and ask about, is it? 'I'm interested in research into historical wanking …' Nor could one really contact climate-change organisations and ask for greener alternatives for teenage boys' self-love habits.

These thoughts quite put me off my bun, and I realised my tea had gone cold, when Jane erupted into the café.

'I PASSED!' she shrieked. 'I DID IT! I'M ROADWORTHY, MOTHER! LET'S GO!'

'That's wonderful, darling!' I said. 'I knew you could do it!' I added untruthfully. 'Did you have to reverse around a corner?'

'No,' said Jane scornfully. 'And now I'll never have to. It's, like, a *pointless* manoeuvre.'

'Have you called Daddy and told him?' I asked.

'Not yet, I wanted to tell you first!' beamed Jane. 'Also, you know, thanks, Mum. For taking me out to practise so much and everything.'

It's rare that your children thank you, or appreciate you, or see you as anything other than the provider of food and profferer of unwanted and unsolicited and, in their opinion, pointless and incorrect advice. But on those exceptional occasions when the blinkers of teenagerdom fall briefly from their eyes and they see you as a person, not just a parent, and they show an appreciation for the role you play in their life, it makes the sleepless nights, the Annabel Fucking Karmel purees, the eye rolls and door slams and the incessant furious 'Oh, *Mother*'s spat at you, almost, very nearly, worth it.

'You're welcome, darling,' I beamed, feeling like I was, for once, bloody *nailing* parenting. Of course, it never lasts, either the sensation that you're getting things right or your offspring being civil and pleasant.

We left the café and walked over to where the car was parked.

'So, anyway, I'll be using the car tonight, obviously,' Jane said blithely. 'Just letting you know.'

'Errr, don't you think perhaps you should *ask* if you can use *my* car, rather than just telling me?' I suggested gently.

'Well, I wouldn't have to use your car, would I, if you'd only buy me one of my own!' said Jane indignantly.

'Anyway, you can't use the car till I've sorted the insurance,' I pointed out.

'Oh my *God*, Mother, *why* are you so difficult about *everything*!' snapped Jane, our lovely moment well and truly over.

'I'm not being difficult, it's the bloody *law*!' I reminded her.

'Oh, whatever!' she huffed. 'Well, can't you just get it sorted so I can drive to Amy's party tonight?'

'I'm really not sure about you driving to a party and coming home by yourself late at night,' I fretted. 'You haven't really driven much in the dark.'

'But I won't *be* by myself, will I? I'll have Sophie and Emily and Tilly and Millie. I've promised them a lift!'

'How? How have you promised them a lift? You've literally only just passed your test.'

'I texted them on the way across the road.'

Marvellous. So I wasn't the first person she'd told after all. I comforted myself that at least I was the first *adult*.

'Jane,' I said firmly. 'No. You're not taking my car out to drive home at 2 a.m. with it full of your drunken mates. It's not happening. No. We'll discuss insurance later, but for now you need to go back to school and I need to go back to work. Anyway,' I wheedled, 'if you're driving tonight, you won't be able to drink, will you?'

'I know that, OBVIOUSLY,' said Jane hastily, though I could see from the panic on her face that it hadn't occurred to her that being the designated driver would mean watching her friends get off their tits while she made do with Coke Zero, and that maybe it wouldn't be that much fun after all.

'Look, I'll talk to your dad about us *looking into* how much it would cost to buy and insure and run a little car for you, but Jane, these things are expensive. I don't have unlimited money to pay for all this, especially with you going to university soon.'

'I *know*!' said Jane. 'I'll get a job and pay for my own petrol and … and oil … and stuff.'

I made a note to have an adult conversation with Jane about basic car maintenance and running.

'For now, why don't you just call Daddy and tell him you've passed?' I suggested.

'I was *literally* just about to!' said Jane.

She tapped out Simon's number, and next thing a female voice purred down the line. 'Hi Jane, this is Marissa. I'm afraid Simon can't come to the phone right now, he's driving.'

Marissa. Marvellous. Simon's pert, lithe, glossy-haired and youthful witch of a girlfriend. I mean, OK, she's not *that* youthful, but she's thirty-eight, which makes her youthful compared with me, and I suddenly felt very hot and I had my usual panic that I was starting to get hot flushes, but it turned out it was just a surge of the burning rage that Marissa provokes in me.

I don't know why I hate her so much. I mean, technically, on paper, she's not a bad person. In fact, if one is to be objective about it, she's actually a Very Good Person. She works for a company that produces sustainable alternatives to single-use plastics (admittedly in the accounts department, rather than designing the products, which mainly seem to be very expensive water bottles and coffee cups that they flog to yummy mummies to drink soy lattes out of after yoga class), and she volunteers in her spare time with a charity teaching English to refugees, and she does lots and lots of yoga, too, so much fucking yoga, and she even has a three-legged rescue cat, for fuck's sake, because she's Such a Good Person.

But Jesus FUCKING Christ, she's also incredibly annoying, and patronising. In fact, she's the smuggest smuggety smug fucker I've ever had the misfortune to encounter in my life. I'm not just saying that because I'm jealous of her shiny, swishy hair or her colour co-ordinated Instagram grid where she posts every single goddamned yoga workout and the books she's taught the poor refugees to read in English in double-quick time (in my mind, Marissa's refugees' language skills improve so fast because they too are desperate to get away from her smug little face, but they're probably incredibly grateful and have shrines in their house to St Marissa). She even manages to make the photos of her three-legged cat annoy me, which is remarkable because I love animals, though obviously my dogs Judgy and Barry are much better than her stupid cat. But surely to make a three-legged cat annoying suggests that your smugness is *literally* off the scale?

Part of me fears, though, that my hatred of Marissa (who's even called Marissa? I thought the only people called that were quirky Americans in the nineties, with interesting haircuts and pixie boots, but clearly not) is not so much about her, but is just good old-fashioned jealousy that while Simon has moved on and found someone, and thus is winning at Who Is Better at Being Divorced, I'm still single.

But for a while I was smashing that game, winning effortlessly.

I had my handsome and fabulous boyfriend Jack, and Simon had been rather satisfyingly moony over me still, not least because I'd been an amazing and supportive ex-wife extraordinaire, holding the fort at home and looking after his children almost full-time when he took a six-month sabbatical after his father was diagnosed with prostate cancer. Simon had to go and stay with his parents, who had retired to France, so he could take his dad to medical appointments because his mother 'doesn't do foreign driving' (I mean, in fairness, neither do I, but I also didn't move to a country where it would be a necessity), and generally support them. I'd also arranged flights for his children to visit him and their grandparents, and dropped off and picked up from airports, and overall just been a very good person. So really it was only fair that Simon realised what a terrible mistake he'd made in letting me go and had suffered for it, especially when he saw how very happy I was with Jack.

Then, in a move typical of my luck, my perfect boyfriend Jack packed his bloody thermals and buggered off to his Dream Job in Antarctica, just after Simon came home from France. France had suited Simon. He was all tanned and he'd lost weight, and he'd bought some rather chic clothes and was generally looking annoyingly hot, which might have had something to do with the fact that the next thing I knew was that he popped up with fucking Marissa one day. Marissa, all pert and perky and ten fucking years younger than me, which is actually a terrible worry because she's still of childbearing age, and will be for some time, as my best and oldest friend Hannah evidenced by finding herself upduffed at the age of forty-six and producing a rather unexpected bundle called Edward, who's now two and a wrecking ball in human form.

I don't think I could actually stand the smugness from Marissa if she were to get herself impregnated by Simon. I just *know* she's the sort of person who would beam things like 'We're pregnant!' rather than 'I'm pregnant.' Simon once told people 'we' were pregnant, and I snarled that 'we' were not fucking pregnant, *I* was pregnant, but if he wanted to recreate the sensation of pregnancy then that could be arranged by strapping a concrete weight to his stomach, repeatedly punching him in the bladder, denying him anything nice to eat or drink EVER, making him swallow acid to recreate the delightful sensation of pregnancy heartburn, then finishing off the experience by cramming a pineapple up his arse sideways and making him shit it out. And for extra fun, I could rip his dick open and sew it up for him. Then I burst into tears and Simon had to take me home, as everyone else at the party was staring at me oddly. I didn't cope well with pregnancy. Marissa, though, would doubtless glow when with child, and float around in white cheesecloth dresses, smugly stroking her perfect little bump and not getting piles.

Anyway. I mustn't let Marissa wind me up so much. Jane asked her to put Simon on the speakerphone, and duly imparted her momentous news.

'Oh, that's *wonderful*!' squealed Marissa, before Simon could even say a word. 'You must be so excited, *well done*, Jane, darling.'

'Er, yeah, well done, darling!' echoed Simon.

'So Mum says that you and her are like going to buy me a car?' announced Jane.

'What!' said Simon.

'I did not!' I said indignantly, grabbing the phone off Jane, as Marissa cooed, 'A car, Jane, darling? I mean, it's *marvellous* that you've passed your test, it's a very useful life skill to have, but getting a car of your own will only increase your carbon footprint and encourage unnecessary journeys. Why don't you get a bike? It's a really efficient mode of transport, and super eco-friendly.'

Jane was making mutinous noises about a bike when Simon interrupted Marissa.

'Why would you say that, Ellen?' he huffed. 'You can't just make promises like that on my behalf.'

'I just *said* I didn't say that!' I repeated. 'What I told Jane was that I'd discuss it with you and we'd see if it was financially viable for us to do something between us, that's all.'

'And me!' chirped Marissa. 'I have a lot of valuable input to offer too.'

'Why?' I asked. 'Are you going to contribute to a car for Jane?'

'Well, no, but I can send you some information about how many miles of rainforest are destroyed per new car built, and also I've done a lot of research into bikes, so I can help with that, which I really think is a better solution and –'

'But I don't want a bike, I want a *car*,' whined Jane. 'I've *got* a bike. It's rubbish.'

'Yes, but Jane, if you had a really super-duper high-end bike, I think that would make a lot of difference,' insisted Marissa. 'Just think about it, OK, Jane? Promise me you'll think about it.'

'I think Marissa's right,' said Simon heartily. 'A really good bike sounds a great idea, darling.'

Jane made huffing and non-committal noises about thinking about a bike, and decided to move on to the next battle to be fought.

'Why aren't you at work anyway, Dad?' said Jane. 'Mum says I have to go back to school after this. Do I really?'

I strained my ears to listen.

'We've both taken today off because we're going on a couples' retreat in Dorset,' said Marissa.

'A *couples'* retreat?' said Jane incredulously. 'Ewww. Is that, like, threesomes and sex parties and stuff? That's *totally* disgusting, Dad!'

'No, of course it's not like that,' said Marissa in her calmest, nicest, I-Am-a-Very-Good-Person-and-Shall-Not-Get-Annoyed-by-the-Inferior-Beings voice. 'It involves a weekend of connecting as a couple, strengthening and deepening our bond through intense work with counsellors and trust exercises and –'

'Do you meditate?' interrupted Jane.

'What? Yes, yes, couples' meditation is one of the workshops,' said Marissa smugly.

'It sounds a pile of wank,' said Jane cheerfully.

'Oh, Jane,' sighed Marissa. 'Don't be so quick to judge what you don't understand. It's vital to couples' well-being to nurture and care for their relationship. You have to be proactive about relationships, you know, if you don't want to end up alone. You often find that the reason a person has a string of failed relationships behind them is because they just couldn't be bothered to put the work in.'

Was that directed at me? That was definitely directed at me. Ouch! Oh, Marissa's good, I'll give her that – sweetness and light and discreet little barbs, just sharp enough to sting, but subtle enough that if you objected you'd either look paranoid and over-sensitive, or Marissa would look at you caringly and say, 'Of course it wasn't about you, but it seems to be resonating with you for some reason. Why do you think you feel that so personally? Would you like to talk about it?' OF COURSE I DON'T WANT TO TALK ABOUT IT, I'M BRITISH. And if I DID want to talk about it, it wouldn't be with you, with your stupid shiny hair, and your head on one side doing your special Caring Look. Single I may be, failed relationships I may have, but given the choice between being a sad, lonely, ageing singleton, and going on couples' retreats filled with people like Marissa, spending the rest of my life with just me and my discreet box from Ann Summers under the bed doesn't actually seem so bad …

'It sounds expensive,' said Jane. 'Sounds like it probably cost as much as … ooh … say a car? Maybe if Dad wasn't off spending all his money on wanky weekends, he could buy me a car!'

'Firstly,' Marissa said, 'you can't actually put a price on emotional health, and secondly *I* paid for it. It was an anniversary present for your father.'

'Lucky Dad,' said Jane sarcastically. 'Anyway, I was actually asking *him* a question, not you, Marissa, so if you could, like, stop interrupting? So, Dad, *do* I have to go back to school?'

'Don't be cheeky to Marissa, please. And if your mother says you have to go back to school, then you have to go back to school,' said Simon firmly, still nonetheless making *me* out to be the bad cop.

'She has A levels!' I shouted down the phone. 'She needs to work. They don't pass themselves.'

'Oh my *God*, Mother!' snapped Jane. 'I *know* I have A levels. How could I forget? I've only just finished my Mocks, and also you've *literally* talked about nothing else for months. *Fine*! Since no one cares about *my* emotional health, I'll just go back to school. Don't anyone worry about my individuality or being allowed to *express* myself at any point. No, that's *fine*!'

'Jane, I need to go. There's a very tricky junction coming up and I need to concentrate. But well done, darling, and I'll call you tonight, OK?'

'No mobiles are allowed at the retreat,' put in Marissa.

'Oh, for fuck's sake,' Simon sighed. 'Anyway, bye, darling, talk soon,' and he hung up.

'God, Marissa is a fucking annoying cow!' said Jane.

'Mmm,' I said noncommittally, not wanting to make the mistake of bitching about Marissa to Jane, only for Jane to repeat it all back to Marissa at some point in the future when I was in Jane's bad books and Marissa had bought her goodwill with ASOS vouchers. 'And don't swear so much, darling.'

'Well, she *is*! Anyway, Mum, *seriously*, why do I have to go back to school?'

'Because, darling,' I repeated for what felt like the eleventy fucking billionth time, 'this is your A-level year, and your A levels are very important.'

'The Queen hasn't got any A levels,' interjected Jane.

'That's because she's the fucking QUEEN!' I pointed out. 'She didn't need A levels. You don't become Queen because you were top of your class at Queen School.'

'It would be more democratic that way?' suggested Jane.

'But you aren't going to be Queen,' I said despairingly. 'And all those other hugely successful people who've got to the top despite not having A levels are the *exception*, not the rule. They'd have been successful anyway, and it might have been an easier path if they *had* had A levels, and for every millionaire A level-less entrepreneur, there are a million other people who never realised their potential because they didn't get any A levels. In most cases it's not because they didn't bother to work for them, but that they never got the chance to, and given that there are billions of people in the world who are forced to work in dangerous, low-paid jobs because for one reason or another they'll never get an *opportunity* to get a decent education, who would in fact give their right fucking *arm* for the educational breaks that *you* take for granted, then it's in fact rather morally reprehensible of you to not take your education seriously and make the very most of it that you can!'

I was rather proud of my little speech – it almost moved me to tears – and surely, surely somehow it would get through to Jane that she really needed to knuckle down and start working.

'Oh my God, Mother,' sneered Jane. 'Have you actually just given me the educational equivalent of the "There are starving children in Africa, so eat your peas" talk? *Sad!*'

'Just get in the fucking car,' I said.

Once a still-grumbling Jane was deposited at school, and I'd fortunately received no phone calls from the school complaining about a lack of a Peter, suggesting that through some miracle he'd managed to disconnect himself from the online world and made it to the bus in time, I drove on to work.

I do rather like my job. I worked bloody hard to get there and, as jobs go, I've had far worse. I'm good at what I do, plus I have a great team to work with, and – an important point that's never mentioned in school careers talks – no one in my office has killer BO (it's astonishing the effect on morale That Person can have).

Our company seems to be full of complicated politics, though, and that side of things is a bit pants, with Shakespearean levels of intrigue and backstabbing over everything from who gets the better desk to who has the more comfortable office chair, and ridiculous levels of virtue signalling over what fucking brand of coffee to buy for the office. ('This is Fairtrade'; 'Yes, but this is Fairertrade'; 'This one is grown by a co-operative of blind orangutans orphaned by the evil palm oil trade'; 'But THIS one is grown by blind, ONE-LEGGED orangutans orphaned by NAZIS and palm oil'; 'THIS one is grown by blind one-legged orphaned orangutans still traumatised by Dominic Cummings driving to the zoo where they lived, to taunt them about his SUPERIOR EYESIGHT.' No one ever seems to make such a huge, show-offy fuss about tea, do they? It's always the coffee drinkers carrying on.)

If we could all be left alone to get on with our jobs, instead of being summoned to pointless meetings about bastarding coffee, we'd probably be a lot more productive. In fact, if certain people didn't spend so much time wanking on about stuff that doesn't have anything to do with what the company *does* do, just to make themselves look important, we probably wouldn't have a threatened merger hanging over our heads, potentially risking all our jobs.

I'd thought when I started at my current company that perhaps this would be the job that I found a passion for – it's an achingly trendy technology company, with 'thinking spaces' where creative types draw on the walls (while drinking the hotly argued-over coffee) and have 'blue sky moments', whatever the fuck they are. I'm not achingly trendy, nor am I creative, and after years of child-rearing I have to bite my tongue to stop myself shouting at the hipster creatives in their braces and beards and too-short trousers that drawing on the walls is NAUGHTY and I'll smack their bottom if they do that again. Mainly what stops me is that Daryl, who has the biggest beard and the shortest trousers, looks rather like he'd enjoy a spanking from a woman old enough to be his mother.

Despite my normal-length trousers and the fact that I prefer to play Buzzword Bingo with my colleague Lydia while the creative sorts are whanging on about how, going forward, they'll be reaching out to take ownership of the synergy outside the box and drilling down to circle back to make this happen in a transparent and diverse value-added paradigm, blah blah blah, wank wank wank, I've done rather well at this company. The short-trousered ones come up with things they want to make, and my team and I provide the software to make this happen. I'm in fact now the head of my department, which means that I get an office with a window (and the comfiest chair), and also means I'll be the first one sacked if anything goes wrong.

I'd be pretty devastated if I lost my job, actually, quite apart from the financial impact it would have. I try to tell myself that I have many transferable skills, and would easily find something else, but I'm forty-eight and I don't want to start over at a new company where I don't know that you mustn't mention After Eights in front of Eric from Marketing because of an unfortunate incident at the Christmas party, and where I don't know where the toilets are.

Of course, if I got made redundant, perhaps it would be an opportunity to do something completely different. I like my job, but it would be wonderful to have a vocation, something you spring out of bed in the morning raring to go out there and do – something I *love*. I invented a very clever game app once that made me quite a lot of money – not retire-on money, but enough to make my finances less precarious, until I decided to get divorced, which made things a little rocky again. I'd thought that app invention might have been my vocation, but it turned out all the other ones I tried to invent were rubbish. But it would be nice to have the sort of job I could talk about at length at dinner parties and people would find hearing about it interesting. The trouble is, the older I get, it turns out that the things I love and that might be my vocation mainly seem to be watching rubbish TV, eating cake, sleeping, talking nonsense to my dogs, reading Jilly Cooper, and drinking wine, gin and vodka. I've tried and tried to see how I could turn any of these things into a vocation or a paying job, but so far I've not come up with anything.

I've also tried to expand my hobbies, to see if perhaps I could find my calling that way. Mostly, I found that I really like Vesper Martinis, which not only make you feel very sophisticated when you're drinking them, but are also an excellent drink choice for ladies who perhaps were not quite as vigilant with their pelvic floor exercises as they might have been. They're very small, you see, but also extremely potent, so they get you extraordinarily pissed for a very little amount of liquid. Unfortunately, Hannah and I tested this theory to the max when she got a Saturday after-noon off from Little Edward and abandoned him to his father so that we could go out and be ladies what lunch, and we drank four of them after wine at lunch and then we couldn't speak. Jane called me 'disgraceful' when I got home, and also 'a shameful example'. In my defence, I never ever claimed to be a *good* example and always held to the theory that since I wouldn't be a good example, I'd better stand as a terrible warning instead. Of course, on the Day of Shame with all the Vesper Martinis, I was quite unable to communicate this to Jane, being forced instead to mumble that it must've been something I ate, and that I needed a 'lil lie-downy'.

I've tried rather more adult ways to find my vocation as well. I always quite fancied being an archaeologist, and thought for a long time that perhaps that would have been my vocation if only I hadn't done computer science at university to spite my mother, who thought it sounded like my course would be full of bespectacled boys in nylon anoraks and how would I ever find a decent husband on such a course, and who would want to marry someone doing such a *male* course? My mother thought I should do English Lit like nice girls do, and try to bag a law student early, or maybe a nice doctor. Secretly, of course, since I went to Edinburgh, where all the posh boys that don't get into Oxford or Cambridge go (or they *did* before Prince William went to St Andrews), she was hoping I might manage to snag myself a title, but failing that, a lawyer or doctor would be acceptable. Or some nice chap who was going into the City. I don't think it ever occurred to her that perhaps I was going to university to further my education and pursue a career. As far as she was concerned, the only possible reason for a woman to go to university was to find herself a rich husband, like she did.

Since I'd been so unreasonable and clearly scuppered my chances with the lawyers and doctors by tainting myself by association with the beige-anorak brigade (who were actually perfectly nice and normal and didn't wear beige anoraks at all), she was relieved I did at least manage to get myself an architect in the form of Simon, though I was annoyed at myself that to some degree I *had* followed my mother's formula and met a nice boy at university and gone on to marry him. In my defence, I probably had a lot more casual sex with random blokes than my mother ever did in her day, and when I met Simon I was so utterly head over heels in love with him that getting married just seemed the natural next step, because *of course* we wanted to spend the rest of our lives together, so why *wouldn't* we get married?

I always had a hankering for archaeology, though, especially after it turned out that Simon and I wouldn't be spending the rest of our lives together after all, and so I took part in a community dig in our village a couple of years ago. It turned out that archaeology wasn't my vocation. I'd thought it would involve careful sifting through priceless artefacts and then perhaps some *Indiana Jones*-style adventures with a rugged and dashing archaeology sort in a tweed jacket with leather patches on the elbows. I had a vague vision of myself with my hair in a prim bun, and some academic-looking spectacles, and at some point I'd take down my hair and remove my glasses, and the rugged and dashing sort would exclaim, 'Why, Miss Green, you're *beautiful*,' and then we'd snog loads while fighting off the bad guys trying to steal our amulet or something.

It wasn't like that. There was a lot of mud. Archaeologists' clothing turned out to tend much more towards sensible man-made fibres than tweed jackets, and even if there had been a rugged and dashing sort there, there would have been no snogging, since there were also twenty-five OAPs getting in the way and telling me off for using my trowel wrong. They made me draw pictures of stones. I don't know why I had to draw the stones and we couldn't just take a photograph. I suspect they made me draw the stones to give me something to do and stop my overenthusiastic trowelling, even though I don't even see how you CAN trowel mud wrong. I lost a pencil and got told off. I did see a shrew, though, and I liked the shrew, and also I like my dogs, of course, and I have three chickens who only semi hate me, so then I wondered if maybe zoology was my calling, but I googled it and it turns out the top job for zoologists is not being David Attenborough but being a zoo keeper, which even I can guess probably involves dealing with a lot of poo, especially if you get the elephant or rhinoceros enclosures. So it was back to the drawing board again.

FEBRUARY

Friday, 1 February

So. We have a development. Margaret, who lives in the cottage down the road from me, put her house up for sale a few months ago, and when I popped in for a drink with her tonight, she told me it's been sold.

'To a nice, young, single fellow, my dear. He was very handsome when he came to view the house, and rather charming.'

'How do you know he's single, Margaret?' I asked, as she refilled my gin glass with a splendidly heavy hand. I shall miss Margaret. I found her rather terrifying at first and felt she was very disapproving of my single mother/divorcee lifestyle and considered me the Village Jezebel for having Gentleman Callers (well, Jack. It wasn't like I had a constant stream of men clamouring for my favours, worst luck), but in fact Margaret is just disapproving of everyone until they've proved themselves worthy of her. Luckily, it's easy to prove yourself worthy of Margaret, as worthiness mainly comes in the form of furnishing her with gin and being enthusiastic about her endless supply of local gossip. Since gin and gossip are two of my favourite things, Margaret was soon established as a Kindred Spirit.

'And not too heavy on the tonic, it's the only way. Well, for a start, there's only his name on the bumpf from the lawyers,' she said.

'Well, that doesn't prove anything,' I objected. 'He could still have a girlfriend. Or a boyfriend. Actually, knowing my luck, he'll definitely be gay. It would be too much to hope for that a single, straight, eligible man would literally land on my doorstep!'

'He's not got a girlfriend or a boyfriend,' said Margaret firmly. 'He came back today to look at the garage roof, which the idiot who did the survey claims is leaking, which is *patently* nonsense, and I asked him, because I worry about you, all by yourself, dear. What would you do if your garage roof started leaking? Hmm?'

'Probably call a roofer, same as most people. And *what* exactly did you ask him, Margaret?' I said faintly. Margaret is not known for beating around the bush. 'Please tell me you didn't say, "Ahoy there, handsome chappy, do you like guys or gals, and if the answer is you like the ladies, are you available because Ellen down the road is gagging for some cock?"'

'Of course I didn't,' said Margaret indignantly. 'I asked him if it would just be him living here, and he said it would, and *I* said what a shame a nice fellow like him didn't have a lovely wife, or even a girlfriend, and he said he just hadn't met the right woman yet. So there you go, he's just the ticket for you … oh, and he's forty-nine, by the way, and has a jolly nice bottom.'

'Margaret, you're seventy-eight, you shouldn't be ogling men's arses at your age,' I said.

'Don't be ageist, dear,' said Margaret sternly. 'Even an old lady like me can still appreciate the benefits of a nice bottom. That's why I keep my spectacles on this handy string so I can pop them on to have a proper look.'

'Anyway,' I said. 'Forty-nine, and never once met the right woman? Clearly there's something wrong with him. He's either got killer halitosis –'

'He doesn't.'

'Or he's been living with his mother until now because he can't wash his own pants, or he's one of those men who rants on the internet about how unfair it is that women aren't obliged to have sex with them because sex is some sort of right they're owed and then they wonder why no woman ever wants to have sex with them, or he's the sort of man who has a ridiculous checklist of qualities a woman must have, like cooking his dinner every night and not swearing and not having shagged anyone else, or else he just murders people and keeps them under the floorboards, and that's why he can't get a girlfriend because she'd complain about the smell. Either way, he clearly has *issues*!'

'Oh, I say, he'd jolly well better not keep murdered people under my floorboards!' chuntered Margaret indignantly. 'It took me *years* to badger Jim into taking up the carpet and sanding them down. I didn't go to all that trouble just to make it easier for someone to store bodies! Anyway, I'm sure he's awfully nice, Ellen, and there's bound to be a super reason why he's still single. Perhaps he's been Doing Good Works with orphans in the Third World and never had time to meet someone? Now, what would you say to another little gin, dear? And do you have any ciggies? My granddaughter confiscated mine yesterday. Can you believe, she said it would take twenty years off my life. I told her I was nearly eighty and in robust health, and the twenty years I'd lose would probably be me being gaga and in a home, so it was no great loss. But she was quite horrid and took them anyway! Are you all right, Ellen? You've gone an awfully funny colour.'

'I'm just a bit warm,' I said. 'You have the heating up very high, Margaret.'

'I know, dear,' said Margaret smugly. 'Jim always made a dreadful carry-on about the thermostat and he'd never let me put it up above 18°, so I'm making the most of having it as hot as I like. Are you sure it isn't the change of life, though, dear?' she added sympathetically. 'At least you're single, and don't have to put up with a man and all his silly nonsense while you go through that. I nearly stabbed Jim when he asked me if it was really necessary for me to make such a fuss. I said, "James Langdon, when you feel like every fibre of your body hates you, when your womb is trying to turn itself inside out and the soles of your damn feet are on fire, *then* you can talk about unnecessary fuss."'

'Margaret, you literally had me round tonight to set me up with a stranger, a man I've never seen and you've met twice, just because he has a good bum, even though he might be a serial killer, and now five minutes later you're telling me that actually I'm better off without a man!'

'Mmmm,' said Margaret. 'Well, I forgot you were getting to that stage. I thought it might be nice for you to have some company. Someone to *do the crossword with*, if you know what I mean, my pet.' (Margaret accompanied this seemingly innocent remark with a salacious wink that suggested she wasn't meaning that I needed help with my cryptic clues so much as I did with 'one down'.) 'But then, on second thoughts, I remembered that sometimes men are more of a nuisance than one can really be bothered with, and after all, you've got your children and your lovely doggies.'

'The children will be gone soon,' I pointed out gloomily. 'I barely see them as it is. Perhaps a man *would* be nice. I've really given up hope, though, since Jack left. I'm too old for dating sites. Men my age are looking for a dolly bird, and the ones who want someone "more mature" are in their dotage and basically want a free nurse, and even then, they'd rather have some young popsy.'

'Well,' said Margaret stoutly, 'it's lucky there's more to life than men then, isn't it? Like gin, for example! I vote we have a little one for the road, don't you think? Now, did I tell you that Nicola in the shop has apparently been on a swingers' website, dear? Brenda's son found her. He said he'd come across the site by mistake, looking for something else, which is a likely tale if you ask me. It's like when Brenda found all his *Playboys* and he claimed he'd bought them for the articles!'

Saturday, 16 February

Hannah came over today. I've known Hannah almost my whole life, or certainly long enough that the few years we didn't know each other for are irrelevant. Hannah's fond of saying that we have to stay friends now, no matter what, because we're too old to ever make another friend that we've known for longer than we haven't known them, and that we'll be dead before that can happen again. Of course, we have to stay friends as well because we know each other's deepest, darkest, most sordid secrets and don't judge each other for them. Hannah doesn't really *have* any deep, dark, sordid secrets, mind you, because she's a better person than me, and in fairness, even my deepest, darkest, most sordid secrets aren't that interesting. It's not like I have a body count or anything.

My shameful secrets tend to extend more to having sex with unsuitable boys in my youth. I was married to Simon for twenty years, though, give or take, and Hannah knows far more about me than the man I lived with, slept next to every night, the man whose children I carried. Hannah knows, for example, that I once shagged a civil engineering student who kept his condoms in his calculator case (sexy). And Hannah knows that although I ended my marriage to Simon over *his* infidelity, I did come very close once to straying myself, and if the man I'd been tempted by hadn't been such a nice person, things might have turned out very differently, and so in fact there was an element of hypocrisy in my reaction to Simon's own indiscretions.

But she doesn't judge me for being a slapper, and has never ever suggested that I was perhaps a bit unfair to Simon, instead robustly condemning his man-whore ways (not that he really was a man-whore – he had a single one-night stand, but alas, it was the final nail in the coffin of a marriage already crumbling under the pressures of bringing up children, never having enough time for each other, his addiction to *Wheeler* Fucking *Dealers*, and the endless, *endless* bastarding piles of laundry).

I sometimes worry that Hannah, being a Good Person, brings far more to our friendship than I do, and that I'm a Bad Friend, as it often seems to me that my main contribution to our relationship was spending our younger years holding Hannah's hair out of her face while she puked, as she was a notorious lightweight. But I don't even have to do that anymore now that we drink Sauvignon Blanc and Rioja, rather than vodka mixed with Hooch lemonade (I frequently complain of this, but seriously, Hooch lemonade? Why did we think that was a good idea? Potent alcoholic lemonade that we blithely used as a mixer and added more booze to! Truly, nothing makes you stupid quite so much as your youthful misplaced faith in your own invincibility).

Of course, I did hold Hannah's hair out of her face when she was vomiting with morning sickness too, especially with her older two children when she was married to her horrible first husband, Dan, but in reality, my role in Hannah's life is the same as could be played by a decent-quality hair bobble and an Alice band. I did mention this to Hannah once, that I felt our friendship was a bit unequal, and she seemed surprised.

'But Ellen,' she said, 'you do the same for me. You never judge me, you're always there for me, you've always got my back, and I sometimes feel like we're unequal because you're so much more outgoing than me, and I'm just the boring one trailing along in your wake, that people only talk to me because I'm with you. And I don't even offer the hair-holding-up sick service, because you never throw up from too much booze, except for that one time in 1995 when they had a vodka disco in the Union and it was 50p for vodka and Coke and you had thirty-six, which was why we realised they must water the vodka down because otherwise you'd have been dead. But even then you puked alone in the cubicle, and when I came to see if you were OK, you told me to go and get you another vodka.'

'Yeah, that wasn't actually my finest hour,' I reminded her. 'In fact, those thirty-six vodka and Cokes might have had something to do with me going home with Condom Calculator Boy –'

'No, that was at a whisky ceilidh,' supplied Hannah helpfully.

'See? You know *all* the secrets,' I sighed.

Ultimately, I suppose, that's the nature of friendships – it's your differences as much as your similarities that bond you together. Where one is loud and talks too much, the other is quieter and more thoughtful. Where one pukes, the other hair-holds. One of you is practical and makes things happen, including offers of finding dubious pubs where murderers can be hired cheaply if someone hurts the other one, and one of you is more sensitive and can put themselves in other people's shoes and remind you why frequenting Murder Pubs is probably not a good idea.

It was lovely to see Hannah today, though, as we haven't seen much of each other recently, since adorable Baby Edward, Hannah's little Late in Life Surprise, stopped being a cherubic, rosy-cheeked baby and hit the Terrible Twos with a vengeance, transforming almost overnight from an adorable poppet whose single-minded aim in life was to achieve his great goal of successfully cramming his own chubby foot into his ear, or, failing that, eating it as a tasty snack, into Conan the Destroyer of Houses.

As a result of Edward's extreme destructive tendencies, Hannah has stopped going out much with him, as there was an unfortunate incident when he was banned from Mummy and Me Music Class for setting off the fire extinguisher ('I literally loosened my grip on him for *one second* to "Point to the ceiling, point to the floor" in "Wind the Motherfucking Bobbin Up", and he was off!' wailed Hannah), swiftly followed by another bijou event in the local coffee shop when Edward threw his babyccino at the waitress and called her a fanny, a word it transpired his older brother Lucas had thought it hilarious to teach him.

Hannah is also shit scared of going to other people's houses because of the carnage that Edward leaves in his wake – our lovely friend Katie, who has two sweet little girls and had never experienced the almost Old Testament-style whirlwind of annihilation that is a toddler boy, was left aghast by a visit from Edward, whimpering, 'Are … are they all like that?' as Hannah and I grimly assured her that not *all* toddler boys are like that, but a good proportion are.

Katie means extremely well, but Hannah confided in me that it was just too stressful watching her twitch every time Edward set off on one of his kamikaze runs around the room – Edward does everything at high speed, there are no low gears for him – and so until he could be civilised somewhat (I laughed, hollowly, because although he's stopped running into things full tilt and smashing them, I'm still not entirely convinced that Peter can be described as civilised), then she would just maybe not go over to Katie's house.

I, however, a) don't have many nice things for Edward to break, b) can just about remember those relentless toddler days, and c) am Hannah's oldest friend, so my house is one of the few places she can escape to that's not the park, which can be very wet and windy at this time of year, or fucking soft-play, which is hell on earth and a fetid health hazard filled with distressing amounts of strangers' bodily fluids.

Nonetheless, I'd forgotten how you must barricade your home against small children on account of their amazing ability to turn almost anything into a lethal weapon and damage themselves on apparently harmless objects.

My own children were no exception, of course – Peter once managed to cut himself on a cushion. I mean, how do you even cut yourself on a cushion? He limped through, clutching his bleeding knee and dragging one leg behind him, doing a more than passable impression of a dying Victorian crippled urchin, as the slightest wound or infirmity always renders Peter in need of a fainting couch and some *sal volatile*. Beth on her deathbed in *Little Women* has nothing on an injured or ailing Peter. When I howled, 'What have you done now?' and he whimpered, 'The cushion, Mummy, it was *sharp*,' I was torn between fury (he'd got blood on my Laura Ashley cushions, which was very galling, even though I got them cheap off eBay and not actually from Laura Ashley, because their prices are fucking ridiculous, even though their things are lovely) and a grudging admiration that he'd seemingly managed the impossible and injured himself on the soft furnishings in what was basically a padded cell. Apparently, he'd somehow jammed his knee against the zip with sufficient force to break the skin. But he staunchly insisted it was *my* fault, for putting the cushions there in the first place.

You forget all this, though, once they finally move past that terrifying kamikaze stage; you forget that literally everything and anything remains a potentially lethal hazard. Sometimes you only find out years later that you were endangering your precious moppets on a daily basis and had no notion you were even doing it! I'd no idea until Jane started school that grapes were a choking hazard and should always be cut up for small children. Astonishingly, Jane had managed to survive this and hadn't choked on a grape just to spite me, though I did think some of the mummies at the school took the whole 'killer grapes' thing just a *little* bit too far when they were still insisting on the grapes being cut into tiny pieces for the Year 6 Leavers' Disco 'because you can never be too careful'. My argument that if their children were still not capable of chewing their own food at that age then maybe they weren't ready to go out into the world and get the bus to Big School all by themselves, or wipe their own arses or, you know, *function*, was deemed 'unreasonable', and so I was put in charge of crisps, which apparently their children *could* chew.

I was well prepared for Hannah's visit, though, and was determined she should be able to relax.

'It's all fine!' I said cheerfully, as Hannah came through the door, clinging desperately to Edward's hand. 'I've child-proofed, all is safe, nothing can be broken, he cannot break himself! Behold, I'm practically the baby whisperer!'

'Really?' said Hannah doubtfully.

'Oh yes!' I insisted, airily gesturing around me. 'Look! I've got a stair gate and everything!'

'Oh Ellen, you shouldn't have gone to so much trouble and expense for us coming,' said Hannah.

'Oh, I didn't,' I assured her. 'I bought it off one of those mad Facebook sites where people try to sell their old cardboard boxes – it was a pointless attempt to stop the dogs going upstairs after Barry developed a delightful habit of bringing presents into the house and letting them go in my bedroom.'

'I thought it was cats that did that?'

'So did I, but Barry does it too. It's quite disconcerting when your giant wolf dog streaks upstairs with a protesting baby blackbird in his mouth and generously deposits it on your bed, beaming happily at you, as if to say, "Look! Am I not clever? I am helping, I have brought sustenance to contribute to the pack, please love me, please!" I think it's because he's a rescue dog.'

I was all set to wax lyrical about Barry, and how hard it is to be cross with him because he's a rescue dog, and he's so desperate to be loved, and even after over two years of living with us, he's so anxious to not do anything wrong, lest he be punished or sent back, that it's truly heartbreaking (*obviously*, I'd never punish my dogs, but someone clearly has been very unkind to Barry in the past, poor boy, which just adds to my conviction that Most People Are Awful and Dogs Are Better). Judgy is a rescue dog as well, but unlike Barry he doesn't give a shit.

We made many allowances for Judgy's attitude and behaviour when we first had him, because he'd not had an easy time either, having been rehomed four times in his first two years, and so we put his grumpy arseholeness down to that. Time eventually revealed that it was probably nothing to do with his rough start in life, and everything to do with the fact he's just a bit of an arsehole. But he's still my baby and I love him dearly. But Edward had no intention of listening to my soliloquy about my Wunder Dogs and began to scream and writhe furiously.

'Coat OFF! MY GO! OFF! OFF NOW!' he bellowed.

Hannah was still attempting to take Edward's coat off when he made a break for it, hurtled towards the stair gate and scaled it like Spider-Man before we could stop him, then charged up the stairs, while we, considerably less agile and thus unable to simply vault the gate like him, wrestled with trying to get the damn thing open.

Obviously, thinking Edward would be contained downstairs, I hadn't bothered to shut any upstairs doors, and so Edward had free rein in his campaign of terror until Hannah and I could get up the stairs after him (stair gates, like childproof caps, proving more of an impediment to adults than to children). Edward, obviously, had made a beeline for Jane's room.

'My painting!' he announced in delight, as we burst in to find him smearing Jane's treasured Urban Decay lip gloss over the carpet. 'My painting NICE, Mummy! See? NOOOOOO! MY PAINTING! MINE!' he roared as Hannah wrested the lip gloss off him and I dabbed at the carpet, whimpering, more terrified in truth of Jane's reaction to her wrecked lip gloss than the state of the carpet, which was already ruined by Jane's many spillages of fake tan and foundation.

'I'm so sorry!' whimpered Hannah. 'I don't know how he's so fast. He just seems to go into some kind of warp speed. I'll buy Jane a new one.'

'No, no, don't worry, it's *fine*!' I assured her, words I'd say many times over before the afternoon was done.

We dragged a reluctant Edward downstairs and corralled him in the sitting room.

'He'll definitely be OK in here,' I assured Hannah. 'There's nothing for him to break. Or for him to hurt himself with,' I added as an afterthought. 'See! I didn't have any of the plastic socket-cover thingies, because I threw the last ones out when Simon and I split up because the children were hopefully past the stage of sticking forks in the sockets, but I've moved the furniture strategically to cover the sockets, and all the breakable objects are on high shelves.'

'Thank you, Ellen,' sighed Hannah. 'Are you quite sure it's safe to let him go?'

'Oh yes, it's fine!' I said confidently.

'It's *fine!*' I beamed a few minutes later, as Edward wrenched my beloved copy of *Riders* in two, although it was the second copy I'd had to buy, as Peter had eaten the first copy when he was roughly the same age as Edward is now.

'It's FINE!' I ground out, as Edward briskly disassembled his childproof Tommee Tippee cup and drenched the carpet in the juice he'd blackmailed out of Hannah with promises he'd quietly watch *PAW Patrol* on her phone if she gave him juice instead of water.

'It's *FINE!*' I insisted in unconvincing tones when Edward clutched his choccy biccie until it melted, then smeared his face and hands over the Laura Ashley cushions, before roaring with red-faced fury because he wanted his choccy back NOOOOOOWWWWWW!

'It's *not* fine, though, is it?' wailed Hannah. 'It's not, look at your house! We've been here less than an hour and he's wrecked Jane's room, and your sitting room, and, OH GOD, EDWARD! LEAVE the doggy! LEAVE HIM! NO, we do NOT play horsey with the doggy. THAT'S NOT NICE!'

Fortunately, Edward had chosen Barry to torment, not Judgy,

who'd wisely removed himself from the carnage to hide on my bed. Judgy's opinion on small children is that they are all very well, but he couldn't eat a whole one, whereas Barry views them as useful snack dispensers and likes to follow them around, hoovering up any crumbs and matter they strew in their wake – he had in fact been attempting to lick the chocolate off the cushions, despite being told it's bad for him, when Edward decided to clamber aboard. Barry had taken this in his stride and seemed to feel it was a small price to pay for contraband chocolate. Judgy probably would have had Edward's hand off, although a bijou maiming would at least have impeded his path of destruction!

'It *is* fine!' I lied valiantly. 'Barry doesn't mind, and I'm sure the carpet won't stain and the cushions will wash. I get red wine on them all the time. And *Riders* will tape back together and I just won't even *tell* Jane about the lip gloss. I'll deny all knowledge and say she must have lost it at a party. See? It *is* fine!'

'No,' sobbed Hannah, unexpectedly bursting into tears. 'It's not fine. It's not. It's constant. He's relentless. From the minute he wakes up, till the minute he goes to bed, he's destroying something. He's even stopped having daytime naps. They were my one respite to try to tackle the mess, or just draw a breath without being on high alert for what the little fucker is doing now. But no, he's even taken that from me, the little bastard!'

'Bastard!' put in Edward helpfully. 'Bastard bastard bastard bastard. You is a bastard, Mummy. Doggy is a bastard. Ellen is a bastard. BAAAASSSSTARD! Daddy is a bastard!'

'Oh God, NO, Edward, we don't say "bastard", it isn't nice!' implored Hannah through her tears. 'Please, darling, promise Mummy you won't say that again, especially not to Daddy!'

'Bastard!' said Edward cheerfully.

'Fuck,' said Hannah.

'Fucking bastard!' chirped Edward.

'Oh Hannah!' I said, handing her a box of tissues, and passing Edward another chocolate biscuit on the basis that my cushions were already fucked, and since Barry had survived stealing several Easter eggs last year, a couple of Hobnobs probably wouldn't hurt. 'Why didn't you tell me you were struggling?'

'Because we don't, do we?' sniffed Hannah. 'Because if you say it's hard, everyone tells you to be grateful, that you're so *lucky*, there are so many people who would give anything for a child, that I should just be glad that Edward's healthy when there are millions of people out there whose children are terribly ill, and really, I need to count my blessings with a roof over my head and enough to eat and a husband who loves me and three children, and I have nothing at all to complain about. And then I feel awful.'

'Who says that?' I demanded. 'Who?'

'Well, WebMums,' said Hannah.

'Hannah!' I said in horror. 'What were you doing on WebMums?'

'I just … I just wanted to know if anyone else found it so hard with their two-year-old,' said Hannah. 'I just asked if it was normal to feel like it was all a bit overwhelming, especially since I don't get much respite from him, with Charlie working such long shifts at the hospital, and trying to juggle Emily and Lucas and what they need from me, as well as trying to keep some kind of spark alive with Charlie, and if anyone else could relate, or if anyone else was trying to deal with a toddler and teenagers at the same time. And then I just got a huge barrage of people telling me how awful I was to want a break from Edward, and why did I even have children if I didn't want to spend time with them, and how he won't be little long and I'll miss these days when they are gone, and how they have twenty-five children from the age of one day old to forty-three, and they have never, ever struggled for even a single second because children are a blessing and clearly I'm a selfish bitch.'

'Oh Hannah! I mean, I don't want to say, "I told you so," but seriously, what did you expect from WebMums? You should know better than to do anything there except read the AIBU boards occasionally, hoping for another Penis Beaker thread! Why didn't you talk to *me*, if you were finding it so hard?'

'I dunno,' mumbled Hannah.

'Bastard fuck!' interjected Edward merrily from the corner, as we looked up to see him attempting to shove a Duplo brick up poor Barry's arse, while Barry tried to cling on to a last semblance of dignity by pretending there was nothing at all happening Down There.

'Don't you remember, years ago when Jane had just been born, and my mother saw her for the first time and re-marked what a pity it was that she wasn't as pretty as her cousin Persephone, because *of course* Jessica's baby, the First Grandchild, was Perfection Personified, and then she asked if I'd spoken to the doctors about the possibility that Jane was "a bit backward" because she wouldn't smile at the old witch, even though she was only three weeks old, and also, who could bloody blame her? And I thought it would be a nice, supportive place, an online forum full of mums, so I made the mistake of posting to ask if I was being unreasonable to be a bit upset by this reaction to my beautiful new baby, and I just got absolutely *slaughtered* by dozens of women telling me I was a selfish bitch, because their mothers had all died in freak accidents involving penis beakers and making a chicken feed a family of six for a fortnight, or something equally ridiculous and WebMumsy, and how they would give ANYTHING to have their mother come along and insult their child's appearance and intelligence.'

'Oh God, yes!' said Hannah. 'And I signed up and tried to defend you, and they all shouted at me as well! I know, I just thought, you know, the internet was still quite young back then and people maybe didn't know how to behave. And all these years later, it might have got better. But it hasn't. If anything, it's got worse. I'm sure I recognised some of the usernames, too, from when they shouted at us. They must have spent the last seventeen or eighteen years literally sitting online telling strangers to stop being selfish and being smug about how much better they are at life than everyone else!'

'Honestly, Hannah,' I said firmly. 'Never go there for advice again. You're probably actually better off reading the comments on the *Daily Mail* than you are admitting you're finding it tough and asking for help there. That's what *I'm* for.'

'I know,' said Hannah. 'I *know*! I just … I didn't want to be a burden, you know. I feel like I'm not much fun these days. I come over, Edward trashes the place, I moan. I'm not exactly bringing a lot to the party, am I? Except a half-eaten packet of Jammie Dodgers that Edward fished out of my bag in the car and opened.'

'That's not what I'm here for!' I exclaimed in horror. 'I'm here for *you*. Whatever you need me for. Whether it's a party, or a shoulder to cry on. That's what we do, remember? When Tony Morrison dumped you for being too spotty, when James Evans told everyone I had given him a blowjob when I hadn't, when Mrs Thompson gave you a detention unfairly because Caroline Walker had flicked a rubber at her and she thought it was you, when my parents got divorced, when Dan left you, when Simon cheated on me, when your dad died and then my dad died. Hannah, we're always there for each other. Always. We can fix this, Hannah. There's nothing we can't fix as long as we have each other.'

My rousing and touching speech was somewhat spoiled by Edward roaring, 'TUUUUMBLE! TUMBLE NOOOOWWWW!'

After Peter had been grudgingly summoned from his bedroom to turn on the fiendishly complicated television, and Edward was happily ensconced in front of *Mr Tumble*, a third biscuit clutched in his chubby paw as he lolled decadently on Barry, staring blankly at the screen as Mr Tumble waved his spotty bag around in a disturbing manner, and Peter, for reasons I could not fathom, settled down happily to watch it too, until I chivvied him out of the room with the lure of a bag of Doritos, Hannah and I were able to resume our interrupted conversation without a lurking teenager eavesdropping.

'I know you're right,' said Hannah. 'And I know I should have talked to you, but I just feel like I'm shit for everybody at the moment. I don't know how to fix this. Edward is Edward, but he's so full-on I have no time for Emily and Lucas, and by the time I get into bed at night I really can't muster the energy to talk to Charlie or even have a cuddle, let alone anything else. But I can't unEdward Edward.'

'This passes, though,' I reminded her. 'We've been here before. You know it's not forever.'

'I don't know,' sighed Hannah. 'I'm so much older now. What if it doesn't pass? I'm already terrified people will think I'm Edward's granny when he starts school.'

'Oh God, don't say that,' I said. 'I still have mortifying flash-backs to that time I asked a woman at Toddlers group if she was just looking after her granddaughter for the day, and it turned out she was younger than me and it was her kid. In my defence, she had a very unflattering haircut!'

'I thought staying at home with him would be easier,' sighed Hannah. 'I wouldn't feel guilty about going back to work like I did with the older two, but mainly I just feel resentful that Charlie can swan off at any point he likes during the day and have a shit in peace. I can't even pee in peace. I either have Edward watching me, or I come out of the loo to carnage! The other day, I left him for less than two minutes, in a fully child-proofed room, and in that time he immediately zeroed in on the only sharp object I'd missed, which was the underside of the lamp base, sliced his thumb open and managed to finger paint my entire sitting room *in his own blood*! Surely that's not normal? And Charlie just laughed when I told him, and said how clever Edward must be. I was thinking more along the lines of what a psychopath he must be.'

'Toddlers aren't normal,' I reassured Hannah. 'I don't think anyone can understand how their brains work, because toddlers are inherently evil and cunning.'

'Oh Jesus, it's such bliss to talk to someone who understands that! Everyone at the baby groups I go to seems to think their children are perfect, even when they're running amok like demon hell beasts. And it's difficult when Charlie just doesn't see how hard Edward is either, or rather he doesn't want to see. He's out at work all day, so when he's with him he just wants to be fun daddy, not disciplining him or doing the boring stuff, just winding him up before bedtime. This leaves me having to be the bad cop again, which means that I'm even more annoyed and resentful of Charlie, and honestly, I sometimes feel like Edward is the only thing keeping us together right now.'

'That's a pretty big thing to keep you together,' I pointed out. 'And I keep saying this, but Charlie *isn't* like your first husband, Dan the Rancid Streak of Weasel Piss! He's a good man. You need to talk to him, Hannah. You need to tell him that he has to step up and help more. This is his first child. You need to explain that parenting isn't just shits and giggles. Sometimes it's giant steaming turds in the bath that someone has to scoop out, often with their bare hands, and that he can't leave all the boring stuff with Edward up to you. He has two parents and Charlie has to pull his weight, he can't be fun dad all the time and let you be mean mummy. I'm sure if you tell him you need more help, he'll understand.'

'When, though?' said Hannah. 'When do I find the time to have that conversation? I'm so tired, or I'm rushing about trying to drop off Lucas or pick up Emily, and I just feel we're drifting apart. I can't even remember the last time we had sex; he just doesn't seem interested. I thought I should try to make an effort there, and we'd maybe feel closer. I even bought a Thing to try and spice "it" up a bit, you know, but I've been afraid to bring it out. It's quite alarming, and I haven't even managed to put the batteries in it yet, because I keep having to put them in Edward's toy phone because he screeches like a banshee when it doesn't light up and make annoying noises.'

'A Thing?' I asked.

'You know. A *Thing*! From *Ann Summers*!' Hannah whispered conspiratorially.

'Do you mean a *vibrator*?' I whispered back, whispering less out of prudishness and more out of fear that Edward would seize the opportunity to add yet more unsuitable words to his vocabulary. The last thing Hannah needed was Edward shouting, 'Fucking bastard dildos, Mummy!' in the middle of Sainsbury's.

Hannah nodded. 'It seems very complicated though!'

Even at our all-girls school, Hannah was famed for her unworldliness when it came to matters of sex. While the rest of us avidly pored over the mysterious copy of *The Joy of Sex* that had been a fixture of our sixth-form common room for generations (thankfully, being an all-girls school, none of the pages were stuck together), Hannah recoiled in horror from the contortions of the beardy man and his curiously be-mulleted partner. We widened our eyes over *More* magazine's Position of the Fortnight, and *Cosmo*'s insistence that we looked at our lady's bits with a hand mirror, but Hannah still claimed she only bought those magazines for fashion tips, and not for the exotic rudenesses contained within. Thus it was not really a surprise to me that Hannah had reached her late forties still considering a vibrator to be a complicated piece of kit.

'How is it complicated?' I asked gently.

'It has a remote control!' hissed Hannah. 'Why does it have a remote control? Surely the point of sex is that you are *right next* to each other, not that someone is downstairs or on the other side of the room? Or if it's just you on your own, you definitely don't need a remote control, do you? So what's it *for*?'

'Um, I'm not totally sure,' I admitted. 'I mean, when you're on your own, it's quite handy to be able to see the buttons, instead of having to contort yourself to reach the on switch. One doesn't get any more supple with age, obviously. Unless that's why so many old ladies are so keen on yoga – they've all got old-fashioned vibrators that don't have remote controls, and there's no need to buy a new one, because things were built to last in their day!'

'Or they could just switch them on *first*?' pointed out Hannah.

'Oh yeah. Good point! Damn, I thought I'd cracked the riddle of why every yoga class is full of octogenarians.' I said in disappointment.

'Anyway, I don't want to think about Gladys and Doris and their sturdy sex toys,' said Hannah. 'You know about these things, you can tell me. I'm afraid to google. It has all these different settings on the remote – what are they for? How are you supposed to know? It didn't say in the instructions.'

Bless Hannah. Possibly the only person ever to carefully study the safety leaflet and instruction manual that came with a vibrator.

'Well, I think that's because different settings do different things for different people,' I suggested. 'As far as I know, you just run through them till you find one that does it for you. Though I have one like that, and it's a bit like trying to find the only cycle on the Christmas tree lights that isn't likely to trigger an epileptic fit in an unsuspecting guest.'

'What do you mean?' said Hannah in horror.

'Well, you know how you always go past the setting that you want when you switch the lights on, and then you have to run through all the other settings about five times before you actually manage to stop in time on the one you were looking for?'

Hannah nodded.

'Well, it's like that. I mean, you get there in the end, but sometimes it takes a while and you start to think you should just have watched another episode of *Stranger Things* instead. But Hannah, if you're so tired, why are you worrying about vibrators and sex anyway? Do you think that's what Charlie really wants? What do *you* want?'

'I don't know,' said Hannah miserably. 'I just want it to be like it used to be. I had this vision, you know, that I'd whip the *Thing* out one night and Charlie would be carried away with passion and we'd have a sex life again, and then we'd find time to talk, and everything would be all right. I don't know. You're right, we should probably talk first, and the rest will follow, but I just feel like everyone else is doing it and it's another thing I'm failing at. *How* do other people manage to have exotic sex lives? Amanda at Baby Music smugly informed us that they have a Date Night every single week and she schedules sex on her Outlook Calendar.'

'Why would she even tell you that at Baby Music class?' I asked in bafflement.

'She overshares,' said Hannah darkly. 'It's actually a hideous cross between good old-fashioned oversharing and humble-bragging. "Oh, I'm soooo tired today, I must look *awful*. I stayed up *far* too late last night trying to choose the handles for my new Poggenpohl kitchen, and then, well, you know, Mark reminded me it was the anniversary of when he proposed to me in Paris, in the Presidential Suite in the George V, so we had a little *celebration* of our own when we went to bed." She's one of the yummy soy milk mummies with one perfect child who completely fulfils her. There aren't any others like me there. There's either the perky smug twenty-eight-year-olds who've snapped back into shape, or there's some older mums, but they're all on their first babies too and all insist how grateful they are to have them. One even told me that her baby was more special than mine because she'd had her through IVF. There's no one else trying to juggle teenagers AND a toddler. They all look at me like I've got two heads while they're being #SoBlessed and #TreasuringEveryMoment.'

'Firstly, Amanda needs to be killed,' I said firmly. 'There's still that option of that Murder Pub in Dundee someone once told me about. You can hire a hitman for £300! We could see if they'd do a BOGOF for Amanda and Marissa.'

'Ellen, we've been through this. You can't just have people killed because they annoy you. And Marissa's not that bad. Also, you'd have to go to Dundee. Dundee is far. Have you ever been to Dundee?'

'Well, no,' I admitted. 'It's *quite* far, I suppose. It's got a new V&A, though. We could make a weekend of it.'

'No,' said Hannah. 'Absolutely not. I'm too tired to go to Dundee and hire an assassin, even for Marissa and Amanda.'

'Well, anyway, secondly, you *know* none of them are as perfect as they seem. I can guarantee you at least half of them are trying to resist the urge to smash their head on the floor repeatedly to make the hell of music class stop, or wondering if anyone is considering just poking themselves in the eye with a maraca to distract themselves from singing "Wind the Fucking Bobbin Up" for the eleventy fucking billionth time in their life, but they've paid for the term so they have to see it through. And even if some of them are still smug as fuck about what perfect parents they are and are judging the others, their time will come! Oh yes, the judgy perfect parents' time will come, and they'll be ritually humiliated and shamed by their offspring, and they'll realise that you're all just doing your best.'

It's a bit like when I was pregnant with Jane, and I'd drift around the supermarket, pushing my trolley full of nice, posh food, smugly stroking my bump and judging the harassed parents of screeching toddlers mainlining Wotsits while attempting to throw themselves out of the trolley and grab anything they could reach off the shelves to hurl at other shoppers and I'd think, self-righteously, 'Those parents should be *ashamed* of themselves. Why don't they set some clear boundaries for that child?

That's *obviously* what they're crying out for. *My* baby won't ever behave like that. I'll simply explain, calmly and clearly, what we're doing and why, and why they must sit nicely in the trolley, or in the café, and I'll *engage* with them so they aren't bored, and I certainly will *never* use food as a reward or as a bribery. Children are not *dogs*, and that's just setting them up for a lifetime of an unhealthy relationship with food. And I most definitely will never, ever allow *my* baby to eat anything as awful and unhealthy as Wotsits. That's just disgusting, it's practically child abuse!'

And then when Jane was born, I got over that smug self-righteousness, and realised that actually those parents I'd thought so *dreadful* were doing their best and the stupid parenting manuals that witter on about engaging with your child and explaining and not bribing and having boundaries HAD CLEARLY BEEN WRITTEN BY SOME FUCKWIT WHO'D NEVER MET AN ACTUAL CHILD!

Those books would be all well and good if only your child had read the book as well. If, when you explained that they must sit nicely in the trolley because Mummy was going to buy some lovely food, they didn't then proceed to ignore your anguished pleas of 'Look darling, apples, you love apples, don't you, yummy apples, shall we buy some yummy apples, sweetie, what do you think, sweetie, please listen to Mummy darling, she's trying to fucking engage with you and make sure you feel heard and that your voice is valued, yes, I know you want out, darling, I know. But you can't get out, you need to sit nicely, like Mummy explained, remember, when we talked about what we were going to do today, and no you can't get out, because you can't, BECAUSE I FUCKING SAID SO, all right? If I give you a nice rice cake will you stop screaming? Hmm, yes, look, lovely rice cake, yum yum, DON'T THROW THE FUCKING RICE CAKE

AT THE LADY, OH JESUS FUCKING WEPT, where did you even GET a jar of turmeric, I SAID DON'T THROW, OK, OK, Wotsits? Yes? Wotsits? Oh God. Now you're bright orange with Wotsit dust and it will stain and yes, I know you've finished them, darling, I know, but you can't have any more, what about some fruit? OK, OK, STOP SCREAMING, I know you don't like fruit but that pregnant woman over there is totally judging us, so I have to pretend to make it look like I'm not giving in. Look, please, JUST STOP SCREAMING FOR ONE SECOND till we get into the next aisle and Mummy will give you some chocolate buttons, OK? Yes, chocolate buttons, DON'T THROW THE MOTHERFUCKING OLIVE OIL, IT'S EXTRA VIRGIN, oh shit, there's judgy preggers woman again, well, just you wait, lady, JUST YOU WAIT, your time will come, when your neat little bump is transformed into Beelzebub himself but you've run out of bastarding bog roll and so have no choice but to brave the shops with your Demon Spawn and see how you like THEM apples, madam, no darling, no, Mummy isn't getting apples, no, Mummy knows apples are evil, as is all fruit in your opinion, Mummy will not sully your trolley with apples, oh Hallefuckinglujah, it's the booze aisle.'

'You don't ever regret not having a third then?' asked Hannah drily.

'Fuck no. I mean, it's a bit bloody scary actually thinking what on earth I'm going to do when they leave home, but no. Anyway, this is about you, not me. How can we sort things for you?'

'I don't know, and Mr Tumble will be over in five minutes, and then I'll have to take Conan the Destroyer of Houses home because otherwise his dinner will be ten minutes late and he'll try to eat the cat again. You don't think the vibrator is a good idea then?'

'I think talking to Charlie about how you feel is a better idea.'

'It's just that was the advice *Cosmo* always gave for "spicing things up", but I'm not even sure *how* it's supposed to do that?'

'Well,' I said airily. 'You just … use it on each other, I think.'

'On each other? Like, I use it on Charlie? But how? Where? Oh my God, do I put it up his –?' Hannah broke off in horror.

'I think so,' I said, slightly uncertainly. 'I mean, I'm not 100 per cent sure. I only got one after I was single. I've not actually done anything with it with anyone else. But I'm pretty sure that's what *More* magazine would say. Or, you *could* just google it, Hannah!'

'I can't google it!' said Hannah in horror. 'I can't! What if I died in some freak accident afterwards and I hadn't cleared my browsing history properly, and Emily and Lucas went onto my laptop, maybe to download some touching family photos to remember me by, and there it was in my recent searches? "Do you put dildos up men's bums?" They'd be traumatised for life!'

'Well, there's probably worse things you could have on your search history,' I said cheerfully.

'Like what?'

'Well,' I said, gesturing at the TV, 'apparently, there are forums out there devoted to women who want Mr Tumble to do unspeakable things to them.'

'No! NO! Surely not!' squeaked Hannah.

'Oh yes!'

'How do you *know* about these things?' moaned Hannah in disgust.

'I'm single. I get bored. I spend too much time on Reddit. Someone mentioned it on there. I didn't look it up, obviously, I don't want "Mr Tumble Sex Forums" on my search history, nor do I want to see what sort of depravity goes on there. But according to the posters on Reddit, the women on the sex forums have a thing about his hands …'

Bang on cue, Mr Tumble signed 'Yes' in Makaton, and Hannah and I both gagged slightly.

'Riiiiiiight!' said Hannah. 'Well. That seems to be Mr Tumble finished. Thank fuck. Come on, Edward, darling, time to go!'

After much pleading and bribery and promises of 'seeing Daddy and Emily and Lucas' and a bag of Wotsits and the obligatory knee in the stomach to fold him sufficiently in half to jam him into his car seat, Hannah wrestled Edward into the car and set off home.

I went upstairs and hammered on Peter's door. To my immense surprise he opened it, instead of just mumbling 'Wha'?' through the door.

'Peter!' I said, trying to hide my shock. 'Pasta OK for dinner?'

'I'm, like, going out?' he mumbled, as I resisted the urge to tell him to stand up straight and get his hair out of his eyes, or suggested he borrowed a kirby grip or an Alice band from his sister.

'Oh. Where?'

'Like, Toby's? He's got the new *World of Warcraft* download and we're all gonna have a marathon.'

'Who's "we all"?'

'Like, everybody? Lucas and Olly and Greg and Tom and Marcus?'

'Who are Greg and Tom and Marcus? Is that Marcus Collins?'

'No, Mum.'

'And what about dinner? Does Sam know you're coming over? Has he got dinner for you? Do you need a lift? I'll run you over.'

'Nah, s'cool, Mum, I'll get the bus, I said I'd meet Lucas on it,' said Peter, lolloping down the stairs and making the whole house shake, and grabbing two bags of Doritos out of the kitchen as he galumphed past.

'But when will you be back? Hannah was just here. You could have got a lift over to hers and met Lucas there and then gone to Toby's. Peter! PETER!'

But I was bellowing at the closed front door, Peter having dropped a rather patronising kiss on my head and vanished with a 'Laters, Mother,' and slammed out without even acknowledging, let alone answering, my many anxious maternal queries. At least, I consoled myself, he was going to Toby's, son of my dear friend Sam, so I could check if he was there or if he was roaming the streets having joined a gang. Gang joining was unlikely for Peter, though, I thought hopefully to myself, as by its very nature it involved a degree of sociability and partaking in outdoor activities that did not come naturally to him.

It's strange, really, that I've spent so many years facilitating my children's social life, arranging play dates, and carefully vetting their friends so as to steer them away from the frenemies and mean girls, and for what felt like a very long time, mainly only being friends with people myself because their children were friends with my children, and then all of a sudden, one day – it's over! I mean, they still expect me to provide a regular late-night unpaid taxi service for them, but the days when I knew all their friends nearly as well as I knew my own children are gone, and they're 'hanging out' with a group of ruffians that I don't recognise, except sometimes one of the giant youths looks up from his canoe-sized trainers and you realise that it's Noah Robinson who was sick at Peter's sixth birthday party after an enthusiastic game of musical chairs followed his over-indulgence at the party buffet.

Or one of the terrifyingly glamorous girls sweeps her curtain of hair back, and under all the contouring and 'on fleek' eyebrows (seriously, what the actual fuck is with the eyebrows?) you spy Ella Wilson, who once wet her knickers while sitting on your sofa (why did my children always befriend the kids who seemed to have difficulty keeping their bodily fluids to themselves?).

Even worse, you go to buy a couple of bottles of wine on a Friday night (to last the whole weekend, *obviously*) and then you realise that the girl on the till is Susie Evans, who has got herself an evening job in Sainsbury's, and you try to laugh it off and explain that *obviously* this wine is for the WHOLE WEEKEND, Susie, and how is your mum, and she just sighs judgementally and says she has to get authorisation to sell alcohol as she's under 21, even though you only have to be eighteen to buy it. Then you can clearly see her looking at you pityingly and thinking that two bottles of Sauv Blanc and a family-sized bag of Kettle Chips are your dinner, because you're a sad old lush, and fuck it, maybe they are, Susie, MAYBE THEY ARE, but we ALL know it was you who pooed in the ball pit at Monkey Mayhem Softplay, Susie, so don't you judge *me*, young lady. Obviously, one doesn't say that. But then the next time you see Susie's mum, she gives you a very pitying look, and then in future one has to buy one's wine in Asda, where so far none of your children's friends are working. Yet.

I've spent eighteen years intricately involved in every detail of my children's lives, listening to the endless tales of what Milly said to Tilly, and so then Sophie said, and not that Millie, Mummy, *Milly*, and being asked what my favourite Pokémon is and then being told why that's wrong, and longing with all my heart for them to shut the everlasting fuck up and give me five minutes' peace, and then all of a sudden – they do! It's a miracle! And also rather strange.

I find myself these days in a peculiar limbo between mother-hood states. They need me, yet they don't. My house is still frequently crammed with noisy, smelly, ravening creatures, yet I'm permitted to know nothing about who they are, what they're doing, where they're going, or why they think it's acceptable to leave fifteen empty crisp packets balanced on top of the bin, like they're playing some complicated game of Bin Jenga. I'm their mother, yet at the moment, in many ways, they seem like strangers. I know literally every single thing about them, and I don't know who they are at all. Deep down, I know this is partly because *they* don't really know who they are either – they're still in that transition period between the children they were and the adults they'll become, but that isn't much consolation.

What it is, though, is confusing. This isn't what I wanted. I just wanted them to stop wittering on at me, and eat vegetables with-out complaining and let me go to the loo in peace and learn to make a decent gin and tonic. It genuinely never occurred to me when they were little that this would ever end – each day stretched for an eternity of *Teletubbies* and Duplo and *In the Night* Bastarding *Garden* and shitty arses and screaming, and I couldn't see that there would ever be an end in sight. But now there is. And despite the busybody old women who used to pop up as if by magic whenever I was having a bad day and tell me I'd miss these days when they were over (my favourite was stand-ing in the middle of Tesco with Jane screaming because I wouldn't let her open and drink from a bottle of tequila while Peter projectile-vomited down my cleavage, and it was all too much and I burst into tears myself and wailed out loud, 'Oh God, I hate this! I can't do it anymore,' and some old biddy actu-ally patted me on the arm and said, 'You should make the most of these days, dear! You'll miss them when they're gone!' At which point, I did nearly brain her with the said tequila I'd just wrestled off Jane. It was a toss-up, really, between battering her with it, and just standing beside my trolley and doing shots), I don't miss those days at all. I've literally never stood wistfully in the supermarket and thought, 'Oh, how I *wish* someone was trailing behind me constantly whining, "Mummy, can I have, Mummy, can I have, Mummy, I want, Mummy, why can't I have?" while another precious moppet tries to climb out of the trolley so they can land on their head and we can end up in A&E. Again.'

Nor do I sadly think of how nice it would be to have someone's arse to wipe, or long for the halcyon days when glitter glue lightly crusted almost every object in the house, like a sexually incontinent unicorn had spunked everywhere. But it's discombobulating to go from being the very centre of two people's worlds – the answer to every woe, the salve to every pain, the provider of wisdom and comfort and fun – to barely having my existence register with them. Oh, they still need me on occasion. If Jane misses the last bus from town, I'm supposed to bend space and time to be with her instantly to chauffeur her home, or if Peter can't find the cheese in the fridge ('I didn't know you meant THERE when you said, "Right in front of you," did I?') or if it's raining and either of them need to be somewhere, or if they need money, obviously, then they remember the woman who gave them life, tended their every childish need and devoted herself to their happiness and well-being. Usually when I already have plans of my own.

Fuck me, sometimes they even say thank you! Not often, though. Usually they just take my assistance for granted and tell me not to speak to them in front of their friends due to how mortifyingly embarrassing my very existence is. Naturally, I respond to this by loudly calling them 'sweetie darling' in front of their mates and assuring them at length that Mummy loves them very much. There has to be *some* recompense to having children, after all, and if you don't deliberately and maliciously embarrass them in front of their friends, then are you even a parent?

I once hit upon the great ploy of making them both help round the house more and keep their rooms tidy by threatening to not wear a bra when they had friends over. Oh, that was a happy week. Until they realised that I'd also be mortified by my tits flobbing around in front of a bunch of teenagers and would never make good on my threats, and so normal service was resumed. Jane was also utterly horrified by me the day I knowingly and unkindly told a group of her friends that I 'wasn't a regular mum, I was a cool mum'. That was one of my finest parenting moments. Oh, how I laughed, as Jane seethed with fury.

I've spent years and years thinking, if only I had time for this or that or the other. If only there was time for me. And now at some point in the tangible future, not just 'one day', there will be time. But I've spent so many years juggling everything, doing things at superhuman speed, multitasking to try to fit everything in, that I don't know what I'll do with all that time. With time to spare, I might have to stop and look at who I am, who I've become. And what if I don't like that person very much? What if all I see is a boring middle-aged woman, who's become that person whose life revolved around her children, and now that they're gone, she has nothing left so she tries to keep interfering in their lives? What if I have no inner resources? Or what if I once had inner resources, but they've been lost?

As part of one of their many money-wasting exercises at work, the powers that be decided to bring in a counsellor once for us all to have an interview with to make sure we were all sane and normal and no one was planning on running amok with an industrial-sized hole punch. As part of our 'chat', she asked me to name ten things I'd like to do, just for myself.

'Ha ha ha!' I chortled. 'Only ten! The problem will be limiting it to ten! I'd have a bath in peace. I'd read a book all afternoon with no interruptions from my children, either in person or by text when they're with their father. I'd … um … I'd …'

'Take your time,' the counsellor said kindly.

'No, no,' I bluffed. 'Just trying to choose. I'd … I don't know. I don't know what I'd do. Oh my God, I don't know!'

The counsellor assured me it was fine, that people often found that list much harder than they'd initially thought, and instructed me to go away and think about it, and find time to do more for myself to help me 'de-stress'. Obviously, I promptly put it to the back of my mind, and gave it no more thought, but perhaps this is the time I should start compiling the list of things I'd do for myself. A Nile cruise, perhaps? Though I'd be disappointed if there was no murder. I could go on a riding holiday I once saw advertised, galloping across the desert to Petra! Except I can't ride and I'm scared of horses.

I was still mulling this over as I made a futile attempt to rear-range the furniture to cover the stains from Edward's Ribena (which turned out to be much harder to shift than red wine) and tried to remind myself that the prospect of a Saturday night to myself was a Good Thing, since Jane had texted to say she wouldn't be home either, because she was sleeping over at Olivia's, and I stopped myself from asking if I could speak to Olivia's mum to check that was where they really were and told myself yet again that Jane is very nearly eighteen, and there was nothing surer to push her away and stop her confiding in me than not trusting her, and anyway soon she'll be at university and I'll have no idea what's going on in her life unless she actually tells me, and oh God, please just don't let her get pregnant or hooked on drugs before that. I mean, obviously don't let her ever get hooked on drugs, not just before university. Anyway, I just hope she does manage to get into university, as everything hinges on her actually passing her A levels, as she is *still* extremely nonchalant and trotting out the 'Just *chill*, Mum' line every time I gently suggest that perhaps a tiny bit more revision and a smidgetionette less partying might be in order?

I settled on the sofa and started breaking out the white wine and crisps for my healthy and nutritious dinner for one, while wondering how many episodes of *The Witcher* I could manage before I fell asleep on the sofa and if Henry Cavill would take his clothes off again in many of them. Apparently one is not meant to think such thoughts, as it objectifies men. One should not refer to Henry Cavill as 'top totty' either, for similar reasons. It seems men don't like being objectified, or so I read in an interview with Aidan 'Shirt off, Cap'n Poldark' Turner. I feel, though, that after a lifetime of arsehole men shouting 'Nice tits, love' and ordering me to give them a smile, if I want to ogle bare-chested chaps on the telly, I damn well deserve to, and in fact, it's another blow struck against the patriarchy, even if it could lead to accusations of double standards. In fact, I think men owe women several thousand years of being objectified and leered over before we can finally say we're quits and agree that one should not reduce a human being to nothing more than his extremely nice pecs and his Very Big Sword.

I stared at my phone and wondered if I'd the strength to make a duty call to my mother. I decided I didn't. Phone calls with my mother at the moment consist of lengthy witterings detailing the

many and stellar qualifications of the various tutors my sister
Jessica has hired to get her Most Precious of Precious Moppets,
Persephone the First Born, the Golden One, the First and
Incomparable Grandchild, the best possible results in *her* A
levels, so that she can dazzle at Cambridge, like Jessica did,
before becoming the youngest ever prime minister. Jessica and
Mum were a bit sniffy when I pointed out that the average age of
prime ministers is fifty-something (yes, I googled), and assuming she spent three years at university, she'd then only have
another three years after leaving uni to find a seat, get elected
and *then* become prime minister if she was going to beat
the record set by William Pitt the Younger, who was only
twenty-four when he became prime minister. Jessica muttered
something about Persephone would probably be fast-tracked,
and then hired extra tutors, while resolutely ignoring
Persephone's pleas for a gap year, and that she didn't *want* to be
prime minister or go into politics, and she didn't even much
want to go to Cambridge, actually, she quite fancied Manchester.

I was just wondering whether there would be another bath
scene in tonight's *Witcher* episode, when Simon rang. My heart
sank. Simon tends mainly to communicate by text, and telephone
calls generally mean Something Serious. 'It's Saturday bloody
night, Simon!' I muttered to myself. 'Can't whatever it is wait and
join the rest of the shit show that's no doubt awaiting me in the
office on Monday morning?' I wasn't too concerned that the
Something Serious would involve some sort of harm to my cherubs, as in any kind of scenario that requires help or rescue, they'd
have immediately called me, despite me repeatedly reminding
them that they have *two* parents that they could call should they
require assistance/transport/bail (not that they've ever needed
bail, of course. Yet. Do you even get bail if you are a minor?).

I picked up the phone and gave a rather terse, 'Hello, Simon, what do you want?'

'Um, well, I wondered if you wanted to have dinner with me?' said Simon brightly. 'Tonight, I mean?'

'What, in a restaurant?' I said suspiciously, in case he was expecting to turn up here and have me magically rustle up 'a nice, simple lasagne', as he always insisted lasagne was so easy to make. Really, claiming lasagne is easy should totally be on the Unreasonable Behaviour list for divorce!

'Yes, in a restaurant. Maybe the Italian place in town?'

'And I presume you'll be paying, since this is your idea?' I enquired. It may be the 21st century, and I'm most definitely a strong, independent, modern woman, but a free dinner is a free dinner, especially in the light of the VERY MANY FUCKING LASAGNES I cooked for Simon over the course of our marriage, so he owes me.

'Yes, of course! So … is that a yes? It's just there's something I'd like to talk to you about.'

Ah. Here we have it. He wants something. Either he's going to ask me to cat-sit Marissa's three-legged moggy while they go on another 'couples' retreat' (unlikely, as I suspect Marissa doesn't trust me with her precious pussy), or he's about to announce that Marissa is With Child, or they're getting married, or both. Actually, they can't get married, because we've not actually got around to finalising the divorce yet. Of course. That's it. 'Ellen, dearest, lovely Ellen, who's so nice and accommodating and like, best ex-wife ever, can we get all the paperwork sorted, so I no longer have any legal links to you and am FREE of the shackles of the endless, dull, drudging days I spent with you that will now be nothing more than a bad memory, but one I will soon forget, because look, radiant, glowing, glorious Marissa has made me the happiest man in the world by consenting not only to become my wife but also to bear me some additional fuck trophies, which I might actually parent properly this time instead of always being too tired or at work and leaving it all up to you because that's a woman's job, but now thanks to Marissa and our couples' retreat and my therapist I'm a new man, who barely even watches *Wheeler* Fucking *Dealers* so these blessed children of my wondrous union with Marissa will grow up to be normal and functioning and enviable offspring, who will not say bugger for their first word and will eat vegetables!'

'Ellen? Ellen, are you still there? Have we been cut off?' Simon interrupted my musings.

'Er, no, I'm still here,' I sighed. 'OK, fine, let's have dinner. But you'll have to pick me up, I've had a glass of wine.'

'OK, I'll get you in half an hour?'

'Better make it forty-five minutes,' I said gloomily. It takes longer and longer to look presentable these days, especially if I have fucking Marissa sitting across the table and looking all doe-eyed and dewy-skinned.

Really, though, I pondered as I slapped on my mascara, making that special Mascara-Face, which for some reason requires you to open your mouth while you put it on, what could I do except agree about the divorce, if they asked? I mean, apart from order the lobster starter *and* the fillet steak main course to at least get my money's worth out of Simon. Maybe I should pretend to be euphoric with joy for them and 'accidently' order very expensive champagne to toast the happy couple, while secretly taking malicious glee in seeing Simon flinch at the thought of the price. Although Marissa will probably insist on ordering Fairtrade ethical wine. She's very hot on ethics, and somehow always manages to make me feel guilty about anything

I eat in front of her, even it's just by dint of her looking virtuous and ordering a superfood salad when I've ordered a big, greasy burger.

Well, I resolved, I'd just tune Marissa and her salad out (my dear friend Sam chastised me once for saying that I hated Marissa for ordering salads and pointed out that salad-eating was not actually the crime against humanity I appeared to be making it), and remind myself that Simon will have to listen to this every day for the rest of his life. I mean, he might not, of course. At one point we thought *we* would be spending the rest of *our* lives together, and look how that turned out.

But if marrying Marissa is what Simon wants, I shall be happy for them and will of course sort out all the legalities from my end. In fact, even if he *isn't* marrying her, I should probably do that. After all, it's really more than overdue that we get all the final rubber stamps and boxes ticked (I'm not sure exactly what's involved in the legal process) and draw a line under things. Closure. Like mature, sensible adults. Though I always preferred the version of closure chosen by the lady who sold her cheating radio DJ boyfriend's Maserati on eBay for £1, and then rang in to his show to tell him live on air …

Simon was very chipper when he picked me up.

'Thanks for coming at such short notice. I wasn't sure you'd be up for it,' he said.

He was also alone.

'Oh. Is Marissa meeting us there?' I asked.

'No. No, she's on a yoga retreat,' he said. 'It's just us. Is that OK?'

'Yes, fine!' I said, while thinking judgemental thoughts about how much younger I'd probably look if I spent as much fucking time 'retreating' from the world as Marissa does.

To my disappointment, when we got to the restaurant the lobster was off, but I decided, in the absence of Marissa, that perhaps this evening was not going to be all about how fabulous their future life was going to be as soon as I released Simon from his bonds of servitude to me, because there was no way on God's earth Marissa would have missed the chance to smirk smugly over her bastarding salad at me during that conversation, not even for yoga. So I ordered pasta instead, because if in doubt, carbs.

'So!' I said, spearing an olive, before remembering that olives might make me feel sophisticated, but inevitably they taste only of disappointment and salt. I've spent twenty years trying to be adult enough to like olives, and am gradually coming to accept that it's probably never going to happen.

'What did you want to talk to me about?'

'Well,' said Simon, looking awkward. 'The thing is, I should probably have talked to you about this before, but it just seemed like a good idea at the time. And now I'm worried you'll feel like I've crossed some sort of a line and trodden on your toes …' He trailed off.

'Go on,' I prompted him, regretting not having learnt from the first olive and taken a second one.

'You know it's Jane's eighteenth birthday in a couple of weeks?'

'Well, yes, I'm hardly likely to forget the day a human head emerged from my fanny, am I?' I said tartly, then realised one almost certainly should not discuss one's nether regions, ruined or otherwise, with one's ex-husband. 'In fact, I usually have to remind *you*!' I added, neatly turning the conversation back to Things that Are Simon's Fault and *away* from my unmentionable bits, though it could be argued that the state of my downstairs lady parts comes under Things that Are Simon's Fault too, as it was *his* children who caused the devastation.

'Yes, yes, I know,' he said. 'But well, the thing is, you know.'

'Oh, do *get* to the point, Simon!' I snapped. 'Just spit it out, whatever you've done. Have you booked a holiday so you'll be away for the momentous occasion of your firstborn child entering adulthood, and now you want me to tell her and smooth it all over and make it OK for you?'

'NO!' he said indignantly. 'Of course not! I've bought her a car. She kept saying she wanted one, *needed* one, and a guy at work was selling his son's car, and I thought that would be perfect for her, so I just bought it for her for her birthday. From us – you and me. It was a bargain too,' he added proudly.

My heart sank.

'But Simon, even if it was a bargain, I don't think I can afford to go halves on a car with you. And I certainly can't afford the insurance for her, and what about the running costs? I'm sorry. You're right, you should really have talked to me about this first. It isn't fair to just go out and buy a car and expect me to conjure up money I already told you I didn't have out of thin air.'

Bastard. I should have ordered the fucking steak. And the expensive wine, not the house red.

'That's the thing, though. I don't need you to give me anything for it. I've bought and paid for it, and my parents are going to pay for her insurance and give her some money for petrol and stuff. I just didn't want you to think I was taking over.'

'Well, you are rather, aren't you?' I said, pretending the lump in my throat was from choking on an olive stone, as tears pricked at my eyes at the unfairness of it all, and also with shame at both my ungenerous selfishness and the fact I could not do this for Jane, because she was going to be over the moon to get a car. But try as I might to feel happy for Jane and pleased at Simon finally making an unprompted grand gesture like this, all I could think was how on Jane's birthday, none of the presents I'd so carefully chosen and bought for her would even come close to the fact that her dad had bought her a car, and frankly that was all she'd see and probably all she'd remember about her eighteenth in years to come – 'What did you get, Jane?'; 'Oh, yeah, my dad bought me a car!'; 'Cool, what did your mum get you?'; 'D'you know what, I can't actually remember!'

'And if I'm not chipping in for it, it's not from us both, is it? It's from you! You and Marissa.'

Despite the fact that I invented that very clever app (which paid off the mortgage on our marital home), and that I earn roughly about the same as Simon, my disposable income is far less than his because the children live with me most of the time, and although he contributes the amount calculated as being reasonable to pay for them, the fact remains that the brunt of financial responsibility for them falls to me. I'm the one who takes them on holiday. I'm the one who buys their clothes, replaces their school shoes when they inexplicably develop holes halfway through the term, provides trousers that fit for Peter as his endless eating leads to endless growing, and supplies Jane with skirts that in my opinion most certainly do not fit and are absolutely not value for money when you consider how little fabric you're getting for that price but that she insists *everybody else* is wearing, and feeds them and all their friends when they descend on the house, and all the myriad little bits of money here and there and everywhere that Simon never has to think about as he pays over his allotted amount every month and then happily gets on with spending the rest of his salary on himself. Or not, in Simon's case – he's quite tight – but the point is, he *could* if he wanted to, whereas I always need some sort of contingency for unexpected child-related financial 'surprises'.

And I know I'm lucky, so much luckier than many millions of people, lucky to earn a good salary, lucky to have an ex that gives enough of a shit to pay anything at all towards his kids without being dragged through the courts, and I'm not *badly* off at all. I just can't afford to go around buying cars willy-nilly, and so it rankled somewhat that on account of *my* care of *his* children, Simon could probably have a garage resembling Cameron's dad's in *Ferris Bueller's Day Off* if he wanted (though it's very unlikely that he would do. Apart from anything else, Marissa probably wouldn't let him on account of the evils of fossil fuels), whereas I was panicking about how I was going to afford Jane going to university, let alone Peter following her in a couple of years.

'It *is* from us both,' Simon insisted. 'I, well, I know things aren't exactly fair financially. You spend more on them than me.'

This time I really *did* choke on an olive stone. Why was I even still *eating* the damn olives? Simon had never admitted such a thing before.

'And also, if you hadn't spent so long working part-time and supporting me when the kids were little, you'd probably be much further on in your career and I probably wouldn't be as far on. So I owe you. So it's from us both, and that's what I want to tell Jane. That *we* bought her a car. Because we did.'

There was a slight interruption at this moment as our food arrived and we had to go through the rigmarole of did we want parmesan and did we want black pepper from the giant phallic pepper grinder because why can't we just have our own pepper on the table, is it more peppery the bigger the grinder? And it's always very awkward, how much parmesan and pepper is greedy and will make the waiter judge you, but on the other hand, what is spaghetti carbonara without shitloads of parmesan and pepper?

Once the crowd of waiters had departed with their kitchen accoutrements, I asked, 'What has brought all this on?'

I mean, I've spent literally *years* raging, screaming, sobbing and shouting at Simon, trying to make him recognise my contributions to our lives, our marriage and our children, and he'd just become defensive and accuse me of 'over-reacting' and insist he did his share and there was nothing inherently unfair or unequal about the division of the burdens on us, whether they were financial, housework or emotional labour.

Simon looked slightly embarrassed. 'Um, well, you know that couples' retreat Marissa made me do?'

'That you were going to when Jane passed her test?'

'Yes. Well, there were some quite wanky bits, but some bits were really useful.'

'Well, that's lovely, but I'm not sure how you and Marissa meditating together or whatever it was has led you to this epiphany, when I banged my head against a brick wall for years trying to get you to see this?'

'We had to do an exercise in "appreciation". Appreciation of our partners. And all the things I appreciate about Marissa, I mean, they're good things obviously, she's a kind person, she's passionate about things she believes in, she's not afraid to speak up for those things, and the sex is –'

'– OK, I think you can stop there, and we'll just assume that the sex is appreciated and leave it at that, THANK YOU!'

'Sorry. Anyway. They're all *good* things, of course. But none of Marissa's good qualities have really contributed to most of my life so far, or where I am now. And also, all those things – I would have listed them as things I appreciated about you once, things that were who you were, not what you did for me. And then I remembered that awful time when we were at the marriage counsellor, and when she asked me to say one nice thing about you, all I could say was that you made a good lasagne. And I felt quite ashamed about that. I was a complete dick that day, no wonder you were upset, and then I rounded it off by telling you that I wanted to take a break from us, and then I was surprised when you started divorce proceedings –'

'– about the divorce –', I put in.

'No, please Ellen, let me finish. I wasn't fair to you, not ever. And you did so much for me that I should have appreciated and I just didn't. You're so much more than lasagne,' he finished solemnly.

'Well. Thank you. Though you still seem to be struggling with the concept of compliments. But thank you for realising I'm "more than lasagne" and finally showing a bit of appreciation. I assume you didn't tell Marissa all this while you were on your retreat? I can't see her being very impressed with that.'

'Well, no. Might have been a bit tactless,' he admitted sheepishly. 'But I *did* want to tell you, you know, that I'm sorry, and I do appreciate everything. And I thought maybe Jane's car would be a small step towards making it up to you. How much I took you for granted.'

'And what does Marissa think of all this, about the car?'

'Oh, she's fine about it. I mean, she'd rather we got her an electric bike, but she didn't go totally batshit or anything.'

'Simon, I'm sure the phrase "totally batshit" isn't politically correct, you know,' I said primly.

'Well, it's a term I learnt from you,' he grinned. 'You used – still use – it liberally when talking about my darling sister!'

'How is Louisa?' I enquired politely.

'Running poetry workshops in a yurt in Coventry.'

'Goodness,' I said. 'Poor Coventry. Didn't it suffer enough with being bombed to bits without Louisa and her poetry descending? What does a poetry workshop even consist of?'

'I don't know!' Simon said impatiently. 'Do we have to talk about Louisa?'

'I quite like talking about Louisa. She makes me feel like a functioning adult.'

'No, Ellen, you like *bitching* about Louisa,' said Simon sternly. 'Anyway, so do you think Jane will pleased?'

'I'm sure she'll be ecstatic. And thank you, for finally recognising my contribution to bringing up the kids. Even if it did take a "couples' retreat" with someone else for you to do that. Who knows what epiphanies you'll have if you go on another one!'

'I don't know how I feel about another one,' he said thoughtfully. 'There were a lot of lentils. I didn't think I was ever going to stop shitting.'

'I'm eating?'

'Sorry. But yeah. Apart from the shitting, it was really helpful, actually. I was a bit sceptical, but I learnt a lot.'

'Good,' I said. 'I'm happy for you. For both of you,' I added, slightly grudgingly.

While Simon was doing the whole adulting thing, I thought perhaps I should do the same, and remind him we did need to actually get divorced.

'Yes,' he said slowly. 'I know. Marissa keeps asking about it too. Is there any great rush? Things are fine as they are, aren't they?'

'Well, yes, but it's all a bit of another grey area, isn't it?' I said. 'I mean, we're not actually divorced, but we're not married either. What if one of us wants to get married again?'

'Well, can't we deal with that then? Do you want to get married?'

'No, I don't, and given I don't even have a boyfriend, I'm unlikely to be getting married anytime soon.' (Oh God, maybe I should get married again, even if it's just to get someone a visa, just so I don't have to use the cringemaking term 'boyfriend' ever again. Not that 'partner' is much better – it's very cold. Why hasn't someone come up with the definitive name for your other half when you're unmarried and over forty?) 'But what if one of us moves to Australia and we aren't divorced, and then the other one wants to get married and has to spend months tracking the Australian one down because they've gone off-grid and are now running a … a dog-grooming salon in a quaint little town in the outback, like something out of *The Flying Doctors*, where the children go to school on the radio, and then they have to do a mad dash across the world the day before their wedding to get the last piece of paper signed so they can legally go ahead? That would be a great nuisance, wouldn't it?'

'Firstly, I'm fairly sure the advent of the internet means Australian children no longer "go to school on the radio", as you put it. Secondly, I'm not planning to go off-grid and move to Australia. Are you? And thirdly, such improbable scenarios only occur in your head and those ridiculous rom coms you're so addicted to, so I think it's unlikely that will happen.'

'It *is* unlikely,' I agreed. 'Especially as in those scenarios, the original couple *always* end up getting stranded somewhere, and while they're thrown together into each other's company and argue wittily, they realise that they've never stopped loving each other and the intended one is actually awful so is never mentioned again, and they get back together and live happily ever after. Ha! Like that would happen!'

'Indeed,' said Simon. 'That's why romantic comedies aren't real, though, Ellen. We've been through this. Anyway, now we've ruled out the possibility of a mercy dash to Australia, you're probably right, we should get divorced. I've just been dragging my feet a bit because …'

Simon paused, awkwardly. Oh no! What was he going to say? *Was* he going to declare his undying love, despite his soulless poo-pooing of romantic comedies? How terribly awkward! Didn't he know you were only supposed to do such things in extreme weather conditions, possibly after a brush with death, when one was looking adorably tousled and vulnerable, and wearing a really good push-up bra? Not over greasy pasta plates when you were wondering if you had pancetta stuck in your teeth!

He took a deep breath and carried on. I cringed in anticipation and considered setting my napkin on fire to deflect from any potential Scenes. 'Well, Marissa has been dropping pretty heavy hints that once I'm divorced, we should get married.'

What? Where was my declaration of undying love? I was already composing kind sentences to let him down gently. 'But surely that's a good thing?' I said crossly. 'Don't you want to marry her? She's all perfect and her hair is shiny and swishy and she Does Good Works and is all caring and stuff. Her pores alone are marriable!'

'Her pores? That's slightly creepy, Ellen. Yes, she's very perfect. Possibly too perfect. I feel like I'm constantly being found wanting by her standards. She tells me things are bad that I didn't even *know* were bad. Like avocados.'

'Well, I've repeatedly told you avocados are bad, they're the Snot of Satan, all green and slimy and ruining otherwise perfectly nice food. Even the *Daily Heil* knows avocados are bad. They seem to blame poor Meghan Markle for the evils of avocados, though I'm fucked if I can work out how they're her fault.'

'Yes, but Marissa knows they're bad because of their carbon footprint. Not just because she has an irrational hatred of them because she once had a club sandwich with them in and has harped on about it ever since –'

'– in fairness, my sandwich was *ruined*. It had slimed over everything. EVERYTHING!'

'Yes, I know, you told me repeatedly. My point is, Marissa is anti-avocado for the right reasons, because she's a good person, and I feel like I'm not good enough for her, and she knows it.'

'Well, obviously not, if she wants to marry you,' I pointed out.

'I sometimes feel like it's not so much she wants to marry *me*, as she just wants to get married,' he said. 'I'm Mr Right Now, not Mr Right. Which is fine, because I *don't* want to marry her either.'

'Because she's too perfect?' I said, not very sympathetically.

'Because I'm not sure she is The One for me either,' he said sadly.

'Well then, it's hardly fair to keep stringing her along, is it, pretending you can't marry her because you're not divorced, when we could get divorced tomorrow? You're stealing her last child-bearing years from her,' I added self-righteously.

'Oh no, she doesn't want kids,' he said with relief. 'Too much of a burden on the planet.'

'Are you sure about that?' I asked.

'Yes,' said Simon firmly. 'She was quite adamant. She's very green, Marissa, hence why she doesn't eat avocados. If she's too environmentally friendly for avocados, she's not going to be secretly yearning for a planet-destroying sprog, is she?'

'Well,' I said, 'as long as you're sure.'

'I'm sure,' he said, with some finality. 'Shall I get the bill? It's getting late.'

MARCH

Friday, 1 March – Jane's birthday

It's finally here. Jane is eighteen. My baby girl is old enough to vote, old enough to drink (legally), old enough to be an MP, old enough to get married without eloping to Gretna Green, old enough to … well, I can't think of any other things you have to be eighteen to do. Technically, she's old enough to watch an 18-rated film, but thanks to Netflix and the internet, it's not like anybody actually pays any attention to film ratings anymore, is it? I'd had some vague idea that with Jane passing into adulthood, I'd feel my maternal responsibilities fade away, and our relationship would suddenly be transformed into one more akin to cool friends rather than mother and daughter, but so far there's been no apparent change, and I'm still uncool, and allegedly 'Only sad people are friends with their mums, Mother.'

She was suitably impressed with her birthday haul, though, especially the bottle of Absolut Raspberri I'd purchased with some misgivings, but it *was* on special offer, so it seemed rude not to. She was also delighted with her ASOS voucher, which she will no doubt use to buy minuscule outfits that will lead to me worrying about her getting a chill on her bladder, while she tells me she's, like, an adult, Mother, so stop going on.

And then Simon drove her car over this morning, and I think it's fair to say that she was quite pleased. There was a lot of squealing and selfies while Simon attempted to give her a lecture on road safety and sensible usage, and offered to show her how to change a tyre and wittered about checking oil levels, and Jane paid not one bit of attention because she was snapchatting photos of HER CAR to Emily and Sophie and the tribe of Millies, Tillies and Olivias.

She was slightly less euphoric, however, when she got in the car and realised Simon had had it fitted with a black box. I'd been unaware of these nifty bits of kit, which are apparently ruining the lives of teenagers across the country by monitoring their driving and ratting on them to their insurance companies if they exceed speed limits, brake too hard, take a corner too recklessly or basically drive like a dick. It also marks down their score for too many short journeys, and if their score falls below a certain level, it invalidates their insurance. What its presence DOES do, though, is vastly reduce the cost of said insurance.

Jane was aghast. A black box was not cool. It did not go with her image of hip young thing about town, zipping hither and thither and yon in her sporty new wheels (aka a slightly battered 1L Corsa). She attempted to argue that it probably infringed her human rights, basically having a 'tracking device' fitted to her without her consent and against her wishes.

'Fine, darling,' said Simon. 'No problem. If you don't want the black box, you don't have to have it.'

'Simon,' I hissed. 'Don't bloody give in to her! Just for once in your life, take a stand and be the bad cop instead of leaving it to me.'

'Thank you, Daddy,' said Jane sweetly. 'I knew you'd understand. And of course I don't need a stupid black box, because I *know* how to drive, and obviously I'll be very sensible and responsible, so it's really quite unnecessary.'

'Of course,' said Simon. 'I totally understand. But unfortunately, if you don't have the black box, you don't have the car either. It's entirely your choice. But since you're SUCH a responsible driver, like you just said, it won't make any difference at all to your driving. It will only confirm what a good driver you are.'

'That's not fair!' wailed Jane. 'You can't give me a car and then be all, "Oh, but there's conditions" about it!'

'Yes, we can,' said Simon grimly. 'Up to you, darling. Car or bus?'

'Car,' said Jane. 'Fine. You win. Thank you, though, for the car.'

'Maybe you could offer your brother a lift to school?' I suggested.

Both children looked at me in horror, with faces that suggested I'd just asked them to shit in their hands and clap.

'I haven't got room, Mum. I said I'd pick up Sophie and Emily and Milly!' howled Jane.

'I'm not, like, going with her. She'll probably KILL me!' said Peter in horror.

'You have got room,' I pointed out. 'And Peter, be nice to your sister, it's her birthday.'

'But Mum, he's too BIG, everyone will be squashed, and then my car will smell of Boy Smell and he'll probably fart in it on purpose and it will just be totally gross!'

'And it will be so embarrassing turning up to school with all of them. Everyone will laugh at me!' insisted Peter.

'Your brother doesn't smell that bad, and I'm sure he wouldn't fart in your car on your birthday, and Peter, I'm sure everyone would think you were very cool, turning up at school with a load of sixth-form girls. People might think one of them was your girlfriend!' I said brightly.

'Mum, no, it really doesn't work like that. He's right, he'd look like a loser, and so would we.'

'Yeah, Mum, Jane's right. Don't make us do this!'

I sighed. At least the children were agreeing on something and conceding that the other was right, which was a small victory. Sometimes it seems that the only thing they ever *do* agree on is how wrong I am about everything.

'Fine,' I said. 'Jane, you'd better go if you're picking everyone up en route, and Peter, you'll miss the bus if you don't hurry.'

'Can't you give me a lift, Mum?' whined Peter. 'I still need to find my PE kit because we've wasted all this time looking at Jane's car.'

'Looking at my car is not wasting time,' squawked Jane indignantly out the window, as she ground the gears, stalled and finally lurched off down the lane.

'Actually, Ellen, I need a lift too,' said Simon. I watched Jane's car jerking into the distance and wondered if I'd ever see my baby alive again. 'My car's still at home. Could you drop me at my office after you've taken Peter to school?'

'Fine,' I said, wondering how it was that Jane getting a car had resulted in me having to provide more taxi services than ever!

I'd spent years planning the wonderful family occasion that I'd create for Jane's eighteenth birthday. I mean, literally years. Sometimes, in the dark days when she was a baby and a toddler and I was utterly convinced she'd never get any older, that for the rest of my life nights would be spent wearily stumbling through to her cot for night feeds or because she'd lost her dummy, and days would be spent wiping her bum and watching *Teletubbies* and singing songs about Dingle Dangle Bastarding Scarecrows in their Fucking Flippy Floppy Hats, imagining what it would be like to have a grown-up child, one whose vocabulary was larger than 'No', 'My not', 'Biscuit', 'Bugger' and 'No like it', was a sort of delirious guilty pleasure.

The Jane of my imagination, of course, bore little resemblance to the reality of Jane. Imaginary Jane was based on a sort of mash-up between Anne of Green Gables and Katy Carr (only without the crippling incapacitation, obviously). A gentle, dreamy creature, sprite-like and slightly fey, yet also practical and kind, with a devotion to duty and family, her head eternally in a book, but always ready to rely on her mother for wise advice and counsel. We'd share hobbies and interests, and perhaps go to the ballet together. We did go the ballet once. I fell asleep, and Jane kept nudging me to tell me she was bored and when was it time for ice cream. In fairness, Imaginary Jane would probably have been quite annoying to live with.

Mind you, real Jane is quite annoying to live with, too, but in a much more stroppy, opinionated, 'OMG Mother, why are you so *stupid*' way, as she dismisses everything about me as pointless, old-fashioned, unnecessary and lame. Maybe one day she'll take my advice, but at the moment she's still very much at the stage where She Knows Best.

Thus it was that Jane's actual birthday bore no resemblance to the merry family occasion I'd envisaged all those years ago. I'd thought perhaps Jane and I would wear not matching, but perhaps complementary outfits (I was not getting a lot of sleep back then), and there would be champagne and canapés and a delightful cake, and Simon and I would beam with pride and make a speech together about Jane and the future, and everyone would think what a perfect, perfect family we were.

Of course, splitting up with Simon was the first problem with the party of my vision. The second was Jane having firm ideas about what her eighteenth birthday should involve and this consisted of having a horde of teenagers to my house for 'pre's' (using full words, let alone entire sentences seems too much effort for today's Youth – apparently, for a generation raised on text speak, that frequently text the single letter 'K', as even 'OK' is too difficult, to actually refer to it as 'pre-drinks' would require entirely too much oxygen, and so 'pre's' they are known as). 'Pre's' basically consist of loading up on as much cheap or parental booze as possible before you leave the house, to avoid the necessity of paying for drinks in the discotheque ('FFS, Mother, stop calling it a discotheque. It's not even like that's what people called clubs in the nineties. You're NOT FUNNY, *Mother*!') rather than the glittering social occasion I'd envisaged. I gently raised the subject of what Jane's friends who were not actually quite eighteen yet were going to do when the rest of them traipsed off to a club, and I just got a withering look and was told that, like, *everyone* has fake ID. I decided not to pursue the matter of fake ID and whether Jane had had some when she was underage, as she now no longer needed it and at least had not been arrested for using it, so we must be grateful for small mercies. I seem to have spent most of the last eighteen years being grateful for small mercies.

Obviously, there was not even a hint of matchingness to our outfits. Even had I been foolish enough to broach the subject, there was no way on earth I'd have worn anything resembling Jane's dress. I use the term 'dress' loosely; I'm not sure there was enough fabric for it to be really classed as much more than a handkerchief. Simon was horrified when he saw it, and hissed at me to persuade her to put on a 'nice warm cardigan'. But shortly before everyone arrived, Jane did come downstairs where I was frantically laying out glasses and plates for everyone and said, 'Um, like, Mum?'

'Yes, darling?' I said vaguely, trying to count the glasses and work out if I had enough, or if some people would end up drinking out of my ever-growing collection of empty Nutella jars.

'Mum, can you, like, just stop a minute? I'm trying to talk to you!'

'Of course, darling, sorry,' I said, my mind still on napkins and whether Peter had found the Kettle Chips stash.

'I just, like, wanted to say thanks, Mum,' Jane mumbled.

'For what, poppet?' I said. 'Do you think I've bought enough pizzas?'

'Mum! For, like, *everything*.'

'Everything?'

'Yeah. I know it's been pretty hard for you the last few years and all that, and well, thank you. For the lifts. And everything else. For being my mum.'

'Oh *darling*!' I said, totally choked up. 'You don't have to thank me. It's what mums do!'

'Well, you're pretty good at it. So thank you!'

'Oh sweetie. Shall we have a hug?'

'Um, no. And Mum?'

'Yes, angel?'

'Is that, like, what you're wearing tonight?'

'Yes. Do you like it?' I said, proudly smoothing down my sequined top, seeing our beautiful bonding moment extending into a lovely chat about fashion and style.

'It kinda makes you look like Joe Exotic?'

'Who? Is that a good thing?'

'MUM! How have you not watched *Tiger King* yet? And no, no it's not.'

'Oh. Should I change?'

'Well, only if you want to. Wear it if it makes you happy.'

I didn't really know how to take that, but I didn't have time to change, so the sequined top had to stay.

All in all, though, everything went pretty well. The teenagers got loud and giggly on Prosecco and Budweiser, and demolished the eleventy billion pizzas I'd bought in lieu of elegant canapés (I thought it wise to provide blotting paper), and then to my immense surprise and slight annoyance, as Jane had made it very clear to me that under NO circumstances was I to say anything in front of her friends, and to Jane's immense mortification, Simon insisted on making a speech.

He banged his glass with a knife, and turned to Jane and said, 'Darling, I can't quite believe we're here already. It doesn't seem five minutes since you were born, and here you are, eighteen years old, and ready to go out into the world and show them all how it's done. Don't worry. I did plan a PowerPoint full of embarrassing photos, with equally embarrassing anecdotes to match, but Peter persuaded me out of it, so I'll keep this short and sweet. Jane, you're strong and independent and fearless, and I could not be more proud of you if I tried. And now, please everyone, raise your glasses to my beautiful daughter Jane. May you continue to kick arse everywhere you go, my darling!'

Jane glowered a bit, but grinned as well, and maybe the speech wasn't quite the one I'd once envisioned, but it was very nice, and Simon had even managed to do it without embarrassing her too much. On the plus side, Marissa's face when Simon made his speech! She looked like a bulldog with a smacked arse and a mouth like a cat's bum licking piss off a nettle, and if I'm mixing my metaphors, it's because one on its own doesn't do justice to the look she had.

The taxis arrived to take the teenagers into town to cause carnage in the local nightclubs, and we were left with just Simon and Marissa, Hannah and Charlie (Little Edward had been left in the tender care of Charlie's mum), Hannah's mum, the eternally splendid Mrs P, and my lovely friends Sam and Colin, father and stepfather to Jane's other best friend Sophie and Peter's mate Toby. Peter had, of course, wangled Lucas and Toby staying over, and they'd long since slouched upstairs with industrial quantities of crisps to create noxious smells and wage virtual war upon demogorgons or something. Apart from the odd alarming thump, they were mostly quiet anyway, which was the main thing.

'Well done, darling!' said Mrs P. 'You did it. I always knew you would. Nearly there now. One down, one to go!'

'Mum!' said Hannah. 'I hope you didn't feel that way about me.'

'Of course I did, lovey,' said Mrs P comfortably. 'Raising children is a bloody hard slog, as well you know. And certainly for the first twenty years or so, almost totally thankless and consisting entirely too much of other people's bodily fluids. But oddly enough, after a few years, you do look back and only remember the good bits, and you seem to miss them. Of course, then you have grandchildren and get to exact a splendid revenge on one's own offspring through the medium of strategically feeding them Haribos just before they go home!'

'I KNEW you did it on purpose!' said Hannah, aghast.

'I don't know what you mean, sweetie,' smirked Mrs P. 'Anyway, I must go, it's past my bedtime. The Fucking Oldness, you know. Buggers everything up. Unfortunately, you young things will all find this out soon enough. I'll see you all soon, I've got some Fangtastics for Edward!' And she departed, chuckling to herself, into the night.

'Shall we open another bottle of wine?' said Simon.

'No,' said Marissa sharply. 'I thought we agreed we weren't drinking on Friday nights because we have an early CrossFit class in the morning. We should go, or we'll be too tired for the gym tomorrow.'

'Chill, Marissa,' said Sam. 'The night is young, and in the eyes of Mrs P at least, so are we, so we should make the most of it before the Fucking Oldness descends. A couple of glasses of wine aren't going to make much difference.'

'And it's my daughter's eighteenth birthday, not just any Friday night,' said Simon, picking up a bottle. 'So I think maybe the world won't end if we just miss fucking CrossFit tomorrow.'

'Oh God, don't open any more of that!' I said in horror, wrenching the cheap Prosecco off him. 'That was for the undiscerning teenage palate. I've got some decent stuff somewhere. Hang on while I go and find it.'

I had in fact hidden the drinkable plonk in the shed, where marauding teenagers were unlikely to look, and then I suddenly had the fear that in my haste to get ready for Jane's party, I had not properly locked the door of the hen house, where my morose Speckled Sussexes – Oxo, Paxo and Bisto – resided in splendour and luxury, producing perhaps three eggs a year each and glaring at me balefully the rest of the time. Nonetheless, despite their bad temper and the fact that each egg cost about £60 when you took into consideration all the outlay for them (if you'll pardon the pun), I was very fond of them, as was Jane, and having them eaten by a fox, or Judgy given half the chance, as they're sworn enemies, would have put something of a dampener on her birthday.

I was just checking the door when I heard raised voices drifting out the kitchen window, which I'd had to open to disperse the smoke from when I accidentally chargrilled a couple of the blotting-paper pizzas.

'All I'm saying, Simon, is that it's a matter of respect. You made a commitment to me that we'd go to CrossFit *together*, and now, any old excuse and you're just not going to bother. I find that quite disappointing. I just don't feel like you're taking our relationship seriously.'

'Oh, for Christ's sake. You're always disappointed in me. Nothing's ever good enough. So now I'm not taking our relationship seriously because I want to have a glass of wine with some old friends to celebrate a milestone in my daughter's life and somehow it's all about you, because I might not want to go to the fucking gym with you tomorrow? Why can't you just relax? Have a glass of wine yourself!'

'I *can't* have a glass of wine, because some of us honour our commitments, and I said I wasn't drinking on Friday nights so I have a clear head in the morning. And also, because now I have to drive home, because *you've* had a drink. And you want to stay with your ex-wife and HER friends. And have you asked her about the divorce? Why hasn't she done anything about it?'

'They were my friends too. Leave the car, we'll get a taxi home and pick it up tomorrow. And I hardly think my daughter's birthday is the time to start nagging Ellen about the sodding divorce. We're all just trying to have a bit of *fun*, Marissa!'

'Firstly, I don't need alcohol to have fun, and I didn't think you did either. Frankly, if we leave now, you'll thank me in the morning when you're not hungover and you're buzzing after

CrossFit. You *love* CrossFit, and you're doing so well at it. Don't mess it up now for the sake of too much cheap wine. And secondly, it's unfair to say I'm always disappointed in you and nothing's good enough. I've *never* said that, and I'm sorry you feel that way. And finally, my idea of *fun* is not sitting with that old lush Ellen and her equally reprobate friends, listening to them all bore on about their bloody children!' spat Marissa.

I thought I should probably stop eavesdropping at this point, before I heard something even worse about myself. What I'd heard was bad enough. Old lush? Was that how people saw me? I didn't think I talked about my kids much at all, but apparently, I do nothing but bore on about them. Before Marissa could expound further on my failings, I crashed through the door with the wine, as Simon exploded, 'For fuck's sake, Marissa!'

'Here we are!' I trilled brightly, dumping the box on the table. 'Much more drinkable stuff. Not like I'm an *old lush* who just drinks anything she can get her cronelike claws on, ha ha ha!'

Marissa did have the good grace to look slightly embarrassed at my 'old lush' reference, and Simon glared at her.

'Shall I open that, Ellen?' he offered.

'Nope. *Perfectly* capable of opening a bottle of wine myself,' I said firmly. 'Marissa, wine?'

'No,' said Marissa sulkily.

'Marissa's just leaving,' said Simon.

'WE'RE just leaving,' insisted Marissa.

'Actually, I'm going to stay and have a drink with everyone, then help Ellen clear up,' said Simon, gesturing round at the pizza and glasses and plates strewn everywhere. 'You go on, I'll get a taxi later.'

'Honestly, Simon, it's fine,' I said. 'I can clear up myself. You go with Marissa.'

'No,' insisted Simon. 'It's hardly fair to leave you with all this mess from Jane's friends, is it?'

'Trust me, I'm used to it.'

'And I should stay till they all come home, make sure no one's too drunk,' said Simon virtuously. 'Give you a hand if they're out of control.'

'Again, really, I'm used to it. I've had multiple pissed-up teenage girls sleeping over every weekend the kids aren't at yours. They might be a bit OTT tonight, but I've got plenty of extra kitchen roll and carpet cleaner and the Marigolds on standby. You two go home, don't worry about me!'

Yes, fuck off home you pair of smug twats, so I can at least have a drink with my friends without you sitting there judging me as a sad old lush with no conversational skills, because occasionally we all need to offload about the frustrations of our children, not that either of you would actually know what that is like because Marissa not having kids means she judges everyone else's parenting, and Simon because he's never really had to parent because he's always just left it up to me. On the weekends he has the kids ('weekends', HA!), he picks them up on a Saturday lunchtime, takes them to Pizza Express for dinner and returns them to me by lunchtime on Sunday.

Inevitably, if there are parties or sleepovers or other social occasions, the children will elect not to go to Simon's so they can have all their friends here, or have me chauffeur them around without Simon grumbling about it, or it getting in the way of their bloody *CrossFit* or something. It wasn't just opening wine I was perfectly capable of doing by myself, it was bloody everything. And if I was exhausted and weary sometimes, and felt a longing for someone to share the load with, I knew I didn't actually *need* anyone, because I could do it myself, like the Little Red Hen.

Obviously, I didn't say all that out loud, as Marissa would probably have just considered me deranged, as well as a boring old lush, and Simon would immediately launch into listing the many times he *had* actually been a responsible parent, and hadn't left it all to me, despite the fact that if you can come up with all the examples of your excellent parenting to prove a point, then there probably aren't that many, and also, I really couldn't face a row. Jane's birthday and our conversation earlier had left me strangely emotional, and hearing Marissa's opinion of me had hurt more than I thought it would, and if Simon started on at me now, there was an excellent chance I'd just burst into tears and wail, 'It's not FAIR,' like Little Edward. Possibly with or without the lying on the ground screaming and kicking part, but hopefully definitely minus the shitting myself with fury bit.

Luckily, at that point Colin came into the kitchen.

'Ellen, did you find the wine? Otherwise, I'll soon be desperate enough to drink the battery acid Prosecco, and surely you wouldn't do that to me, would you? Oh!' he said, suddenly noticing the slight tension in the room. 'Everything OK, Ellen, darling? Here, give me that,' and he yanked out the cork I'd been trying to stop Simon noticing I was struggling with.

'Marissa and Simon are just going home,' I announced.

'Oh, what a shame!' said Colin, managing to sound not even slightly regretful. He had never been a big fan of Simon, and he was a good-enough friend to agree to dislike Marissa on my say-so, despite trying to point out that she didn't really seem so bad.

'Actually, Marissa's going home, but I'm going to stay, give Ellen a hand to tidy up after everyone's gone, and make sure the girls are all right when they come home and that she doesn't need any help with them,' said Simon.

'How nice,' said Colin faintly, tipping most of the bottle into his glass. 'Ellen, we're going to need some more wine if Simon is staying then, aren't we?'

'Simon –' began Marissa.

'Just go home,' said Simon. 'Please. Don't make a scene. I'll call you tomorrow, if I don't see you at CrossFit.'

'But we haven't finished talking about this, though. And we brought your car, remember,' said Marissa.

'I'll get it tomorrow!' snapped Simon. 'I'll deal with everything *tomorrow*! Just give me one fucking night off, OK? One night. To have a drink and a laugh and a chat with some old friends. Everything doesn't always have to be so serious, Marissa. We don't have to talk about everything. Sometimes, there's a lot to be said for British reticence and emotional repression.'

Colin and my eyes met, and he raised his eyebrows questioningly, while I fought the urge to giggle. This is one of the best things about Colin; sometimes, even without saying a word, he can take you from the verge of tears to laughter in an instant. If Marissa takes everything seriously, Colin takes nothing at all seriously. 'Life's too bloody short,' he's fond of saying. Sam says this is all well and good, but it gets annoying sometimes when Colin uses it as an excuse for not taking the bins out again.

'Come on, Ellen,' he said. 'Grab another bottle, and let's go and top your guests up. Hannah needs to make the most of her night away from the Devil Child, and Sam's having kittens because he's just seen on Sophie's Instagram stories that they've found a bar doing 2-4-1 Pornstar Martinis, and he's convinced she's going to get alcohol poisoning or pregnant because of this, so we need to numb his pain.'

We left Simon and Marissa glaring at each other and retired to my gracious drawing room (slightly more shabby than chic sitting room, shabbier than ever after Edward's recent visit). Some more raised voices drifted through, but we couldn't hear what was actually being said – the curse of living in an old cottage with thick stone walls. There's a lot to be said for the lack of soundproofing in modern stud walls.

Then the whole house shook as someone slammed the front door with a violence worthy of Jane in her worst teenage tantrum, and Simon came through from the kitchen.

'Unfortunately, something's come up and Marissa's had to go home,' he said slightly sheepishly. 'Needs to feed her cat. And she's got an early start and all that. Err, is there any more of that wine?'

Obviously, we were all very British and pretended that a) we were devastated that Marissa had had to go, and b) it was due to some unexpected turn of events that definitely wasn't anything to do with the massive barney we'd just heard them having in the kitchen.

Much later, after everyone but Simon had gone, and we'd tidied away the mess from the party, and the dishwasher was on (it was a lot faster with two people to tidy up, I had to give him that much) and we'd decided to have maybe just one more glass of wine, he suddenly said, 'Ellen, can I say something?'

Everyone knows that anything that needs to be preceded by 'Can I say something?' is never going to be good. It's not quite as bad as 'No offence, but …' or indeed any statement that's followed by a qualifying 'but', though as some wise person once said, nothing that's said before the 'but' actually counts, it's only the words after the 'but' that are important (e.g. 'You've got a really pretty face and great sense of humour, BUT you've also got a big fat arse, so I don't want to go out with you').

'It rather depends what you want to say?' I said warily.

'Well, I didn't want to say anything in front of Jane, because it's her day, and I didn't want to take the focus off her or anything, but I did want to say that you've done a really fantastic job with the kids. I've been a shit father. I throw money at the problem, and hope for the best. You're the one who's really brought them up, wiped their arses, mopped up their puke, given them confidence and resilience and strength. You're why Jane is so tough and independent. She sees your example, and she knows she can be anything she wants to be. If she grows up to be half the woman her mother is, I'll be even prouder of her than I am now. And that's all down to you. So … I wanted to say thank you. Thank for you listening to them, making them into the people they are. The people they will be.'

'Shut up!' I said awkwardly. I'm not good with compliments. Especially not from Simon. And especially not from Simon about my bloody parenting, which he seemed to have spent most of the last eighteen years criticising and sniping about. 'Anyway, you weren't a shit dad.'

'I wasn't as good a dad as I could have been. Yes, I worked hard to provide for them, no, they've not wanted for anything. I love them dearly, and I'd do anything for them, but I was never there for them like you were. Are. I never knew what to say to them. Not when they were little and endlessly droning on, not now, when I'm always so worried about saying the wrong thing. And you were always so good at it, that I would just think, "Oh, Ellen can deal with it," and run away and hide.'

'In your shed!' I reminded him. 'Is this sudden new perspective due to you still not having a shed to hide in? Because you've made me feel like a pretty shit mother plenty of times before. And I wasn't good at it. Quite often I wanted to claw my own ears off rather than listen to another long story about how they saw an ant at nursery, or if a random combination of creatures fought each other who would win, but I just got really good at tuning them out and nodding and smiling and going to my happy place.'

'Bollocks,' said Simon. 'You were good at it. You still are. So thank you.'

'How about instead of thanking me, you try to be a better dad?' I suggested. 'If you think you're a shit dad, be better.'

'But how?' he said. 'I suppose I've been a dad like mine was – go to work, earn the money, pay the bills, don't talk about feelings, stiff upper lip, get on with it. I can't just start being all touchy-feely now!'

'No one's asking you to be touchy-feely. But it's a pretty feeble excuse that you can't do any better because your dad didn't. My mother wasn't much of a mother. It's not like I'd a great role model there, but I managed. Mostly by trying to be less like her and more like Mrs P. You just need to take an interest in them. Do stuff with them. Go to some awful gaming convention with Peter or something. Take Jane out to lunch on her own and treat her as an adult, not a little girl. Start small. I dunno. You saw a therapist when we broke up, what would she advise? I'm just muddling through here as best I can, I don't know what *you* should do.'

'Yes. You're right. This is my problem, not yours. I was just trying to say thank you for giving me such great kids, and now I've just given you more crap to deal with, trying to help me be a better father. Sorry. That wasn't my intent.'

'Just google it?' I suggested. 'You can find anything on Google. Except where to hire a hitman. Not that I've googled that!' I added hastily.

'You have totally googled how to hire a hitman,' he said. 'You're a terrible liar. That's why you could never actually murder someone.'

'That's why I would need a hitman!' I pointed out.

'Anyway,' I said chirpily. 'You can put all the lessons you've learnt with our children into practice with being a better dad to Marissa's baby.'

'I told you!' said Simon. 'She doesn't want kids.'

'I think you're wrong. I bet she does want kids,' I said. 'Tom at work got married and told us all that they didn't want kids, that his wife had said before they were married that she definitely didn't want children, bad for the environment, over-populated world, yada yada. That was four years ago, and he's got three under three now, and I saw his internet search history, which consists of things like, "How can I get a vasectomy in secret?"'

'Do you mean she's lying?' Simon said in horror.

'Not LYING as such, no, I shouldn't think,' I said, determined not to inadvertently bitch about Marissa to Simon, despite their massive row earlier, because I still wasn't convinced he wouldn't end up married to her while she popped out sprogs left, right and centre.

'I'm sure she believes she doesn't want kids right now, but why else would she be so keen for you to get divorced? And even if she genuinely doesn't want them now, once she knows she's in a secure relationship, maybe she'll feel otherwise, clock ticking and all that, and hey presto, you'll be standing in Tesco at midnight doing the emergency Calpol run again. Mmmm, remember the smell of Calpol puke, Simon? It's a unique aroma, so sugary sweet going in, so rancid when they bring it back up five minutes later.'

Simon was sweating. 'You're sick, do you know that?' he hissed. 'I try to say something nice, and you turn round and start on scenarios like that!'

'Yes,' I said cheerfully. 'I'm just giving you a glimpse of the possible future. You wouldn't be the first man to think their partner doesn't want children and find things are very different a few months down the line.'

'She's stopped drinking,' said Simon slowly. 'She said it was for health and fitness reasons. She wants me to stop drinking altogether too. Said it would be much better for me.'

'Well, your boys do swim better when they're sober. Personally, I think there's a lot to say for being sloshed myself.'

'Oh God!' said Simon in despair.

We were interrupted at that point by Jane and the other girls arriving home somewhat earlier than we'd expected, in a state of high indignation.

Apparently the only club willing to accept the dubious fake ID from the underage members of the party was a complete dive, filled with dodgy men, and unfortunately Jane's 'Birthday Girl' badge had attracted most of them around her. Simon turned puce at this, and when Jane announced that one of the sleaze bags trying to chat her up had turned out to be fifty (what are fifty-year-old men doing in nightclubs on a Friday night, let alone chatting up teenage girls? Why aren't they at home wearing fleeces and watching *Wheeler* Fucking *Dealers*?), a vein actually began to pulse in his temple.

'Shall I go find the bastard and kill him?' growled Simon.

'God, Dad, shuddup! You're like sooooo embarrassing! I *dealt* with it, OK?'

'You were brilliant, Jane!' said Sophie.

'Did you knee him in the balls?' I asked.

'Mum! No! I'd be done for assault. No, I asked him how old he was, and then I said did he know that he was older than MY MUM, and didn't he think he should be ashamed of himself, and he got all embarrassed and walked off, and then Emily shouted, "Yeah, fuck off, Grandpa, go and buy a bag of sweets like a proper paedo," and he looked like he was going to cry.'

'And then this other guy kept hassling Sophie to "Smile", so she told him that she didn't have to smile just to reaffirm his fragile masculinity and also that he was a dickhead, and then it was all just too much hassle with arsehole MEN, so we went and got chips and came home!'

'Chipsh is betterer'n men, anyway!' mumbled Emily happily.

Monday, 4 March

Despite the fact that there was a huge deadline looming and my team were under some pressure, we all spent the morning perched on uncomfortable chairs in the conference room while we were given a pep talk by a jolly American sort brought in by HR to motivate us by talking about energy vampires and how to avoid them.

We were all rather uncertain exactly how wasting an hour and half eating indifferent biscuits (would it kill them just for once to get Mint Clubs in?) and listening to Chad tell us how he used to be fifty pounds heavier and work a desk job before he discovered that energy vampires were holding him back, and so he lost the weight and took up Motivational Speaking instead, and now he's a super-successful globetrotter from doing his Motivational Speaking, was going to actually increase our productivity or motivation. But HR had sent round a snippy email making it clear that attendance was 'expected', and who are we mere warm-blooded mortals to argue with the powers that be if they think that 'energy vampires' are a problem in the office?

Maybe I should become a motivational speaker? I mused. After all, 99 per cent of 'motivational speakers' didn't seem to have any qualifications other than the ability to talk a lot of bullshit. Of course, there were a small number of people who were truly inspirational, who'd overcome terrible adversity to do amazingly heroic things and then went on to become motivational speakers, but Chad definitely wasn't one of them, and if he could do it, surely I could? I spent half my life giving motivational talks, either to my children or my team, so I was completely certain that I could Buzzword Bingo up the basic message of 'Get your fucking finger out and get on with it or you'll fail your exams/fuck up the project, and ruin your life/get sacked' and be a brilliant motivational speaker.

Slightly more alarming than Chad's witterings was the email that arrived from my old boss, Ed. Ed used to do my job until he got a big, important promotion and buggered off to the head office in California, and I got his job, which was nice, and all the bullshit that goes with it (less nice).

Ed's email did not bring tidings of joy. Instead, it was a heads-up that the potential merger that we'd all been worrying about seemed almost certain to be going ahead, in which case there would be 'significant restructuring'. Which is, of course, a nice way of saying, 'Yeah, they're gonna sack y'all and give your jobs to their own staff.' Still, it was good of him to let me know and give me some advance warning that I was probably going to be out on my ear shortly, as I fear the people who'll keep their jobs are the fuckers like Daryl in the short trousers who know the right things to say, rather than saying, 'Well, my team hits every deadline we're given and we do it ON BUDGET and we've not fucked anything up, caused any product recalls or international incidents, so really, what the fuck more do you want from us? We're all good at our jobs and actually would be even better at them if the people in the wanky trousers would just leave us alone to get on with it.'

Note to self. Do not mention wanky trousers when they're restructuring. Possibly I should even invest in a pair of said trousers myself to try to look hip and cool and happening. Perhaps I should consult Jane about the trousers and what the Young People Are Wearing? Assuming she would deign to give me fashion advice, of course, and doesn't just roll her eyes and tell me to go shop in Boden or tell me it's all Carole Baskin's fault (I finally watched all of *Tiger King* over the weekend with a very hungover Jane, and now get what everyone else is talking about).

Every stage of employment seems like such a battle if you're a woman. First you're young and pretty, and everyone thinks you probably only got the job because you shagged someone, and you have to put up with sleazy men creeping over you and be told their inappropriate sexual innuendo is just 'banter' and to 'take a joke'. Then no one wants to employ you, or promote you because, heaven forbid, you might go off and have babies, how very dare you? Then if you do have children, you're expected to juggle everything and be the perfect mother and Employee of the Fucking Month, with society judging you for working and your colleagues convinced you can't possibly be pulling your weight because you're a 'working mother'. And can we talk about the whole 'working mother' label too? How many men are called 'working fathers'? None. Every single bloody interview with a successful woman who also has kids asks her a patronising question about how she 'juggles' being a 'working mum' with her career. No one asks successful men that. Ever!

And then, you get past the stage of hurtling between the office and the school run and sneaking out for the afternoon because you can't bear the thought of your kids being the only ones with no one supporting them at Sports Day, or at their very boring assemblies, and then you're old and invisible, and no one takes you seriously because you're not hot anymore, even though when you *were* young and hot, no one took you seriously *because* you were attractive. And after all that, your pension will probably be worth less than a man's.

Of course, it's not only in the workplace that it's shit to be a woman. Men can bleat on as much as they like about how awful it is to be a man in the 21st century, because they can't comment on your boobs whenever they like. But maybe things are changing and I should take heart. It might be too late for me, but maybe we've made things a bit better for our daughters, at least, fought battles they'll never have to fight and smashed glass ceilings that they'll never even know existed.

Bleak as things might seem to me right now, the world Jane is growing up in is so very different to the one Hannah and I knew when we were her age. When we were eighteen, we still had one very old-fashioned teacher who insisted that we should never go out with a boy in shiny shoes, in case he used them to try to see up our skirts in the reflection. In an age of upskirting, dick pics, sex tapes and nude selfies, the thought of some spotty youth casting aside his scuffed Doc Martens or his skanky Adidas Gazelles in favour of polishing up his patent spats to get a glimpse of our stout M&S cotton gussets is even more ludicrous than it was then (Hannah's mother informed us that in her day, they were told to avoid going to dinner with a chap in a restaurant with white tablecloths, lest they remind him too much of bed sheets and inflame him to uncontrollable ardour, which obviously wouldn't be his fault, poor fellow). But although technology has brought in ever new and inventive ways for men to be sleazebags, at least this generation of girls seems much less inclined to simply accept the casual everyday sexism and abuse in the way that we were taught to. For them it's not just 'one of those things' if a man puts his hand on their leg, or a builder shouts, 'Show us yer tits, love,' or a colleague makes unwanted advances towards them.

Despite some misogynists claiming the #MeToo movement is about snowflakes who really need to get a grip, and the poor, put-upon menfolk wailing that they just can't say *anything* to women now, can they, lest they take offence (usually the sort of men I suspect who also say things about how Piers Morgan talks a lot of sense and Laurence Fox makes some good points), I think it's all a most excellent thing.

I wouldn't say I'd ever been properly sexually harassed or assaulted or abused, but when so many women started speaking out, most women of our generation realised how inured we were to casual sexism, to men's uncomfortable comments, to modifying our behaviour to placate men, so they didn't get angry or turn nasty, and really, how very wrong that was.

From leering bosses staring at your tits, to lying to taxi drivers about your address because they made you feel so uncomfortable with their personal questions, to drunk men in bars and clubs who bought you drinks you didn't want and hadn't asked for but that they thought entitled them to your time and attention, we were conditioned to smile, to be nice, to be a good girl, not to be a bitch, not to upset them. Because deep down, we were scared what would happen if we did upset them.

But Jane and her friends are so much more fearless, partly, I think, because the shift was coming even in my generation. We didn't want our daughters to grow up like us. We wanted to smash those glass ceilings so they didn't have to, and break taboos so they could have a more equal world than us, and I hope it's paying off. I sent Jane to ju-jitsu lessons where my mother sent me to ballet ('It might make you more ladylike, darling,' she cooed when I objected. 'So you can break both his arms first and ask questions later,' I told Jane when she asked why she was going to ju-jitsu). But more than that, Jane just takes no shit off anyone. Admittedly, this is a pain in the arse when she turns that attitude on me, but her bravery is one of the things I'm most proud of about her.

Jane is never going to let sweaty youths paw her because she's afraid they might think her rude if she tells them to stop. She will not tolerate jokes from colleagues about how she 'must be on the blob' if she objects to their crude behaviour. She will not be called 'sugar tits' or smile anxiously in the hope they just fuck off and leave her alone when some arsehole says, 'Come on, love, give us a smile then.' She will tell all those twats where exactly they should get off, and where they can stick their misogynistic comments, and then, quite possibly, break their arms and knee the fuckers in the balls (obviously, I hope that she's never in a situation where she has to *use* her ju-jitsu skills, but should the worst happen, I did take her every week for ten years, and should she put them to use, I hope she goes to town and at least gets my money's worth – is that wrong of me?).

It's not just Jane, of course. I see her attitudes mirrored in her friends, too, in Emily and Sophie and all the Millies and Tillies and Olivias. I'd never have stood up to the sleaze bags on Jane's birthday like they did at that age. I'd have smiled like they told me to, and just hoped they'd go away if I was Nice and Polite. But why should I have had to be? The girls were quite right to tell them where to get off. And hopefully, there will be enough tough, strong girls like Jane and her friends, and boys like Peter who have been brought up to respect women, not least by living with sisters like Jane, that any men left who still think it's OK to be a misogynistic wanker will quickly learn that it's most certainly *not* all right, and will modify their behaviour at least, if not their mindset, for fear of the consequences, so that the girls who have not been as lucky as Jane and Co., who for so many reasons don't have their confidence, their strength and their courage, do not still get treated like shit either.

I spent so long musing on all this that my computer had shut down, unfortunately leaving me staring at a blank screen, when the annoying HR woman marched in to enquire if I'd finished filling in the evaluation of how useful I'd found this morning's motivational speaker, and if not, why not? I assured her I was *just about* to do it, and then, when she seemed poised to sit in my office and watch me do it, reminded her that it was supposed to be confidential, and chivvied her on her way. I stared at the stupid evaluation for a while and then pulled up my long-neglected CV. At least Ed's heads-up had given a bit of extra time to get working on it before the official announcement. It was time to try to be positive and remember that I'm a team player with a go-getting attitude whose main fault is probably being a perfectionist and caring too much.

Oh God. What sort of wank are employers looking for on CVs these days? And WHY do we have to jump through such stupid fucking hoops, pretending that we're people we're not, with hobbies we don't give a monkey's about? Why can't we just say, 'I want this job because I like being able to eat and pay my bills, and I think I'd be quite good at it because I have all the necessary skills. And so if you just leave me alone to get on with it, I know I will give you the results you're looking for and I might be able to go on holiday, thanks very much,' instead of pretending your imaginary passion for hang-gliding is in any way relevant to your job (unless, of course, you're applying for a job as a hang-gliding instructor, in which case it's probably quite important). It's like internet dating in a way (though at least when you've had enough of that, you can simply walk away from it with nothing more than your pride hurt, unlike gainful employment, which if you decide you've had enough of it, you might lose your house. Of course, the same is occasionally true of those who engage in internet dating with Nigerian generals).

APRIL

Saturday, 6 April

Well, that's the end of an era and the start of a new one. Margaret up the lane moved out yesterday, after about three different 'goodbye' parties, and went off to her little retirement flat with great glee about how cheap her heating bills will be and with high hopes of pulling some unsuspecting retiree at a wine and cheese night. I quite like the sound of Margaret's retirement village. 'I think it'll be rather like a cruise!' said Margaret cheerfully. As a leaving present, she gave me a beautiful pair of vintage binoculars that had belonged to her grandfather, and made me promise to visit regularly to quaff gin and provide contraband cigarettes.

She gave me a lascivious wink as she gave me the binoculars and informed me I might find them useful for 'looking at the local wildlife', by which, given the wink and the nudge that followed it, I assume she means I'm to use them to spy on the mysterious new Handsome Man who's moving into her house.

I told Sam and Colin all this when they came round for dinner this evening, and they were most thrilled at the prospect of A Romance on the horizon. I attempted to cool their enthusiasm, pointing out the many flaws in the plan, including the fact I'd not yet even SEEN this man, let alone met him, he might be a complete arsehole, I almost certainly wouldn't fancy him, and it was even more unlikely that he'd fancy me, and there was also an excellent chance he was a serial killer and I'd end up in some sort of grisly Bluebeard's cupboard.

'Also,' I pointed out firmly, 'he hasn't even moved in yet! I saw a car there briefly earlier, but it went away and hasn't returned, let alone a van or a removals lorry.'

Unfortunately, right on cue, a car rumbled past and stopped outside Margaret/New Mystery Man's house.

'Come on!' said Sam, grabbing a bottle of wine out of the rack. 'We're going to be neighbourly!'

'What?' I said. 'No! Wait! We can't. The chicken's in the oven. I still need to make the salad. We can't just barge in there.'

'We're being welcoming!' said Colin firmly. 'Come on, Ellen! Live a little! You won't do internet dating, you won't let us set you up on a blind date, but Jack got you over all the awkwardness of getting naked with a stranger after years of marriage. Do you want to be alone for ever more?'

'Yes,' I said. 'The last man who saw me naked moved to Antarctica. What does that tell you about me? I'm resigned to being on my own. I'm fine with it. I have the dogs. And the chickens.'

'Ah, but do the dogs and chickens keep you warm at night?' wheedled Sam.

'Yes, actually. TOO warm sometimes, when Judgy decides he's going to sleep on my head and Barry forgets he's the size of a Clydesdale and tries to snuggle too.'

'Stop making difficulties, and just come and say hello,' said Colin bossily. 'What have you got to lose? You'll have to meet him some time, you're going to be neighbours. And just think how romantic it would be, two lonely souls, eyes meeting, your cold and shrivelled hearts unthawing in the glow of each other's love … Little did either of you know, when you did your neighbourly duty on that balmy spring evening, that it would end in you … well, doing your neighbour.'

'I think you are getting a little bit ahead of yourself,' I pointed out. 'We haven't even met him. We only have Margaret's word that he's attractive and her eyesight isn't what it used to be. It's probably not even him. It's probably a plumber or something, come to do some work before he moves in, and also you seem to be forgetting about the whole possibly a serial killer thing I mentioned.'

'In my experience, the chance of a plumber coming out to look at some work at this time on a Saturday night is entirely non-existent, but in the event it IS a plumber, look on the bright side. You'll clearly have discovered the most dedicated plumber in the country, which can only be a bonus. And the potential serial killering is all the more reason to go round there NOW when we are with you. He won't murder us all!'

'I think the whole point of serial killing is multiple murders, so he might!' I objected. 'I could do with the number of a decent plumber, though. I asked Simon if he had one, what with him being an architect and overseeing buildings being built all the time, because the kitchen tap was leaking, and so he offered to fix it and then he said it couldn't be fixed and I'd have to replace the whole kitchen and so I'd need a kitchen fitter not a plumber. But I'm not sure I believe him. He always talked bollocks when it came to DIY, and I can't see how a dripping tap would necessitate the whole kitchen being replaced. I think he just didn't know how to fix it, and didn't want to admit it.'

'Yes, but while we're standing here talking about Simon's lack of practical skills, someone else might snaffle him next door.

Come on!' said Colin. 'You said it would be half an hour before dinner was ready. Let's go get you some cock!'

'I think it might take more than half an hour to do that. And wait!' I said. 'What wine is that? I don't want to waste good stuff in case he's a wanker, but I don't want to give him the scary Tombola Bottle of Doom that's been in circulation since 1973, in case he *is* all right and he judges me for my dodgy Black Tower! £5.99 Rioja? That'll do.'

'Right, let's go!' said Colin.

'Hang on!' I yelped. 'Do I look OK? Is my nose shiny or hair weird, is the light bouncing off my crow's feet making me look hag-ridden? Have I got gravy down myself?'

Colin and Sam looked me up and down for a moment.

'Maybe brush your hair and powder your nose and put on something a little less covered in dog hair?' suggested Sam.

'With a bit of cleavage,' added Colin. 'Might as well set out the wares while we're about it.'

'Rude!' I said. 'I'm not getting my tits out till I know he's worth it.'

Nonetheless, I DID put on a clean shirt, as the jumper I was wearing was not only very hairy looking, but also had a distinctly doggy whiff to it too, due to Judgy sitting on me while he was wet, as he regards that as a perfectly valid way of drying himself.

'No no no no, WAIT!' I squawked again as Sam and Colin beetled down the path.

'What now?' said Sam in exasperation.

'What if he thinks we're weird sex people? Like we're some kind of commune or polyamorous or something? Like we live in some sort of threesome? Actually, it would be even worse if he *is* a plumber and he thinks that, because he might think we want him to join in with some very clichéd porn scenario about coming to fix the washing machine and then he might blacklist me on the Plumber's Guild or something, and I'll never get a plumber and the tap will drip forever until it drives me mad, and I turn into Miss Haversham or the first Mrs Rochester and live in my nighty and burn the house down.'

'Yes, I see your point,' said Colin. 'Because obviously that's the only explanation as to why a woman would have two males to dinner on a Saturday night, isn't it now? Because they are "weird sex people". Honestly Ellen, you're clutching at straws now! Just COME ON! We'll drop into conversation that we're simply friends of yours, and that we're a couple and thus not that way inclined, and dispel any confusion, OK? Also, has anyone ever told you that you overthink things?'

We shuffled down the lane, and jostled each other on the doorstep like schoolchildren, Colin and Sam trying to push me to the front, while hissing at me to at least undo a button and stand up straight.

I rang the doorbell. The door flew open, and BLIMEY! He WAS rather nice. So nice in fact that Sam nudged Colin and me rather sharply as we were staring slightly slack-jawed. Tousled, floppy blond hair, slightly salt and peppery, blue BLUE eyes behind some rather intellectual-looking glasses, and oh bliss, he was actually wearing a tweed jacket with leather patches on the elbows. He looked extraordinarily like Indiana Jones in the bits where he's being a university lecturer and not stealing ancient artefacts and losing his hat, only a bit older. And if he could look like that sort of Indiana Jones … well, there was much potential for him to look like a down-and-dirty Indiana Jones … I wondered if he had a hat?

'Hello,' said the Vision. 'Can I help you?'

I gulped and attempted to speak, but made a strangulated noise instead. Colin and Sam both nudged me this time. Unnecessarily hard, in my opinion.

'Hello,' I squeaked, 'um, we're from next door – *I'm* from next door, I mean, ha ha ha – and we came to say hello, and brought you a housewarming present.' I thrust the bottle of wine at him unceremoniously.

'Oh,' he said, looking slightly discombobulated. 'Er, thank you. I'd ask you in, only there's no furniture or anything yet. I'm just sort of camping here tonight until everything arrives tomorrow. I can't even offer you a cup of tea, because the water's been turned off and I can't find the thingy to turn it back on again.'

'The stopcock?' I said brightly. Nice. The second sentence I ever say to possibly the most handsome man in the world and I manage to include the word 'cock' in it. Cockadoodlefuckingdoo. 'I know where it is, do you want me to show you?' I clutched my right hand with my left to stop myself leaning forward and smoothing his floppy hair out of his glorious blue eyes, and licking him. I adore a man with floppy hair. Simon and Jack both failed miserably on that count. Though it is, of course, a fine line between Hugh Grant in *Four Weddings*-style floppy and just unkempt.

'Oh. Well, actually that would be helpful. I'm Mark, by the way.' Mark. Mark was a good name. I was very much in love with a Mark when I was about ten. I sat next to him for spelling, and he used to steal my rubber and refuse to give it back, but despite this, I adored him and planned to marry him when I grew up. He had floppy hair too. Perhaps that's where my fascination with it began. I never saw him again after we left primary school, but I did look him up on Friends Reunited when internet stalking first became a thing, and he'd gone bald very young. Obviously, it was very shallow of me to mind about that, but he just wasn't the same without hair. Given the unrequited passion for/early baldness of First Mark, though, was this man being a Mark a good omen or a bad omen?

While I goggled at him, still slightly open-mouthed, and regretful of the stopcock comment, Sam took the initiative and ran with it.

'Hi Mark! I'm Sam, and this is my husband Colin, and this is Ellen. Colin and I don't actually live next door, we've just come over for dinner with Ellen. Hey, if you've no furniture, Ellen always cooks for the 5,000, and she's a great cook. Or just come round for a drink. Get to know the neighbours. Ellen's a fabulous neighbour by the way, always brings her bins in as soon as they're emptied, and definitely no nude sunbathing at all and no rowdy parties – that was Margaret's *pièce de résistance*. Actually, so was the nude sunbathing. Oh, and no male callers, ha ha ha.'

Thanks Sam, you're really selling me to THE MOST HANDSOME MAN IN THE WORLD EVER! If he doesn't now have some sort of vision in his head of me bin-wrangling in the altogether, with drum 'n' bass thumping in the background, possibly with a Transit van up on bricks on the driveway, then he'll think I'm some repressed, pearl-clutching spinster, probably constantly firing off letters to the parish council about parking issues and dog poo and noisy children.

'I don't have cats!' I burst out, in an attempt to dispel the twin-setted spinster image at least.

'Right,' said Mark. 'But I'm sure I'd be intruding if I came round, though.'

'No, of course not! Ellen was just saying how quiet it will be without Margaret, and that she was looking forward to getting to know the new neighbours,' beamed Colin.

'Sorry, who's Margaret?'

'This is Margaret's house. Well, it's yours now, obviously, but Margaret is who you bought it from. She didn't sunbathe in the nude, Sam's just being silly,' I explained. FOR FUCK'S SAKE, ELLEN, NOW YOU'VE MOVED ON FROM COCKS TO TALKING ABOUT NAKED PENSIONERS, WHAT THE ACTUAL FUCK IS WRONG WITH YOU?

'Ohhh, right,' said Mark. 'Yes, she was quite a character! Anyway, so you know where the stopcock is?'

I showed him the stopcock, cunningly hidden behind an invisible panel in the bathroom (Margaret had sent me to turn off her water one day when she had a burst pipe; I don't make a habit of investigating my friends' stopcocks), and tried not to giggle like an inane schoolgirl, while glaring at the Greek chorus of Sam and Colin in the background, who were obviously dying to make a variety of cock-based comments, but were heroically resisting.

We went back downstairs and Sam returned to the attack. 'So, Mark, Ellen's made roast chicken, if you fancy it?'

Mark hesitated. Of course he wasn't going to accompany this strange raggle-taggle gang that had just appeared on his doorstep. HE probably thought WE were serial killers. Either that, or he'd make a polite excuse about being a vegetarian, or already having eaten, or 'lots to do' in his almost completely empty house or something.

'Oh no,' he said. 'I couldn't possibly, I'd be intruding.'

'Come for a drink, then,' said Colin, who was clearly not going to take no for an answer. 'Just a quick one.'

'Yes,' said Sam, getting in on the act. 'Come on. Quick drink to be neighbourly.'

Poor Mark hesitated, but he was helpless in the face of Sam

and Colin's determination to drag him next door for my viewing pleasure.

'I … I suppose I could come for one?' he said uncertainly.

'GOOD!' bellowed Colin. 'Excellent. Come on then!'

They hustled him out the door and down the path before he had a chance to change his mind, and before the poor sod really knew what was happening, he was sitting on my sofa clutching a large glass of Cab Sauv. Fortunately, I probably made a better impression than I would have if the children were at home, but they were at Simon's. And since I'd known Colin and Sam were coming over, I'd tidied up and made the place look semi-respectable.

As Mark drank his wine very slowly, he told us a little more about himself. He was an archaeologist! My faith in the universe was restored. There *are* hot archaeologists in tweed jackets out there! Hollywood did not lie to me! Oh, how marvellous. He was taking a sabbatical to write a book about … well, actually I tuned out a bit there, because it wasn't anything terribly interesting like cursed amulets or holy grails, something about Neolithic or Palaeolithic or the like. Stones, basically.

'You dabbled a bit with archaeology, didn't you, Ellen?' asked Colin.

'Um, not really.'

'Yes, you did. Last year. You were convinced it was going to be your new vocation,' said Sam unhelpfully.

'Oh yes?' said Mark politely. 'What were you doing?'

'Er, it was just a community project thing,' I mumbled.

'Oh fascinating, it's amazing what they can turn up,' enthused Mark. 'What did you dig?'

'A hole,' I replied.

Mark looked slightly less enthusiastic. 'Well, obviously. But what for?'

'Not sure, really. Sort of old village remains. But we didn't find anything.'

'What, nothing at all?'

'Well, stones and stuff. They might have been bits of wall, the archaeologist said, but he didn't seem very sure. We didn't find anything good, like treasure.'

'Oh, but that's the beauty of archaeology, those stones *are* treasure!' insisted Mark. 'They're a link with the past, someone put them there. It's all part of a bigger picture.'

'Mmm,' I said doubtfully. 'I was quite hoping for something shinier. Or at least a pot or something, you know?'

Colin tactfully changed the subject at that point to what plans Mark had for the house, before I revealed myself to be a total archaeological philistine.

But overall, he seemed very nice, though slightly nonplussed by us, and I don't think I was quite as 'in there' as Sam and Colin insisted, as he was resistant to their efforts to top him up and left after one glass, insisting he'd a lot to do the next day.

'So!' said Sam as we sat down to dinner. 'What do you think?'

'Well, he's very attractive,' I admitted.

'I'll say!' put in Colin, before being quelled by A Look from Sam.

'But even so. He still might be a serial killer. And even if he isn't, why is he single? Why hasn't he ever had a relationship?'

'Oh, I asked him about all that when you were in the loo!' said Colin cheerfully. 'You were ages, so I managed to get quite a lot out of him.'

'I wasn't pooing! I just had a wee, then I went to tidy up my face,' I felt the need to clarify.

'Well, good,' said Colin. 'Anyway, Margaret wasn't quite right in her insistence that he'd never had a girlfriend. He's had two long-term relationships, one in his twenties, which ended because she wanted to settle down and have babies and he wasn't ready, and another one in his thirties because HE wanted to settle down and have babies and SHE wasn't ready, and since then there have been a few semi-serious dalliances that haven't really come to anything, and he's resigned himself to the fact he'll probably never be a dad now, but he's still hopeful of meeting someone to spend the rest of his life with.'

'Blimey! I didn't think I was in the loo *that* long,' I said. 'Imagine what you could have got out of him if I *had* gone for a poo! Oh God, do you think he's an over-sharer? Do you think he likes to constantly talk about feelings? He'd probably make you sit down and have adult conversations about things that annoyed you instead of passively–aggressively sulking about it for days until you lose your temper and shout a lot, like *normal* people do!'

'That's not really what normal people do,' pointed out Sam. 'That's what you do. Some people might say that there are actually better ways to deal with your issues.'

'I'm trying!' I said. 'You all keep telling me I need to talk about things, and I'm trying. It just doesn't come very naturally to me, and anyway, emotional repression has worked fine until now. Simon never had a problem with it.'

'Simon was *almost* as emotionally repressed as you, darling, and also, the fact that you and Simon are now getting divorced somewhat suggests there's something to be said for talking your issues through,' said Colin. 'Anyway, we're not here to talk about Simon, are we? We're talking about the rather delicious Mark. He might be an over-sharer, I'll grant you that. I think it was more probably the fact that moving house is a very stressful and emotional time, and he had quite a large glass of wine on an empty stomach.'

'Oh well, that's all right. Everyone over-shares when they're pissed,' I said in relief.

'I think he likes you, though,' murmured Sam slyly. 'He asked quite a lot about you, when you weren't in the room ...'

'Shut up!' I said. 'No, he doesn't! He's gorgeous. He knows about history and stuff. He can hold proper grown-up conversations just about stones. Why would he like *me*?'

'Stop fishing for compliments, it's very unattractive,' said Colin sternly. 'You know perfectly well there are many reasons why he might like you.'

'Huh, he was probably just quizzing you to find out my daily habits so he could work out the optimum moment to serial killer me without being caught,' I said sulkily. 'I mean, he has an entire career that basically gives him an excuse to dig holes, not to mention a lot of digging practice. We can't rule out the serial killing yet!'

'I mean, most serial killers aren't attracted to it for the hole-digging,' said Sam. 'Hole-digging ability isn't a prerequisite for the job. According to the True Crime channel, most of them tend to go for more imaginative ways of disposing of bodies than the good old-fashioned hole in the ground. Why are you so convinced he's a serial killer anyway?'

'Well, it would be just my luck,' I sighed. 'A handsome, solvent, interesting, intelligent SINGLE man moves in right next door to me, but I've finally realised that life does not pan out like it does in rom coms or pink chick-lit books with shoes on the cover. He will not fall in love with me at first sight but be unable to tell me for Implausible Reasons, thus leading me to believe that he doesn't like me, before he finally reveals, just as I have Given Up All Hope that in fact it's me he loves, it has always been me, and thus everything that's wrong with my life is resolved with a snog, and we all Live Happily Ever After. There's clearly *something* dodgy about him, because right now he's just too good to be true, and I might as well set the bar low and assume the issue will be serial killing, because then anything else is a bonus, because it's unlikely to also affect the value of my house. Can you imagine trying to sell your house if someone had been serial killing next door? Oh dear, the wine's finished! Shall we have some whisky?'

'Ellen, when did you become so cynical?' asked Sam gently. 'You've always pretended to be so hard-headed and made out you were Miss Tough Independent, but deep down you always believed in love, and hoped there was someone out there for you. What happened that the best you'll hope for from an apparently perfect man arriving on your doorstep is that he doesn't have too high a body count?'

'Life,' I said shortly. 'Life happened. My ex-husband turned out to be a fucking cliché who had an utterly predictable midlife crisis involving shagging someone else and then getting a younger girlfriend, and the last man to be interested in me moved to Antarctica – fucking ANTARCTICA.'

'Why did you never think about trying to do the long-distance thing with Jack, though?' asked Colin. 'You just announced one day that Jack was going to Antarctica and that was that.'

'What was the point? It was Antarctica. For two years. Two years of what – weekly phone calls? I barely knew him. He barely knew me. Phone calls for two years weren't going to sustain that. It would be like having a relationship with someone in prison – worse, because I think they get conjugal visits, don't they? I mean, even if he'd gone to Australia, I could have gone there on holiday and braved the killer spiders to go on a tour of the *Neighbours* set, and maybe visit Summer Bay and the

Sydney Opera House and all the other cultural highlights of Australia.'

'Your fixation with Australian soap operas is quite remarkable,' said Sam. 'Do you know that apparently Australian people get quite annoyed at British people's obsession with Australian soap operas, and say that basing your ideas of Australia round them is like Australian people thinking that all of the UK is either Albert Square or Coronation Street?'

'Well, I don't think they realise the effect the constant diet of Aussie soaps had on nineties' teenagers here. When it gets dark at 4 p.m. and it's cold and grey and swimming is something that happens in sweaty, chlorinated municipal piss-pools and the sea is so cold you can actually feel your internal organs contract when you go for a paddle, the golden, sunny, barbecued worlds of Ramsay Street and Summer Bay with backyard swimming pools and surfers' beaches, not to mention the strange lands of *A Country Practice* and the *Flying Doctors*, were literally like something from another planet, weren't they?

'Even the shit ones were good, like *Sons and Daughters* and *The Sullivans*, and, the grimmest one of all, *Prisoner: Cell Block H*. Australian prisons seemed so glamorous, with their Top Dogs and trouser presses. And anyway, this is all academic, because Jack didn't go to Australia, he went to Antarctica, which is the one with the penguins, not the polar bears, though at least his departure means I now know why polar bears don't eat penguins. And I realised we don't all get a Scott to our Charlene, and there's no Prince Charming coming to save the princess in the tower. Even fucking Shrek isn't coming. You have to save yourself, not rely on someone else to do it for you.

'Rapunzel would have saved herself a whole lot of grief if she'd tied one end of her plait to the bed and abseiled out of that

window down her own sodding hair, then given herself an adorable pixie cut at the bottom, punched the witch in the tits, told
her parents to get to fuck for selling her for a CABBAGE, and
gone off and kicked some arse in the world. Even the Little
Match Girl, who always made me cry with her pathos and aban-
donment, freezing to death in a doorway – she should have lit
her matches and then posted them through the door of the
bastards who wouldn't buy them, and burnt their houses down,
then she could have warmed her hands on the blaze and been
toasty-roasty!'

'That would have been quite a different story,' said Sam
doubtfully.

'Also, they'd probably have hanged her for arson, so she'd have
died anyway,' added Colin.

'Well, maybe, but the point is, she'd have been the agent of her
own destiny. Rapunzel too. Instead of just passively waiting for
someone else to change their life, they'd be taking control of
their futures, whether for better or worse. It would have been in
their hands, not someone else's. If I can't be happy by myself,
someone else isn't going to solve that problem for me. Yes, it
would be nice to have someone to come home to, yes, it would
be lovely to have someone to share the load with, it would be
amazing to have a relationship like you two have, and yes, I
know things aren't perfect with you, and your snoring pisses off
Colin, Sam –'

'– I do NOT snore,' objected Sam.

'Yes, you do,' said Colin.

'– and Colin's running commentary every time you watch a
TV programme drives you mad, Sam.'

'I'm SHOWING AN INTEREST IN WHAT WE'RE
WATCHING, that's all!'

'– but overall, you two are probably about as perfect as it gets. You share interests, you support each other, you respect each other, you love each other and care about each other's happiness, not just your own. And it feels great when you're with someone like that, and I did have it once, with Simon, in the early days, but somehow it all went wrong. The kids came along, we didn't have time, we didn't *make* time to work at things, maybe in the end we just didn't love each other enough to stick it through the bad times, I don't know. But I thought once upon a time that he was, I dunno, if not a soulmate, then at least a Kindred Spirit, even though he could be very FUCKING annoying. But then it all went tits up, and you know what? I'm OK. I'm OK by myself. I don't *need* a soulmate or a kindred spirit.

'It's like a fancy stereo in a car. It's nice to have, but the car drives fine without it, and sometimes it can actually be a distraction and cover up the fact that the car's making bad noises and something's wrong with it. So, yes, Mark is nice. He's fucking gorgeous, and, if I'm perfectly honest, I'd probably shag the arse off him given the chance, but realistically, he's probably not The One. And I'm getting to an age where, frankly, I've realised there's no point in living for a Future You that you think will be better. You need to live for *now*, not think, "Oooh, if only I were thinner" or "If only I had a boyfriend" or "If only I won the lottery". You just have to make the most of what you've got, and who you are. Though winning the lottery *would* be nice. God!'

I finally paused for breath. 'Whisky makes me really profound, doesn't it?'

Sam appeared to have nodded off.

'What!' I said indignantly. 'Didn't he hear anything about how fucking wise and deep and meaningful I just was?'

'No, darling,' said Colin. 'Welcome to my world. Do you think *you'll* remember anything about how very clever and enlightened you just were in the morning?'

'Almost certainly not. Maybe I should write it down?'

'The last time you tried to do that, you texted me the next morning complaining you'd woken up face down on sixteen pages of A4 that appeared to be covered in illegible Satanic symbols. I'm sure you'll remember the *gist* of it, though. Shall we go for a little cigarette while we wait for Sleeping Beauty's carriage to arrive before he turns into a pumpkin?'

'Mixing metaphors is one thing,' I said. 'But mixing fairy stories is unforgiveable.'

'Says the woman who wanted to turn the poor, tragic Little Match Girl into an arsonist chav!'

Friday, 12 April

I shoved my head into both children's bedrooms before I left for work this morning and despaired.

In Peter's room, one has to try not to gag on the stench. Why *do* teenage boys smell so bad? WHY? I make him shower daily, I change his bed weekly and his towels every couple of days, I open all the windows and empty endless cans of Febreze in there, but it still HONKS! It's even worse when he has friends over, and he's not forgiven me yet for the shame of putting Oscar Wilson's trainers in the wash because he left them at the back door and they made the whole house stink. Apparently I crossed a line, but it was much pleasanter afterwards.

In Jane's room, I just winced at the piles of clean laundry dumped on the floor that would doubtless shortly reappear in the dirty-washing basket, because she couldn't be arsed to put them away, but at least her room only smells of fake tan and too much perfume. My boldness in venturing into the pits of hell was a valiant attempt to rouse the beasts from their lairs in order to do some revision, as EXAMS are looming ever closer on the horizon. My exhortations to please, please, get up and do some work, even though it's the school holidays, were met by snarls and growls that they would do so 'soon' and to 'stop going on'.

I *must* 'go on', though. For my own good, as well as theirs. I keep reading terrifying articles about how millennials can't afford to move out and so will be forced to live with their parents forever. I'm never sure where the generational lines lie. As far as I can work out, I'm Generation X, my parents were Boomers, then there are millennials, and I *think* Peter and Jane are Gen Z. But anyway, that's not really the point. The point is that the prospect of having a thirty-year-old Jane and twenty-eight-year-old Peter still living with me, still cluttering up my space, taking up all my broadband width, hogging the bathroom and leaving my Sophie Conran mugs (TK Maxx, excellent bargain) festering and gathering mould in their bedrooms fills me with dread.

Part of me is unconvinced by the whole 'millennials can't afford to move out' thing, though, and suspects they could perfectly easily afford a room in a rat-infested shared flat somewhere, but they don't want to do that. They want to live in comfort and ease, in the conditions they've become accustomed to at home, and so they simply stay on, and thus it's in some part the parents' fault for letting them stay and making life too cushy for them.

I mean, obviously I'm not saying put your kids out on the street. But Kevin from Accounts was talking to me the other day and was in despair about his son ever moving out – at twenty-nine, his son lives at home, has all his washing done, meals made and pays no rent. Why the fuck *would* you move out if you have all that done for you?

Anyway, I'm *determined* that this will not be the case with my children, and the first step on the path to independence is to ensure that they get some qualifications, so they can get a reasonable job, so they cannot claim they're too poor to ever leave. This is thus far not going entirely to plan, as Jane managed to do rather well in her GCSEs without a lot of effort, and therefore thinks that her A levels will be the same, despite me trying to get it through to her that A levels are a totally different kettle of fish, and Peter is of the impression that since his sister did well in her GCSEs, he will too. I don't know how he thinks that will work, possibly by some kind of osmosis-like process involving sibling knowledge being absorbed by him? He's also still claiming that he can totally become a professional gamer and make millions à la DanTDM or whoever the latest cool gamer is (I stopped listening several years ago when DanTDM was still the flavour of the month, but no doubt things have moved on considerably since then).

It's slightly alarming, though, to think that in just a few short years I could be living on my own. I've never actually lived by myself. I lived with my mother, spent weekends with my father after they divorced, and then I went to university and lived with flatmates, and I met Simon at university and so then I lived with him, and we got married and had children, and now I live with the precious moppets. The idea of a house where there's no one else to make a mess, no one to move stuff from where you left it, where your pristine, freshly wiped countertops will not immediately be covered with someone else's crumbs, where no one will be wanting something from you as soon as you walk in the door, is, dare I say it, rather a lovely one.

I mean, there's the whole scenario where you fall over putting your trousers on and hit your head and die, and no one realises or finds you until the neighbours start complaining about the smell. And then your bloated corpse is finally found, still sprawled on the floor in your knickers. But at least the house will probably be clean and tidy (apart from the smell) when someone finally breaks in and finds you, so they won't be able to judge you for that. Perhaps, if the day ever comes when I live alone, I'll have to buy nicer pants, though, and throw out all the fraying, greying, saggy elastic ones, just so I make a respectable dead body if the worst comes to the worst.

Anyway, it's not like I'd really be living alone anyway. I'd still have the dogs. Barry is extremely well meaning and would probably do a Lassie and alert someone to my plight before I actually died. Judgy wouldn't, though. He'd probably just sprawl in state on my bed, going, 'Ha ha, bitch, this is MY BED NOW!' Actually, he already does that, and growls at me when I try to remonstrate with him. Judgy is very much lacking in loyalty. If I lived alone, there would be no impediment to getting more dogs – loyal, good dogs – nor to eating toast most nights for dinner, and sharing it with the dogs.

But before I need to worry about any of that, I need to get the children to actually move out! I told myself I'd done my best with my rousing pep talk of, 'Get up out of your beds, you lazy wretches, and do some revision or you'll be stuck here with me forever and I'll make a point of embarrassing you in front of your friends by whatever means necessary, and also go and walk the dogs and empty the dishwasher because I'm not your bloody slave,' before I went to work.

There's still been no official word about the looming, dooming merger, and I'd be starting to wonder if perhaps Ed was mistaken, or it was his idea of a funny joke or something, except other people are starting to mutter about rumours that they've heard, and ask me if I know anything more. So I fear that it's true, and they're just biding their time before officially announcing it.

It was an otherwise uneventful day, though I was unimpressed but unsurprised to return home to find the dogs unwalked, the dishwasher unemptied and a dirty protest from Judgy in the sitting room that 'no one had noticed'. I sighed, dispatched Peter to walk the poor, bursting dogs and Jane to empty the dishwasher, and I tackled the dog turd myself, as the last time I tried to get the kids to clean up something like that, they trod in it while 'looking for it'. Another glamorous Friday night for me!

Jane then came in, wittering something about the black box in her car and her points being down because Reasons, and how she needed me to drive it for a bit because having a responsible driver drive the car somehow improves your ratings. I protested that I was just about to have a glass of wine, that couldn't it wait until tomorrow, that I was tired and the last thing I wanted to do was to drive around aimlessly for no reason other than because Jane had been arsing about in the car. I suggested she could drive herself to her father's house and ask *him* to do it, because she did actually have two parents after all, but that was also not an option apparently. In the end, it seemed easier to do what Jane wanted and come home to a glass of wine in peace instead of listening to stomping and door-slammings and wails of why everything was just SO UNFAIR.

I returned, parched, with visions of ice-cold wine splashing gently into a glass, condensation sliding down the sides, almost tasting that first sip already, to find a beautiful bunch of flowers sitting on the hall table. I glowed with delight. Peter must have bought them while he was out, to say sorry for not walking the dogs sooner! What a kind, thoughtful boy he was, and clearly I must be an excellent mother to have brought up someone so sensitive and caring (if you overlooked the fact that he'd yelled 'DIE IN A HOLE' at his sister as he left the house). I charged up the stairs, even forgetting about my wine, ready to have a long and heartfelt chat with Peter about how much he meant to me, and how small gestures like his can make all the difference to people.

I burst into his room, still clutching the flowers. 'THANK YOU, DARLING!' I cried. 'You really didn't need to do that, and you shouldn't be spending your money on me, but I'm so touched. You've no idea how happy these have made me!'

'Wha'?' said Peter, not looking up from the screen.

'Oh, sweetheart, there's no need to be embarrassed, it was a lovely thing to do for me.'

'Didn't do anything,' he mumbled. 'Don't know what you're on about.' Oh bless him. So bashful.

I stepped in front of him and brandished the flowers at him. 'You don't need to pretend to be Mr Cool with me!' I said jovially. 'You bought me some lovely flowers, didn't you, poppet?'

'Mum!' he hissed in horror. 'Everyone on my network can hear what you're saying. Shut up!'

'Sorry, darling,' I stage-whispered. 'I just wanted to say thank you.'

Peter finally disconnected himself from the screen and turned around. 'I've muted it. They can't hear you now. Thank you for what?'

'The FLOWERS!' I said patiently.

'What about them?'

'Thank you for buying me flowers!'

'*I* didn't buy you flowers. Why would I buy *you* flowers? You're my mum. That'd be, like, *weird*!'

'Well, where did they come from then?' I asked, but he was already turning back to the screen.

'Man,' he grunted.

'What do you mean "man"?' I demanded.

'I just SAID! A MAN brought them,' he said exasperatedly.

'What man? Who? Did he say why he was bringing me flowers?'

'What?'

'Who brought the flowers?'

'A MAN!'

'WHO WAS HE?'

'Dunno.'

'Well, what did he say? What was his name?'

'Can't remember?'

'Peter, for Christ's sake. It can't have been more than half an hour ago. Try to think? Was it a delivery man?'

'Maybe. No, I don't think so. It might have been, though.'

'Well, what did he say?'

'I've forgotten.'

'Any distinguishing features?'

'What?'

'WHAT DID HE LOOK LIKE, PETER?'

Peter mumbled into his headset and shot a zombie.

'Peter?'

'I'm like *thinking*, OK?'

He finally pronounced. 'Glasses. He had glasses. And he said something about next door.'

Mark? Could it be Handsome Mark from next door, bringing flowers? Maybe I was in with a chance of a shag, even if he wasn't my soulmate. Which would be nice. Batteries aren't cheap, you know. But what if it wasn't Mark? What if it was a mistaken delivery for someone else and nothing to do with Mark? Or what if it was a delivery man with flowers FOR Mark as a housewarming gift, and I said, 'Oh thank you for the flowers,' and he said, 'What flowers?' Then I'd have to move house because otherwise it would all be Too Awkward, and I like my house and it would unsettle the chickens and make them hate me more than ever.

'Peter, please. Did he say anything else?'

'Ummm. I think he left a note for you?'

'You *think*? Well, where is it? There was no note with the flowers!'

'Dunno.'

Oh, sweet, suffering fuck. Preserve me from bloody teenagers!

Saturday, 13 April

I was going through the pockets of Peter's jeans this morning (always a rather tentative process. I'm contemplating starting to don the Marigolds to do it. I haven't found a dubiously encrusted tissue *yet*, but I wouldn't put it past Peter to put such a thing in his pocket, instead of down the loo), when I found a crumpled note. I knew, of course, that it would be a gross invasion of his privacy to read it, and I should just return it to him, but I felt as a responsible parent (i.e. I was nosy), I should at least have a quick look at it. It was a bit sticky with unknown substances after its sojourn in Peter's pocket, but this didn't overly concern me. Since babyhood, everything that has come into contact with Peter has picked up a slightly sticky patina. I smoothed it out and squinted at it. Fuck, I really must get an eye test soon.

'Ellen,' I read. 'Sorry I missed you. Thanks for the drink the other night. Wondered if I could return the favour – give me a call or text. Hope you like the flowers. Mark.' Then his number at the bottom.

Well. It *was* Mark. I don't have to move house. But what to do about it? After all, I've been doing just fine on my own, so why would I complicate things with another relationship? But on the other hand, I *did* find him attractive and what if I was wrong? What if he was my soulmate and I never knew because I was too scared to risk finding out? At the very least I should go for a drink with him and see if there were any more hints as to soulmate/serial killer, and really, there was a very good chance he'd be neither. At best, he'd probably turn out to be a new friend and a good neighbour.

Either way, I had to reply, obviously, but I needed to play it cool. Then again, it's not like I went charging round there last night to fling myself into his arms and declare my undying love for him, and he didn't know that was because Peter hadn't passed the note on. Maybe he thought I was super-Busy and Important, with a glittering social life. Then again, *he* had taken nearly a week to even bring the wretched flowers over, so maybe I should leave it a bit longer before texting back. On the other hand, the poor bloke had just moved house, he'd probably been quite busy trying to find his cutlery and clean pants, and maybe he couldn't go to the shop or pop by until yesterday on account of an underwear crisis that meant he could not mix with the general public. I chided myself for my ridiculousness. I'm a mature, intelligent woman. I should not be childish about this and trying to score points about who likes who more by how long it takes to text back. That's something I'd tell Jane off for. I texted him, keeping it quite brief and businesslike.

> Hi Mark, thanks for the flowers, you really didn't have to. Hope you're settling in and have managed to get unpacked. Ellen.

I dickered for a while about whether to add a kiss. I usually add them to almost all my texts, and occasionally to emails by mistake as well, but it's different when you actually fancy the person you're sending kisses to. Then it seems inappropriate. I've no idea why it seems fine to send kisses to my hairdresser and not to someone I'd quite like to snog, but those are the rules, I didn't make them. Well, maybe I did. I decided to consult Jane on the matter.

Jane was unhelpful. She was lying on her bed, messing about on her phone, but as soon as I said, 'Darling, can I talk to you about something?' she immediately insisted that she was busy revising.

'It won't take long,' I said brightly. 'I just wanted to ask you about adding kisses to texts! You know, when it's all right to, and when you probably shouldn't?'

'Why?' said Jane loftily.

'No reason,' I said quickly. 'I just wanted to know about text etiquette, that's all.'

'Why do you want to know? Are you sexting someone? Because that's really not a good idea, you know. Not to mention it's also inappropriate and can be classed as sexual harassment in some cases. And FFS, don't send anyone photos of yourself, not even on Snapchat, because they can download them and use them for revenge porn!'

'Yes, OK, I mean, I'm not actually sure how we got from text kisses to revenge porn, but I'm not sexting anyone. I wouldn't know what to say, for a start!'

'Mother, all you need to know about sexting is that you shouldn't do it!'

'Well, I do have a grasp of basic internet safety, darling. If you recall, I was the one who told you never to send nudey pics –'

'Please don't call them "nudey pics", that's so mortifying!'

'Well, anyway, you know what I mean. I just wanted to know your opinion on sending text kisses.'

'But why?'

'No reason.'

'You must have a reason. Who are you texting?'

'NO ONE! I just WONDERED!'

'Huh,' said Jane, looking entirely unconvinced. 'Well, I'd say a good rule of thumb is if you're wondering if they're a good idea or not, they almost certainly aren't. All right? Does that help? Can I get back to studying for what you keep telling me are the most important exams of my life now, as your burning question has been answered? Yeah?'

'OK, darling, thank you, byeee!' I trilled brightly. 'You're actually revising, then? Only it does look like you're on Instagram?'

'I was having a break! I'm allowed to have a break, aren't I? You're the one who insisted on coming in to ask me weird questions.'

'OK, OK, I'll leave you in peace.'

I decided to leave the kisses off the message to Mark.

Nonetheless, he binged straight back.

Glad you liked them. House is nearly sorted, but I'm getting cabin fever. What's the local pub like – respectable or murderous dive?'

Well done on getting house unpacked! The pub's quite nice, no one has been murdered there as far as I know.

Great. Fancy joining me for a drink tonight?

Well, he doesn't waste much time, does he? Such a prospect is both quite thrilling (OMG, maybe I'm not totally past it and still retain an element of sexpot) and also terrifying (OMG, maybe he's just keen to get the serial murdering underway in his new locale). But either way, TONIGHT? Surely not. I needed warning. I needed to shave my legs and put on a face mask to attempt to de-hag the crow's feet and make myself look glowingly youthful! Tonight? Maybe I could do it. I could be spontaneous, couldn't I? After all, I hadn't been done up to the nines when he met me last week, and he didn't seem entirely repulsed. Also, it was only a drink. Maybe he was just being friendly or neighbourly, in which case how embarrassing if I got myself all gussied up and he'd just been expecting a quiet pint with a pal, and there I was with six inches of lip gloss on. Yes. Maybe it was better this way, to just keep things casual. Make it obvious I wasn't a desperate old slapper, no matter what perky-titted, swishy-haired, just-off-to-fucking-CrossFit Marissa might think of me. But what if that was what other people thought of me too?

I've been worrying about this ever since I overheard the 'old lush' jibe at Jane's birthday. Maybe I *am* past it. Maybe what I see as retaining some kind of sense of style, others see as mutton dressed as lamb (though I'm sure my darling children would be quick to tell me if there was any hint of inappropriateness in my attire). My idea of still being funny and witty and amusing perhaps comes across to others as just a ranting mad old bag, and my 'social drinking' is apparently lushdom.

Once again, it's easier for men. They just trade in for a younger model (à la Simon and Marissa) and make crass jokes about how 'You're only as old as the woman you feel' (ugh), while women are bombarded with articles about how fifty is the new forty, and emotionally blackmailed into buying Wunder Creams to restore lost youth, banish eyebags and crow's feet and sagging jowls and laugh lines. For Christ's sake, you even get a cream promising to restore the 'youthful pink' appearance of one's unmentionable parts, which, it seems, turn an 'unattractive grey' with age (and I'm NOT talking about pubes, either). Who knew? Both that one's bits were no longer fashionably pink and that one should be ashamed and start remedying this with a grim product called 'My Pink Button'? Not only that, but the other day I saw an advert for earring backs to rectify the apparently socially unacceptable problem of your earlobes sagging with age. As if we didn't have enough to worry about, now we're supposed to worry about our FUCKING EARLOBES sagging!

And meanwhile, as women are cajoled to stay as youthful as possible, to perk and primp and preen in pursuit of our lost youth, the men we're supposedly doing this to be attractive for just fuck off and get themselves someone ever younger, like those disgusting old men trying to pick up Jane and her friends – the sheer *arrogance* of some men, thinking that an eighteen-year-old girl is going to want to get off with a fifty-year-old man, because men sag and wrinkle and grey too, they just aren't publicly shamed and chastised and targeted by unscrupulous advertising to try to make them defy it. There's a lot to be said for the idea of a matriarchal society where wisdom and experience are valued over youth and physical beauty.

Anyway, I roused myself from my dark musing about the patriarchy to think about getting ready in the limited time I had available. There were some benefits to this, as in the (unlikely) event that he *was* interested and didn't think me over the hill and past it, if I hadn't shaved my legs or tackled any of the other rather luxuriant foliage, then there would be no chance of me getting carried away and doing anything untoward on the first date. I would have to go home alone, and be virtuous and pure. Not that I made a habit of bonking chaps on the first date. I hadn't done that since ... well, since Simon. Though technically I'd only actually done the sex thing with one other chap since Simon, and that had all been rather daunting, though it had gone well enough in the end. Well, until he went to Antarctica, anyway.

Hopefully Mark will not find sex with me such a traumatising experience that he moves hemispheres, though. I mean, assuming he wants to. Assuming *I* want to. He's very nice to look at, but I hardly know him, and there's still plenty of potential for statements like 'I'm not racist, but ...' or other such attractive passion-killers. He's probably a *Daily Mail* reader. Maybe he even leaves mad comments beneath articles online. Or maybe he doesn't find *Blackadder* funny. A man unable to quote from *Blackadder* is not a man I could give my heart to. Oh dear, that's very shallow of me, but a shared sense of humour is important. Maybe he wears socks with sandals. Perhaps his current, rather sexy, tousled floppy hair is because he's growing it out so he can wear a man bun. Now a man bun would *definitely* be a deal breaker.

I was still running through all Mark's many possible shortcomings (maybe he had no willy? He still could be a serial killer.

Maybe he was a serial killer with no willy, that was why he killed people, because he was annoyed about having no willy?) when Peter thundered down the stairs and into the kitchen.

'What are you doing?' he said in surprise. 'Why are you just standing in the middle of the kitchen with your mouth open? I'm *starving*. There's no food, Mum, what can I eat?'

'There's plenty of food, it just requires some degree of preparation, rather than just being shoved in your mouth,' I pointed out. 'Peter, I might go out tonight. Is that OK?'

'Yeah, whatever. Can I have Lucas and Toby over then? And can we order pizza?'

'Have you done any revision at all? You go back to school on Monday, and then the exams start in a couple of weeks. I don't think having your friends over for an all-night gaming session is exactly a great idea so close to your exams.'

'It'll be a *study* session, obviously,' said Peter unconvincingly, through the third slice of bread he'd shoved in his mouth in under a minute. 'Just chill about the exams, Mum, it'll be fine! I'll go tell them to come over.'

'Wait! I didn't say they could come over! If they come, you'd better study! And get some sleep.'

It might have been nice, I reflected, if Peter had shown some interest in where I was going and what I was doing. But then again, I could hardly say that I was going to throw myself at the hot neighbour, if he did not find me a repulsive crone, provided he could satisfy my exacting criteria with regards to acceptable hairstyles and nineties comedy programmes, could I? Also, if the children told me to 'chill' one more time about these sodding exams, I will not be responsible for my actions. I really feel like I'm the only person in this family who actually gives a shit about them!

I'd arranged to meet Mark at the pub, to conserve conversation, lest by the time we'd walked there it turned out we'd nothing more to say to each other, and we were forced to sit in awkward silence for the space of a G&T until we could make our excuses and escape.

In the event, though, I needn't have worried. Mark was wearing normal shoes when I arrived, and one of the first things he said when pushing his hair out of his eyes (which was actually rather damn sexy) was something about needing to get a haircut, so a man bun is obviously *not* on the horizon.

I was determined to be an erudite and charming conversationalist, with no wittering about otters, which is my default setting when nervous, nor making crude and somewhat bawdy double entendres, thus proving some point in my head to fucking Marissa about how very unboring I am and how very many interesting topics I can discuss.

I started by asking Mark about his very interesting archaeology job. Although I was quite hazy about the difference between Neolithic and Palaeolithic, it was quite fascinating, and I managed not to ask him about whether he had ever encountered Nazis or cursed amulets. He'd been on a dig in Petra, and it sounded amazing.

'I've always wanted to go on a riding safari to Petra across the desert,' I mentioned casually, though I wasn't entirely sure where that had come from, as hitherto it had been a vague 'thing I'd like to do if I could ride and wasn't scared of horses', but I was saying it out loud, with authority, as if I were the sort of person who went on adventures like that, instead of two weeks in the summer lying by a pool in Portugal or Spain drinking all-inclusive cocktails.

'Wow,' said Mark. 'That would be quite a trip. Not sure about the riding part of it, but you definitely should go to Petra.'

'Yes, I might do that next year,' I lied, hastily changing the subject and asking, 'Where would you go, if you could go anywhere?'

'I'd love to go to Vietnam,' said Mark. 'It looks amazing.'

'Oh yes, it looks fantastic,' I agreed knowledgeably, basing this entirely on Susan Lancaster from school's photos on Instagram of a recent trip.

I steered the conversation onto literature.

'Have you read any interesting books recently?' I enquired (SUCH A PROPER PERSON I AM).

'I don't actually have a lot of time for reading outside of work stuff,' said Mark. 'But I did read a really interesting biography of Wordsworth recently.'

'Oh, the daffodil man?' I said without thinking.

'Yes, but he was so much more than that!' said Mark earnestly. 'He was involved in the French Revolution, he was quite a radical, he changed the way people think. It was fascinating.'

'Goodness,' I said. 'I had no idea! I must read that.'

'I really recommend it!' said Mark.

This truly was an educational evening. I was learning a huge amount about all sorts of different things, as well as having a very nice view to admire. Mark was the sort of man I'd been waiting for all my life – interesting, intelligent, with a wide range of interests and a collection of tasteful knitwear. Jack had been lovely, of course, but he'd never really encouraged me to stretch myself or leave my admittedly quite shallow intellectual comfort zone. I had visions of Mark and me in the future giving witty little dinner parties for fellow intellectuals. He might read French poetry aloud. Perhaps we wouldn't have dinner parties at all, but would hold *salons* for our clever friends to attend and discuss art and literature and philosophy! I necked the rest of my gin in excitement at the dazzling future that lay ahead for Mark and me.

'Do you want another drink?' he said, looking slightly surprised.

'Oh yes,' I said happily.

Another gin later, Mark suggested we headed back. I readily agreed, because I'm NOT a sad old lush, and we walked along the lane towards our houses, me fighting the urge to point out who lived where and fill him in on the scurrilous village gossip, because that's not what high-minded intellectual sorts like me do.

We got to my house and I had a mild panic about what to do next? WAS this an actual date, and would he be expecting to be invited in for 'coffee'? Or were we out as friends and neighbours, and he'd think me a strumpet? What would an intellectual do? Did I even *want* to ask him in? Actually, it occurred to me that the problem was somewhat out of my hands. I couldn't ask him in because my house was full of teenage boys tonight, and no doubt there would be stinking trainers by the door and the place would be a tip, despite my leaving it clean and tidy a few short hours ago. Also, it would be of Poor Moral Standing to bring a gentleman caller round on one's first date when one had a house full of Other People's Children, though I feared these attitudes were probably sadly bourgeois and I should attempt to be more bohemian.

We got to the gate, and I said, 'Well, this is me! Ha ha, obviously, you knew that! Anyway, I'd better go, got a houseful of teenagers, need to go and see what carnage they've caused! Thank you, that was a nice evening.'

'Oh.' He looked a little crestfallen. 'Yes, it was very nice.'

Aren't we all just so *nice* and polite. Nicey nice niceness. How on earth do we make the jump from 'That was nice,' 'Yes, very nice,' to 'Ride me sideways, big boy'? Maybe we should be more like the Dutch. Apparently, they just *talk* about sex. Without sniggering or euphemisms. It must be very liberating to be Dutch. Though terrifying as well, if one is British. Just *talking* about sex! The very idea!

'Anyway, I'll see you!' I trilled, and scuttled off up the path. I got to the door when he called.

'Ellen?'

'Yes?'

'When is bin day?'

Oh, for fuck's sake. Bin day? I bet a Dutch person wouldn't need to ask that. Nor is that very intellectual. Bin day indeed. Would Keats have asked Mary Shelley about bin day?

'Tuesday,' I said. 'You should have a complicated rota about what goes in what bin and what bin is collected on what date. I'll send you a photo of mine if you don't have one.'

'OK, thanks. Or maybe you could just bring it round for me to look at? I could make dinner for us? One night next week?'

Had he really asked about bins just to give himself an excuse to ask me to his house for dinner? Perhaps his flaws were beginning to reveal themselves.

'Won't you need it before Tuesday so you know what bins to put out?' I pointed out.

'Well, yes. I've probably got one somewhere, it'll be fine. Soooo, what night would suit you to pop round?'

Blimey. He actually seemed quite keen (unless he was just eager to get the local serial murdering under way, of course). 'Well, how about Wednesday?'

'Wednesday it is, then. It's a date!'

'Right. See you then!'

An official date, no less. I'd better shave my legs before Wednesday then. And find my push-up bra. I haven't needed it in a while. I suspect it's lurking somewhere at the back of the drawer with all my Good Pants (the sort that don't have stout and greying gussets, but do have a distressing habit of wedging themselves up your arse crack). Oh, and read some clever books.

Wednesday, 17 April

Dinner with Mark was divine. I had hastily skim-read the Wordsworth biography he'd recommended and, in the absence of time to do anything else, quickly watched some *Horrible Histories* about the Georgians and Victorians so I had some historical context within which to discuss it.

It was a very welcome distraction from work problems, actually, as two members of my team had handed in their notice today, in the wake of the merger and redundancies rumours, having landed jobs with our biggest competitor. I, too, am wondering if I should just jump ship before I'm pushed, while another part of me says, 'But they can't sack *everyone*.'

I didn't bore Mark with all this though, as a) I didn't want to think about it anymore, and b) how do you explain all this tedious corporate nonsense to someone who's more accustomed to dreaming spires and living in the past, and who's taken a year off to write a book. I did blurt out a lot of my concerns to Simon when he rang me before dinner to find out where he was supposed to pick Jane up from on Saturday, as his repeated pleas to be texted Millie A's address, where Jane's staying after a party, had fallen on deaf ears. He was remarkably sympathetic, and didn't start bossing me around and telling me what to do, which was most unlike him. He did, however, point out that there was no harm in sorting out my CV, and maybe having a chat to a few recruitment agencies and seeing what was out there. I didn't actually have to *leave* my job yet, but it would be useful to get the lie of the land if I did leave.

He sounded a bit odd, actually. Like he was very tired. Usually he'd tell me at great length if he was very tired, and explain how much more tired than me he was, because being Busy and Important is so very exhausting, and in fact no one knew what tired felt like like Simon did. I was a bit worried about him, and was going to ask if he was all right, but then I reminded myself that these days Simon is Marissa's problem to worry about, not mine. Maybe he's coming down with something, in which case she can dose him up with Lemsip and listen to his enfeebled croakings as he googles his symptoms and diagnoses himself, 'Competitive Illnesses' being one of Simon's favourite games. No sooner would I remark that my throat felt a bit scratchy and maybe I needed a Strepsil, than Simon would be collapsing dramatically on the sofa, clutching his own throat and gasping that he thought he had diphtheria. Or maybe polio. Could be a touch of TB. Simon used to take umbrage at my lack of sympathy for his many life-threatening conditions, despite me pointing out repeatedly that he was in fact one of the most robustly healthy people I'd ever met!

Dinner was delicious, though. Mark's an excellent cook, and he casually tossed together some most impressive pasta with truffles and anchovies and various other exotica that Simon would never have dreamt of adding to pasta. Mark's also something of a wine connoisseur, pouring me a large glass of something jolly nice from a rather expensive-looking bottle. It was very good, and definitely a cut above my own usual plonk (I suspect my 'housewarming gift' might have gone down the sink if Mark's accustomed to the finer things), but I fear my uneducated palate did not quite appreciate its subtler nuances. I felt that perhaps a second bottle might have assisted with educating my palate, but Mark showed no signs of opening one, and made coffee after dinner, which is clearly far more sophisticated and exactly the sort of thing one would do in one's highbrow *salon*, even if it did result in me lying awake until 3 a.m. with a headache. But one must suffer for one's art.

And Mark has suggested we go to the theatre next weekend! How utterly cultured. Colin has been bombarding me with texts wanting to know if I've shagged him yet, but Mark is a gentle-man, not the sort of person who just leaps into bed with people. Though hopefully there will at least be a snog after the theatre. Not a snog, obviously. Mark is too cultured to snog. A tender and poetic kiss may occur, however.

MAY

Friday, 3 May

I popped round to Hannah's tonight for a very long-overdue wine-soaked Fuck It All Friday.

I rang the door at 7 p.m., as arranged. There were several crashes and bangs from inside and some ear-splitting screeches, but no one answered the door. Eventually I went round to the garden and let myself in the back door. Hannah's kitchen, usually so immaculate, was a scene of carnage. There was a strong smell of banana and something burning.

I opened the oven and extracted some kind of blackened brick. The screeches continued to emanate from somewhere upstairs. I went to the bottom of the stairs and shouted, 'Hannah? Are you there? Are you OK?' just as the smoke alarm went off, due to the clouds of smoke that had issued from the oven when I opened it.

At the sound of the smoke alarm, Hannah appeared at the top of the stairs wailing, 'Oh fucking HELL, FUCKING HELL!'

'Hannah?'

'Oh God, Ellen! What are you doing here?'

'It's Friday, Hannah. We arranged to have a #FIAF night?' I said as I flapped a tea towel at the indignant smoke alarm and managed to shut it up.

'I know, I know. I just can't believe it's that time already. Oh shit, Edward's in the bath. Hang on!' and she belted out of sight again.

I went upstairs to further scenes of chaos, as Edward had managed to hurl most of his water out of his bath over the floor during the thirty seconds Hannah had been on the landing.

'Edward!' she shrieked. 'WHY did you do that?'

Edward chuckled.

'Oh, Jesus fucking wept!' Hannah muttered. 'Another thing to clear up. How did you get in, Ellen?'

'Back door.'

'Oh shit, you'll have been in the kitchen then. I meant to clear it up after I got Edward to bed, before you came. And, oh buggering shitsticks, the fucking banana bread! It's still in the oven!'

'I took it out, though I think it's beyond salvation. Get Edward dried and dressed, Hannah, and I'll mop up in here.'

I cleared up the bathroom and went downstairs, while Hannah was still waging what sounded like World War III as she attempted to wrangle Edward into his pyjamas while he bellowed 'NONONONONONONONO!' and howled like she was sticking pins in him. I opened the wine I'd brought and poured a large glass, which I took upstairs to Hannah.

'Here!' I said. Hannah was back in the bathroom, with Edward clamped under one arm, jabbing a toothbrush round his mouth, a process slightly helped by Edward's open-mouthed roaring.

Hannah took a grateful glug.

'I've still to do his story,' she groaned over the cacophony. 'Charlie was supposed to be home to do all this, but he's had to work late, and I can't even bloody complain, can I, because he's a doctor. He's out there saving lives, not lurking in an office tinkering with spreadsheets.'

'Drink your wine while you do the story, and I'll see you downstairs in a bit.'

I started clearing up the kitchen, while Hannah put Edward down. There was a lot of banana thrown around, and industrial quantities of flour and sugar over the floor. Three times I heard Hannah close Edward's door and get as far as the top of the stairs before his door flew open, and she had to go back and start the process all over again. She slammed the door and roared dire threats through it about what happened to little boys who didn't stay in bed.

The kitchen restored to order, I put a wash on and made a start on folding the piles of clean laundry while I waited. When Hannah finally came downstairs, she burst into tears when she saw this.

'Oh, fuck my life,' she sobbed. 'You shouldn't be doing that. We're supposed to be having a nice night drinking wine and having fun, not you cleaning up my bloody mess!'

'Sit down,' I said sternly, gesturing at the table with one hand and waving the bottle at her with the other.

'No, I need to –'

'SIT!' I thundered.

Hannah sat. I refilled her glass and returned to the laundry.

'Drink your wine,' I ordered.

'I can't just here drinking wine while you do that!' she said despairingly.

'Yes, you can. What are bestest friends for? Now, why don't you tell me about it?'

'I just … there's no time. No time to do anything properly. No time to clean the house, because Edward needs me. No time to focus properly on him, because I need to do laundry or clean the house. And no time for anything else. I dream about just getting one night to myself,' she said wearily. 'Just a few hours' peace. To have a bath. Something to eat. I could read a book! I mean, I probably wouldn't, my concentration is shot. But I could maybe have a stab at *Heat* magazine. Or watch *Love Island* – my intellect's probably just about up to that. But Charlie works such long shifts at the hospital, and he's so tired, and when Emily and Lucas were little, Mum used to take them for a night, or even a few hours. But I can't ask her now, she's just not quick enough to keep up with him, and she certainly can't pick him up, and if I left him with her, she'd probably break a hip. She's definitely at that age when you don't just fall over, you "have a fall", and I don't think I could cope with that on top of dealing with Edward. And Emily does nothing but scream at me that I have no idea what it's like for her, and tells me to shut Edward up because it'll be my fault if she fails her exams because she couldn't get peace to concentrate. And Lucas just shuts himself in his room on that infernal headset chatting to God knows who –'

'Mainly Peter, I think,' I put in, trying to be helpful.

'And Charlie just comes home from work and falls asleep after he's had his dinner, and then I want to stab him because bloody Edward never sleeps. I give him the soothing lavender baths and read him his story, and we have quiet going-to-sleep time, and then up the little bastard pops up twenty minutes later, bellowing for drinkies or claiming scary things in his room or wanting cuddles, and rampages till 11 p.m. He'll be up again in a minute, you wait and see, and then he gets up again at 5 a.m. He's two and a half – he should need at least twelve hours sleep a night, minimum. How the fuck is he functioning on six hours when I'm an adult and feel so tired I'm almost dead on that much sleep?

'I just feel like I have to be everything to everyone, and it's just so hard trying to meet the emotional needs of teenagers and toddlers at the same time, and oh God, I'm sorry. I'm sorry. We're supposed to be having a catch-up, and I haven't seen you in ages, and every time I do see you, all I do is moan and forget to even ask how you are! How is Gorgeous Mark? Are you madly clever and intellectual now? Have you had sex with him yet? Did you find out if he has a willy yet? Do you remember Thomas Younger, who we knew at school, who everyone said didn't have a willy? So it could definitely be a Thing.'

'Hannah,' I said, when I could finally get a word in. 'Calm down. It's OK. You don't have to ask about me if you're having a shit time and need to unload. Now, between us, tonight, we're going to sort the house out, while drinking wine, so that's one less thing to worry about when you get up tomorrow. And you need to be easier on yourself. Get a cleaner. Send Edward to nursery one day a week. If Charlie's hours are too long to let him help you, then get some help from somewhere else. You don't have to do all this yourself.'

'But that's what we are supposed to do. Won't Charlie think me a failure, if I can't even manage to run the house and look after my children?'

'Firstly, I don't give a fuck about what Charlie thinks. This is about you, and if he does think that, well, that's his problem for being a prick, not yours. Secondly, have you talked to him yet about how you're struggling? And thirdly, if things were the other way round, would you think I was a failure? What would you say to me, if I were in your position?'

Hannah wiped her eyes and took a slug of wine. 'Probably all the things you've said to me?' she said quietly.

'There you go then. No one thinks you're a failure. Talk to Charlie, OK? Now, the washing machine's finished, so I'm going to stick that load in the drier, put another load on, then we'll open another bottle and tackle the sitting room. And I have another idea, as well. Why don't *I* take Edward for the night? Maybe you and Charlie could even go away somewhere for the night, have a proper break where you don't have to think about housework or cooking. You can lie in a bubble bath and drink champagne!'

'I couldn't ask you to do that!' said Hannah.

'You haven't asked me to do that. I've offered. Totally different. Go on, just do it!'

'But you don't even *like* children,' said Hannah.

'That's not true,' I said indignantly. 'I like my children. Mostly. And I like your children – they're practically my children anyway. Either send the older two to their useless father, or ask Colin and Sam if they can stay over, or to be honest, Emily is very nearly eighteen. You could probably just leave them at home. It will do you good, Hannah.'

'I don't know,' she said doubtfully. 'He's quite a handful!'

'Hannah, I've coped with two children myself before, you know. It's not like I don't know what I'm doing! When Jane was Edward's age, I was dealing with a newborn too. I think I'll manage one small boy for the night without too much difficulty.'

'Yes, well, I've dealt with two other children too, including the toddler/newborn combo, and it wasn't like this! I don't know if I'm just too fucking old, if this is the first hint of the Fucking Oldness that Mum talks of, that my knees cracking when I stand up and getting *twinges* in my back are Mother Nature's way of saying love, you're too fucking old to have a baby. But then again, this whole situation was largely Mother Nature's fault, so she can fuck off, the evil bitch. Or maybe it really is Edward. Maybe the first two were just much easier and I didn't realise it at the time, or maybe he genuinely is a lot more *spirited* – that's what Charlie's mum calls him. I said he was feral in front of her, and she chastised me and said, "Oh no, dear, he's just *spirited*," but she's not the one who has to apologise at Messy Art because he had a dirty protest in the modelling clay and then stripped off because "My gonna paint my bum so I like a *fucking baboon*!" That's not being spirited!

'And then afterwards in Tesco, I had him strapped in the trolley, *not* without some difficulty, and at the check-out he got out his willy, I don't even know how, and waved it at the check-out lady while yelling, "I got a great big willy! I got the biggest willy in the world! Lookit my WIIIIILLLLLLLYYYYYY!"'

'Can you go back to Messy Art?'

'No. Never. So he's won, because he told me he didn't want to go, but I'd paid for the term, so I wanted to get my money's worth, so I made him go, and those were the consequences. He's *two*. What will happen when he doesn't get his own way when he's twenty-two? And after the modelling clay, I daren't even take him to soft-play to wear him out, because I know for sure he would be the ball-pit shitter. No one wants to be the ball-pit shitter's mum, and I can't face being barred from anywhere else, because I can't go back to Tesco either!'

I was trying not to laugh at the thought of Edward shitting in the modelling clay so he didn't have to go back to Messy Art. It really wasn't funny, but there was definitely a hint of Evil Genius to it.

'Look, we won't leave the house,' I promised. 'I'll take him to no public places, there will be no opportunities for him to expose himself or defecate anywhere he should not. It will be fine, really.'

Charlie came home about 9.30 p.m., and I took my leave of them, hissing 'Talk to him!' at Hannah as I left.

Saturday, 11 May

I'm all of a quiver and floating on air. There have been developments in the Mark department. Kissing developments, to be precise. Tonight we went to a jazz concert, which admittedly is not really my sort of thing, but it was outdoors, it was a perfect early summer's evening, there was the smell of new-mown grass, Mark brought one of his lovely bottles of wine, and even the jazz was quite bearable, which is clearly a sign of how urbane and cultured I'm becoming, and was nothing at all to do with me getting to drink most of the wine because Mark only had a glass since he was driving.

Afterwards, when Mark dropped me off, he got out of the car and walked me up the path to my house. He stopped at the door, brushed my hair out of my eyes and cupped my face in his hands.

'Oh, Ellen,' he breathed. 'I can't help myself, I'm going to have to kiss you.'

It was very fucking Mr Darcy-esque, I can tell you!

It was a very good kiss too. I practically swooned, until the noise of the dogs hurling themselves against the door in outrage that I hadn't come in yet brought me back down to earth.

'Do you want to come in?' I whispered afterwards.

He kissed me on the forehead.

'Not tonight,' he said softly. 'I'm crazy about you, but I don't want to spoil things by going too fast. I've made that mistake before. I'll call you tomorrow, yeah?'

And then he kissed me again, and left, and I stumbled inside to the indignant dogs, too blissed out even to mind that Judgy had shredded a cushion in fury at being abandoned.

It was all so utterly magical that I decided to write a poem about it, but it turned into a dirty limerick instead, so maybe poetry writing isn't my hidden talent either, as there was something a little lacking about:

There was a hot archaeologist called Mark,
Him and me had quite a spark,
We snogged at the door,
I'd've shagged him on the floor,
Though ideally with the lights off so it was dark.

The concerns about him not having a willy were proved unfounded, though, as there was quite a lot of evidence to the contrary as he pressed himself romantically against me.

Thursday, 16 May

Well, that went well. Peter and Jane both had their first exam today. I've been attempting to be a loving, helpful and supportive mother, and since they both strenuously rejected my offers to help them revise or test them on their subjects (possibly because Jane grudgingly let me see her Maths GCSE past papers last year to go through them with her, which ended in me shouting, 'What's this buggering bollocky nonsense they're teaching you? That's not how it was done in my day. How on earth are you supposed do algebra with this idiotic method?', which led to Jane calling me a 'dinosaur' and 'unhelpful'), I resolved that if they wouldn't allow me to nourish their minds, I could at least nourish their bodies, and therefore banned all junk food in favour of healthy, home-made, brain-friendly food. This did not go down entirely well.

'Mum, like, what is this even meant to be?' complained Peter on the first night of my new regime, poking suspiciously at his quinoa and broccoli bake with seared salmon (everyone knows fish is good for the brain). 'And you know I don't like fish.'

'Rubbish!' I said briskly. 'You love fish fingers. Just imagine it's deconstructed fish fingers, and the salmon is the inside and the quinoa is the breadcrumbs! Yummy!'

'Ewww. It's like, nothing *like* fishfingers,' Peter insisted.

'Just eat it. It's good for you.'

'Can I put ketchup on it?'

'No, ketchup is full of sugar, and it will undo all the health benefits of the delicious meal I've just lovingly prepared for you!'

'If you're going to go all high-protein health nut on us, can't we at least have steak?'

'Fish is extremely good for you. Fish oils! Omega 3! I'm trying to help, and also steak is bloody expensive, especially in the quantity you eat.'

And so it went on, until I was forced to compromise by returning to the children's usual diet of mainly pasta with pesto, although I reverted to my toddler tricks of whizzing up various vegetables into the pesto, only for them to regard it with suspicion and complain of 'bits', but to make me feel like I'm nourishing them, a bowl of cherry tomatoes is placed on the table under the pretence they might eat some. Obviously they don't, but we all keep up the pretence that they *might*, or at least that they could possibly absorb some nutrients by merely being in their proximity.

Today, though, I thought I'd better ramp things up a notch and make sure they had a good, healthy breakfast before their exams. I got up early, and made fruit salad, scrambled eggs and wholemeal toast, thus providing vitamins, protein and complex carbs so they'd be firing on all cylinders and ready to go out there to dazzle the world with their brilliance. When they're world leaders and Nobel Prize winners, they might make speeches about how they would not be here today without the nurture, care and wisdom of their loving mother.

'Behold!' I cried. 'Breakfast of champions!'

Jane nibbled a piece of toast and pushed her scrambled egg around her plate. Peter complained about the lack of Pop-Tarts and settled on his usual brimming bowl of Weetabix, before then polishing off the scrambled eggs and toast as well, but declining the horror that was actually eating some fruit. Meanwhile, Judgy nudged me to remind me that if my so-called real children were too ungrateful to appreciate the breakfast I'd so lovingly made, he, Judgy Dog, was quite partial to scrambled eggs, and though it would be a struggle and a great personal sacrifice, he'd be willing to consider taking them off my hands. But he was too late, as Peter had scoffed the lot, including Jane's. I feared for the poor child sitting next to Peter after he'd consumed all that fibre and then the best part of six eggs.

'So, darlings,' I said brightly. 'How are we feeling about today? Confident? Prepared?'

'Mum, seriously, can you just stop *wittering*,' snapped Jane. 'I need to concentrate. Think. I can't *do* that with you going on all the time!'

'Oh. Sorry darling. What about you, Peter? This is all new to you, isn't it, poppet? Are you feeling OK? Nervous? Anything you want to talk to me about?'

'No. Please, Mum. Just stop talking, and let me eat my breakfast.'

'OK, OK, I'll be quiet. Can I get you anything else? Do you need any snacks? Remember to take a water bottle. And remember to drink it. Hydration is key!'

'MUM! SHUT UP!'

With that they both slammed out of the door, leaving me to scrape the remnants of the scrambled-egg pot into the dog bowls, and wonder why it was that the harder I tried, the more I just seemed to annoy them. Maybe that's the problem. I don't really remember my mother paying much attention to my exams at all, other than making it abundantly clear, having gone to some trouble and expense to pay for my overpriced education, that Failure Was Not an Option. She certainly never worried about my balance of complex carbs and protein for optimal brain function, and I doubt she knew what exam I was sitting on what day, let alone had a large colour-coded timetable pinned to the fridge. Actually, would it have bloody killed her to take an interest? I might have *liked* to feel that she cared about what was going on. I mean, probably not, as I suspect my teenage reaction would have been similar to Peter and Jane's, but if she HAD been more hands on, and I HAD won a Nobel Prize, I'd definitely have mentioned her in my speech. So perhaps there's hope.

Not that there IS much hope of a Nobel Prize, mind you, given the utterly foul mood both children were in when I got home from work.

'FINE!' snarled Peter, when I asked him how it had gone, and 'I DON'T WANT TO TALK ABOUT IT!' yelled Jane. I bit my tongue to refrain from saying, 'Well, I did *tell* you to do more revision,' and just got on with steaming some broccoli for them to not eat for dinner.

Still. Only another three weeks of watching my precious moppets piss their lives away and having all offers of help rejected. And then, no doubt, they'll find some other reason to hate me and tell me why I'm wrong about everything.

I tried to ring Simon to see what he thought about our children's future, or lack of it, but his phone kept going straight to voicemail. Hannah and Sam and Colin assure me that they're getting exactly the same attitude from their teenagers too, almost word for word, and surely they can't *all* be about to fail *all* their exams. I'm tempted to ask my dear sister Jessica how her perfect offspring Persephone and Gulliver are coping, but there's little point, as doubtless they'll be merrily mainlining goji berry smoothies and sailing through it, and even if they aren't, she'll just lie to me and claim everything's perfect and marvellous. Either way, I'll be left feeling more inadequate than ever.

Sunday, 26 May

I. Am. Broken. Normally, the utterance of these words on a Sunday indicates that I had a very good Saturday night, possibly involving Patrón XO Cafe tequila and dancing on tables doing my finest rendition of Kate Bush's 'Wuthering Heights' (I've made up my own dance routine for it, which personally I feel is an improvement on Kate Bush's. She just waved her arms around a lot, while mine is a great deal more *interpretive*, as I mime trying to get in windows and how coooooold I am. Colin said 'improvement' wasn't necessarily quite the word he'd have used, but it was definitely 'different').

However, I spent my entire Saturday night completely stone-cold sober, without so much as a SNIFF of a nice cold Sauv Blanc to get me through it. This is because this weekend was the much anticipated Visit from Little Edward. I'd promised Hannah that it would 'be fine', and 'It will be fine' proved to be famous last words, for FML, Edward is, indeed, 'spirited'. It didn't help, of course, that I'd forgotten just how utterly relentless toddlers are, that they need to be busy every single second of the day and virtually the only currency you can deal in to try to buy their compliance is refined sugar, so obviously that backfires every time you beg them to just do as you ask and then they can have a 'nice sweetie'.

Hannah dropped him off mid-morning, wreathed in smiles and gratitude.

'I'm wearing Spanx,' she whispered as she handed him over. 'I've even got *mascara* on. On both eyes! Oh my God, Ellen, I can't thank you enough. We're going to have such a lovely night, just Charlie and me. You really are the best friend ever.'

'Why are you wearing Spanx?' I said. 'This weekend is about you recharging your batteries, not glamming up for Charlie?'

'It's not for Charlie, it's for me! I never thought wearing Spanx would be a luxury, but to wear knickers that it will take me five minutes just to wriggle out of when I go for a wee is a novel sensation. And they make my dress look better! It's wonderful to look in the mirror and not see my bulges in leggings. I feel like a proper grown-up again.'

'Well, have a fabulous weekend being a grown-up, but for God's sake don't get carried away and get yourself knocked up again,' I warned her. 'I'm not taking two of them. I'm a good friend, not a bloody idiot!'

'Oh no!' said Hannah firmly. 'I've got condoms, and femi-doms, and I'm on the Pill, and I did try to get a coil fitted too, but they said there was no need if I was on the Pill, and I couldn't very well explain that I seemed to have given birth to Chucky and I wanted to be 100 per cent certain that there was *no* chance of any such thing ever happening again. Anyway, give me a call if there's any emergencies, but I'm sure you'll be fine. You're right, you've done all this before.' Then to Edward she said, 'Bye, darling! Be good for Ellen! Mummy see you tomorrow!'

And Hannah leapt in the car and sped off, just as it dawned on Edward that Mummy was leaving him, and he let out the most almighty bellow.

Dear little Edward, with his cherubic blond curls, turned out to have quite the set of lungs on him, not to mention an impressive range of noises that sounded like something appalling was taking place in a farmyard. At first, he contented himself with merely roaring like a wounded bull, but tiring of that, he quickly moved on to the sort of noise I imagine an angry donkey would make if its bollocks were being chopped off with a rusty saw.

By now, of course, he was lying kicking and screaming on the path, and I was fearful that the volume of his rage was such that the rest of the village would think I was torturing this poor innocent moppet. Attempts to cajole him indoors were useless, so I resorted to picking him up bodily and heaving him in, receiving a hefty kick in my left tit in the process for my trouble. How are such small children so strong and so heavy in relation to their size?

I rather regretted bringing him indoors, as he shifted the pitch up a notch, and started shrieking like a semi-garrotted tomcat. This was not a pleasant noise in a confined space. Judgy agreed, and felt the best way to convey his displeasure was by yapping as shrilly and loudly as he could. Barry, uncertain as to what was going on, but always keen to be a good sport and do his best to please, decided that since everyone else was making a fearsome din, he'd better do the same, and started baying at the top of his voice. My ears began to ring.

Despite his apparent distress, though, it hadn't escaped my notice that not a single tear had made its way down Edward's rosy little cheeks. This was not, of course, my first time at the rodeo, and I remembered well these bouts of fury, where it appeared that the world was about to end, yet no tears were shed, thus suggesting that there was more than a small element of being 'at it' and that Edward was not so much broken-hearted at Hannah and Charlie deserting him, as he was testing his boundaries as to exactly how far he could push this poor sucker he'd been abandoned to. My suspicions were augmented by the fact that, periodically, Edward would pause to take a breath and peek over to make sure he was still the centre of attention.

I got down on the floor so that I was on his level and he'd feel like we were more equal, and embarked on my best Supernanny impression.

'Edward!' I said brightly. 'Edward, that isn't really a very nice noise, I'm afraid, and it's upsetting my doggies. Look, Edward, the poor doggies really don't like that noise, could you stop, please?'

Edward continued to screech. The pitch of his screams were really quite impressive, as dimly, above the barking, baying and bellowing, I could hear my grandmother's crystal vase on the hall table ringing (just what I needed – even the fucking bric-a-brac was getting in on the act).

'Edward,' I said in my best Firm but Fair Voice, 'if you want to make that noise, that's OK, you can keep doing it, but I'm going to take the doggies into the garden away from it, all right? If you'd like to stop, though, you can come and help me feed the chickens and we can have a play on the swing, and then we'll have some lunch, and after lunch, you can watch *Octonauts*, and maybe even have some chocolate buttons!'

The cacophony dropped a notch. One baby blue eye opened and regarded me cannily.

'*OCTONAUTS* NOW!' roared Edward. '*OCTONAUTS* AND CHOCCY BUTTONS NOW!'

'No, Edward. Not now. After lunch, *if* you're a good boy!'

'NOOOOOWWWW! *OCCCCCCTOOOOOOONAAAAA-UUUUUTS*! NOOOOOOW.'

'No. Now, if you will stop that horrid noise, we will go outside and have a lovely time in the garden. Won't that be fun?'

'NOOOOOOOOOOOOO!'

'OK, Edward, well, I'm taking the doggies into the garden now. When you decide you'd like to get up, you can come outside and find us, and then we'll have a play and feed the chickens and go on the swing, yes? But not until you can stop making that noise.'

With that, I stood up, summonsed my poor puppers, then strode briskly into the kitchen and out the back door.

'BYE, EDWARD!' I cried cheerily, before shutting the door ostentatiously loudly so he knew I'd really gone.

Obviously, I'm not the sort of irresponsible person who simply walks out of the house and leaves a distressed toddler alone. Although I did quite often walk off and leave Jane screaming on the floor of the supermarket, when all attempts at consoling her tantrums had failed. One old lady followed me in outrage, insisting, 'You can't just leave her there. I shall call the NSPCC!' as I hissed that I was only around the corner of the next aisle, where she couldn't see me but I could keep an eye on her. We were still arguing when a tear-stained but by now sunny-faced Jane came skipping round the corner to say, 'We get rest of shopping now, Mama, yes?'

Sadly, this technique didn't work so well with Peter. He wasn't a screamer like Jane, but incredibly stubborn, and utterly immoveable when he'd decided he was going no further. I tried bodily dumping him in the trolley, but he'd simply climb out and sit back down in the middle of the aisle; I tried lugging him, but he'd kick his way out of my stranglehold – I mean, loving embrace – and plonk himself back down again. And attempts at walking away and leaving him left him quite unmoved. I once peered around the end of the aisle to see him happily opening a £9.99 bottle of olive oil and, after attempting to take a swig, merrily tipping it over the floor and reaching for another one. I couldn't go back to that Waitrose for years.

I was confident, however, that my tried-and-tested tantrum technique would work on Edward. I hovered outside the back door, peering through the glass at the furiously kicking little legs. Within about one minute of me exiting the house, the flailing stopped. Another minute later, and the noise also ceased. I smiled smugly to myself. By Jove, I thought proudly, truly I was a Toddler Wrangler Extraordinaire! I wondered if I could gently give Hannah some hints for dealing with the little shit, or if she might take it the wrong way. Perhaps I could write a seminal book full of practical tips on how to cope with small children, and it would be a *Sunday Times* bestseller and I could give up work and go on *Lorraine* as a parenting expert?

After all, most of the fuckwits they roll out as parenting experts have no more qualifications on the subject than having a couple of fuck trophies themselves, and one woman I saw on *Good Morning Britain* the other day was dispensing advice based solely on having a three-year-old and a six-month-old, both with angelic blonde curls, whom she dresses in matching and impractical white clothing to photograph in bastarding sunlit cornfields for her Instagram account, which has a stupid name involving the word 'Mummy', because heaven forbid anyone not realising that she's a mummy. She's a mummy, you know. She no longer exists outside motherhood, only as a mummy. Her Mummy account is filled with photos of her moppets looking implausibly clean, and herself wearing sweatshirts saying 'Mama' (because again, SHE'S A MOTHER, YOU KNOW), with twee captions about how her #MamaHeart is living her #BestLife #MakingMemories, and reminding us to #LiveInTheMoment and to #LiveLaughLove, all while shilling us vastly overpriced face cream (#NoFilter) and unnecessary baby gadgets (#ObsessedWithThis #SwipeUp) and fugly dresses that NOBODY wanted to know where they came from (#SoManyOfYouHaveAsked #AffiliateLink #Gifted #SoBlessed).

And her life-changing, revolutionary 'parenting advice' that she was prattling on about on *national television* was to blend vegetables into pasta sauce to make sure they get their five a day, which all parents have been doing since the dawn of time, since Mrs Caveman worked out that if she gave the dubious vegetation she'd gathered a bash with a rock, the little Cavebabies would not whinge that they didn't like the mammoth stew, because there were bits in it, and Mr Caveman would not complain that it didn't taste like his mum's and had she put bits of that bush in it again, she *knows* he doesn't like that bush. Mrs Caveman didn't feel the need to put up any cave paintings of herself bashing said vegetation and #TreasuringEveryMoment because #They'reNotLittleLong (though in the case of the Cave family, that was generally because they got eaten by sabre-toothed tigers).

But I could do way better than that stupid Instagram Mummy. I've been through the fire of every stage of the little cherubs, and have many top parenting tips, like the cunning sleight of hand required when the Tooth Fairy 'forgets' to come, and you chide your precious moppet for 'not looking properly', before triumphantly bringing a shiny pound coin out from beneath the pillow! How to get puke out of your car upholstery, whether it's caused by too many fizzy drinks at the cinema, or too much vodka at a teenage party. How to best revenge yourself on other parents who have pissed you off by filling their children's party bags with Pure Evil (Haribos and vuvuzelas and, ideally, if the Pound Shop stretches to it, some tiny craft kit requiring parental involvement and containing many pieces the perfect size to insert into an ear or a nostril and just sharp enough to make you swear like a bastard when they're left on the floor and you stand on them). How to chip Weetabix off the ceiling. My parenting tips are endless – I'd be excellent at this.

I was still smirking at the thought of the brilliant new career awaiting me, when the little legs suddenly vanished. Shit! Where was he going? I decided he was probably sitting up just out of sight and taking a minute to collect himself, and any second now he'd come trotting out, trustingly place his chubby paw in mine, and we'd spend a magical afternoon, as I introduced him to the wonders of nature that abounded in my garden, and in years to come, when he became the next David Attenborough, as he accepted his Lifetime Achievement BAFTA to add to all his many other awards and accolades, he'd say, 'Really, I owe it all to Ellen. You know, Ellen Green, the *Sunday Times* Bestselling, World-Famous Parenting Guru. It's not surprising that Ellen is loved and revered by children and parents alike, for her wisdom is unparalleled. But to me, she wasn't just the star of her own award-winning TV series. She was also a wonderful friend of my family and me, who taught me about chickens and plants and bees. I still remember that first astonishing afternoon that Ellen taught me you can eat dandelions, and we explored all the different forms of life that flourished in her marvellous garden. That's when I knew I wanted to be a naturalist!'

Hang on, though. Isn't 'naturalist' another name for nudist? Not a naturalist, obviously. Well, I mean he might be a naturalist, but it will be nothing to do with *me*. There are laws against that sort of thing! What *is* David Attenborough, apart from a National Treasure. Does anyone know what his official title is? Also, we probably shouldn't eat the dandelions – the dogs have almost certainly pissed over them. And more to the point, where actually was Edward? He should have appeared by now. Oh God, maybe he'd pulled over the coat stand as he tried to get up and was lying smothered! I belted into the house, praying desperately that I'd not broken or maimed Hannah's baby in the first fifteen minutes I'd been left in charge. That really would not be the sort of thing a Toddler Wrangler Extraordinaire did! My new career would be in jeopardy before it had even started.

Everything was quiet. This was bad. Quiet toddlers are the worst sort. Edward was not in the hall, but the coat stand was upright, and no other furniture appeared to have been moved, so hopefully he'd not yet been crushed or smothered.

'Edward!' I yelled. 'Edward, where are you?'

There was no response, but I heard a faint noise coming from the sitting room. I flung open the door, to find Edward sitting cross-legged and catatonic in front of *Octonauts*, covered in chocolate from the jumbo packet of chocolate buttons I'd bought to act as currency for the weekend, and had left on quite a high shelf on the dresser. Somehow, in the few moments I'd been standing outside the back door waiting for him to collect himself, the little fucker had scuttled in here, scaled the dresser (thank God it didn't collapse on him), turned on the TV, and ripped open and consumed almost the entire packet of buttons! How had he even done that? Was he a Time Lord to have somehow accomplished all of that in the brief window he'd had? And also, how the everlasting *fuck* had he not only managed to turn on the TV, but put CBeebies on? He's *two*, for crying out loud!

I'm forty-eight, with a degree in computer science, and my bastarding smart TV still outwits me several months after purchase, leading to much random pressing of buttons, crying, swearing, making hollow threats at the horrible thing about throwing it out the window, before either giving up and fetching one of my children to make it work for me, or watching my programmes on my laptop. To have a child that still shits itself regularly manage to work the television with such ease suggests that the problem is not in fact that the TV is a 'useless bit of crap that clearly has something wrong with it', but that I may be the problem. Oh God, the next thing I'll be jabbing hopelessly at my phone, before requesting a Young Person assist me, and shouting into it extra loudly if I'm making a long-distance call, so the words will travel further. Then, I shall probably develop an unhealthy interest in soup, and become fretful if I miss *Countdown*, while complaining that it's never been the same since Richard Whiteley died. I had more pressing problems than the encroaching Fucking Oldness, though.

I marched over to Edward and prised the now rather choco-latey remote from his clenched fist. Edward twitched slightly, but did not otherwise react. Then I attempted to retrieve the remains of the chocolate buttons. He tightened his grasp, but did not look away from Captain Barnacles rescuing a depressed barracuda. I decided to tackle one thing at a time, and left him clutching the packet, and instead pressed the 'Off' button on the remote (the only one I knew how to work).

'Come on, Edward,' I said sternly, as I pressed it. 'We said *Octonauts* and chocolate buttons *after* lunch, didn't we?'

All hell broke loose. The tears that were not shed for Hannah's departure poured forth over being denied knowing how Dr Shellington would treat the dejected fish. Heels were drummed and the chocolate buttons packet hurled, scattering the remaining few in the direction of Barry, who immediately hoovered them up, having been hovering close by, clearly remembering Edward as a rich source of treats from his last visit.

After five minutes of this, there was no sign of the storm abating. My pleas, my threats, my promises, my abject begging on my knees for Edward to please, please just stop screaming for one second made no difference at all. Unlike the previous fake tantrum, when I'd spotted him regularly eyeing me up to make sure I was paying sufficient attention, his eyes remained firmly screwed shut, and there was now a definite damp patch on my carpet from his tears. He was a most unpleasant shade of puce, and even though I'd already googled 'Can a toddler scream hard enough to rupture something?' (apart from my eardrums) and the answer was 'No', I was starting to worry that Google was wrong. I was genuinely afraid he'd still be lying there screaming tomorrow, when Hannah and Charlie came to pick him up, a dehydrated husk, having squandered all the moisture in his body on tears. There was nothing else for it. I hated myself, but it had to be done. I picked up the remote and pressed the 'On' button, hoping against hope that it hadn't been off long enough to forget what channel it was on and that it would take me back to CBeebies. Oh hallelujah, happy day!

'Bye bye, Benny Barracuda!' cried the weird cat that was one of the Octonauts, for no apparent reason, despite all the other crew being at least semi-aquatic animals.

Like someone flipping off a switch, Edward's bawls ceased. He sat up, as if nothing at all had happened, and resumed his viewing.

'My likes *Octonauts*,' he announced with a slight hiccup, which apart from his wet scarlet face was the only sign of the storm of emotion I'd just been subjected to. 'Is mine *best!*'

Then, with a sudden snort of outrage, he demanded, 'MY BUTTONS! WHERE MY BUTTONS?'

'Finished, Edward, darling. Edward ate them all,' I hastily assured him. He looked at me with some suspicion.

'Ellen not eated my buttons?'

'No, poppet, you ate them *all*,' I insisted. Fortunately, he seemed to accept this, giving only a warning glare through narrowed eyes, and an insistence that 'You not eat my buttons,' and he returned to the delights of CBeebies, where Big Andy was now hunting for dinosaurs.

I collapsed in a chair and looked at my watch. 12.03 p.m. Edward had been here for less than half an hour, we were already two tantrums and a packet of buttons in, and he'd won the first battle over the TV hands down. Just another twenty-four hours to go then. I started to think my new career as a Parenting Guru might need to be reconsidered. Though of course, the thing about being a Parenting Guru is that you just look on from a distance and tell other people how to deal with the little bastards. You don't actually have to be hands-on yourself.

Big Andy and the dinosaurs over, I hastily turned off the TV before Mr Tumble made an appearance. I've not been able to so much as look at Mr Tumble since the distressing discovery about the internet forums devoted to women who would quite like to fumble with Mr Tumble. It raises altogether too many questions about his Spotty Bag.

Edward at least accepted the end of CBeebies with equanimity this time, although he took a worryingly deep breath when he spotted Barry still hopefully licking out the chocolate buttons bag.

'Doggy eated my buttons!' he shouted in outrage.

'No, darling, no. The doggy is just licking the packet. *Edward* eated, I mean ate, all the buttons, remember? Now, are you going to come and help me make some yummy lunch for us?'

Edward looked at me suspiciously for a moment, clearly under no illusions that this was a blatant distraction device, but fortunately hunger won over his need to thwart me.

'OK,' he said, grudgingly.

Hannah had warned me that Edward was a very picky eater, but I was quietly confident (being as I was a Toddler Wrangler Extraordinaire) that I had a few simple techniques that would make him happily yum down whatever was put in front of him. Firstly, he could help me make lunch. It was a well-known fact that when children participated in cooking, they were *always* willing to eat the results. It made them feel included and important and listened to, and so *naturally* they couldn't wait to gobble down their creations! I mean, OK, it hadn't actually worked for Peter and Jane – if anything it had made things worse because they'd been able to see what had gone into the delicious concoctions we'd cooked and also, the kitchen always ended up in a godawful mess – but maybe I just hadn't been patient enough, and now, using my Special Toddler-Taming Voice, I would bend Edward's palate to my will.

'So, darling,' I announced. 'We're going to make lovely cheese toasties! Won't that be fun?'

'Yes,' agreed Edward happily. 'Fun!'

Ten minutes later, Edward had somehow managed to scatter grated cheese on every surface in the fucking kitchen, including the ceiling. Judgy and Barry were doing a sterling job of cleaning up, which made my heart sink slightly, as Judgy in particular suffers from an unpleasant affliction we simply call 'cheesy bum' when he eats too much dairy.

I was attempting to dissuade Edward from grinding the remnants of the cheese into his hair, when I realised the bread was burning under the grill. I dived across to save it, and Edward took advantage of the moment to pick up the grater and grate his finger.

'Ouchy!' he howled, 'Got ouchy!' as he held up a bloody finger. 'Eeeelllllleeennnnn! OUUUUUUCHHHHHY! NOOO-OOOOO!'

'Oh God, OK, sweetie, it's OK.'

'AAAAAAARRRRGHHHHHH!' screamed Edward, staring at the small nick in his finger as one might an entire severed limb. I slapped a plaster on it, was chastised for not having Octonaut plasters, compromised by adding another two plasters to make up for my plaster inferiority, and then the smoke alarm went off.

'Looooooooud!' howled Edward, as I flapped a tea towel under the smoke alarm and made soothing noises at him.

I fished the charred toast out from under the grill and started again.

Eventually, Edward and I were sitting down in front of two delicious oozing cheese toasties. Edward had not only grated the cheese but had sprinkled it onto the toast, sandwiched the bread together and cut his toastie into dinosaur shapes using the old cutter I bought for Peter years ago.

'Doesn't that look yummy, Edward,' I said encouragingly. 'Dinosaur toasties. Come on, try a bit.'

'No,' said Edward firmly. 'My no like it.'

'But you haven't *tried* it, sweetie. It's in *dinosaur* shapes! Come on, just one bite!'

'No. Like. It. Want my Dairylea sangwidge. Not yucky dinos!'

'But you had such fun making it!' I reminded him. 'We talked about it while we were making it, and you said you were going to eat it. You agreed it looked yummy.'

'Not yummy. Not like it. Want Dairylea!'

'All right, look. How about if you try one bite, and then if you really don't like it, I'll make you a Dairylea sandwich? Hmmm? One bite?'

'No.'

'Please?'

'No.'

'If you try one bite, you can have more *Octonauts* after lunch?'

'No.'

'JUST TRY ONE BITE! I SPENT ALMOST AN HOUR WITH YOU MAKING A TOASTIE! A TOASTIE, DAMMIT! I could have knocked up an actual proper meal in that time, not a bloody hot sandwich!'

Unfortunately, my use of the word 'bloody' reminded Edward about his Ouchy Finger, and he started crying again about it being sore and needing another plaster.

'If I give you another plaster, will you eat your nice lunch?'

'Yes.'

'OK, here you go. Come on, just try it!'

'No. Dairylea.'

We wrangled on. My own toastie was now stone cold. Had Edward been one of my own precious moppets, by this point I'd have hissed, 'Fine, go hungry. *Starve* if you want, see if I care!' But it's frowned upon to not feed Other People's Children, even when they're the fruit of your best friend in the world's loins.

I had one final try.

'I hear Captain Barnacles *really* loves cheese toasties in the shape of dinosaurs,' I wheedled. 'They're his favourite.'

'No. Cap'n Bar'cles likes Dairylea too. *Not* yucky dinos!'

I gave up. I was too hungry to argue anymore. I made Edward a Dairylea sandwich.

'No, traingles! Want traingles!'

I assumed (hoped) he meant triangles, and not his sandwich cut into the shape of Ivor the Sodding Engine. I made him another sandwich, this time in triangles.

'There,' I said wearily.

'Thank you, Ellen!' he said sweetly.

I was just taking a bite of my now stone-cold and congealed toastie when an aroma drifted across to me.

Edward looked up and said brightly. 'My done a poo, Ellen! Ellen change my bum now?'

FML. I unstrapped him from the booster chair, carried him upstairs, as at arm's length as I could manage, and tried not to actually vomit over him as I cleaned him up. Why does other people's children's shit stink so much worse than your own? I mean, I'm not saying my own were exactly fragrant – I had a fair few gagging moments with them too, and then there was the terrible day Peter had to sit in a butternut squash poo for a while before I could get to somewhere to change him, and he was left with a bright orange bum like a baboon for a week – but however horrendous one's own offspring's deposits are, other children's are a million times worse. Maybe it's like how your own farts never smell as bad as other people's? Unless you're Judgy, of course. When he has cheesy bum, he's been known to leave the room in disgust at the pong!

Back downstairs, offending nappy firmly in the outside bin (after Barry showed distressing interest in having it for a tasty snack), with windows now open to try to clear the smell, I wearily ate the rest of my cold toastie. Edward had taken a small bite out of the centre of each sandwich and declared himself, 'All done now!'

I wiped him down (how do children cover themselves in so much food while eating so little?) and agreed to his demands for more CBeebies, leaving him happily watching *Sarah and Duck* while I cleaned up the kitchen. To my dismay, I found I'd already reverted to toddler mode – mindlessly consuming their half-chewed leftovers – having shoved in two of Edward's crusts before I even realised what I was doing. What was wrong with me? He wasn't even my child! I didn't even have the excuse I had when Peter and Jane were little that sometimes those pre-slobbered leftovers were the closest thing I'd get to a meal all day, and eating them was a matter of basic sustenance.

That's another thing no one tells those smugly pregnant women, so sure of how right they're going to get everything – that one day a time will come when a child spits a half-eaten jelly baby into your hand because they've just realised that they'd inadvertently taken a green one, and instead of being revolted by the very fact you have a slimy sweet covered in someone else's saliva in your hand, *you just eat it yourself*, because a) it's the easiest way to get rid of it, and b) well, why not? And what's more, none of the other parents around you will even blanch at the disgusting thing you just did, and in fact may be rather envious of your impromptu and unexpected snack.

In fairness, the dogs had done a sterling job of cleaning up the floor (everyone with toddlers should have a dog; it's the only way to keep the floor clean), but it still took a little while to clean up the rest of the mess on the countertops and up the cupboards (how? HOW?). I kept up a cheery flow of chat to Edward as I wiped, to ensure he didn't wander off on some kamikaze mission of destruction. This meant that tidying up lunch took about five times longer than it should have, which was another thing I'd forgotten: just how long everything takes when you're also trying to stop a toddler from killing themselves/their siblings/burning down the house/cutting up the goldfish. Even leaving the house, something I now take totally for granted, would be a military operation. For a start there was packing enough supplies for the day, including snacks, changes of clothes in case of 'accidents' – either bodily fluid related or, in the case of Peter, because of a near-fatal ability to manage to fall in any body of water within about a five-mile radius, from small puddles, which he liked to faceplant, to Windermere, where he managed to kick off his wellie into the water, then attempted to plunge in after it.

But even once you'd assembled your supplies for the day, you still weren't ready to leave the house, as you then had to catch and clad the children, who would suddenly decide that shoes were evil and that it was a much better idea to try to kick you in the face on account of your unreasonable request that they didn't walk through puddles, broken glass and Unidentifiable Matter in their stockinged feet, or that you would much rather they didn't get hypothermia by going out in the snow in a swimming costume. Then, after loading the car, or the buggy, attempting not to hang so much stuff off the back of the buggy that it tipped up, or forcing them into the car seat, off you'd finally go, sweating and furious and still merrily singing 'The Wheels on the Bastarding Bus' to your darlings in the hope that maybe, possibly, just perhaps, your very best efforts *might* result in some #HappyMemories for them one day.

Hopefully, they'd forget the bit where you called them a little fucker under your breath or the time you dropped their most treasured, beloved, unable-to-part-from-ever-even-for-washing cuddly toy down an extremely dubious public toilet, having insisted on holding it yourself because you didn't trust the child not to drop it down the bog. Peter does remember that, unfortunately, and still references Super-Hippo's impromptu swim and the fact he was never quite the same after his thorough boil washings when he's pointing out my many failings as a parent, *even though it was an accident* and I've been apologising profusely about it for the last twelve years.

I finally finished wiping down the surfaces and popped back to see Edward. He'd vanished again. Why? How? Did *Postman Pat* not meet his viewing requirements? I could hardly blame him – a fucking postman with a helicopter! Also, the new CGI *Postman Pat* is scary and not a patch on the old ones from my own childhood.

'Edward!' I yelled anxiously. 'Where are you?' It had only been two minutes since I had last checked on him. Literally two minutes. I heard a giggle and the flush of the toilet upstairs. Oh God. How had he got into the bathroom? What was he doing? Hopefully he hadn't drunk TCP or tried to brush his teeth with the loo brush or flooded the bathroom or *drowned*! Well, obviously he hadn't drowned, because he'd just flushed the loo. Unless he'd flushed his own head down the pan. On the other hand if you're foolish enough to bog wash *yourself* and drown in the process, there's an element of Natural Selection and the Darwin Awards about it.

I belted up the stairs and burst into the bathroom as Edward attempted to flush the toilet again. Luckily, the cistern hadn't filled up yet, because the loo was brimful of water. Why? What had he put down there?

'Splashy!' chortled Edward. 'Splashy splashy WHOOSH!' And with that he lobbed a pair of my pants down the toilet.

'Edward!' I shrieked. 'Noooo!' I dived over and fished them out. They were my stoutly gusseted, greying, elasticated granny pants that, although hideously unattractive, are extremely comfortable. Floating just below them, though, were my Best Pants – the rather saucy black lace ones that get wedged up the crack of my arse, but I feel are rather more alluring than the M&S bloomer-style drawers that stay where they're meant to and stop you getting a draught on your nether regions. I'd been wearing my Best Pants when I had dinner with Mark on Thursday night, just in case anything happened, though, he once again politely declined my invitation to come in for coffee, as he always does, which is starting to become rather alarming, and makes me wonder exactly what is going on between us.

Anyway, I certainly did not have time to think about that now, as the bowl was about to spill over and I could see what looked like another pair of pants poking out of the U-bend. Edward laughed with glee again and smacked his hands into the water in the toilet bowl.

'Splashy,' he whooped. 'Pantsies are playing fishies! Fishy pantsies!'

There were so many things wrong with that sentence, not least the fact no woman wants the words 'fishy pants' ever uttered in relation to her undergarments, even in innocence by a toddler who's decided to flush them down the lavatory for some inexplicable reason. He must have dived into my bedroom on his way to the bathroom and swiped them off the top of the pile of clean laundry sitting on my bed. Well, at least it was clean ones he was playing with.

As I grabbed him and tried to drag him away from his fun new game, Edward snatched the loo brush.

'I do fishing!' he cried, walloping the brush into the water and drenching us both.

'NO!' I yelled. 'No fishing! Toilets are dirty, Edward, we don't play with them.'

'FISHING!'

This time he attempted to poke me in the eye with the brush.

I finally wrested it off him (toddlers are freakishly strong, especially when in possession of contraband items that they don't wish to relinquish, and we were both already rather wet and slippery now). 'NO!' I said again, 'NO, EDWARD!'

Edward was outraged. 'MINE!' he roared. 'ELLEN SHARE! SHARE!'

Oh, for fuck's sake. I declined to 'share' the loo brush and flung Edward into the bath fully clothed, but not before he'd managed to flush the toilet one last time. There was an unpleasant gurgle, the pants that had already been flushed vanished altogether and the water spilled all over the floor.

'Is the sea!' beamed Edward, his fury at my theft of his 'fishing rod' forgotten in his glee at the tidal wave now coursing across my bathroom floor.

'Edward, that is *very* naughty!' I hissed, as he attempted to climb out of the bath, crying, 'Edward go swimmy in his sea!'

'STAY THERE!' I bellowed at him. 'STAY THERE AND DO NOT MOVE, or … or … I'LL BURN THE TV AND THERE WILL BE NO MORE *OCTONAUTS*!'

This was the best, albeit completely futile, threat I could come up with, the only other thing that sprang to mind being to threaten him that Mummy and Daddy would never come back unless he stayed there. But giving other people's children nightmares and traumatising them for life is also Frowned Upon.

Luckily, I must have looked serious, as Edward subsided back into the bath, while I plunged my arm down the toilet in a desperate attempt to unblock it. I've never put my hand down a U-bend before. I never wish to again. I think it's safe to say that plumber is not on my list of potential future careers.

I eventually grasped the stout gusset and gave it a yank, and the toilet thankfully drained. I looked around at my lovely bathroom, which I'd finally had refitted last year, which was supposed to be a haven of peace and tranquillity, when Jane wasn't spending hours in there having unfeasibly long showers and clogging the drain with hair, or Peter wasn't having a mammoth shit and leaving a great deal of evidence of his activities behind him. So. I had three, no, four pairs of sodden pants that had been flushed as 'fishies'. I had one drenched toddler currently corralled in the bath, who now appeared to be making growling noises at me and demanding to get out. I had toilet water flooded all over my tasteful tiles and seeping into my hall carpet. And I myself was soaked to the shoulder and liberally sprinkled with said toilet water also.

One thing at a time, I decided. I sloshed across the floor and got the old towels out of the airing cupboard that I kept 'just in case'. I'd never been sure just in case of *what*, but now I knew. I dumped them on the floor to start soaking up the water. Edward watched me, then suddenly stood up and announced, 'My help, Ellen!' and grabbed my lovely John Lewis Egyptian cotton bath towels off the towel rail and hurled them into the water too.

'For fuck's sake, Edward!' I yelled in fury.

'Fuck's sake!' he parroted merrily. '"Fuck" is bad word, Ellen. You naughty Ellen. You go on naughty step, ha ha ha!'

'Edward, I had extreme provocation,' I said sternly. 'No, you stay in that bath. I'm going to take your nasty, dirty clothes off now.'

I stripped Edward off and ran him a bath. I looked at the soaps, bubble baths and various other unguents, lotions and potions I possessed to cleanse, calm, soothe and clarify mind and body, and then tipped half a bottle of Dettol into his bath. After a moment's thought, I added a good dash of TCP, just to be on the safe side.

'Poo!' said Edward. 'Smells yucky!'

'Yes, well. It will make you nice and clean and disinfected, you filthy child!' I said.

'Poo,' said Edward again.

'Yes, I know, but that's what happens to grubby little boys who play in toilets!'

'No, POO! I done a poo!'

I paused while scrubbing those cherubic blond curls, and looked down. There was indeed a large floater there, winking merrily up at me. How had he produced something that big? It appeared to be twice the size of his sodding head! Was that even biologically *possible*? Surely it's not normal to produce poos that are so out of proportion with the rest of you?

I sighed. I was by now beyond horror and rage, and merely resigned to surviving the next twenty-four hours without getting cholera, despite Edward's best efforts. I hauled him out, put on the Marigolds from under the bathroom sink, fished out the poo, binned the Marigolds and got a new pair, thanking my lucky stars that I kept extra cleaning stuff in the bathroom cupboard so I didn't have to turn my back on a semi-disinfected, wet, slightly poopy child, scrubbed the bath with bleach while issuing lengthy threats to Edward about the dire consequences should he move off the loo seat where I'd perched him, ran a new bath, added even more Dettol and TCP, and started again.

Edward clean and dressed again, I sat him on the landing with the iPad and unlimited access to Netflix, and a packet of elderly dolly mixture I'd found at the back of the kitchen cupboard and set aside for emergencies (they were a bit hard, having gone out of date two years earlier, but I reckoned sugar was a preservative, so they'd be fine. They'd just take him longer to eat) while I cleaned up the rest of the bathroom.

Then the only offending article in need of a good scrub was me. This was a dilemma. I didn't dare leave Edward alone while I had a shower, but equally, I didn't really feel I could just bring him in the bathroom with me, like I used to with my own children, as although I wasn't really sure of the protocol about nudity and other people's children, I was pretty sure it's not the done thing. Also, I'm British and am not good with nudity at the best of times. Such things are all very well if you're all Scandinavian or Dutch and liberal about such things, but I like things buttoned up, both literally and metaphorically.

In the end, I settled for draping a towel over the shower screen so that I could peer round and see Edward, but he couldn't see me, as long as he stayed in the corner where he was put. I'd had quite a bad enough day without those blue eyes looking innocently at me and him asking me why my hairy bottom was so wrinkly or something equally crushing yet awful. My self-esteem was low enough already, what with Mark's strangely platonic approach to 'things'.

I instructed Edward to sing a lovely song, so that even if I took my eyes off him while I washed my hair, I could still be sure he was where I'd left him and he hadn't escaped to cause more carnage. Hannah's description of him as Conan the Destroyer of Houses was starting to seem very apt.

We settled on 'Twinkle, Twinkle, Little Star' as a suitable song for Edward's bathroom concert, although the only song currently going through my head at this point was Kevin Bloody Wilson's marvellous song 'An Absolute C*nt of a Day', but I didn't think Hannah or Charlie would thank me if he came home humming that and started belting it out at Little La La's music class next week.

Edward duly sang. I scrubbed. And scrubbed. Edward kept singing. My soul started to dissolve. But I was clean. I resolved that perhaps we should go out for a walk, somewhere far from my home, where Edward could destroy other people's possessions and sanity, and where there would be witnesses, should I find my patience tried further, so I would be forced to still refer to him as 'Edward, darling' and not shout, 'What the fuck have you done now, you feral pig troll?'

'Lovely song, Edward,' I said encouragingly as I stepped out the shower. 'Keep singing, darling, while Ellen gets dressed quickly, yes? Good boy!'

And then I stopped. And sniffed, a very familiar smell. And froze at a horribly familiar sight.

Edward, still lustily belting out 'Twinkle, Twinkle' at full volume, had nonetheless sidled out of his corner, evidently doing it gradually enough and with ninja cunning so I hadn't noticed the source of the sound had moved *ever* so slightly, gone into his changing bag, which, FOOL that I was, I'd left on the floor after I'd got him dressed, and retrieved the Sudocrem.

'What are you doing?' I asked faintly.

'I helping, Ellen,' said Edward cheerfully. 'I put bum cream on. Bum cream make things clean an' nice, Mummy say. So I put bum cream on dirty floor for you! S'clean and nice now, see? I's good boy, so I have buttons and *Octonauts* now, yes?'

Edward had liberally smeared Sudocrem over the landing carpet, just outside the bathroom door. Sudocrem does not come out of carpets. It's the most viscous, clinging, oily, foul substance known to humanity, and I knew it doesn't come out of carpets because Peter and Jane had both done the same thing. Edward was also thickly coated in it.

'I very helping!' he said firmly.

I briefly considered just burning the house down, and walking away, abandoning the problem of the Sudocremed carpet and the mountain of wet towels and clothes covered in typhoid water waiting to be washed. But I'd still have the problem of the Sudocremed toddler to deal with. I sighed, put on my dressing gown and ran a third bath for Edward. It was only half past three.

By teatime, I was giving serious thought to ringing Hannah and begging her to come back and take Edward away. The only thing stopping me was the realisation that today was Hannah's life every single day, and so I couldn't actually ruin her one brief escape into a world of adult conversations and baths without disinfectant.

After the final bath – well, I hoped it would be the final bath for the day – Edward and I had gone on a nice walk to the shop. It was not quite the relaxing experience I'd hoped for. Edward alternated between walking very slowly and suddenly speeding up and belting off into the distance like Speedy Gonzales, while I hurtled after him, shrieking for him to come back. We passed a mind-numbing half an hour in the park, with me see-sawing him up and down, and pushing him on the swings and trying to catch him at the bottom of the slide before he landed face first in the mud and I had to take him home for a fourth bath. An old woman passing with her dog stopped to chat to him and asked him if he was having a nice day with his granny.

Edward replied sweetly, 'Ellen not nice. Ellen say "fuck" 'cos she naughty. My not say "fuck". Does you say "fuck"?' and the old woman beat a hasty retreat.

'You got a fat bum!' he yelled after her in a chatty tone.

In fairness, she *did* have a fat bum, not that one would have been so rude as to mention it, though I was quite close to telling her to fuck off myself for mistaking me for a granny. Do I look like a granny? I know it's the 21st century and grandmothers come in all shapes and sizes and ages these days, and being a granny doesn't automatically conjure up white-haired old ladies knitting and going berserk with their bus passes, off their tits on Werther's Originals, but even so. I surreptitiously sneaked a look at myself on my phone camera. Even allowing for the hideousness of the selfie mode, I *did* look quite haggard after a day with Edward.

I managed to persuade Edward out of the park with promises of a 'treat' at the shop, as I could no longer feel my feet with the cold, and I felt I was pushing my luck to stay there much longer without Edward managing to hurt himself or another child after he pushed a little girl down the slide, complaining she was 'too slow'. I had in mind perhaps a packet of Wotsits or similar, but Edward had other ideas and demanded a comic costing £4.95 because it had a plastic piece of *Octonauts*-themed tat taped on the front. I was attempting to remonstrate with him and he was just taking a good lungful of air in to do his bellowing wounded-bull impression at the injustice of it all, when Mrs Fat Bum from the park came into the shop and I was forced to capitulate lest I became known as the cruel and mean granny as well as the naughty, sweary one, if Edward took it upon himself to document more of my crimes against him in public (I wouldn't have put it past him to have claimed I washed him in the toilet, just to blacken my character further), or worse, started insulting the other clientele with that marvellous toddler honesty.

Outside the shop, Edward immediately ripped open his comic, extracted the shitty piece of overpriced plastic and broke it. Wailing commenced. As did a long, slow, cold walk home with the wailing one as I brightly informed passers who stopped to enquire about his welfare that 'he was just over-tired'. At least, if *he* wasn't over-tired, I most certainly was. Eventually, unable to bear the sluggish, sob-punctuated pace of the trudge home, I offered Edward a piggyback. This resulted in Edward snottering in my hair and kicking me in the kidneys for half a mile, while I wondered if my spinal column was actually collapsing under his immense weight.

Unfortunately, we met Mark in the lane, who seemed slightly surprised to find me With Child.

'Oh,' he said. 'Um, I was on my way home and thought I'd pop in to see if you wanted to come round for dinner, but I take it you're busy. Who is this little chap?' he added, in the forced jovial way that people who are unaccustomed to children think makes them sound like they're good with children.

'Edward,' I said wearily, casting longing looks at Mark's posh paper carrier bag from the posh local deli, which clearly had at least two bottles of wine poking out the top and probably contained nice cheese of the sort you don't put in toasties or let toddlers rub into their hair. 'He's staying the night. He's my friend's little boy.' Some kind of insanity then clearly gripped me, as I went on to suggest, 'You could always come round to mine for dinner after he's in bed, if you want. It *must* be my turn to make you dinner – you always seem to be cooking for me!'

Even as I said the words, I was wondering what was *wrong* with me. When I finally got the demon hell fiend to bed, the *last* thing I'd want to do was to start cooking another meal. I'd want to slump on the sofa with an enormous gin and a packet of pickled onion Monster Munch and watch mindless TV, not pretend to be a proper person over complicated pasta.

I was very relieved when Mark immediately said, 'Oh no. No, thank you. I've got something on.'

I was slightly insulted by the speed of his refusal, though, but it was not exactly a glamorous offer I'd made, nor, I felt, was I probably looking my most alluring (and my Good Pants weren't exactly Match Ready either, after being flushed by Edward).

I trudged into the house and deposited Edward (who fortunately had contented himself with only staring menacingly at Mark) on the floor.

'Dinner,' said Edward.

'I need to feed the doggies first,' I said as kindly as I could, which wasn't terribly, given that Edward was not the only one who was cold, hungry and fed up. 'Poor doggies are very hungry.'

'Dinner NOW!' insisted Edward. 'Or buttons,' he added cunningly.

'No buttons, and dinner *soon*, as soon as I've fed the poor doggies!' I said firmly, feeling a brief pang of smugness that it wouldn't hurt Edward to wait and would help him not to grow up spoilt if he learnt that animals are always fed before people, even recalcitrant toddlers. And also, I still had to heat up Edward's dinner, which Hannah had luckily provided, as all he'll eat for dinner is Hannah's fish pie, made in precisely the same way each time, so it always tastes identical. Any attempt to get him to deviate from this apparently involves *Exorcist*-style tantrums, a lot of food being thrown and quite possibly projectile vomiting if any of the offending dish actually makes it into his mouth by some miracle.

So Hannah had brought a Tupperware pot full of Edward-approved dindins. With my earlier hubris, I'd entertained notions of whipping up some exotica to tempt Edward's developing palate and then blithely informing Hannah of how much he'd enjoyed it. But now, the fight had quite gone out of me, and if all Edward wanted was fish pie, he could have fish pie, as it required no effort from me whatsoever.

I dumped the dog food into their bowls and shoved the fish pie in the microwave. I heard a furious growling and turned round to see Edward on all fours, snarling at poor Barry and chasing him away from his bowl, as Edward shoved a handful of kibble in his mouth.

'EDWARD!' I yelled, snatching him up from the floor and thanking my lucky stars he'd chosen Barry to go full-on Wolf Boy at. Judgy would have had no truck with such nonsense, and by now they'd probably have been rolling on the floor, trying to tear each other throats out and howling at the moon. Poor, timid Barry, despite his enormous size, will always avoid a fight if it's at all caninely possible.

'My a doggy, my have dinner!' insisted Edward.

'You are *not* a doggy. And we do *not* steal food out of my poor dogs' bowls. That's not nice, and you're lucky you didn't get bitten!'

'I BITE! I'm doggy. Grrrr! Want my DINNER! GRRRRR-RRRR!' snarled Edward, struggling to get down and continue with his impromptu snack.

Luckily, the microwave pinged with his actual dinner, and I wrestled him into his booster seat and plonked the fish pie down in front of him.

Edward recoiled.

'Yuck!' he said firmly.

'Not yuck!' I said equally firmly. 'Yummy. Yummy fish pie. You *love* fish pie!'

'Nooooooo! My not! My not like it! My like *Mummy's* fish pie!'

'This *is* Mummy's fish pie,' I said soothingly. 'Just try it. Mummy made it just for Edward.'

'Is NOT Mummy's fish pie, is *bits*, is YUCK! WAAAANT the doggy food, doggy food is YUMMY, not YUCK! Dis YUCK!'

Marvellous. A new low. An absolute new low. Arguing with a child so fussy he'll not even taste the food in front of him about why he can't eat the dog food he was so merrily cramming in his gob not one minute earlier.

'You can't have dog food. You're not a dog.'

'I IS!' he insisted.

I approached with a spoonful of fish pie and many blandishments and aeroplane noises and promises about the wonderful things that awaited boys who ate fish pie. Edward bit my hand, while managing to get no fish pie in his mouth.

'I IS a dog,' he said darkly. 'See?'

In the end we compromised yet again. Edward had a bowl of dry cereal for his dinner, which he insisted on eating off the floor, like a dog. I was no longer sure where this stood on the scale of responsible adulting. On the one hand, I was allowing him to use his imagination and explore his environment through role play, and not constraining his developing view of the world by forcing him to conform to my own narrow stereotypes of how children should behave. On the other hand, I was feeding him on the floor. Like a dog.

'Finished!' said Edward triumphantly. 'You tell me I good boy!'

'Good boy,' I sighed.

'An' now I poo in garden, like the doggies!'

'NO!' I said. 'Absolutely not.'

'Why not?'

'Because,' I said desperately, 'it's cold. It's too cold. You haven't got a hairy bottom to keep you warm like my doggies. Your bum will *freeze off* and then you'll never be able to poo ever again!'

Edward considered this. 'My not want my bum to freeze off,' he said eventually. 'My not poo outside now.'

A small victory. A very small victory.

'Can I sleep in the doggies' bed?'

'NO!'

'MY WANT TO!'

'Well, the doggies don't sleep in their bed,' I said. 'They sleep in my room, where Edward is going to sleep too. So if you go to sleep in there, you'll be just like the doggies.'

'I *am* a doggy.'

'Yes, yes, so you can do the same as them and sleep in Ellen's room, OK?'

'Like the doggies?'

'YES.'

'OK. CBeebies now?'

'Doggies don't watch CBeebies,' I said unkindly, and really quite stupidly, as CBeebies was currently the only thing buying me some precious moments of sanity, so why the fuck would I refuse to put it on to score some ridiculous point about whether Edward was or was not a dog? But that's what toddlers drive you to. Eventually you're sucked into their insane little world, where reason and good sense go out the window, and you find yourself having some bizarre and meaningless argument with them, because, GODAMMIT, you'd MAKE them admit you were right, and you'd thwart them JUST ONCE THAT DAY!

I read a book once that advised you to pick your arguments with your toddler, and just let it go if it's something unimportant. Does it really matter if they insist on the blue cup for milk and the red cup for juice? Does it *really* make any difference to you if they insist on wearing odd shoes? No, of course it doesn't. But … sometimes, you just need to win. You really just need to *win*, when every sentence you utter is met with the response 'NO!' or 'MY NOT!' or 'NO LIKE IT', when you've spent twenty minutes trying to persuade someone who can't wipe their own arse why they need to wear trousers, when you've been hit in the face with a wooden shape sorter because you suggested that them trying to cram Duplo into your bra really wasn't that enjoyable an experience for you. Sometimes you just need to fucking win one argument, just to make yourself feel better, and feel, even just for a moment, that you're actually the one in charge.

I capitulated, obviously, and put CBeebies back on. There was a God, however, as Tom Hardy was reading the bedtime story. Wearing an unnecessarily ugly anorak, but after the day I'd had, any Tom Hardy was better than nothing.

Edward had a fourth bath – my attempt to create a soothing and peaceful bedtime atmosphere – followed by a glass of milk, which he refused to have from a sippy cup and so tipped all over himself, because I'd forgotten that you never fill the cup full for a small child, so then he had a fifth bath (luckily Hannah had included multiple spare sets of clothes and pyjamas) and I popped him in his travel cot.

'No,' said Edward, climbing out with alarming ease. 'I sleep like the DOGGIES! NOT in cot. Where doggies sleep?'

Well, obviously, the dogs slept on my bed, but I didn't really want a starfishing, thrashing, sweaty child hogging the bed. Judgy is bad enough for taking up far more than his fair share of space, and Barry *tries* to make himself as small as possible, but the fact is that he's still enormous, even when curled in a ball.

'On the floor,' I lied, hoping this would tempt Edward back into his cot.

'I sleep on the floor too then!' he said firmly. 'Why the doggies not going to sleep?'

'It's not their bedtime.'

'Then Edward not going to bed, 'cos Edward is a doggy.'

I summoned the dogs. Judgy looked at me, snorted in disgust and stomped off. Barry, though, good soul that he is, lay down obediently next to the pile of blankets I was making a bed for Edward out of on the floor.

Edward curled up happily, and I read him *Where the Wild Things Are*. He declared it to be rubbish, and demanded another story. I raided Jane's room and retrieved her ancient Dr Seusses, but Edward howled and said NOT *Cat in HAT*, a DOGGY story. I ransacked the house and found an old Spot the Dog book. It was very dull, though, so I made up a story instead about a dog that went to sleep as soon as it was told to, so that it had magical adventures in its sleep, and it never got out of bed when it had gone to bed because it was such a good dog and the adventures wouldn't happen if it got out of bed. Edward seemed unconvinced, and asked why the doggy was playing with a ball in the pictures when I said it was sleeping. I snapped that it was part of the dream, and with great restraint refrained from adding the words, 'Don't question me, you little motherfucker.'

Finally, I tucked him in. Barry gave me a plaintive look, but I bade him to stay, just till the devil pig fell asleep. I sat on the landing outside, and waited for the next onslaught. I could hear Edward babbling away in my bedroom. I crept closer to the door, and heard him telling Barry a long and involved story. Barry occasionally made the rumbling sound that's his version of talking when he's happy and relaxed, so I assumed he didn't mind.

At last, Edward fell silent. I left it a few more minutes and tiptoed in to rescue Barry. Edward had left his nest of blankets and was curled up asleep between Barry's long legs.

'Come on, Barry!' I whispered. Barry looked at me and did not move.

'Come on!' I tried again. 'Come get cheese.' Barry sighed. He loves cheese. But he just settled down more comfortably around Edward and did not get up. I tried to pick Edward up to return him to his blanket bed, but Barry headbutted my hand reproachfully. It seemed he'd decided Edward was his puppy and his responsibility, and he'd be staying put. Because I've seen children poke their fingers in Barry's eyes, and pull his tail, and in one unfortunate incident with my sister-in-law Louisa's hell beasts, cut his whiskers off, all while he sat quietly and let them, I knew Edward would be quite safe with Barry. Judgy sneezed reproachfully at me from outside the door, though, as he'd heard the word 'cheese' and didn't see why Barry's noble sacrifice meant that he should go without. I put a blanket over Edward, who was quite cute when he was asleep, but not as adorable as my beloved Barry curled protectively round him.

The utter goodness of Barry's heart never fails to astonish me. His first few months had been hell. When he arrived at the shelter he was covered in cigarette burns and someone had kicked him so viciously they'd broken his ribs. He was still only a puppy then, and all he'd ever known was pain and fear and cruelty. He'd be quite justified if he hated humans, if he could never get over his mistreatment and could never trust anyone. And yet, he'd nothing to give but love. From the day I brought Barry home, all he ever wanted was to be loved and to love back in return. He had the very nicest nature of any dog or human I'd ever met; he asked for nothing at all and he gave everything in return. Of course, everyone thinks their dog is the best dog, and everyone is right, but to be able to give a dog like Barry – who deserved so much and had been given nothing but brutality – somewhere he can feel safe and loved, somewhere he can show that he might not be the most beautiful on the outside (though he *is* the most beautiful to me), but that his pure and loving soul far outweighs his physical looks, *that* is the great privilege that comes with getting a rescue dog, one you just can't get from buying a puppy from a breeder, however reputable they might be.

Judgy interrupted me from my fond gazing at Barry with another angry sneeze to remind me that *he* is also a rescue dog, thank you, and a rescue dog in dire need of that cheese that was mentioned, *if* you don't mind. I wearily followed him downstairs to dispense cheese and shut up my chickens (and sneak a bit of cheese up to Barry as well, of course).

I barely lasted till 10 p.m. before I followed Edward up the wooden hill to Bedfordshire, my eyes drooping. How the hell did Hannah do this, day in, day out? How the hell had *I* once done this for years on end? It was a reminder that, really, although it feels like things don't get easier, as every stage brings its own challenges and it seems like you've just exchanged the toddler tantrums for the teenager rants and door-slammings, actually nothing is as physically draining or even as mentally taxing – being simultaneously mind-numbingly dull yet in a constant state of high alert – as those early years. And at least when they grow up a bit, they can wipe their own bums too!

Fortunately Edward slept through the night, but he was up at 5 a.m., with a rather anxious-looking Barry dancing beside him, as poor Barry had not even left Edward to go for a bedtime pee. He hurtled down the stairs to the back door, making 'Please hurry up' whuffling sounds at me as I dashed down to let him out. The look of relief on his face was palpable as he relieved himself against the lavender pot beside the back door. It was a beautiful morning, though. I looked at the sunrise and took a few deep breaths. Then I became aware that the splashing sound of Barry's enormous widdle had been joined by a second stream.

Edward beamed up at me, having abandoned both my instructions to wait in the kitchen, and his nappy, as he too pissed joyously into the lavender pot.

'Let me guess?' I said. 'You're weeing like the doggy?'

'YES! My love the doggy. I live here with the doggy now! Don't I, doggy?' he said to Barry.

Judgy and I made twin strangulated noises of horror at the thought of a full-time Edward. Barry, however, grinned at me, as if he rather liked the idea. Sometimes Barry, although entirely full of love and kindness, and with the biggest heart in the world, is lacking in brains. But I decided Edward's new abode was an argument Hannah and Charlie could have with him when they came to pick him up.

Breakfast was accomplished with relatively little fuss, through the simple means of feeding Edward on the floor again with the dogs and letting him eat from the bowl on all fours. However, he then demanded to go out into the garden and see the chickens while I was still finishing my first, much-needed, cup of tea. It was still only 5.30 a.m. My chickens were not early risers, much like myself, and I'd no intention of going cavorting around the garden in my jammies until I'd had at least one more cup of tea. I informed Edward of this. Edward ignored me, reached for the door handle and announced, 'MY go sees the chickens by myself then! BYEEEE!'

'EDWARD!' I thundered 'BAD DOG! SIT!'

Edward sat, to my immense surprise. As did Judgy and Barry. I gave the dogs a biscuit each as a reward, and attempted to fob Edward off with a Cheerio, but he wanted a dog biscuit too. I gave him a charcoal one, as he'd spent the night farting extremely loudly.

I tried a new command.

'Edward,' I said. 'I'm going to get dressed. Are you a good dog?'

'YES!' said Edward. 'Edward is a VERY good doggy.'

'OK,' I said. 'Well, GOOD dogs stay when they're told to stay. If I put on CBeebies for you and say, "Edward, good dog, STAY," you have to stay where you're sitting without moving. Do you think you can do that? Can you be a good dog?'

'Of *course* I can be GOOD dog,' said Edward scornfully.

'Remember, good dogs don't wee in the house either,' I added hastily, lest the dog persona get the better of him. 'Right, come on, I'll stick the TV on, and then when I say, "STAY", you must not move, and if you STAY like a good dog till I come back downstairs, you can have another dog biscuit, OK?'

'YES!' said Edward. 'I good doggy and I love the doggy biccies!'

I plonked him in front of *Topsy and Tim*, gave a stern 'STAY! GOOD DOG!', hoped I wasn't creating the scenario for either a lifetime of therapy or sexual deviancy, and hastily belted upstairs and threw my clothes on. To my astonishment, Edward was still sitting happily where I'd left him when I came back down.

'See?' he said. '*Good* doggy! Biccie now!'

'Very good dog,' I said, handing him a Bonio, and wondering why I'd never tried this approach before. I always said that children were a bit like puppies, in that they needed regular feeding, plenty of exercise, and were inclined to piss over your house and wreck the furniture, but it had never occurred to me to implement an actual dog-training routine on them. If you think about it, though, that was really what Captain von Trapp had done with his hundreds of offspring, with all of them marching about, trained to the whistle. I wondered if it was too late to get a whistle for Peter and Jane. I suspected so, especially now that Jane was eighteen. I'd perhaps missed my training window with her.

Of course, as happened every time I thought I'd nailed this parenting/adulting/life-hacking business, I peaked too soon. Edward, initially relishing the novelty of being a 'good doggy', quickly decided it was far more fun to be a 'bad doggy'. He decided to test this theory by digging a hole in the middle of the lawn when I was feeding the chickens, while Barry looked on and made remonstrative noises, and Judgy, disloyal as ever, decided to join in. When I attempted to object about this, Edward growled and bit me on the ankle. I gave serious thought to smacking him on the nose with a rolled-up newspaper and shouting 'BAD DOG!', but that was probably taking the dog/parenting theory just a little too far, as was rubbing his nose in any puddles he might make.

Instead, I grabbed a protesting, muddy Edward and hauled him in for bath number six of the nineteen hours he'd so far spent with me. Edward's visit, I feared, would have quadrupled my energy bills for the quarter, between the constant baths and the washing machine having been going non-stop since Toiletgate the previous evening.

I had three more hours to fill before Hannah and Charlie arrived to pick Edward up. I suggested another walk, which Edward agreed to enthusiastically. Unfortunately, he was only willing to go for a walk if he was allowed to continue in his role as a doggy, i.e. on all fours, and with a collar and lead on. I was starting to suspect that a successful career as a Tory cabinet minister might be awaiting Edward.

Since he point-blank refused to leave the house without a collar (he'd discovered the basket of spare collars I'd bought for Judgy at various times that he'd declined to wear, as they were too frivolous for a Proud and Noble Border Terrier, so he'd just tear them off every time I attempted to deck him out in jaunty tweed or seasonal loveliness, and was now parading around wearing three collars and a canine tweed bow tie), I ran through the potential activities I could contain him with until his doting Mama and Papa finally relieved me of him, because in all conscience I could not sit him in front of a screen again.

For a brief and foolish moment I considered baking, but thought of the mess created by the toasties the day before.

I'd thrown out the last of the Play-Doh years ago, evil nasty stuff that it is, but for a mad second I considered googling a recipe for a home-made version, before I remembered its propensity to lodge in every crack and crevice in your house, as well as setting like concrete under your nails.

Painting? Toddlers have a remarkable habit of getting paint on every surface *except* the paper, and also the only paints in the house were the rather nice ones Jane had got when she was doing GCSE Art, and I didn't really want to waste them on Edward painting pictures of poos.

Jigsaws? Jigsaws are stimulating and fun, and, more importantly, are quiet and involve no liquids. A jigsaw would the perfect way to entertain him.

'Do you want to do a puzzle with me, Edward darling?' I asked.

'No,' said Edward flatly. 'No pussle. Pussles rubbish.'

'But look,' I wheedled, showing him the box I'd unearthed from the bottom of the board-games cupboard. 'It's got a lovely picture on it of a doggy!'

'No. Rubbish.'

A board game? The trouble was that I'd got rid of all the games that were suitable for a toddler, and the ones that remained were either full of tiny pieces that were the perfect size to cram up a nostril, or else were not age-appropriate, though even if Edward could read, Cards Against Humanity was probably *still* not quite the thing for him.

Also, toddlers cheat like UTTER BASTARDS at board games. I still recall the utter soul-sucking misery of trying to play Snakes and Fucking Ladders with Peter, who would simply blithely ignore what he'd thrown on the dice, move his counter wherever he pleased and shove mine off the board before shouting, 'WIN! I WIN!' and crowing about it and demanding choccy biccies ''cos my had winned!' I got my own back when he was a bit older and I thrashed him six times in a row at Connect 4, and shouted 'Loser' at him so many times he started crying. On reflection, that was perhaps not my finest parenting moment, but at the time the victory was so very, very sweet.

Edward crawled around, barking a bit more, and added a festive holly berry collar to his attire. Then inspiration struck.

'Edward,' I said. 'Do you want to play dressing up?'

Edward pondered for a moment. 'Yes,' he finally said.

Ha. Dressing up. Quiet, creative, liquid-free. I *was* a Genius Parenting Guru Extraordinaire after all!

Off we duly trotted upstairs and rifled my wardrobe for my Primarni finest garb. At first I tried to find things that Edward could put on to create a more masculine outfit ('Here, darling, why don't you pretend this is armour?' I trilled as I proffered a rather terrifyingly bling sequin jacket at him), but it was quickly apparent that all he really wanted to do was pile on as much glittery stuff as possible, and bollocks to pretending he was anything but fabulous. And why not, he was two? If you can't get away with a tiara, a sequin shrug, a feather boa and four-inch heels that are six sizes too big for you when you're two, when can you? On second thoughts, I removed the heels from him on health and safety grounds, after he tripped and nearly smacked his head on the corner of my dressing table. There's being fabulous, and there's getting blood on my sequins, and anyway, he'd already ruined my landing carpet, which was quite enough for one weekend.

I'd completely forgotten how much fun dressing up is. When I was little, my very favourite thing in the world was to be turned loose in my grandmother's bedroom to ransack her cupboards. She never threw anything away, and she had dozens of glamorous evening dresses, a few of which must have dated back to the Second World War. Some of them would probably be worth a fortune to a vintage clothes collector now, but after Granny Green died, my father was foolish enough to ask my mother to sort out her clothes, and Mum threw everything away, apart from the odd treasure I was able to salvage. I found some of them now, including a pair of full-length turquoise satin evening gloves.

I still remember being about seven, and parading up and down Granny's garden in these gloves, and an emerald-green satin dress that was at least two feet too long (a problem I'd solved by tucking it into my knickers), a scarlet pill box hat, complete with veil, approximately six ropes of various pearls and jade and turquoise beads, and a jet choker, with far-too-big silver dancing sandals on my feet, which my toes kept sliding out of and getting muddy. I was swinging a gold mesh bag round like a microphone and belting out 'Super Trouper', and it was one of the last times I remember feeling truly, utterly, totally unself-conscious, and convinced I was stunning. Mr Briggs from next door popped his head over the wall to see what all the noise was about and looked a bit nonplussed, but Granny just said, 'She's having fun, Bernard. Are you coming round for a gin?'

The week after that, I overheard my other grandmother, my mother's mother, tell my mum I was like a little barrel and she should put me on a diet, and Sandra Evans told me that boys only liked girls with blue eyes and blonde hair and so I'd never get a boyfriend, and a lifetime of insecurity about my looks began. But looking at those gloves, for a moment I was trans-ported back to that little girl in that back garden, and Granny and Bernard Briggs knocking back the gin and Dubonnet and puffing on cigarettes (Gauloises for Granny, B&H for Mr Briggs) and applauding my 'performance'. I didn't find out until long after Granny and Mr Briggs were both dead that they'd become 'a bit more than good friends' after the death of Grandpa Green and Mrs Briggs. I'd always wondered why he'd come round for breakfast so often, and thought he must get up very early in the mornings.

I have, of course, tried very hard not to pass all these insecu-rities about my body and my appearance on to my children, but

I fear that in trying to avoid the mistakes of the past, we just make new ones and create different hang-ups and issues. God knows what mine will accuse me of in years to come.

Edward interrupted my musings to shout, 'I PRETTY, Ellen!'

'Yes, darling, Edward is very pretty.'

'I put on STICKLIP!' he announced as he made a beeline back for my dressing table, and I slightly regretted removing his heels, as they did slow him down considerably. I rugby tackled him just in time to rescue my precious Dior lippy from his grasp. There are lines I draw when it comes to dressing up, and smearing himself in twenty-quid lipstick was one of them. It wasn't a sexist thing, that he couldn't wear it because he was a boy. It was an economy thing, because I didn't want my good make-up ruined.

Edward was displeased. 'GIMME STICKLIP!' he demanded.

'No. It's MY lipstick, it's not for children.'

'MY WANT STICKLIP TO BE PRETTY!' he roared. 'MY WANT IT! YOU MEAN! GIMME!'

'NO!'

'NOT FAIR!'

'Look,' I said, trying to compromise while waving my powder brush at him. 'Why don't I put some of this on you to make you pretty? Hmmm?' Obviously I had no intention of brushing my equally eye-wateringly expensive powder on him, but I was confident I could trick him into thinking I had.

'NO. Rubbish! Want RED STICKLIP!' he insisted.

I was saved by the doorbell ringing, and Judgy and Barry deciding we were under attack and barking their heads off. Edward was distracted from the lipstick and remembered he was a dog, and he started barking too. I shepherded the three of them downstairs and opened the door to Hannah and Charlie, who looked slightly baffled by the sight of their son, sitting in the middle of the hall, head thrown back and baying loudly, dressed in a lurid selection from my wardrobe, topped off with a silk scarf tied Rambo-style round his head.

'Hello, Edward,' said Charlie. 'Have you had a nice time? We've come to take you home now.'

Edward paused in his baying to look at Charlie scornfully.

'I not. I live with Ellen and the doggies now, 'cos I IS a doggy. AaaaaaWOOOOOOOOO!' he howled.

'Ah,' I said. 'About that …'

Sometime later, after Edward had finally been dragged to the car amid great wails that he was not a boy, he was a DOG and he NOT GO HOME NOW (to Barry's immense consternation that his puppy was being mistreated), all was silence. Hannah had given me a quick hug and a bottle of artisan gin, and said, 'I can't thank you enough. It was bliss! I'm human again!' before returning to wrangle Edward, who'd put on a collar and lead again and was insisting that was the only way he'd go to the car.

Peter and Jane were not due home from Simon's for another couple of hours, and the house was suddenly very quiet with no kamikaze toddler roaring round. Barry had collapsed into a state of depression without Edward, and Judgy was taking advantage of this to sit on top of him. I decided I'd better tackle the carnage of my house.

Several more loads of washing on the line and a thorough hoovering and wipe down of everywhere Edward had been to dispel the crumbs and stickiness small children leave in their wake, and I trudged upstairs to my bedroom to start putting my clothes away.

I really did have too many clothes. I seemed to have inherited Granny Green's inability to throw anything away. There at the back, luckily unspotted by Edward, was the hideous taffeta confection that was my wedding dress, a proper 'meringue' number if ever there was one. There was the skirt I wore on my first date with Jack, which was probably now cursed, and the dress I wore out to dinner in Paris when Simon took me there for my fortieth birthday. We didn't quite dance by the Seine in the moonlight, but we did hold hands, which by that stage was exceptionally romantic for Simon. And, oh God, next to the Paris dress was an old sheepskin jacket I'd bought second-hand in the *nineties* that Simon always complained smelt of dead sheep. I gave it a tentative sniff. Actually, it *was* a bit whiffy. The suit I wore for my very first job interview – oh dear God, it was vile. My old school tie; why on *earth* had I kept that? I *hated* school.

I decided I needed to have a proper sort-out. I'd tried to do this when I packed everything up to move here, but I was still quite raw and emotional about the end of my marriage – not really in a place to make rational decisions – and had just ended up crying a lot and keeping almost everything. It was time to let go of the past. I started sorting things into three piles: to keep, for the charity shop and to bin. It was actually very therapeutic. Finally, I came to the back of the cupboard and my wedding dress. I sighed. Really, what was I keeping it for? It was revolting. It had been the height of style at the time, and I'd been convinced I looked like a princess, complete with Anne of Green Gables puffed sleeves and a bow on the bum. There was no way Jane would ever contemplate wearing it for her wedding. All it was, really, was a reminder of what had once been, and of bad nineties fashion. No. It could go as well. I'd put in the charity shop pile – someone might get a bit of fun out of it for a fancy dress party.

Before I chucked it, though, a vain little niggle nagged at the back of my mind. I wondered if I could still get into it. Maybe not do it up, but at least shoehorn it on. Had the Zumba classes I was taking every week in an attempt to cancel out the Sauv Blanc and crisps done their job?

I stripped off and struggled into it. To my astonishment, it very nearly *did* do up, though I almost gave myself a hernia in the process, and breathing appeared to be an optional extra. I was looking at myself in the mirror, trying to remember how on earth I'd gone for a pee in this confection, when I heard a fearful chuntering from the chickens. I rushed to the window and saw Nigel, the evil ginger tomcat from the top of the lane, in the chicken run. It appeared that Nigel might have bitten off more than he could chew, as his anticipated chicken dinners were furiously rushing him and attempting to peck his eyes out. Sometimes there's a lot to be said for Oxo, Paxo and Bisto's anti-social, bordering on psychopathic, tendencies. Nonetheless, I felt I should come to their aid, and so I flew down the stairs as fast as I could when hampered by approximately eleventy fucking billion yards of ivory silk taffeta getting caught round your legs.

Since it turned out that Nigel was all mouth and no trousers, the chickens had him cornered and in fear of his life by the time I got to the chicken run. I didn't even have my wellies on to wade through the mess to rescue him, but I didn't feel I could really sacrifice Nigel for the sake of wearing flip-flops, so in I plunged, my wedding dress hitched up to mid-thigh to keep it out of the mud.

I shooed off the chickens, who were most indignant at having their prize removed from them, and attempted to peck off my toes instead, and grabbed Nigel, who was not one bit grateful to be rescued, and instead of a fond purr at me for my kindness, yowled in my ear and scratched my cheek, before shredding the front of my dress with his hind claws as he took off for freedom as we exited the chicken run. Bastard. Next time he can fend for himself.

Then, of course, the dogs wanted to pee, which involved sniffing every inch of the garden first in order to find the optimum spot to relieve themselves, and the chickens started squawking for food, because why else would I be in the garden other than to provide them with corn, and I needed to rinse off my flip-flops after their encounter with the chicken run, and then, as I finally walked back into the house, Peter and Jane burst through the front door, followed by Simon.

'MUM!' yelled Jane. 'MUM! Dad's here! He wants to ask you about –'

Jane came to an abrupt halt as she caught sight of me, bedraggled, bloody and dripping, clutching my torn dress over my bosoms in an attempt to preserve some modesty.

'Oh holy fuck, Mother, what *are* you wearing?'

'Her wedding dress,' said Simon grimly from behind her.

'It's gross!' said Jane. 'Don't even think about keeping it for me!'

'What's for dinner?' demanded Peter.

Simon was still staring at me in horror.

'Jesus, Ellen, what *happened*?' he hissed.

What, really, could one reply to that? On what level did he mean it? What happened, as in, why was I muddy, bleeding and damp? My fucking menagerie, obviously. Or what happened to me, as in, where had his radiant bride gone, to be replaced by this dishevelled crone? Because I didn't know the answer to that one. Either way, though, I was quite mortified enough by the situation without dignifying him with an answer of any sort.

'Did you want something?' I said, with as much cold dignity as I could muster under the circumstances.

'Um, no, it's OK, I'll text you,' said Simon, backing away and almost running out the front door.

Marvellous. So now, in addition to having turned my best friend's youngest son into a cross-dressing dog, my former husband is now under the impression that when our children spend the weekend with him, I wander the house in my wedding gown doing my best Miss Havisham impression and pining for my lost love, only with not so many cobwebs because Standards. Quite low Standards, but still Standards.

Fucking fuck my fucking life. I definitely deserved an enormous drink.

JUNE

Wednesday, 12 June

The official announcement of the merger has been made at work. On the plus side, this means people are no longer sidling up to me to ask if I've heard anything concrete, or if I can give them any sort of heads-up about what's happening. On the downside, everyone's shitting themselves that we're all about to be out of a job.

A very jolly American sort from the new joint head office came into our department to give us a pep talk about what an exciting time this is, and how delighted he is to be part of it, and how everyone is looking forward to the new *streamlined* company and the great things it will achieve.

So, 'streamlining' is the buzzword they're going with, as opposed to 'rationalising' or 'restructuring', and it's now something we are to be positive about! Yay! Happy happy fun joy! How nice for them that they've found a nice, cheerful word to describe at least half the workforce getting the sack, but before they do get sacked, having to endure the ritual humiliation of being interviewed for their own job first, and *then* told they're shite and being binned! Huzzah! But it's OK, because it's *streamlining*! It's all about efficiency and *moving forward* and the *future*. Except for us poor bastards, who probably now have no future.

I must at least try to be positive, though. I've not been sacked *just* yet, and I suppose there's a slim chance I might actually retain a job, though probably not the one I have, and so I'll be demoted and have a peppy young managerial sort to micromanage me and tell me how everything I do is wrong, while I look at the utter bastard and realise they were probably actually born in the nineties! How do people born in the nineties have positions of power and responsibility? They're *children*! I suppose I'd better go and look up the company mission statement so I can spout the appropriate corporate wank as I desperately try to cling onto my job. And also investigate the possibility of remotely installing a load of porn on the irritating HR woman's computer if I do get laid off.

Saturday, 22 June

A very long two months of shrieking, 'Drink water! Revise! Get some sleep! Eat some fucking nutrients for the love of God, please!' and rattling bottles of Omega 3 and multivitamins and lobbing apples at my precious moppets are finally over, as are enduring the outraged wails when I blocked all their devices from the Wi-Fi at night so they were forced to sleep instead of whiling away the hours on social media.

Peter's final exam was last week, and he was most annoyed to find he was expected to go back to school this week, and Jane's last exam was on Thursday. Alarmingly, this means that, apart from the 'graduation ceremony', which seems to be what was called 'prize giving' when I was at school, and a few 'optional' classes on coping with life as an adult ('How to open a bank account', 'How to not burn a house down', 'How to deal with the realisation that life is now just a meaningless trudge towards the grave and there's nothing to look forward to but your body sagging and your mind going' – OK, maybe I made the last one up), Jane has now effectively left school.

To celebrate the end of exams, which we all agreed seemed to have taken far more of a toll on us as parents than they did on the children actually sitting them, who seemed astonishingly blasé about the whole thing, Hannah and Sam and Colin and I went out.

One of the best things about my friends is that we long ago abandoned the foolish notion of ordering wine by the glass, and we just go straight for the bottle, not even pretending that it's just because it's slightly better value (apart from Sam, who likes to pretend he's well 'ard by drinking pints. But of Italian lager, because he's not as Ross Kemp as he likes to think he is).

We congratulated ourselves on surviving another round of exams and tried not to think about the fact that we'd one more round of this to go with our younger poppets' A levels in a couple of years.

'Ha!' snorted Hannah. 'You only have to do it *once* more! Think of me! I've still got to go through A levels with Lucas, and then I'll have to do it *all* again from scratch with Edward in fifteen years, when I'm –'

Hannah paused as she tried to work out how old she'd be in fifteen years after she'd drunk the best part of a bottle of Pinot Grigio. 'Fucking old!' she concluded.

'Maybe they won't even sit exams then,' mused Sam. 'Maybe they'll just, I dunno, do a data download from your brain to make sure you have all the relevant knowledge stored there and that will be it. Maybe they won't even have to revise to learn all that shit, they'll just plug a memory stick into their ear and transfer everything across. By the time Edward's of an exam-sitting age, children will probably basically be sentient robots, controlled by the government. Either that, or we'll all be living in a post-apocalyptic dystopian nightmare, where the only things that count are basic survival skills, and it doesn't matter how you find the hypotenuse of a right-angled triangle –'

'That would still be quite a useful skill for building shelters,' I objected.

'OK, fine!' snapped Sam. 'They might still need that, but they won't need to write critical essays on the bastarding imagery in "Ode to Autumn", because all the books will have been burnt and culture eradicated!'

'Well,' said Hannah. 'Thank you for painting this happy vision of the future that awaits our children. Especially my youngest, who's apparently either going to be some sort of Orwellian government drone, or living off rats in an underground tunnel, attempting to stay alive amid the shattered ruins of our civilisation!'

'Yeah,' said Colin. 'Bit depressing, babe. We're meant to be celebrating. What's up with you?'

'Oh, I don't know,' said Sam gloomily, staring into his Peroni. 'The Fucking Oldness, I expect. Or maybe Peroni just has the same effect as gin. But none of us know what the future holds, do we? It's all a Great and Ineffable Mystery.'

'Oh, for fuck's sake!' said Colin crossly. 'As if it wasn't enough that we had to stop you drinking gin because it made you maudlin, now bloody lager does it. You're the only person I know who can get depressed on lager!'

'I'm not getting depressed, and I'm not drunk,' said Sam with some dignity. 'I'm merely reflecting on the conundrums of this complex modern world.'

'And predicting our children will end up eating rats,' put in Hannah. 'Which is quite depressing.'

'Right. Enough! We're celebrating. I don't care how fucking old we are, I'm going to get the shots in and get the barman to play Gloria Gaynor, and then we'll all feel better for a couple of tequila slammers and belting out "I Will Survive"!'

'Will we?' murmured Sam sadly into his beer.

'YES!' said Colin. 'It's a medically proven fact that tequila and "I Will Survive" make EVERYTHING better. Everything! Even if future generations *do* end up living in a subterranean pit, should they one day stumble across a forgotten bottle of Patron and an ancient Walkman with just enough battery power left to wheeze through "I Will Survive" one last time, they'll find themselves perked right up, and positively looking forward to their rat on a stick for tea! OK?'

'OK!' we all said obediently, because Colin did make a very good point. And also, as long as we were still able to do shots and retained some control of our bodily functions, like speaking and walking, then the Fucking Oldness had not won yet.

Sometime later, I tottered to the loo, my control over walking only minimally retained. As I washed my hands afterwards, I gazed blearily into the mirror, checking I didn't have lipstick on my teeth or that my eyeliner hadn't gone full-on Alice Cooper with the tequila sweats.

A strange woman was looking over my shoulder, staring at me intensely. It was unnerving, and also rude. I swung round to tell her where to go, but there was no one else in the bathroom. I looked back in the mirror and there she was again, scowling out at me. I peered closer. It was *me*. I hadn't even recognised myself, this haggard creature, with eyebags and crow's feet.

Who was she? Who am *I*? I thought in horror. The picture I'd always had in my head of myself was not this woman in the mirror, who looked so tired and faded. If I'd passed her in the supermarket, I'd probably have felt a bit sorry for her, and wondered if there was a tactful way of recommending a good moisturiser.

I staggered out to the bar and sat down heavily.

'Are you all right, babe?' said Sam. 'You look a bit pale.'

'I think I'm having An Existential Crisis!' I announced dramatically.

'Wha'?' mumbled Hannah. 'Doesh come with chipsh? I fuckin' love chipsh! Can we getta kebab an' chipsh on way home?'

'No!' I said fretfully. 'An Existential Crisis, Hannah! I'm having An Existential Crisis!'

'Is tha' like a Sex on the Beach? Is vodka, innit?'

'NO, Hannah! Me! *I* am having An Existential Crisis. Me! Not a drink, not a lard blanket on the way home, my very existence and reason for being is IN QUESTION! I DON'T KNOW WHO I AM ANYMORE!'

'You're Ellen Green!' Hannah informed me smugly. 'You musht be pished! Ha ha! An' you says *I'm* the lightweight!'

'I know my name!' I wailed. 'I know my name is Ellen Green. But I don't know who Ellen Green is! I know who she *was*! I know who the girl who was Ellen Green was, before she married Simon and became Ellen Russell, but I'm not Ellen Russell anymore, and I'm not that other Ellen Green anymore. I've spent more than half my life being someone's wife, or someone's mother, or someone's employee, and now, now I'm not a wife and soon I won't be a mother – and *don't* tell me I'll always be their mother, because you *know* it won't be the same when they leave home – and soon enough they'll be bickering about whose turn it is to come and see me, sitting there in a puddle of my own piss.

'And shortly, I probably won't even have a fucking *job* to define me. You, you have Charlie, Hannah. And Sam and Colin, you have each other, and soon I'll have no one and nothing except myself. I'll have nothing to anchor me. It's fucking lonely by myself, and soon I'll be floating free like a fucking *helium* balloon that an irresponsible toddler has let go of, only there will be no one to cry if I float off over the horizon, because it will just be *me* and I DON'T KNOW WHO I AM ANYMORE!'

I snivelled a bit. Really, I'd wanted to burst into full-throttle tears, but it's not seemly to do such a thing in an upmarket gastropub.

Everyone rushed to assure me that I was *fine*. I was *fabulous*. That I wasn't on my own, I had them to anchor and ground me, and they would definitely cry if I floated over the horizon. They reminded me that Mark was still on the scene, even though he was still insisting on 'taking things slowly', so we hadn't actually Done It yet, and it was starting to be less romantic and a bit frustrating, actually, especially since everything else about him, including the kissing, suggested that the sex might be rather excellent. And if it turned out that actually he was a crap shag and that was why he was putting it off (though Hannah was still weirdly fixated on him having no penis), there were many other men.

They reassured me that I was a *catch*, that anyone would be lucky to be with me. Colin rubbed my back. Hannah attempted to give me a hug but missed, and luckily was caught by Sam before she hit the deck. Everyone was kind and lovely, and it's impossible not to feel a bit better when everyone's being so nice to you. And yet the image of that strange woman's face looking out at me, the sensation of 'Who *are* you, and if you're me, then who am *I*?' stayed with me.

Sunday, 30 June

You know how they say if something's too good to be true, then it almost certainly is? Well, they're right. I was surprised and delighted and felt my years of shrieking, 'Please will someone walk the bloody dogs now?' every weekend had finally paid off when Peter sauntered downstairs this morning with Toby, who'd spent the night, and they announced they were taking the dogs for a walk. Unasked, unnagged, uncajoled. I hadn't even had to haul them out of bed or lure them down with the smell of bacon. They'd arisen, unbidden. They even looked like they'd brushed their hair, and they'd definitely deodorised and also seemed to have doused themselves in aftershave. I was choking on the cloud of Lynx Africa and the Dior Sauvage I'd bought Peter for Christmas as they trotted out the door dragging Judgy behind them, who wanted to sniff every gatepost, and were towed along by Barry, who is eternally Very Excited by Walkies.

I should have known something was up. It was too out of character. If nothing else, the aftershave ought to have given it away. I don't think Peter had even opened the aftershave bottle before today. But, naïve and ever hopeful, I simply made myself a cup of tea and sat down to enjoy the peace and quiet. Forty-five minutes later, my phone rang. It said it was Toby. Toby has never rung me, ever. He shares all teenagers' uncontrollable fear of actually using their phone to talk to someone.

'Hello, Toby,' I said.

There was a pause, then Toby said, 'Um, Ellen? Like, well, um, the thing is, like, it's just that, um.'

'WHAT is it, Toby? Spit it out.'

'Um, Peter's, like, sort of hurt his foot a bit?'

'What do you mean?'

'Well, he was, like, standing on a wall, and he sort of fell off and it's hurt?'

'What was he doing on a wall?'

'Standing on it?'

'You said that. Oh, for goodness' sake. It can't be that bad!'

'He, like, says he can't walk home?'

'Well, could he hop? It's not that far?'

'Dunno. There's a lady says she's going to call an ambulance?'

'Oh, for fuck's sake! Why do people always over-react? Right, I'm on my way. I suppose I'll have to come and pick him up if people are making such a fuss. He's probably just jarred it. Walking on it would probably help ease it off, but don't worry, I'll come and get him!'

I jumped in the car and drove to the park, chuntering to myself about my stupid son and also whatever bloody drama queen was threatening to call an ambulance. Boys fell off things all the time. If I called an ambulance every time Peter fell off something and claimed to be in agony, I'd have singlehandedly crippled the NHS.

I screeched to a halt outside the park and went in search of the boys. They weren't hard to find, as quite a crowd had by now gathered around them.

'Honestly, Peter,' I said crossly, as I strode up to them. 'What *are* you playing at? I'm sure you can get up. Just pull yourself together!'

Peter was lying on the ground, a packet of frozen sweetcorn that turned out to have come from Mrs Jenkins's shopping on his ankle. He was quite pale.

'It's very sore, Mum,' he whispered.

'Oh really, Peter, it can't be that bad. You only need to walk to the car.'

'I can't, Mum, I honestly can't,' he groaned.

'Well, hop then. Just hop to the car, it's not far!'

At this point, Frank Watson, the designated first aider for the Village Hall and St John's Ambulance Member, removed Mrs Jenkins's sweetcorn from Peter's ankle and looked at me sternly.

'I'm afraid it looks like his ankle is broken,' he pronounced solemnly. 'He won't be walking anywhere; the ambulance won't be long.'

'Oh, for God's sake –' I snapped furiously, then actually looked at Peter's ankle now the sweetcorn had been removed. It was all sort of bent at a funny angle. And about four times the size it should have been. The crowd stared stonily at the mother who'd tried to make her broken son hop to the car.

'There, there, darling!' I said weakly. 'Mummy's here! It'll be all right. Don't worry, poppet. Mummy's here,' I repeated, so as to sound like a caring and loving mother, which of course I *am* (it's just that Peter does have a track record for being a hypo-chondriac. He gets it from his father).

'Where are the dogs?' I whispered to him. I noticed actually he was a bit more than pale – he was a rather nasty sweaty green colour.

'Toby has them.'

I saw Toby lurking on the outskirts of the crowd, trying to stop Judgy peeing on the remnants of Mrs Jenkins's shopping, which she'd discarded to join the drama.

'Toby, could you take the dogs home, please? Here are my keys. I'll call Jane and get her to come home, and I'll get your dad to come and pick you up.'

Toby duly trotted off with the hell hounds, and the ambulance arrived. They tutted a lot at the state of Peter's ankle, gave him some gas and air for the pain, and stretchered him into the ambulance. I was given special dispensation to abandon my car and go with him, which was quite exciting as I'd never been in an ambulance before. It was actually a bit rubbish; they didn't do lights and sirens for a broken ankle, apparently.

The nice ambulance man, who fortunately hadn't witnessed me trying to make Peter hop to the car, and so was convinced I was a good mother, smiled at me reassuringly. He was quite hot, a small, shallow part of me noticed.

'Don't worry,' he said kindly. 'They're tough at this age. He'll be fine. How's the pain, mate? Do you want some more gas and air?' he added to Peter.

'OK,' said Peter faintly. He took a large draught of the gas and air, then took the mask off in disgust.

'Oooh, I don't much like this,' he slurred. 'Makesh me feel a bit funny. Mum, you alwaysh shay you LOVE gas 'n' air, you shaid it made you feel all pished. Here, do you wan' some?'

I did, actually. I very much wanted a toot on the lovely gas and air, just to take the edge off the worry over Peter, and the stress of being in an ambulance, and the nasty feeling that was still with me from the judgement of the crowd. The hot but kindly ambulance man, however, was looking at me somewhat less kindly after Peter's announcement, and I felt forced to decline, even though gas and air is the only good thing I remember about giving birth. After nine months of sobriety, its delicious blur was very welcome. Of course, it did fuck all for the pain involved in a baby emerging through your unmentionables, but it somehow made you care a bit less about it. After Peter and his extremely large head was born, they let me keep the gas and air while they stitched me up, then they forgot to take it away. I left Simon holding the baby, quite literally, while I lay sucking away in a glorious haze. Half an hour later, a midwife came in to check on us, and was horrified to see I still had the gas and air. By this time I was well away with the fairies, though, and became quite fighty when she tried to take it off me. But somehow, I didn't think this anecdote would endear me any further to the ambulance man.

At the hospital, they wheeled Peter in, while I gave his details to the lady on the front desk, and quickly rang Simon and suggested he might want to come, asking him to ring Jane and tell her to go home and dog-sit, and Sam or Colin to go and pick up Toby. I was quite pleased with how calm I was remaining in the crisis and how well I was dealing with it.

When I went in, Peter had already been taken to X-ray, which astonished me, as all you hear on the news is about people sitting in A&E for eleventy billion hours waiting to have their severed limbs reattached. But actually, this hospital seemed to be running very efficiently, which is yet another reason why one shouldn't read the *Daily Mail*. A nice nurse showed me where I could wait, and before Simon had even arrived, Peter was back from X-ray and we'd been put in a cubicle to wait for his results.

'Peter, what happened?' I said, as this was the first time I'd been alone with him to actually find out what had taken place.

'Well, I was like on the wall, and then I sort of fell off,' he said slightly sheepishly.

'Yes, I gathered that much. But what were you *doing* on the wall?'

'Chicks.'

'Chicks? Was there a nest? Were you trying to rescue a baby bird or something?'

'No, Mum, *chicks*. Girls!'

'Chicks? Seriously? Firstly, I didn't think that was a word your generation used, I'd have thought it was far too uncool, and secondly, Peter, how many conversations have I had with you about respecting women, about how the language you use to describe them is important, and here you are, describing girls to me as *chicks*! Honestly! I thought better of you, I really did.'

'Mum, I'm, like, lying in a hospital bed, can you spare me the lecture on the sisterhood?' groaned Peter.

Something clicked with me. 'Peter, did you and Toby take my dogs to the park to try to use them to pick up girls?'

Peter looked shifty.

'You *did*, didn't you?'

'We read this article about how chicks, sorry, I mean *girls*, love dogs, and it's much easier to start talking to them if you've got a dog. But it didn't work with your dogs, because every time we saw some girls, Barry would stop and do a big shit. He shits a *lot*, you know.'

'Well, good. I'm glad my dogs at least are striking a blow against the patriarchy!'

'Yeah, well, girls don't want to talk to you when you're picking up huge dog shits. So then we thought if we climbed up on the wall, Tilly Johnson and Milly White from school would notice us, and they'd maybe talk to us then because they don't at school, only then I fell off. And so now they'll never talk to me because they'll think I'm a total loser! And it wasn't just that, Mum.'

'What? What else did you do?'

'Well, you probably couldn't see when they put me on the stretcher, but I caught my jeans on a branch when I fell off the wall and I ripped a big hole in the bum.'

'Oh dear.'

'Yeah. And all the girls saw my pants.'

'Well, that's not so bad. At least you were wearing some.'

'I'm wearing the Spider-Man pants you got me for Christmas. It's so uncool! Mum, I need to change schools!'

Part of me was obviously very sorry for my son, both for his broken ankle and for being in that awkward phase of adolescence where the opposite sex is a mystery that you're more desperate to crack than the Five Find-Outers and Dog were to catch kidnappers and gangs of coiners, yet you're utterly baffled as to how to go about it. And part of me was bloody furious at him for using words like 'chicks', trying so cackhandedly to impress girls, and mostly for involving my innocent dogs in his seedy plans!

Simon arrived as I was explaining to Peter why he most certainly wouldn't be changing schools at the start of his A level course just because some girls had seen his cartoon pants, and we had to go through all the explanations again, though Peter did at least have the wit not to say 'chicks' yet again. Then the doctor came in to discuss Peter's X-rays.

The doctor was very nice, but he was twelve. It was almost impossible for me to take him seriously. I wanted to ask if his daddy was in, and could I please speak to a grown-up. I fear this is another sign of the Fucking Oldness. I found myself thinking the same thing about a policeman the other day.

Alas, the child-doctor pronouncement was not good (maybe he *was* a child, I mused. Maybe it was like *Doogie Howser, M.D.*, and he was a child prodigy who'd gone into medicine, and I wasn't old, he really *was* twelve. Then I reminded myself that fanciful children's TV programmes are fanciful children's TV programmes for a reason, and that reason was because they weren't real, and I tried to listen to what the boy doctor was saying). It turned out that Peter, usually so lazy and half-arsed about things, took a different approach to breaking bones, and had not only broken his ankle, but had broken it so badly that he needed to have it pinned back together.

Luckily, the orthopaedic surgeon was free, he announced, and Peter would be going to theatre imminently. In under two hours, we'd gone from Toby's vague, 'Peter had sort of hurt his foot' to Peter being about to be wheeled into surgery. Of course, this was a wonderful reflection on our health service and its marvellous staff, even under the immense pressure put on it by government cuts, but it was also a bit of a headfuck for me as a mother. Astonishingly, this was only the second time my children had ended up in hospital, and the first time was only for Peter to have a pea removed from his nose, so it barely even counted. Now, he was going to have a general anaesthetic and be sliced open and have his *bones* pinned back together.

There wasn't really time to think about that, though, between signing forms, and lovely doctors and nurses explaining things, and keeping Peter calm and making sure he knew enough about what was going on to understand, but not so much that he would freak out. He'd have to stay in hospital for a night, but one of us could stay with him, because he was under sixteen, and someone could go into theatre with him while he had the anaesthetic.

'Mum, please,' said Peter, looking terrified. 'I want Mum. Please come with me, Mum, I need you there!'

'Of course I will,' I said soothingly. 'I'll stay as long as they let me. Don't worry, darling, you're going to be fine.'

Finally, we were in the theatre, and the anaesthetist started administering the anaesthetic. I'd thought it would be like watching Peter fall asleep. It wasn't. It was horrible. One minute he was there, talking to me, the next he was just … gone. As soon as he was unconscious, a lovely nurse whisked me out of the theatre so they could get on with the operation, and that was when it turned out I wasn't coping very well at all, because now that Peter wasn't there for me to hold it all together for, I just fell apart and burst into tears. Simon was waiting outside the theatre and pulled me into his arms.

'It's OK, it's OK,' he kept whispering. 'You've done so well, it's OK, I'm here now. Come on, darling, it's OK, he's going to be fine.'

Even as I sobbed, I couldn't help but feel how feeble and ridiculous I was being. Peter was going to be *fine*! He was having amazing treatment in a first-world country *for free*! I reminded myself about all the parents and children who weren't nearly so lucky as us. All the parents of children with terminal or chronic or life-limiting conditions, whose lives revolve around hospitals and watching their children in pain and being unable to do anything to stop it. I'd nothing whatsoever to complain about at all, but despite that, nothing really prepares you for how it feels when it's your child lying on the operating table, no matter how positive the prognosis. I've always known how lucky I am that the children are so robustly healthy, but this really brought it home to me. Unfortunately, that made me sob even harder, until I was a dissolving, hiccupping mess. I finally got enough of a grip on myself to go and get a cup of tea with Simon, because after all, we're British, and all crises must be addressed with tea. Or gin, if it's after 6 o'clock.

In the canteen, still sniffling slightly, I suddenly realised Peter's timing had been impeccable as always.

'Oh shit!' I said. 'We're supposed be to be getting a team coming in about the merger tomorrow, to "observe" us all at work. Well, I'm definitely for the chop then, since I won't be there to dazzle them with my brilliance, efficiency and employability!'

'Why won't you be there?' asked Simon.

'Because I can't be in two places at once!' I snapped. 'After I stay with Peter tonight, and then he gets discharged in the morning, and I take him home and somehow get him upstairs to his room – God knows how if he's on crutches – then he won't be able to go up and down stairs, someone will have to stay with him until he can go back to school. You heard the doctor – it'll be a week before he can have a proper cast that he can walk in because of the swelling, so someone will have to be with him! In theory, I suppose Jane could, but I can't leave Jane with an invalid Peter. She'll just torment him. So, I'll have to take at least the next week off. It's just awful timing. But I'm his mother, it's what we do, however old they are. We have to be there for them.'

'*I* can stay with him tonight, and then he can come back with me,' said Simon. 'I can just work from home for the next week or so to look after him. I've got a couple of meetings, but I can either reschedule them, or if Peter's at my flat, there's no stairs to negotiate inside and a lift to my floor. I'm sure he could manage to get to the loo by himself if I have to go out for a couple of hours.'

'You?' I looked at him blankly. '*You* take time off to look after Peter?'

'Why not? You're the one always complaining they have two parents, you can't do everything yourself. And neither should you have to. He's *our* son, he's *our* responsibility, not just yours, so you shouldn't be the one who has to take the time off and risk your job over this. I'm his father, I should be there for him every bit as much as you. It won't make any difference to my job if I'm not in the office next week, but you're right, it could make a lot of difference to yours if you're not there to fight your corner. It's my turn to step up, Ellen. You've given up enough for *my* career in the past, and I haven't forgotten how you were there for me a few months ago, so I could go and look after my parents.'

'Oh,' I muttered. To be brutally honest, Simon taking time off to look after Peter was simply not a solution that had even occurred to me. He'd never, ever, taken time off in the past, claiming his great Busy and Importantness precluded this, and leaving me in the lurch trying to rearrange meetings into conference calls and pour Calpol down sweaty feverish children while attempting to concentrate on what was being said at the other end of the phone and not overdose the children. The one time I'd asked him to watch the children while I had a phone interview as part of the process of getting a new job, he'd abandoned them because he had 'really needed a shit'. And that's before we even get into all the business trips he'd simply inform me were happening, with zero consultation about how we'd manage childcare while he was away, or even checking his diary to make sure I didn't have a trip scheduled myself.

'Why would you do that?' I asked suspiciously, waiting for the 'But'. 'I'll look after Peter for a week, BUT then I'm going to Outer Mongolia for six months and he'll be your problem,' or 'I'll look after Peter for a week, BUT then Marissa and I are taking a year-long sabbatical travelling round Asia and taunting you with our Instagram feeds while you ferry my son around and feed his endless appetite and wash his skidmarked Spider-Man pants. Enjoy! I'll be watching the sun rise at Angkor Wat and gazing romantically into Marissa's eyes, before we spend the days in

self-indulgent sightseeing and the nights making love languor-
ously, and you sit outside a party waiting for Peter and his
drunken friends to emerge and hope they don't puke on the way
home!'

'Because it's about time I pulled my weight,' he said. 'Mum
said when I was over there last that it was no wonder you are
divorcing me. The only surprise was that it took you so long. She
doesn't like Marissa.'

'She didn't much like *me* when we were married,' I pointed
out. 'She probably only dislikes Marissa because she's the latest
competition for her darling boy, and now I'm safely off the scene,
she can be nice about me.'

'She *did* like you!'

'She accused me of cheating at Trivial Pursuit, she said I was
too stupid to have known the answer, and insisted I must have
gone through the box and memorised the questions and
answers!'

'Well, that's how she shows she likes people. She doesn't
accuse just *anyone* of cheating at Trivial Pursuit. That's her way
of showing you're one of the family. She's never accused Marissa
of cheating, even at rummy. Anyway, so are we decided? I'll stay
with Peter tonight and he can come home with me tomorrow,
until he can go back to school. Even afterwards, if it's easier for
him to manage at the flat without stairs? You could maybe pack
a bag for him, and get Jane to drop it off tomorrow, if you don't
mind?'

'I suppose so,' I said, still convinced that Simon was just
planning on hitting me with the news he was buggering off
with Marissa for months and I wouldn't be able to object because
of his immense sacrifice in looking after his broken son for
a week.

We went back up to the ward to wait for Peter to come back from theatre. He was very woozy, but the operation had gone well, he was alive, and he would make a full recovery. I very nearly cried again with sheer relief. Peter was unfazed by the news he was going to live with his father for a week.

'Dad has better broadband anyway, Mum. And you'll bring my computer and my Xbox and my PlayStation and my Nintendo Switch, won't you?'

'Yes, Peter,' I assured him. 'And clean pants.'

'And my chargers, Mum, don't forget my chargers, and remember all the power supplies.'

Peter's priorities were at least unaffected by his trauma, I reflected.

JULY

Saturday, 6 July

It's been strange without Peter here. I haven't actually spent this much time apart from him since he was born. I miss him, but I'm coping better than I thought I would without him at home, and it's done wonders for the supplies of food and toilet roll. Since Jane is out most of the time, too, I spend a lot of time talking to the dogs, and am facing up to the fact that there's a very real chance I will turn into a Mad Dog Lady when the children have gone. Of course it's not quite like it will be when I'm alone and abandoned. I've seen Peter a lot, as I go to Simon's every night after work for a chat, and I have dinner with them. It's been a bit awkward, because Marissa is usually there, with a face like thunder, but Peter insists I stay and have something to eat, and even Marissa could not deny the invalid child.

Jane, naturally, has been spectacularly unconcerned about her brother, going so far as to suggest that if he were to make a permanent move to Simon's, she could take over his bedroom as a dressing room. I pointed out to her that hopefully, if her A level results are good enough, she'll be leaving home in September to spend most of the year elsewhere, therefore booting her only brother out of his bedroom might be considered unnecessary, and had she got a summer job yet? Jane merely snorted.

Anyway, the 'observers' have been prowling around all week at work, sitting in on meetings ('Pretend we're not here. Carry on exactly as you normally would') and generally making everyone very twitchy.

This twitchiness, combined with us racing to finish one of the biggest projects we've ever done while we're still short-handed, on account of the people who left over the merger rumours, means that I feel a bit like I'm back in exam time with the children again, cajoling everyone along, trying to reassure them that it will be OK, keeping morale up, and putting a bright and brave face on things to make sure we all just keep buggering on, and we get this done to the best of our abilities, no matter what the future holds.

It's exhausting and draining trying to keep everyone going, on top of my own usual workload, but it seems to be what women, especially if they're mothers, end up doing all the time. However much stress we're under, however worried or scared we are, we keep going, to make it all OK for everyone else. What I'm doing for my team at work right now is really no more than I've been doing for my children for years, through splitting up with Simon, through the exams, constantly reassuring and smiling and not letting the mask crack, because if you're not OK, then how can they be OK?

It's a shame you can't translate things like that onto a CV, really. I've been trying to work on mine in the evenings, to get it into a decent state to send off to start looking around for a new job, just in case, and there are so many things I'm good at that I've learnt from being a mother that have been hugely helpful in the workplace as well. But motherhood is still sorely underrated as a career move. If I'd been on some expensive course for negotiating skills, no problem, I could whack that down, and everyone would be most impressed. Yet if you put, 'Look, mate, I've got negotiating fucking NAILED, because once you've mastered persuading a furious toddler that their blue cup is the blue cup they asked for, the same blue cup they had yesterday, and in fact it has not been swapped for a different, EVIL blue cup, then you've got all the tools you need to bring peace to the Middle East, quite frankly' (only obviously in more wanky CV speak), then no one cares at all. Ditto, the multi-tasking, the organisational skills, the motivational speaking.

It's all well and good if you've spent three days in a corporate hotel in Swindon having a callow youth talk at you about these things – people will then feel you're bringing something pretty serious to the table. But when you've learnt these skills by being able to simultaneously wipe up dog vomit, make packed lunches, kick all the crap out of one corner of the house so you can have a Zoom meeting, while yelling at children to get off the fucking internet and stop hogging all the bandwidth and find their own damn shoes, because saying 'I can't find it' isn't the same thing as actually looking for it, then you might as well write, 'I'm good at arse-wiping' on your CV, for all the difference it will make.

Marissa informed me I was being melodramatic when I said this over dinner, and asked me if I'd ever considered retraining as a teacher if I had all these wonderful life skills with young people. I said I hadn't, because I'd be a terrible teacher as I have no patience, and teachers need certain saintly qualities to stop them murdering their charges, qualities I definitely don't possess, and also, half the teachers out there already can't find jobs, so how would that possibly help? Marissa gave her little laugh and murmured something about how at 'my age' retraining and learning new skills probably would be very difficult. I considered stabbing her in the eye with my fork, but decided that witnessing a bloody murder over the penne all'arrabiata was probably not conducive to Peter's recovery.

Sunday, 14 July

Men, frankly, are by and large ridiculous arseholes. They're just more trouble than they're worth.

I was looking forward to a chilled-out Sunday. I was going to walk the dogs, pop over to see Peter, who's in a walking cast and back at school, but still staying with Simon as Simon's shower is apparently easier to use, and also I suspect because Simon doesn't shout at him about his five-a-day fruit and veg, and lets him live on Doritos. Then I thought I might see what Sam and Colin were up to, and possibly go for a civilised drinky with them, like grown-up people do, and then I'd efficiently meal prep for next week (thriftily, since I might soon be unemployed and even boring mince will be a luxury food), have a nice bath and go to bed.

Instead, Simon turned up at about eleven o'clock, just as I returned with wet and muddy dogs.

'What are you doing here?' I said in surprise. 'Is Peter OK?'

'Peter's fine. He has some malodourous youths visiting. They're all shouting at a computer, one of them has the smelliest trainers I've ever encountered – I don't think I'll ever get the smell out of the flat – and I never have any milk, but Peter's fine. I came to see you.'

'Why? You'll see me later when I come to see Peter.'

'I know, but I wanted to talk to you. On my own.'

Ah ha. Here we go. This is where he hits me with his demands for nursemaiding Peter. I *knew* it.

'You better come in,' I sighed. 'You can help me dry the dogs.'

I thought I might as well spin this out, make him sweat before he got to finally make his requests. Why make it easy for him? I kept up a steady stream of wittering to Barry and Judgy while we dried them ('Is 'oo best boy? Is 'oo my bestest boy? Is 'oo? 'Oo IS! Is muddiest boy? Is 'oo muddiest boy? 'Oo IS!'), so he couldn't get a word in. I was damn well going to make him look me in the eye while he said whatever he had to say, not get away with mumbling it over a muddy dog.

Then I took my time making us some tea and finding some biscuits (I'd have faffed around with a doily just to annoy him if I'd had one), and finally we were sitting down at the kitchen table because the wet, smelly dogs were not allowed in the sitting room until they were dry and so were lying on our feet.

'Go on then,' I said, taking pity on him, as he'd been looking more and more hangdog the more I procrastinated. 'What's so important that you leave our crippled son to the dubious care of his stenchful friends to come over here on a Sunday morning?'

Simon sighed bravely and then announced, 'I wanted to tell you myself. I didn't want you hearing it second-hand from the children. It's about Marissa and me.'

Ah. An engagement, I presume. Followed by a lengthy honeymoon, no doubt, and then the happy news that Marissa was expecting. After my weekend with Edward, I couldn't help but think that Simon being thrust into fatherhood again at his age would bring me a certain amount of *schadenfreude.*

'Don't worry!' I said kindly. 'I signed the last divorce papers last week and sent them back. You'll be quite legally free any day now.'

'What? Oh, I haven't even looked at mine. That was part of the problem. The thing is, Marissa and I have split up.'

Oh!

'Who dumped who?' I said, reverting back to callous teen-ager. Which would be better? Simon getting binned by Miss Smuggy Smug Pants, or Simon chucking her annoying arse?

'Is that relevant?' asked Simon.

'She dumped you, didn't she?'

'No. If you must know, *I* finished it with her. But we're not fourteen, so that doesn't really seem like the most important thing here.'

I mean, it's *quite* an important thing, but I decided to let Simon have his moment.

'Why?' I said.

'Well, lots of reasons. But mainly Peter.'

'*Peter*? Why did you dump her over Peter?'

'She's been awful about him staying. She put up with the first week, but all this week she's gone on and on and on about what an intrusion he is into our lives, and how inconvenient it is, and just generally been an utter bitch about the fact that *my* son is staying in *my* flat. She didn't like you visiting all the time either. And she was pissed off that I hadn't asked her first before *my* son came to stay with *me* in *my* flat that she hasn't even officially moved into. She's still got her own bloody flat. It's not like I moved him in *there*, is it? Anyway, things came to a bit of a head last night.'

'Oh dear. That doesn't sound great, but I can see that having a teenage boy dumped down into the middle of your life when you're not used to it would take some getting used to.'

'Why are you taking her side? You hate Marissa. Don't be all reasonable about her now.'

'I don't hate her. I just don't see eye to eye with her on everything.'

'You hate her. You're spectacularly bad at hiding it when you don't like someone; you do this forced smile and say, "It's fine" about everything. You hate her.'

'Anyway, this isn't about me and Marissa, this is about you and Marissa. So what happened?'

'You were right,' he said gloomily. I tried to hide my glee. I do like to be right, and Simon rarely admits I am, even though I'm always right. Well, almost always. What had I been right about this time?

'What happened?' I said, trying not to smirk.

'She did want a baby. She had a massive rant last night about how when we have our own child, I won't be able to be so selfish and just dump Peter on her whenever I like, and I said, hang on, who said anything about US having a baby, she said she didn't want kids. And she said she'd never said she didn't EVER want them, of *course* she wanted children, she just hadn't wanted them just then. But she bloody well *did* say she never ever wanted them – she made a massive speech about how overpopulated the planet was, something she now completely denies saying, by the way.

'And also, I told her that was a shitty attitude to have towards my son. That even if I did have a baby with her, he'd still be just as much my child as any kid I had with her, and a new child wouldn't take priority, and she said I was being selfish and unreasonable, and of course *her* new baby would take priority over a teenager nearly ready to leave home, and actually, now we were talking about it, she'd wanted to wait until we were married before we tried for a baby, but since you were taking so long over the divorce she wanted to start trying now, and we could get married later. And I said WHAT THE ACTUAL FUCK, I hadn't even asked her to marry me and I didn't want a baby, and she said I'd never said that, and I said I HAD, I'd agreed with her when she said she didn't want to have children, and she still said she'd never said that, and then she said that I was stealing her child-bearing years –'

'*I* said she'd say that!' I put in smugly.

'– and I said, well, I didn't want her child-bearing years, because I DON'T WANT A BABY, and if she does want a baby, she'd better find someone who does, because it wasn't going to be me. And then we fought a lot more, and she basically kept saying I *owe* her a baby and I tricked her into this relationship if I wouldn't have a baby with her. But *she* tricked me. She was quite insistent she didn't want children, there has been no misunderstanding, SHE TRICKED ME, and oh my God, Ellen, what if she's already pregnant? What if she really *has* tricked me, and she's already up the duff and is just waiting to be sure before she tells me? Oh God, I hadn't thought of that till just now! I read this thing in the *Daily Mail* by some woman who stole her boyfriend's sperm to get pregnant, literally stole his sperm –'

'What? How do you steal someone's sperm? It's not like it's something you can pop in your handbag when they're not looking? Did she put a pair of tights over her head while they did it?'

'I can't remember, I just remember the headline about stealing sperm. I think it was something to do with keeping the johnny afterwards –'

'Ewww. That doesn't sound hygienic. Or very nice, fiddling about with cold jizz. Though I suppose it's just an extreme version of using a turkey baster. Did she put it in a turkey baster afterwards? Do you have a turkey baster? Is that why you think Marissa might have been basting herself? You should probably throw the turkey baster away.'

'I don't HAVE a turkey baster. Why would I have a turkey baster?'

'But did the woman in the article? Is the turkey baster crucial to the sperm stealing? If so, then you're quite safe.'

'I DON'T GIVE A FUCK ABOUT THE WOMAN IN THE ARTICLE OR HER TURKEY BASTER. I'm having a crisis here!'

'All right, has she given you any reason to think she's been making off with the johnnies?'

'Well, no, we don't use them.'

'In that case, you can hardly be surprised if she's up the duff then, can you? What did you expect? You do *know* how babies are made, Simon. And you can hardly accuse her of "stealing your sperm" if you didn't even put anything on!'

'No, she has a coil. She said we didn't need to worry, the coil would take care of it.'

'Well, hopefully she doesn't have the clap then. Seriously, what is it with men and condoms? What's your problem with them? Why do you always think contraception is a woman's problem?'

'Don't give me one of your speeches on the fucking patriarchy. Not now. It was her idea that we went bareback. She said as long as we both got a clean STD test, there was no need to be contributing to landfill with condoms. So don't blame me.'

'Eco sperm-stealing. Clever!' I smirked. 'I assume with her responsible attitude to the environment, she'll be using cloth nappies as well. Nice. Nothing quite like the smell of a bucketful of shitty nappies soaking in NappySan. Lucky you!'

'Are you *enjoying* this?'

'No. Of course not. What do you take me for?'

'Sometimes it seems to me that you get pleasure from my pain,' Simon said darkly.

'Oh, do shut up with your Christian Grey bollocks,' I said.

I mean, obviously, a part of me *was* enjoying it, but I couldn't possibly admit that without losing the moral high ground.

'Do you think Marissa's pregnant?' he pleaded.

'Honestly? Probably not. She would have told you.'

'But what if she is?'

'Well then, whether you like it or not, there will be another child in the world that you helped to create, and you'll have to man up and get on with it.'

'But I don't want to spend the rest of my life with her. I want –'

'If there's a baby involved, it doesn't *matter* what you want. It's about the baby. You don't have to spend the rest of your life with her, but you do have to be there for the kid, which means you'll be in each other's lives forever. Much like we are, whether we want to be or not.'

'But we're more than that,' Simon insisted. 'We're more than just in contact for the children. We've got so much history, I can't imagine you *not* being in my life. When I saw you the other day – oh, never mind. But Ellen, what will happen when the children are grown up?'

It was the first time it had occurred to me that when the children left home, Simon would leave my life. There would no longer be any reason for us to see each other. Maybe once Peter left, I'd see Simon briefly at Jane's graduation, and then probably not again until her wedding, assuming she even got married. That would mean years without ever seeing Simon, talking to Simon … No Simon … The world gave that strange lurch, like it had in the pub a few weeks ago when I hadn't recognised myself.

I was still feeling very cast adrift, struggling to work out who I was these days, and the notion of a Simon-shaped hole opening in my life was rather a daunting one. There were plenty of times when I'd have happily welcomed such a thing, would in fact have heartily booted him through such a hole and said, 'Good riddance.' But he was right. There was so much shared history, so much shared crap, so much shorthand between us that the thought of that not being there at all now made me feel even more lost. The only option clearly was to change the subject and not discuss such matters.

'Simon,' I said firmly, 'why are you here, anyway?'

'I wanted to tell you about Marissa. To see if you thought I'd done the right thing.'

'It doesn't matter what I think. It matters what you think. Why are you asking me?'

'Because … I value your opinion?'

'Is it because I'm always right?'

'You're not always right. You just always think you're right. That's not the same thing.'

'Well, you're wrong there, but why do you want my opinion if not because I'm always right?'

Simon looked sulky.

'Look, Simon, my opinion doesn't matter here. Do *you* think you've done the right thing?'

'Yes. I mean, I think so. Probably. Yes. Almost certainly.'

I sighed. 'Come on, you can do better than that. How do you *feel* about splitting up with her?'

Simon's face took on its customary look of terror at being made to talk about feelings. I'd hoped his time with Marissa and going on the couples' retreats, not to mention the counsellor he saw after we split up, might have gone some way towards curing him of this fear of discussing emotions. But clearly not.

'Do I have to?' he said reluctantly.

'Yes. Tell me how you feel, Simon,' I said maliciously. 'Be a metrosexual new man for once in your life. You can do this. You've had therapy and everything!'

'Yeah, but talking about stuff with people like them isn't like talking about it to real people.'

'Simon!' I snapped. 'Shit or get off the pot. How do you fucking *feel*?'

'If you get made redundant, you could use that caring and compassionate nature to become a counsellor yourself,' said Simon sarcastically. 'OK, fine. I feel embarrassed about another failed relationship. I feel stupid for not realising her agenda all along. I feel bad that maybe I *have* stopped her meeting someone she could have had a baby with, and now if she doesn't have one it might be all my fault. But mostly, I feel relieved. I feel like I can be myself again without being judged. I always felt like I was having to be someone I wasn't to live up to her standards.'

'Is this because she banned you from farting in front of her?'

'No, well, yes partly. I mean, if you can't fart in front of someone, how can you ever really be relaxed around them? But not just that. Everything.'

'To be honest, some of the horrors you let off when we were together, I would have been happy for you to have been tense for our entire marriage. But don't you think if you never felt you could relax or be yourself around her, then maybe this is for the best?'

'Yes. Yes, you're right.'

'I always am!'

'Whatever. Sometimes I think you're the only woman I've ever been able to be myself with.'

'Don't fart in my kitchen.'

His phone pinged. 'I'd better go. Peter wants his lunch and says there's no food, and he's asked me to stop at Nando's.'

'Has he eaten *any* vegetables or fibre since he's been living with you?'

'Well, he must be getting some sort of fibre in his diet, because he's eternally clogging my loo with giant shits!'

'Welcome to my world!'

Later, after Simon had departed in search of chickeny goodness for Peter, Mark texted. Things have progressed no further with Mark than a bit of a snog, and I'd decided that, like Simon, he must either shit or get off the pot. He suggested I came over for dinner. I declined, and countered with him coming to mine. He's never been here since that first night, and always makes some excuse. Tonight, it was that he had 'bought asparagus for dinner'. I like asparagus, but it's not enough to sustain a relationship alone. Imagine the smell in one's lavatory for a start. I suggested a compromise of meeting in the pub for a drink, and we could see what happened with the asparagus later.

After a large gin and tonic, I decided to take the bull by the horns. Or not. Depending on the outcome of Mark's answer.

'Mark,' I demanded. 'What's going on? With us? I'm not sure, you see. You keep talking about taking it slowly, and that's fine, but there's slowly and there's slowly. Because everything else seems good between us, it's just … we seemed to reach a certain point and then we've stalled a bit. So I just thought perhaps we should clarify things. Avoid confusion.'

Mark took my hand and looked earnestly into my eyes. 'I'm glad you've brought this up, Ellen,' he said. 'I really, really like you, and I would absolutely like things to go further, a lot further, but you always jump up and say you have to get home for the dogs, so I didn't know if you were ready or didn't want to, and I didn't want to push things.'

'No, I do have to go home for the dogs,' I said. 'I tend to see you on nights when the children are out, and I have to go home and let them out, and they don't like being left too long. That's why I keep suggesting we go to mine, but you always make an excuse. Oh!' Something dawned on me. 'It's the children, isn't it? You don't want to come to mine because of them. I mean, is it that you feel awkward in my children's home, or do you have a problem with me having children full stop, and you think if we stay at your house you can pretend my kids don't exist?'

Mark looked shocked. 'No! No, it's not the kids at all, they seem charming, I have no problem with them.'

'Well, what is it then? Why do you never want to come in when I ask you, even when the kids aren't there?'

'The dogs.'

'What?'

'I don't like dogs.'

'You don't like *dogs*? Not *any* dogs, or just my dogs?'

'Not any dogs. But yours, well, the little one is quite jumpy. And the big one is quite … big. I didn't know you had dogs the first night I came over, but I just don't like them. I don't like being in a house with them. They're all licky and hairy and dirty.'

'My dogs are *not* dirty,' I said heatedly and untruthfully. 'They're wonderful dogs.'

'I'm sure they are. For dogs. But I just don't like dogs.'

'Cats?'

'Not really.'

'Horses?'

'Very big too. They sort of loom.'

'What about Shetland ponies?'

'Aren't they vicious?'

'Do you like *any* animals?'

'No, not really. But I especially just don't like dogs. I don't know why, they just aren't for me.'

'Oh.'

'It's not really a problem, is it? We can still keep seeing each other, just at my house.'

'And what about my dogs? Who will let them out for a pee, and put them to bed?'

'You put your dogs to bed?'

'They like to be settled down for the night with a Bonio, they know when they get their biscuit and I say, "Night night, it's sleepy time."'

'Do you think you maybe anthropomorphise your dogs a bit?'

'NO!' (I wasn't entirely sure what anthropomorphise meant, but it didn't sound complimentary.)

'Couldn't we see each other when your children are at home and they can deal with the dogs?' he said hopefully.

'Not really,' I said shortly.

'Why not?'

'Well, Jane will hopefully be going off to university soon, and I can hardly leave Peter alone overnight on a regular basis, and, well, Mark, my dogs are a big part of my life. What would happen if things got serious in a couple of years and we thought about moving in together? What happens to my dogs then?'

'Couldn't your ex take them?'

And with that, I was done. Anyone, ANYONE who could just casually suggest that I would give my dogs away, even to Simon, was most certainly not a kindred spirit, and there was no future there. To be honest, I'd known this pretty much as soon as he said he didn't like dogs, but a shallow part of me hoped that maybe he would promise to change, learn to love dogs, at least sponsor a Guide Dog or something, because he was really very handsome. But as soon as he suggested giving away my dogs, he suddenly became rather unattractive.

'No. No, he couldn't. I'm sorry, Mark, this isn't going to work.'

'But why not? Is this really such a big deal? I like you, Ellen, I like you a *lot*. I honestly think things could get very serious between us. I don't see why we can't find a compromise.'

'Mark. I'm forty-eight. My dogs are among the few unconditionally joyful things in my life. There's no compromise to be had. Compromises are about things like what colour you paint the bathroom, not about something so important. I think I deserve to be with someone who shares my passions and joys, not who thinks they're so insignificant I can just give them away. Look, not liking dogs doesn't make you a bad person,' I lied (obviously, not liking dogs made him a *terrible* person in my opinion). 'It just makes you a person not for me. I think I'd better go home. Thanks for the drink.'

I WhatsApped our group chat when I got home.

Me: Found out why Mark doesn't put out.

Colin: Is it because he hasn't got a penis, like you thought?

Me: Worse.

Sam: What's worse than that?

Hannah: Hang on, hang on. Wait till I put Octonauts on for the hell beast, don't start without me!

Sam: Is he insanely religious and won't put out until you've accepted Jesus into your heart and promised to give his weird church 50 per cent of your earnings and you've been married by a minister that looks like a paedophile?

Hannah: OK, he's distracted. Go! So, he does have a cock? Did you see it? Is it a micro dick? Is that the problem?

Me: No idea on the size, large or small, of his cock. We're finished, done, finito,

because I discovered he wouldn't ever come back to my house because ... HE
DOESN'T LIKE DOGS!

Sam: What sort of person doesn't like dogs?

Colin: Oh, babe. Best you found out now.

Hannah: There's always the murder pub in Dundee, Ellen.

Me: You don't think I over-reacted? Binning him for not liking dogs? He even
suggested if it came to moving in together I could give them to Simon!

Hannah: Right, Dundee it is!

Sam: Who would do a thing like that? You can't just give a dog away. He might
as well ask you to give your children away!

Colin: I suspect Ellen would send the children to live with Simon quite happily
before she let the dogs go.

Me: THEY LOVE ME. They love me even when I'm being a dick. No wonder I love
them too.

Me: I mean, don't all rush to tell me I'm never a dick or anything!

I told Simon that Mark and I were over too when I went to see
Peter.

'Must be something in the water this weekend,' I sighed. 'You
and Marissa split up over babies, and Mark and I split up over
dogs. Not that we ever were really a thing.'

'Yes, Jane said you thought he had no penis,' said Simon
smugly.

'Jane really needs to stop listening in to other people's conversations,' I said furiously.

'He was a smarmy git anyway,' said Simon. 'I met him outside
once when I was picking up the kids. All that stupid hair. Mate,
well done on not going bald, but get a fucking grown-up
haircut.'

'He did have stupid hair,' I agreed. 'Anyway, here we are, single
again. But I think I'd rather be single than be with someone just

for the sake of being with them. I feel a bit … lost … right now, Simon, with the kids growing up. Like I don't know who I am anymore. I thought by now I'd have everything sorted, and know exactly who I am, what I am, where I'm going. And I don't know anything, not even who I am. But I do know there's no point in being with someone if they're not right for you. And you don't get much more wrong for me than a dog hater!'

'Do you remember the pigeon?' said Simon.

'The pigeon you transported on a train from Hampshire to Edinburgh from your grandmother's house because I made a throwaway remark about wanting a pink pigeon, not knowing I actually had a massive phobia of pigeons?'

'Yes. How come you hate pigeons but are fine with chickens?'

'Dunno. Something to do with the flappiness. Chickens aren't as flappy. Is this going to be some metaphor about you didn't judge me for hating pigeons so I shouldn't judge him for hating dogs?'

'Fuck no!' said Simon. 'I was just going to say, we thought it was complicated then, didn't we? Life. But actually, it was so very simple if only we'd known. And we thought it would get easier as we got older, but it just gets more complicated. Do you remember how you screamed when you opened the box?'

'Yes.'

'You said you'd rather have found Gwyneth Paltrow's head in there than a fucking pigeon. You always complained I wasn't romantic enough, but is it any wonder I didn't make grand romantic gestures when that was your reaction to my attempt at romance?'

'It was still quite romantic, though.'

'Well, once you stopped screaming. That was the first time I told you I loved you, wasn't it?'

'Yes. Yes, it was.'

'What's that song, about when you remember the first time, but you don't remember the last time?'

'Pulp. It's literally called "Do You Remember the First Time?". I always thought it was about how bad their first shag was, though.'

'I remember *that* too.'

'Do you? We were quite pissed!'

'I remember a lot of things,' said Simon, 'I remember –'

'DAAAAAD!' yelled Peter. 'Dad, I'm hungry and my ankle's really sore. Can you bring me some Doritos?'

'Have an apple!' I yelled back. I wondered what else Simon had been going to say he remembered?

Monday, 22 July

The pre-culling grillings have started at work. I mean the 'streamlining interviews', sorry. I was also summoned to a meeting with the head honchos, and asked to justify the position of everyone in my department. I thought I'd done a pretty good job. There really is no dead wood in my department, we *do* need everyone, they all contribute something unique and we'd struggle without any of them, and I was at pains to point all this out and sing everyone's praises. I felt quite happy afterwards, confident that I'd done everything in my power to save their jobs. It was only later that I wondered if I'd done it wrong, if instead of telling them how diligent Lydia is, and how conscientious James is, and how creative Tom is and detail-orientated Liam is, I should have made it all about me, and spent the time pointing out that *I* was the reason everyone was so good at their jobs and the department ran so well, and explaining how it would all go to rat shit without me, that I was actually probably motherfucking *inspirational* and definitely irreplaceable. But instead, I didn't say a word about what I brought to the department, so hopefully I haven't kept everyone else in a job at the expense of my own.

I asked Simon what he thought when I went to see Peter, who's still declining to return. I found Jane measuring up in his bedroom and googling fitted wardrobes the other day. Simon thought about it for a bit.

'Did they ask about you? What you brought?'

'Not really. They asked about how I got on with the others, and how we all get on with each other, but not really about me, as such. Should I just have been really pushy and kept bringing it back round to me even though that wasn't the question, so they were in no doubt about how indispensable I am?'

'I don't think so. If they were asking about everyone else and how you get along, it sounds like you told them what they wanted to know. If you'd gone on about yourself, it could have looked like you have no real insight or knowledge about your team dynamics and always put your own interests first, and as we're always told, there is no I in Team. On the other hand, if they were proper corporate wank splatters, they might have been looking for you to really pitch yourself to them at the expense of others, to show how power-hungry you were. I don't know, Ellen, I wasn't there. What did they seem like?'

'They seemed nice, actually. And Ed was there. He used to be my boss – he's a pretty good guy. I don't think he'd be deliberately trying to double-bluff anyone.'

'I'm sure it's fine, then. And if it's not, well, there's nothing you can do about it now, is there? Relax and have a glass of wine.'

'On a Monday night?' I said virtuously, as if I hadn't been planning on going home and pouring myself a great big fuck-off glass. I thought how strange that after all those years of Simon and me having conversations largely based around whether or not there was any yoghurt for the children's packed lunches and if not, whose fault it was, we were finally able to have proper, adult conversations about careers and stuff.

'Why not? You look like you need it.'

'What about the car?'

'Get bloody Jane to come and pick you up. She can make herself useful, since I assume she has still failed to get a job.'

'Yes, she was thinking about ringing the pub about the bar job they're advertising, but apparently hasn't found a moment in between shopping and snapchatting and instagramming her latest make-up look.'

'Tell her to stay for dinner. I assume you're staying?'

'What are you making?'

'Stir fry. I thought I'd better get some vegetables into your son.'

'Yum! Are you sure you want to put so much ginger in it?'

'Yes.'

'Aren't you putting any garlic in?'

'Ellen, do you want to do it?'

'I'm just trying to help!'

'Well, drink your wine and don't interfere.'

'What about –'

'Ellen!'

'I'm just trying to give you the benefit of my vast experience. Oh, give me a knife. Look at the mess you're making.'

'No. Just stop interfering. I can cook a bloody stir fry, Ellen!'

'I'm just trying to HELP!'

'Well, don't. You need to realise that sometimes, just because something isn't done in the exact way you'd do it, it doesn't mean it's done wrong. You complain that you have to do everything for everyone, but that's because you can't relinquish control and let people get on with things in their own way. You should try it sometimes, starting now.'

'Are we just talking about stir fry?'

'No, actually. If you want to help, you can get me another glass of wine, and just talk to me without criticising, OK?'

'OK. What about some –'

'Ellen!'

'OK! Here. Here's your wine. Shall I open another bottle?'

'Oh, why the bloody hell not?'

Simon's interference-free stir fry was annoyingly delicious in the end. Maybe he had a tiny point about not everything having to be done my way. Not that I would admit that to him.

Thursday, 25 July

I think Jane has finally turned a corner. She needed a dress for her 'graduation' ceremony tonight and one for the 'Leavers' Prom' tomorrow night (the schools seem determined to Americanise everything for children who grew up on a steady diet of the Disney Channel and Nickelodeon), and actually allowed me some input. This was quite remarkable given the debacle that was finding her something to wear for the Christmas dance last year, whereby she'd sullenly send me a link to a dress, I'd say it was nice, and she would scream that it was a horrible dress, she didn't want it, and I was stupid and wrong and knew nothing.

Eventually, we found her a dress via some fairly basic reverse psychology. She sent me a dress and I said it was vile, and she insisted that was the one she wanted. I then offered to lend her my grandmother's pearl earrings to go with it, and she informed me they made her look like a cheap prostitute, which I don't really think was the look Granny was going for. When I told her the earrings did nothing of the sort, and I'd worn them at my wedding, she just smirked at me, which made me rush to get all my wedding photos out again, to see if I *had* looked like a cheap hooker (of course I hadn't).

This time, though, she approached me with a dress, actually a very lovely dress, and when I said I really wasn't sure about it, her face fell and she said she really loved it, and she'd thought I'd love it too, so I had to lie about needing to see another photo, and pretending that oh, yes, it *was* a nice dress, it was just the other photo hadn't done it justice. And then she asked me what shoes she should wear with it, and she actually took my advice!

We sat through lengthy speeches from school governors, and the headmaster, and an 'inspirational' former pupil, whose main achievement seemed to have been failing repeatedly to make the Olympic shot-putting team, and I was very nearly asleep with boredom when Simon nudged me sharply in the ribs.

'Why didn't you tell me Jane was making a speech?' he hissed.

'Wha'?' I mumbled blearily. 'Jane? She never said!'

But there she was, on the stage, our daughter, clear and articulate and confident and funny, and to my huge relief, not putting her new hobby of portmanteau swearing to use (she's become quite creative in her bad language, and the other day referred to her brother as a dickwanking twat goblin. Which was nice). She spoke about how school had given her more than just an academic grounding, but taught her other life skills as well, and to my immense surprise, also mentioned that her parents had given her a huge amount of support too, but that not everyone was so fortunate. For those children who lacked parental support, she said, the school played an even more important role.

Jane had publicly acknowledged the support we gave her! Jane had publicly acknowledged my existence! I was quite bursting with pride, once I got over the shock.

I rushed up to her afterwards. 'Jane! You never told us you were speaking tonight!'

'Yeah, well, I knew you'd just get all stressy or be embarrassing about it.'

'But you were marvellous.'

'OK, Mum, just, like, chill, yeah? Don't go on about it.'

And just like that, she has officially left, and is done with school. My baby girl is all grown up. I may have said this and become slightly emotional over dinner afterwards, which made Jane tell me to 'pull myself together'. Simon gave me a nice hug after dinner, though, when he dropped us off, and whispered, 'I know how you feel. It's scary. But we did a good job. We've kept her alive for eighteen years, she's not pregnant or in prison, and it's time for her to become an independent person. That's the point of bringing up children, remember?'

AUGUST

Saturday, 3 August

Simon rang me at lunchtime, sounding panicked. His mother and father were over from France for a few days, visiting his sister Louisa at her poetry co-operative in Coventry, and his mum had been admitted to hospital with chest pains, which turned out to be a heart attack. She'd survived, but she wanted to see the children. Of course, I immediately offered to drive Simon and the children to Coventry, but he declined.

'We've had one near-death experience in the family today, I don't think my nerves can stand your motorway driving. But come with us, please? I could use some moral support.'

I could hardly refuse, especially since Simon had been wonderful when my father died, even though we were separated by then, so off we all trundled to Coventry.

When we arrived in his mother's room, Louisa was already in situ, wafting around in a very grubby-looking kaftan, which I was sure couldn't be hygienic in a hospital setting. Though this being Louisa, generally one is just grateful she's wearing any clothes at all and hadn't got naked to invoke the spirit of the Goddess to channel through her to heal her mother. Instead, she appeared to be placing amulets around Sylvia's bed, and her first words to me were, 'Ellen, do you have a lighter? I need to light some sage to smudge the room and cleanse the space. Mummy can't possibly heal here with all the bad energy I can feel. I can sense someone died in here.'

'It's a hospital, Lou, of course someone died in here,' said Simon. 'And you can't light bloody sage. You'll set the smoke alarms off and the place will have to be evacuated. Hello, Mum.'

Poor Sylvia looked very frail and small in the hospital bed, but she'd managed to put her make-up on and drape herself in a couple of scarves, so it seemed likely she'd rally and recover. Sylvia has never been seen without her make-up, not even in the middle of the night – we once were disturbed by what we thought was an intruder when we were staying with them (it turned out to be a fox in the bins), and Sylvia had hurtled downstairs clutching the poker, having taken the time to apply a dash of Red Door Red on her way out of her bedroom, her mantra being if she was going to be brutally murdered, she'd look her very best for the occasion.

'Hello, darling,' said Sylvia. 'Thank you for coming. Oh, and Ellen! You came too, how nice to see you. I'm sorry I look so frightful. And my lovely grandchildren, Peter, Jane, how are you? Peter, what *have* you done to yourself?'

Peter looked sheepish and gestured to his cast, mumbling something about an accident.

Louisa interrupted to dab lavender oil on Sylvia's pulse points. 'To keep you calm,' she insisted, oblivious as ever that the main obstacle to calm in Louisa's presence is not a lack of lavender oil, but Louisa herself.

'Oh no, that's horrid,' said Sylvia crossly. 'Really, it smells like my granny's knicker drawer. What were you thinking, Louisa? Pass me that flannel, Simon. I don't want to smell like an old lady.'

'It's CALMING,' roared Louisa. 'I AM CALMING YOU!'

'I don't *need* to be calmed,' said Sylvia. 'I'm fine!'

'Well, you're not,' said Simon. 'You've just had a heart attack. Kinda the opposite of "fine", Mum.'

'Which is WHY I'm keeping her calm and trying to ward off the bad energy, but NO ONE'S LISTENING TO ME!' shouted Louisa. 'If I could just smudge the room, she'd feel MUCH BETTER!'

'I wouldn't,' said Sylvia. 'Then it would just smell of burnt sage *and* old women in here. And do move these, darling, they're rather in the way.' She handed Louisa back her amulets.

'Well, if you want to do this without the protection of the Goddess, on your own head be it!' huffed Louisa.

'I think I shall trust in medical science, if it's all the same to you, dear,' said Sylvia tartly. Oh good, she was being snippy, which meant she almost certainly wasn't going to die.

'Where's Dad?' asked Simon.

'Gone for a cup of tea. Louisa was annoying him,' said Sylvia.

'I wasn't annoying him. I was just asking him if he'd actually switched to an organic vegan diet like I'd advised him to months ago instead of having chemo, and he got quite shirty with me. Why does everyone get angry with me when I'm only trying to *help*?' whined Louisa. 'How are you, Ellen? Are you menopausal yet? You look quite menopausal. I've been writing some marvellous poems about the menopause. There's a wonderful one called "My Wombs Shrivels, My Yoni Mourns". I'll even give you a special price on my new book!'

'Er, thank you,' I said weakly. 'I'll … bear that in mind.'

Ah, Louisa. No matter what may happen in this ever-changing and fickle world, no matter what fortune and fate may throw at us, one thing remains forever constant, and that is that my ex-sister-in-law will eternally be utterly batshit. Louisa simply careers through life, like an unstoppable force of nature with exceedingly questionable personal hygiene issues, scattering in her wake a random selection of poorly researched and executed alternative therapies; children (in her heyday, pre-womb shrivelling and yoni mourning, Louisa fired out an alarming number of feral children, most of whom she abandoned to their father as they got older and began to question her lifestyle); and dubious self-published books of grim poetry that she attempts to flog to any innocent bystander.

There's a small, mean part of me that lives in fear that one day, Someone What Knows about these things will stumble across a volume of Louisa's poetry, declare it an unbelievable work of utter genius, publishing deals will rain upon her and she'll become a *Sunday Times* and *New York Times* bestseller, sell millions of copies, be showered with literary prizes and we'll all have to eat our words. And possibly some of hers. I realise having been the recipient of several of Louisa's books of poetry, which mainly seem to demonstrate an unhealthy obsession with her reproductive system, that this is unlikely to happen, but it seems there's no accounting for the oddities of the literary world.

How else do you account for the fact that the wondrous St Jilly of Cooper, author of many splendidly interesting, entertaining and informative books, has never won a literary prize, while many dreary and dull books, often about turgid professors having torrid affairs with nubile students, are lauded from the rooftops? So, although it's *unlikely* that Louisa's poetry could be a commercial and literary success, it's not *impossible*. But given that her last book was titled *Anointing the Patriarchy with the Blood of My Womb*, it's really *quite* unlikely.

Louisa was now irritating Sylvia further by waving her hands over her while Sylvia fidgeted and tried to see round her to talk to Simon.

'Keep STILL, Mummy!' snarled Louisa. 'I'm trying to do some healing reiki on you. You'll feel much better if you just keep STILL and let me do what I do best!'

'You haven't got any qualifications in reiki,' objected Sylvia.

'I don't NEED any, because I'm just very naturally gifted at it,' insisted Louisa. 'Now keep STILL. Can't you feel the heat from my hands as I channel the universal energy through you?'

'No,' said Sylvia, looking at Louisa's grimy mitts with some alarm. 'Do you think you should use some of that hand-sanitiser gel by the door, darling?'

'Absolutely NOT!' said Louisa in horror. 'I'm not dousing myself in *chemicals*! Come on, Mummy, you're not even trying. KEEP STILL! There! Don't you FEEL yourself healing?'

'NO!' said Sylvia again.

'Well, you are!' insisted Louisa. '*I* can feel it. Though really, there are so many things you could be doing to help yourself more. You too, Ellen. I see you're still wearing a bra. You really shouldn't. They cause cancer, you know. And you'd just feel much better if you cast your bra aside. It's nothing more than a tool of the patriarchy, because they're afraid of our breasts. That's why they want them trussed up, to cripple and strangle us. I felt so STRONG when I stopped wearing a bra.'

Sylvia made a choking noise that suggested another heart attack might be imminent if Louisa continued in this vein, and Simon turned a shade of purple that made me fear he might join her. Jane and Peter both blurted 'GROSS!' in unison.

'Darlings,' I said desperately. 'Why don't you go down to the café and tell Grandad that we're here?' They fled in relief. Louisa meanwhile prattled on blithely.

'I mean, look at your pants as well!' she wittered. 'I haven't worn pants in years, which is why I'm so creative. Your yoni is the centre of all your strength and power, you know, and the patriarchy know that too, and that is why they're stifling us, making us smother our vital life portal under layers and layers of fabric, so our voices can't be heard, so they don't hear our yonis *sing* –'

Sylvia gave a whimper. But Louisa had warmed to her theme and was now unstoppable.

'– they think that if they stop up the voices of our wombs, of our powerful yonis, then they can stop us. That's why tampons were invented. I don't even use a Mooncup anymore, actually. I just free-bleed, and it's so liberating.'

Simon left the room.

'– not that you have to worry about that anymore, Mummy, or probably you either, Ellen, as of course I'm considerably younger than you.'

'TWO YEARS!' I interrupted indignantly.

'But the power surge you experience when you feel that blood coursing down your legs, when you know your yoni is free and pure and able to SPEAK to the world. I just don't understand why anyone wears pants,' she finally finished.

I had nothing. There was literally nothing I could think of to say to this speech. Sylvia, fortunately, was made of sterner stuff, and rallied herself.

'Louisa,' she said firmly, 'I've never heard such nonsense. One's downstairs area "singing", indeed. Even it could, I don't think I'd want to hear it, so rest assured I shall continue to wear my nice Marks & Spencer undergarments, no matter what you

say, and THAT, I hope, IS THAT! Also, get OFF me! This waving
your hands over me is VERY ANNOYING!'

For most people, that would have been the cue to give up, but
not Louisa.

'Well, I've finished the reiki now,' she said sulkily. 'Next I need
to realign your chakras, but I probably can't – wearing pants
sends them all out of kilter because of all the power and energy
you're stopping flowing through your yoni, and actually Mummy,
that's probably why you had a heart attack. You've blocked
everything up with your bourgeois attitudes and pants.'

'I had a heart attack because I have a genetic disposition
towards heart disease that clogged my arteries, and also probably because I ate rather too much BRIE. It was NOTHING TO
DO WITH MY KNICKERS!' bellowed Sylvia, just as her
husband Michael came back into the room alongside Simon.

'Why on earth are you shouting about knickers, darling?' said
Michael in astonishment, as Simon made frantic 'Don't even go
there' gestures at him and Louisa opened her mouth to explain.

'Where are the children?' I shouted quickly, before she could
start explaining to her father about the patriarchy's gusset-based
oppression. 'LOUISA! HOW ARE YOUR CHILDREN?'

'My children have betrayed me!' said Louisa fiercely, and then
embarked on a lengthy rant about how ungrateful her children
were, with their unreasonable demands for sanitation, education
and a parent who didn't prance round the house starkers with
her tits swinging in the breeze, and how all of them, including
Boreas, the youngest, had therefore sodded off to live with their
father. I think we all just tuned out while this was going on and
gave thanks that she was no longer on about singing fannies.
Fortunately, she left after that, as she had an 'unbreakable
commitment' to an unsuspecting women's group to do one of

her poetry readings. 'I don't tell them I read in the nude. I feel it makes a much more powerful impact and statement when I just come out like that.'

We all breathed a sigh of relief after she'd gone, and Peter and Jane sidled back into the room, having seen Louisa sailing down the corridor, stopping only to harangue a nurse about how modern medicine was killing us all.

After Louisa had departed, the rest of the afternoon passed without event. Sylvia, once a draconian mother-in-law, has mellowed in recent years, and even more so since Simon and I split up. I was very relieved that it looked like she was going to be OK, providing she was sensible and laid off the brie, and stopped insisting it was fine as long as she'd enough red wine with it.

Much later, Simon dropped us at home. Jane dashed into the house to post eleventy fucking billion more selfies on her Instagram stories, Peter hobbling behind her, the novelty of living with Simon having worn off when he discovered just how limited Simon's mealtime repertoire was.

'Try not to worry,' I said. 'She's in the best place.'

'I know,' he said. 'It's just – how do you not worry?'

'Do you want to come in for a drink?'

'Would that be OK?'

'Of course. Abandon the car, Jane can run you home later.'

Jane, obviously, was unimpressed by this plan, but grudgingly agreed on the basis of Simon's mother's near-death experience meaning she should cut him some slack.

We took our wine out into the garden.

'Do you want a cigarette?' asked Simon.

'I mean, I sort of feel like we shouldn't, given they're very bad for you and we just spent the afternoon in a hospital at the bedside of a heart-attack patient, don't you think?'

'Suit yourself,' said Simon gloomily. 'I'm having one.'

'Oh, fuck it, give me one then. If I'm going to be breathing your second-hand smoke, I might as well breathe my own first-hand.'

'Anyway, I need it,' said Simon. 'After today. Fuck me. You think your parents are invincible, don't you? All those years, growing up, you always think they're never going to go anywhere, and yes, they annoy the tits off you, but you still quite like the thought of them being around *somewhere*, and then you grow up and realise that they're not immortal, and they're not going to be here forever. And I should know that by now, after Dad being sick last year and everything, but *Mum*! I just, I never thought anything would happen to her. Stupid, really.'

'Well, you don't, do you? But I'm fairly sure my mother probably is immortal. I'd be entirely unsurprised if she'd sold her soul to the devil years ago, though that would mean she actually had a soul to sell, which I'm not convinced about.'

Simon laughed, then became serious again.

'I just hate the thought that one day this will be Jane and Peter, worrying about us,' he sighed. 'They're our children, we're supposed to worry about them, not the other way round. Parents are meant to *parent*, not need looking after. We seem to have spent a lot of time in hospitals together over the last couple of years, Ellen, sitting at one bedside or another, and soon that will be our children.'

'I know, but that's life, Simon. Our children grow up, we get older, we die. Hopefully, we're not too much of a burden on them first, and hopefully we manage to fuck them up *just* enough that they're sad when we go, but not all consumed and overwhelmed with grief and unable to enjoy the rest of their lives. And it's going to happen to all of us, whether we like it or not. You know what they say: the only two certainties in life are death and taxes. Though I'm not mad keen on either.'

'I know, I know. You can be very practical sometimes, Ellen. I know we can't avoid it. I know my parents are going to die, and sooner rather than later. Oh, fuck it!' He ground out his cigarette. 'If all we have ahead of us is death, Ellen, shall we make a pact that if we're both still single when we're seventy-five, that we'll get married again, so we don't die alone? You know, like people used to when we were young and thought forty was impossibly ancient and decrepit, and they'd promise if they weren't married by forty, they'd marry each other as a back-up plan?'

'No,' I said firmly. 'If I'm still single by the time I'm seventy-five, I'll be far too set in my ways to want to be bothered with putting up with a man again. Weeing on the loo seat and mansplaining things to me and *scratching* themselves. If I'm still single by then, I intend to be extremely rude to everyone and claim it's eccentricity and wear unsuitable hats and have a copious number of dogs.'

'I could put up with that,' grinned Simon. 'You're already rude to me, and you suit hats and I like dogs.'

'NO! The rudeness will be extreme, the hats outlandish and the number of dogs vast. There will be no room for you in the house with all the hats and dogs. You can live down the street and wave when you go to get your paper in the morning and I shall shout, "Piss off" and throw parsnips at you.'

'Why parsnips?'

'I don't like them.'

'Then why would you buy them?'

'To throw at you.'

'That's ridiculous.'

'See? You're already finding faults with my plans for old age –'

'Only the bit where you waste money buying parsnips purely to hurl at me!'

'Which is why there would be no future in us getting remarried at seventy-five.'

'What if we got married and I *grew* parsnips, and let you throw them at me? To save money. We'll be pensioners, so we won't have spare cash to fritter on airborne root vegetables.'

'No. It's a silly plan. Go and bring the bottle out, I seem to have finished my wine.'

Thursday, 15 August

The day of reckoning finally came. Or rather, the Dreaded Results Day for Jane. After months of insouciance and refusing to take either her exams or revision seriously, it suddenly seemed to have hit home. She came downstairs this morning, pale and drawn, refusing all offers of breakfast. She stared at me mournfully as I tucked into my tea and toast, and then heaved a deep sigh.

'Mum?'

'Yes, darling?'

'What if I've failed them all?'

'Do you think you've failed them all?'

'I don't know. But just *say* I have. What then?'

'Well, you'll have to consider your options, won't you? You can go to college and retake them, or you can find a job that doesn't require A levels. And you might possibly concede that your mother was right. Again.'

'What jobs don't you need A levels for?'

'Well, according to you, being Queen. But unfortunately, there's not an opening there at the moment.'

'Mum, you need to take this seriously!'

'Which is exactly what I said to you repeatedly for months, and you told me to "chill". Maybe you should chill.'

'Don't worry, Jane,' said Peter kindly, emptying half a packet of cornflakes and a pint of milk into a bowl. 'I'm going to be super-rich, designing ground-breaking computer games. You can be my cleaner.'

'You still need to pass *your* exams!' said Jane furiously. 'And I'm *not* being your cleaner and picking up your crusty wank socks, ugh!'

'I don't wank in a sock, actually,' said Peter indignantly. 'And I won't need qualifications to be a game designer.'

'"I don't wank in a sock"?' snorted Jane. 'Is that the best comeback you can manage? If you'll pardon the pun? And you really think *you're* going to be able to afford a cleaner? With your level of intelligence?'

'Do we have to talk about wank socks?' I pleaded. 'I'm trying to have my breakfast.'

'She started it. Her and her *stupid* face,' said Peter. 'I bet SHE wanks in a sock.'

'OMG, you have literally no idea about women's bodies, do you?' snarled Jane. 'No wonder you can't get a girlfriend. You fell off a WALL trying to impress a girl, like you were six or something. You're *so* going to be one of those angry incel men on Twitter in a year or two.'

'Like, Twitter won't even probably *exist* by then!' spat Peter, somewhat missing the point of Jane's insult. 'Maybe I'll invent the next social media platform and be the new Mark Zuckerberg, with billions and billions of pounds, and then you'll have to be nice to me, because you'll be my *stupid* sister who couldn't even get any A levels, and I'll introduce you like that when you're cleaning my house!'

'For Christ's sake, SHUT UP, both of you! Peter, you're not helping. Jane, it's too late to worry now, there's absolutely nothing you can do about it. Dad will be here in a minute, and we'll go and find out, one way or another.'

I'd taken the day off, reasoning that either way I should probably spend it with Jane, whether it was in celebrating or investigating clearing, or coming up with a Plan B. Or C or D, depending on the results.

We pulled up outside the school. Jane was ashen-faced.

'I feel sick,' she said. 'But the thing we must remember is that at least we all have our health.'

'Do you want me to come in with you?'

'No!' she said indignantly. 'HOW sad would that look? My mummy holding my hand? Ugh! Stay here. And don't talk to anyone and embarrass me, OK?'

Simon and I sat in the car for a nail-biting fifteen minutes, waiting for her. A stream of teenagers, jaws set, all looking like the condemned, poured into the school. The first ones were starting to come out, some looking jubilant, others shuffling out looking dejected, all the hopes of the last few years clearly crushed.

'Do you think she's all right?' I fretted. 'I should go in and find her. Maybe she's too upset to come out yet. I should go in, she might need me.'

'Stay where you are,' said Simon. 'She'll come out if she needs you. All you'll do by going in there is to mortify her and upset her more. She told you that you were to stay outside. So stay.'

I stayed. I bit my nails some more. Where *was* she?

Emily, Hannah's daughter, passed the car. I put down the window and yelled, 'Good luck, Emily!' Emily grimaced and walked on.

My phone rang. My mother's number. I declined the call.

'Don't you want to talk to her?' said Simon in surprise.

'God, no!' I said in horror. 'She'll just be calling to ask about Jane's results, so she can crow over how much better the Golden Grandchild Persephone's results are, and what a shame that poor Jane didn't do so well. Oh dear, never mind. But not everyone can be as gifted as Persephone, can they? And she's so *proud* of Persephone. It'll be even worse if I tell her that we don't even know yet. It'll be all, "Oh well, *Persephone* was in so early and told everyone how she did *immediately* because she's so fucking perfect!" You know what she's like.'

Another ten minutes passed before Jane came sauntering out. She looked neither up nor down, not dancing with joy like some students, nor sobbing like others. She wandered over to the car, taking her own sweet time, while I resisted the urge to lean out the window and scream, 'Hurry the fuck up and TELL ME WHAT YOU GOT!'

Jane climbed into the car, casual as you like, and said 'What? Why are you staring at me with that weird look, Mum?'

'Just tell me how it went?' I begged.

'What?'

'Jane!'

'Oh, yeah – fine.'

'What does that mean? Fine good, fine bad? WHAT DID YOU GET?'

'Yeah, it was all right, I suppose,' she said, still poker-faced.

'JANE! Just TELL me!'

'Oh, you know. Just two As and a B. No biggy. So, looks like I'll be doing History and Politics at Edinburgh. Anything else?'

'OH MY GOD! THAT'S AMAZING! THAT'S SO BRILLIANT, I'M SO PROUD OF YOU!' I shrieked, while Simon made proud and impressed noises as well, and Jane just shrugged and continued to pretend it was really no big deal.

'We've booked a table somewhere nice for lunch,' said Simon. 'Thought we'd treat you! Do you want to go home and get changed first?'

Jane looked aghast. 'Err, we're all going into town to celebrate! Emily's just ringing her mum – her and Sophie did brilliantly too – but they wouldn't even let Hannah and Sam come to school, so you should be honoured I let you bring me. And then we're all going to go and get completely pissed!'

'Are you sure that's sensible?' I wittered. 'Why don't you have some lunch with us first? Line your stomach.'

'Mum, in about a month I'll be at university hundreds of miles from you. You need to stop worrying and fretting about me. We've had it planned for months, how we're going to celebrate today. Maybe we could all go out tomorrow night and celebrate instead, yeah? But for now, literally the whole year are heading out. It's the last time some of us will see each other. We'll all be going our separate ways soon, so it's like … a last hurrah!'

I sighed. 'OK, fine. I'll see you later. Or if you're staying over at someone's, let me know as soon as possible so I'm not waiting up at midnight convinced you're dead in a ditch!'

'And here,' said Simon, opening his wallet and handing Jane a wad of cash. 'If you don't want to come for lunch, you'd better have a drink on us. Don't do anything stupid, and don't spend it on drugs.'

'Dad! That's actually quite insulting!'

'Just be sensible.'

'I WILL be! OK, bye, love you,' and with that she danced out of the car and off into the first day of the rest of her life, though hopefully the rest of her life won't be filled with dubious cocktails and lurid shots, like today.

'Well,' I said, 'I suppose you'd better cancel that table for lunch.'

'Why? We can still go and celebrate our daughter's achievements while she makes heroic attempts to destroy her liver. Go home and get changed, and I'll pick you up in an hour.'

I'd just finished getting changed when Mum rang again. This was about the sixth time she'd phoned, as clearly she was determined to extract her pound of flesh and have a good old gloat about Persephone's 4 A*s and her glittering upward trajectory towards Cambridge, while blithely overlooking the fact that her other granddaughter had also done BLOODY FUCKING MARVELLOUSLY. I'd been refusing to answer since I was feeling a bit sorry for myself about Jane's imminent departure, and was not really in the mood to cope with my mother. But it seemed she was not to be avoided.

'Ellen!' said my mother crossly. 'WHY haven't you been answering your phone? I have been ringing and ringing you!'

'Sorry, Mum,' I said unrepentantly.

'Anyway, I need to know how Jane did in her A levels.'

'Thanks for remembering!' I said sarcastically. 'She did really well, actually. Two As and a B. So, she's got into Edinburgh.'

I waited for the twittering glee about how nice that poor dear Jane had done so well, but of course, it was nothing compared with *Persephone*! Instead Mum heaved a great sigh of relief.

'Oh, thank God!' she said. 'Oh, I'm so glad.' I felt bad. Clearly,

I'd misjudged Mum, and she did genuinely care about Jane, her future and her results.

'Yes,' she continued. 'I didn't know *what* I was going to be able to say to Antonia at the tennis club if at least *one* of my granddaughters hadn't got decent results. It's all they'll be talking about for weeks, and I wouldn't be able to hold my head up if both my grandchildren had ploughed them.'

Oh. My mistake. She didn't give a shit about Jane, only about how Jane's results reflected on her. But hang on a minute.

'Did you say *ploughed* their A levels, Mum? Do you mean Persephone …?'

'It's just too awful. I don't want to talk about it. Do you know how much Jessica and Neil have spent on Persephone's education? Well over £100,000, and that's not even counting all the tutoring and the music lessons and everything else. And then, she just throws it all back in their faces. It seems she went into the exams and deliberately wrote nonsensical answers. 'How long is a piece of string?' was her answer to one question. Oh, I just can't even discuss it, it's far too distressing. Poor darling Jessica can't stop crying and Neil is simply LIVID! Oh, Persephone! Your cousin has done marvellously, you know!'

'I TOLD YOU I DIDN'T WANT TO GO TO FUCKING CAMBRIDGE!' I heard Persephone yell in the background. 'I FUCKING TOLD YOU ALL, AND NO ONE WOULD LISTEN TO ME!'

'Are you actually there at Jessica's?' I asked.

'Oh yes, Geoffrey and I drove down from Yorkshire last night. We thought it would be so lovely to be here with Jessica and Persephone, but now she's *spoiled* it all, for everyone. Thank goodness for Jane, and her doing so well, even though she went to a comprehensive school!'

'What do you mean, "Even though", Mum? There's nothing wrong with Jane's school!'

'Oh darling, I'm just saying, imagine how well she could have done if she'd gone to a *proper* school.'

'Mum!' I protested, but I was interrupted by more muffled shouting in the background. Mum gave a wail.

'Oh no! Persephone says she's going to go to a sixth-form college to get her A levels, and then she's going to go to some dreadful polytechnic-type university and will become a *social worker*! Oh, I can't bear it. A *social* worker!'

'Mum, social workers are very important. They can literally save people's lives and make a real difference.'

'She might as well become a hairdresser,' sniffed Mum.

'Also a very valuable and underappreciated job,' I pointed out.

'I WANT TO BE A FUCKING SOCIAL WORKER BECAUSE I KNOW HOW IT FEELS TO HAVE YOUR PARENTS FUCK UP YOUR WHOLE LIFE!' Persephone bellowed distantly.

'What does she *mean*?' whimpered Mum. 'Jessica and Neil have given that child everything. Everything! The money spent on her education!'

'Persephone didn't ask them to do that though, did she? She's been saying for ages she doesn't want to go to Cambridge, but she's right, none of you listened. Neil and Jessica have had her whole life mapped out for her from before she was born. She's never been able to make her own choices or decisions, or consulted about what *she* wants. It's always been about what Jessica and Neil wanted for her.'

'Oh, I couldn't possibly expect *you* to understand!' said Mum crossly 'Your children are practically feral. All Jessica and Neil wanted was the best for Persephone.'

'Well, clearly Persephone disagrees, or she'd be drinking champagne and buying a bicycle with a wicker basket ready to be seduced by a dashing and tweedy and only slightly creepy professor at Cambridge right now, wouldn't she? Instead of still trying to make you all LISTEN! And my "feral child", the one you think I did such a terrible job with by actually letting her be her own person instead of who I wanted her to be, is now going off to do what she wants and is happy about it, even if she can't speak fucking Mandarin and has never done a Suzuki violin course!'

'Oh, you do talk nonsense,' snapped Mum. 'Poor Jessica. She's so devastated.'

'And there you go!' I said. 'All you've said in this is "Poor Jessica" and "Poor you" about how Persephone's results reflect on you. Not once have you said, "Poor Persephone", or wondered what drove her to act like that, have you?'

'Oh really, Ellen,' Mum began, but my phone was flashing with another call.

'Mum, it's Jane. I need to go. Stop being so bloody hard on poor Persephone, OK?'

I hung up and answered Jane. She sounded quite hammered already.

'Mum? Mum, Pershephone jusht called me. Mum, she totally fucked up her exams on purpose, and Aunty Jessica and Granny are going batshit at her, and I said just get on a train and meet us at the pub an' we'll go get shitfaced and then she can come an' stay for a few days, and tha's OK, isn't it, Mum?'

'Yes,' I said, 'of course,' thinking that another fucked-up teenager under my roof was JUST what I needed.

Simon then arrived, in a taxi, not his car, saying, 'I thought it might be more fun if neither of us had to drive!'

When we got to the restaurant and sat down to lunch (there were tablecloths and everything), I said, 'Are you going to have a glass of wine, if you're not driving then?'

'Fuck it,' said Simon. 'Let's get a bottle of champagne to start!'

'A bottle,' I gasped. 'Simon, that'll cost a fortune! We've never ordered a bottle of champagne in a restaurant before.'

'Well, we've never had a child pass their A levels with flying colours before either, have we?' He grinned across the table at me. 'And I'm paying, so don't worry about the cost.'

The champagne arrived and Simon raised his glass. 'To Jane,' he said.

'To Jane,' I echoed.

'And to us,' he added.

'Us?' I said in surprise.

'As Jane's parents. To us, for getting her here. That's all,' he quickly added.

'Oh yes, of course. To us.'

Over the rest of the bottle I filled him in on the developments with Persephone and Jessica, and he laughed. 'Is it terrible that I feel rather smug that our daughter has done so much better than your sister's?' he asked.

'No, I feel quite smug too. I mean, obviously, it's awful for poor Persephone, but really, Jessica has always held herself up to me as this shining paragon of motherhood, so there's a part of me that's not entirely regretting seeing her find out she fucked it all up so spectacularly. It's weird, though. Now the A level results are in, I feel like that's another parenting box sort of ticked off, and time's running out and I don't know how that's happened. And now Jane's going to Edinburgh.'

'I know,' Simon said, shaking the bottle. 'I don't know how it happened either. One minute, there they are. The next, off they've fucked. God, it's weird to think, isn't it? *Jane* at Edinburgh. Shit, this is finished already. Let's get another bottle.'

'Oh, go on then! *We're* meant to be the kids at Edinburgh. Not Jane,' I said. 'God, I'm a terrible person to think like that about my own daughter.'

'No, you're not. It's understandable that it feels strange to almost watch history repeating with our children. In the meantime, if you're going to have a houseful of drunk teenagers tonight, you know what they say! If you can't beat 'em, join 'em. Drink up, darling. If you can't get gloriously sloshed today, when can you?'

Another bottle later, we went for a walk along the river to try to sober up a bit.

'We did all right,' Simon slurred drunkenly. 'We din't know what we were doin' most of the time, but we did all right, din't we?'

'We did,' I agreed, equally drunkenly. 'We really did!'

Wednesday, 21 August

Well, given how much time I've recently spent thinking sad thoughts about how strange it will be when it's just Peter and me in the house, once Jane has gone to university and wondering how I'll cope without her, or even worse, how it'll be to be alone altogether when Peter goes too, after a week of Persephone staying and constant phone calls from both Jessica and Mum to harangue me, after Persephone blocked their numbers so they couldn't harangue *her*, I think it's safe to say that I'm really rather looking forward to a house without teenagers and door-slammings and forty-minute showers and wails about unfairness and misunderstoodness, and things being where I left them and food remaining in the fridge for when I'm hungry.

To give her due credit, Persephone has been very nice and pleasant to me most of the time, apart from when I've had to try to persuade her to talk to her parents, at which point she tended to slam out of the room wailing that she couldn't talk to them because they didn't LISTEN to her, which was a fair point because I'd also been trying to talk to Jessica and Mum about Persephone and they didn't bloody listen to me either.

Things finally came to a head today, when Jessica called again to *insist* I send Persephone home, and threatened to call the police and have me arrested for kidnapping – and I snapped. I'd been trying to be reasonable with Jessica, attempting to smooth her ruffled feathers and calm her down, for Persephone's sake as much as to stop her ringing me up and alternately screaming and crying at me, but the kidnapping accusation was really too much to bear.

'FOR FUCK'S SAKE, JESSICA!' I roared. 'If I don't let her stay here, do you really think she'll just go on home to you? She's already said she won't, that she'll stay with friends, or worse. You should be GLAD she has somewhere safe to go, where you know where she is, where you know she's being looked after, that she has people who care about her around her, instead of still trying to force her to do what YOU want. And she's eighteen and here of her own free will, so good luck with getting your own sister arrested for kidnapping her. But you know, don't worry about THANKING me or anything.'

'I just think that if she were at home, we could make her see SENSE!' insisted Jessica. 'You're not helping, you're encouraging her in this ridiculous plan. I've given her EVERYTHING, and she's throwing it back at me!'

'Please, Jessica, PLEASE stop making this about you. Persephone didn't ask for any of the things you did for her. She didn't turn around at the age of two and say, "Oh, Mother dear, please do enrol me in an eye-wateringly expensive school so I can fulfil my lifelong dream of doing a law degree at Cambridge." That was YOUR dream, that you'd turn her into a little clone of you. But you can't do that with children. You have to accept that they become who THEY want to be, not who YOU want them to be, and the best you can hope for is that they don't turn out to be arseholes.

'Jessica, you CHOSE to give Persephone an expensive education and an obscene number of extra-curricular activities, but you can't control what *she* then chooses to do with that. You just can't! And if you keep trying to, you'll lose your daughter, possibly forever. Whereas if you can just take a step back, let her know that you're sorry you didn't pay more attention to what she was trying to tell you, and that you love her and will support her regardless of what career she chooses, then she'll probably end up being very grateful to you for all the opportunities you gave her.

'If you let her make her OWN decisions, and give her a bit of space and time, who knows, she might decide she DOES want to go to Cambridge. She might even decide to do law, though I doubt she'll want to be a corporate lawyer like you, or fulfil your dream of her being prime minister, but she could do lots of humanitarian things with a law degree. But right now, she wants to be a social worker, and whether that's what she *really* wants or whether that's just her kicking against you and trying to piss you off, doesn't actually matter, because you have to let her make her own mistakes and learn from them.'

There was silence at the other end of the phone.

'Jessica? Are you still there?'

'Yes. I was just thinking. I don't want to lose her. And I certainly don't want her sleeping rough or having to traipse round friends' houses begging for a bed for the night because she feels she can't go home. Thank you for letting her stay, Ellen, I've been very ungrateful. And yes, it's her life. I just … what am I going to say to everyone? I've made such a big deal about Persephone doing law at Cambridge for years. I'm going to look such a fool to everyone.'

I sighed. 'Jessica, if you could put a positive spin on this, would you feel happier about Persephone's choices? If you were able to convince people this was a good thing, and that you were happy about it and proud of her?'

'But I'm not.'

'But if you *could* persuade people that this was a wonderful thing for her, would you feel better? Because I think a lot of your anger is about feeling embarrassed in front of your friends and colleagues about her choices.'

'Well, maybe a bit,' Jessica grudgingly admitted.

'That doesn't reflect tremendously well on you,' I said sanctimoniously.

'Oh, shut UP, Ellen. If you're so bloody clever, tell me how to fix this.'

'Easy. Just tell everyone that, of course, Persephone *could* have gone to Cambridge if she'd *wanted* to. But she decided that actually law wasn't for her, and she was more interested in a career in helping people directly, on a one-to-one basis, and you're very proud of her humanitarian instincts and caring nature, and that she wants to use her education to improve other people's lives.'

'That sounds vaguely plausible,' said Jessica doubtfully. 'Do you think people will believe it?'

'If you say it with enough conviction they will. Say she's resitting her A levels to do different courses that are a better fit for her new choices, and isn't it marvellous that unlike most of today's selfish, self-obsessed teenagers, Persephone cares so much about other people? Say it often enough, and you might even believe it!'

'Do you really think so?'

'Look at it like this. What if someone came up to you in twenty years' time and said, "OMG, you're Persephone's mum, and because of her and the influence she's had on my life, I've achieved all these wonderful things, and been able to go on and improve other people's lives in turn, and without Persephone, I'd probably be dead." Would you be more proud of that, or of someone coming up to you and saying, "Oh, you're Persephone's mum, and because of her, I've been able to turn my already privileged life into one of even more obscene wealth, and fuck everybody else"?' (I was *slightly* hazy regarding what corporate lawyers actually did, but I was pretty sure that mostly it wasn't about helping the little guy.)

'Couldn't she do both?' said Jessica hopefully. 'Be a lawyer and just, I don't know, volunteer with a charity?'

'She could. But that's not what she wants, Jessica, that's what YOU want again. LISTEN to what she wants. Do you think you can do that? Actually listen. Or if you can't do that, just tell her you love her and will support her no matter what choices she makes.'

'OK. OK. I can do *that* at least, I suppose. And yes … telling people she *could* have gone to Cambridge might work. It's not even a fib, really. In theory, anyone *could* go there. If I promise not to shout, and just try to be supportive, do you think you could see if she'd talk to me?'

'I'll try. But really, if I get her to talk to you, don't fuck it up, OK?'

'I WON'T.'

After much persuasion, Persephone agreed to talk to her mother. For the first time in her life, Jessica had evidently managed to take my advice, because Persephone came off the phone looking happier than at any time since she'd arrived.

'I don't know how you did it, Aunty Ellen, but she was so nice. She's asked me to come home and said she'll support me whatever I choose. Daddy too. She was sorry for being so angry. She said she'd been very disappointed, but she sees now it's about me, not her. Oh, thank you! I think I'm going to go and pack!'

'I'm so glad, darling. Just one thing – Granny might take a bit more persuading, but we'll all do our best!'

Well, hurrah to me! Maybe if I lose my job, I could get a new career as a negotiator for the UN. If I can manage a truce between Persephone and Jessica, I'm pretty sure I could bring about peace in the Middle East in a jiffy!

Persephone appeared again. 'Errr, Aunty Ellen? Any chance of a lift to the station? And I don't know what time the trains are …'

FML. The sooner I can give up being a taxi and human googling service the better!

Thursday, 22 August

And we're back at the school for Results Day round 2! Peter's GCSEs this time. He was a great deal less concerned than Jane had been, despite my frequent admonishments that GCSEs ARE important, and they DO count, and to please, please just do some fucking revision. Luckily, he'd at least got his cast off last week, though if he celebrated his results with the same enthusiasm as Jane did for her A levels, there was every chance he'd end up breaking something else. Assuming there was anything to celebrate.

He trotted out a lot faster than his sister, though, and being less of an evil puppet master than her, instead of poker-facing us and making us guess, he was jubilant and practically skipping as he returned to the car.

'All good!' he crowed. 'Jane's not the only clever one, is she! Ha! Five As, two Bs and a C. The C was for Art. Apparently they weren't impressed by my robot zombie sculpture, the philistines. Woohoo! Can Lucas and Toby come over for a few beers later?'

'But … nice lunch, family celebration?' I said hopelessly.

'Yeah, great, lunch is good, but can we go to an all-you-can-eat pizza buffet? I'm starving! And then, Mum, can they come round? Will you get us a few cans?'

I sighed, as Simon picked up his phone to cancel the reservation for the posh lunch in favour of watching our son shovel down industrial quantities of pizza, before announcing he was 'off for a tactical' and retiring to the bathroom with a purposeful stride for an unpleasant amount of time, and then returning looking pleased with himself and recommencing the eating.

I capitulated and had the boys round 'for a few beers'. Unfortunately, Toby brought a bottle of vodka and they all got rat-arsed, and I spent the night checking on them every few minutes to make sure they were still in the recovery position I'd placed them in, which was fun.

Friday, 23 August

I went into work this morning half asleep after the antics of the boys last night, and rather apprehensive, as today was the day when everyone found out whether or not the shadow of the workhouse was going to fall on them, complete with eternal gruel.

When I arrived I found everyone in my department jubilant, having ALL received an email informing them that they'd been successful in interviewing for their position and would be continuing in gainful employment.

I felt a bit sick. Unfortunately, all the department heads had already been told that they'd be summoned to individual meetings with Ed and Mike, the American Head Honcho, to be told their fate, instead of receiving an email. I had an hour to go. Surely it would be all right? Ed had got in the lift with me a couple of days ago, and had been perfectly chatty and friendly. Surely he wouldn't have done that if he knew he was about to cast me and my precious moppets out to starve in the street? Would he? Lydia, one of the team leaders, came into my office.

'Isn't it wonderful?' she said. 'I know you kept telling us it would all be OK, but I was still worried. I love working here, especially since you arranged for me to have flexible hours so I wasn't constantly feeling so guilty about missing school assemblies and sports days. I told them about this in my interview, and how much more productive I'd become since you let me do it. I'm so glad we're all staying together. When's your meeting?'

'Ten o'clock.'

'Poor you. The waiting must horrible. But surely there's nothing for you to worry about. If we're all staying, then there's no way they'd get rid of you. Everybody told them how great you are, how you actually listen and care about us, and that you're the one holding it all together. You'll be fine.'

Despite Lydia's positivity, it was a slow hour. What happened when you were made redundant? It had never happened to me before, but it was my understanding from TV programmes that you had to vacate the premises immediately, carrying a cardboard box filled with photos of your children, together with a pot plant. I didn't have any photos of the children. I didn't have a pot plant either. All mine had died. I did have a large stapler and hole punch in my drawer that I could steal if the worst came to the worst. That was something. I'd never actually used them – our department is largely paperless – but everyone knows hole punches and staplers are always useful. I could probably nick a handful of biros, too. I gave myself a shake. Lydia was right – surely it would be fine. I was just being melodramatic.

Finally it was five to ten. I went upstairs and sat down. I was the first one there. I looked around to see if there was anything else I could steal. I wondered if I could fit an interactive whiteboard up my top?

Ed and Mike came in, with the new HR lady, all very jovial and jolly. This was a good sign.

'Any plans for the weekend?' Ed asked me.

I said something about getting my daughter ready for university and what an expensive process it is, to remind them I'd a family to look after, just in case they were making me redundant and I could guilt trip them out of it at the eleventh hour. Ed just laughed and said he knew the feeling, and it was even worse in America.

'Anyway, Ellen!' said Mike. 'Thanks for seeing us. As you know, we're here today to talk about your position in the company. You've done a fantastic job in your department, and really turned the different teams under you into a great coherent unit that work well both together and independently. You should be very proud. But what we observed from watching is that we don't think this role is the right fit for you anymore.'

'What?'

'We don't think your unique talents and skills are being utilised there properly, and so we'd like to promote Lydia into your role. You've been a great mentor to her, and we feel she's ready for more responsibility.'

'But if Lydia's doing my job, what about MY job?' I said stupidly, feeling a sudden inability to breathe.

Ed must have seen the panic in my eyes.

'Don't worry, Ellen, it's OK,' he said quickly.

'Yes,' said Mike. 'We were just coming to that. Like I said, we don't feel you're fully utilised in your current role, but we recognise that you've brought some exceptional skills and talents to the company that we don't want to lose in the streamlining process. All your department spoke so highly of you, of how you motivate them, encourage them all to get the best out of them, and enable them to adapt to individual work patterns to really maximise their potential, while having an excellent grip on the technical side of things as well.

'We're creating a new department, based between California and the UK, developing some new special projects, working with some of the brightest and best young graduates we can recruit, and we think you'd be perfect to head it up. But it would involve a lot of travelling, longer hours, time spent in the States as well as here, although we feel that would be reflected in the very generous package that we'd be offering you with it, including a company car and healthcare, and, of course, a significant salary increase. Is this something you'd be interested in?'

'What if I say no? Lydia's got my old job?'

'No, we haven't approached Lydia yet. We wanted to see if you were interested in this new role first, but we all feel that this is the one you're meant for. What do you say?'

I was dazed. I realised that sitting there with my mouth open, gawping at them like a dying goldfish, probably wasn't entirely the professional image I should be projecting at this particular moment. I pulled myself together.

'I'll need to think about it,' I mumbled. 'I … big decision. Stapler? Will I get a stapler?'

'Sorry?' said Mike, looking baffled. 'Did you just ask if you'll get a … stapler? Uh, sure. If you want one.'

'OK.' I tried to think what one was supposed to say in these situations, other than NOT ask if your big promotion would involve your Dream Stapler of Your Very Own. 'Um, the package? Is that it? Is there any room for negotiation?'

'Well, we think it's a pretty generous package, but sure, there's maybe a little wiggle room.'

I suddenly had an image of Mike, who's quite a large chap, wiggling, and fought the urge to laugh.

'Well, you've certainly given me a lot to think about,' I said. 'I'll get back to you as soon as I can!'

'That's great,' said Mike. 'Don't take too long. We're looking forward to hearing from you.'

I stumbled back to my office, still unable to believe quite what had happened. I shut the door and tried to remember to breathe. I looked through all the papers Mike had handed me (despite his fondness for streamlining, Mike likes things done on paper, not electronically, so there was an excellent chance of a very high-quality stapler being including in the new job). Fuck my old boots. This was literally my Dreamiest of Dream Jobs Ever! And the money was more than I could have ever hoped for! Of *course* I was going to accept it! I'd be insane to turn it down! It was only my attempts at playing it cool that stopped me ringing Mike there and then (or at least his secretary), and shouting 'YES! YES! A THOUSAND TIMES YES!'

My phone dinged. A text from Peter. Peter. Oh God, Peter! I'd forgotten about Peter in all this. Jane was leaving home, but Peter was still there. He was only just coming up on sixteen – I couldn't abandon him for one to two weeks every month to go off and be Busy and Important. I just couldn't. Unless? Maybe Simon would step up? He owed me, after all, but when had that made any difference in the past? His own Busy and Importantness had always taken precedence over mine, but he coped so well with having Peter living with him when he broke his ankle, and it had been lovely seeing them spending so much time together and getting on so well. Of course, Simon had never been much use in the past, but he was different these days. And it would only be for a few days each month, after all. Yes. Simon would help out, surely. That was one problem sorted.

But the dogs? What would I do with the dogs? And the chickens? Well, actually the dogs could go and stay with the lovely dog sitter who lives nearby. I suspected them of loving her more than me, since she feeds them quantities of ham and spoils them rotten, and she's usually happy to feed the chickens when I'm away too, and the chickens won't even notice I've gone as long as they're fed, because they hate me. And if Simon happened to be away at the same time as me, maybe she could just feed Peter when she came to feed the chickens? As long as he had a decent

Wi-Fi connection and some pizza slung at him regularly, would he even notice I wasn't there? But no, I told myself firmly, that's clearly not responsible.

I texted Simon and asked him to meet me for a drink after work.

He'd already got us some drinks when I got to the pub.

'How was your day?' he asked. 'You had your meeting today about redundancies, didn't you? You look pretty happy, so I assume you're not now unemployed and going to have to earn a living as a cam girl or something!'

'What? What's a cam girl?'

'Live sex shows over the internet.'

'No! And how do you even know about that? Do you watch them?'

'No, of course not, but you've led a very sheltered life. There was an article about them in the *Guardian*.'

'Well, at least you've stopped reading the *Daily Mail*. Why would you assume that that would be the only avenue open to me if I'd been made redundant anyway?'

'Sorry. I was just trying to make a joke. Bad taste, you're right.'

'Anyway, I do need to talk to you about my job. I've been offered a promotion. A *fabulous* job, actually. More money. Doing really interesting stuff.'

'That's wonderful, Ellen, I'm thrilled for you. Congratulations!' he interrupted.

'Yes, it's wonderful, but there'll be a lot of travelling. I'll probably be away from home for a week, maybe even two weeks a month.'

'Wow, I mean that'll be hard work, but you'll get used to it, I'm sure. You should go for it, if that's what you want. Well done!'

'You're forgetting one small problem in all this, if I'm away from home for a minimum of a week a month,' I pointed out.

'What?' said Simon in puzzlement.

'Peter. Your son.'

'Oh. Yes. Oh dear. No, well, obviously you can't just leave him, can you?'

'No,' I said expectantly. Come on, Simon, don't let me down.

'Shame this didn't happen in a couple of years, when he was old enough to go to university or something,' said Simon, shaking his head sorrowfully. 'Life and timing never seem to quite match up, do they?'

'No,' I said grimly. How was it not even occurring to him what the solution was? Even if he refused to take Peter, how could he not even *think* it might be an option for us, rather than just sitting there and commiserating with me, without it so much as crossing his mind that Peter could come and live with him while I was away? I was seething.

'Oh, look,' he said brightly, 'we've finished our drinks. I'll get another round. Same again?' And before I could say anything else like, 'Why won't you actually just look after your own son, you useless fucking cockgoblin?' he'd jumped up and gone to the bar. Tosser. If he couldn't even see the answer staring him in the face, there was no way he was going to agree to help me. Help me? Actually, it wasn't 'helping' me, it was taking equal responsibility for HIS child. Not 'helping', like he was doing me a favour. Calling it 'helping me' was like the fathers who call looking after their own children by themselves for an hour 'babysitting'.

And if he was going to be an arsehole, then I wasn't going to humiliate myself begging him to actually be a decent human being for once in his life. Simon always does this. He gives and he takes. You think he's being a good person, he does something nice, and then in the next breath he turns around and shits on you from a great height. All the getting on so well, friendship and companionship, and, dare I say it, actually quite fancying him in an illicit sort of way, of the last few months were entirely cancelled out by tonight's complete tone deafness. I was gathering up my coat and bag, ready to make my excuses and leave, declining a second drink, when he returned to the table clutching a large glass of wine and a beer.

'God, I'm a fucking idiot!' he said, sitting down.

I stared at him coldly. He'd get no disputing that. I couldn't be bothered hearing his amusing tale of how he'd ordered me the wrong thing, or some other tedious tale of his banter with the barman.

'I need to go,' I said.

'No, don't. Wait, I need to talk to you. Like I said, I'm a fucking idiot. I was standing at the bar, thinking what a shame you couldn't take that job, and then I thought, Simon Russell, you WANKER, why can't Peter just come and live with you while Ellen's away? Assuming that's OK with you, and Peter agrees to it, of course,' he added.

'Really?' I said.

'He has two parents. There's no reason why not. Well, except I'll need to have Domino's on speed dial and probably keep a plumber on a retainer to come in once a month and unblock everything after Peter's, you know, exceptional deposits. But this is your opportunity, you should take it. If Peter's OK with it, obviously. We should probably ask him first.'

'Yes, probably,' I said faintly, unable to believe what had just happened.

'It'll take a bit of juggling between us, and working out schedules in advance, but I don't see why with a bit of organisation we couldn't make it happen. Like you always say, it's all about the Six Ps – Proper Planning Prevents Piss Poor Performance. Anyway, you don't have to rush off *just* yet, do you? Finish your drink, at least? We're celebrating after all! And it's your round, now you're going to be super-high-powered and Busy and Important!'

'Maybe,' I said. 'Peter hasn't agreed yet, remember?'

'I'm sure he will,' said Simon cheerfully. 'I've got fibre-optic broadband and a Deliveroo subscription, and you don't.'

SEPTEMBER

Saturday, 7 September

Well, here we are in Edinburgh with Jane. The last couple of weeks have been fraught, to say the least, between everything at work that needed sorting before I started my new role, getting Jane finalised with somewhere to live in Edinburgh, and buying her the vast quantities of stuff she needed to survive, since she's got a place in a student flat, not in halls, which meant many trips to Home Bargains and Ikea for crockery and cutlery and pots and pans and bedding and towels and cleaning products and laundry powder.

There were several unfortunate scenes between Jane and me on these shopping expeditions, including my attempts to buy her a soup maker ('Just think how handy it will be to simply whizz up a nice nutritious soup, darling,' to which she snarled that students don't eat soup, they eat Pot Noodles), culminating in the row to end all rows in the home department at TK Maxx when I insisted on buying her a giant roasting dish, which I swore would be very useful, and Jane swore she would never need, and I shouted, 'WHAT IF YOU WANT TO ROAST A FUCKING CHICKEN, DARLING?' and she yelled back that she'd never found herself with an overwhelming urge to ROAST A FUCKING CHICKEN in her life, and if the necessity to roast a FUCKING CHICKEN happened at any stage in the next four years, SHE'D BUY A FUCKING ROASTING DISH.

People were looking by this point, clearly not having realised that roast chicken or lack of it could be such an emotive subject, as I howled that she wouldn't NEED to buy a roasting dish because I WAS BUYING THIS ONE IN CASE OF ROAST CHICKEN EMERGENCIES and stormed off to the till with it, while Jane trailed behind me muttering I was ruining her university life before it had even started and she would probably be known forever as Roasting Dish Girl, and I snapped that actually, it would probably make her very popular with her flatmates should they want to ROAST A FUCKING CHICKEN AT ANY POINT. I think maybe we might not have been fighting about roast chicken.

I also insisted on buying several other useful items, such as a collapsible bucket ('Why do I need that?'; 'There might not be a bucket in the flat'; 'So?'; 'Trust me, a student flat needs a bucket'), a lifetime's supply of bleach (I remembered the squalor of the shared-flat days), a mountain of loo roll ('Seriously?'; 'You'll thank me for it') and a bottle of vodka ('Awesome, cheers, Mum!').

Despite the wisdom of my knowledge and experience, Jane insisted she was capable of packing up her room herself, even as I wittered on at her to remember to take pants, plenty of pants, did she want me to get her some more pants, and I surveyed the vast pile of stuff in the hall to go and wondered if I should buy her a kettle and toaster for her room in case her flatmates turned out to be the sort of filthy skanks who boiled their knickers in the kettle to wash them, like a thing I'd seen on Twitter about people doing that in hotel room kettles, which is why I'm never making a cup of tea in a hotel room again, and Jane told me to 'chill'.

Even Peter seemed to think the pile of possessions I was sending Jane away with was excessive, and kindly suggested he could help by eating some of the store cupboard essentials I'd bought her, starting with the giant tin of biscuits ('It will break the ice in the flat and help you make friends!' was met with yet another eye roll from Jane).

Simon had looked aghast when he arrived this morning to pack it all into his car (he has a bigger car than me, and also, as mentioned, he doesn't care for my motorway driving) and saw the mountain of Useful Things.

'Dear God, Ellen!' he said. 'What the fuck is all this?'

'I KNOW!' said Jane. 'I tried to tell her!'

'IT IS USEFUL!' I insisted.

'Seriously, Dad, we can leave a lot of this,' said Jane. 'Like this!' She picked up the giant roasting tray.

'No!' I re-added it to the pile. 'You'll be glad of it for the ROAST FUCKING CHICKEN!'

'What roast fucking chicken?' said Simon in confusion.

'Just pack the car, Simon. If you're a real man, you'll be able to get it all in.'

Of course, such a slur on his manhood was all the encouragement Simon needed, and after twenty minutes of sweating, swearing and darkly muttering, the car was packed. Jane's car was being left behind on account of the exorbitant parking fees in Edinburgh, the dogs were already with the dog sitter (Jane having said a lengthy and tearful goodbye to them, including promises to FaceTime them every week), Peter had set off to get the bus to Sam and Colin's, where he was staying while we took Jane to Edinburgh, and we were ready to go.

'Wait!' wailed Jane. 'I haven't said goodbye to the chickens!'

'I'll just go for one last wee, "in case", while you're doing that,' I said and belted upstairs while Simon sat in the car and huffed.

'Don't you DARE even think about tooting or revving!' I yelled over my shoulder at him.

Upstairs, I popped to the loo, and then stopped on the landing (there's still a faint smell of Sudocrem, post-Edward's visit). Jane's bedroom door was ajar. Jane's door is never open – it's always firmly shut and entry is only grudgingly permitted. I pushed open the door and stepped inside. It was bare. The posters were gone, the clutter of make-up on every surface removed, the piles of clothes over the end of the bed and on the floor vanished. I felt like I'd been winded. I'd been so busy trying to get everything sorted for her, to keep going, obsessing over soup makers and fucking roast chicken, that it hadn't really sunk in until now, looking at her bare and empty bedroom, that she was really going, my baby girl really was grown up and leaving me. I sat down on the bed, looked around the little room and sniffed. Strange. The absence of so much utter crap was the thing that had finally brought it home to me. I wiped my eyes. I was going to miss her so much.

The front door crashed open.

'Mum!' yelled Jane up the stairs. 'Are you having a poo? Dad says we need to go, if we're going to miss the traffic. COME ON!' She then thundered up the stairs.

'Mum? What are you doing in here?'

I sniffed and wiped my eyes again, and tried to pretend I wasn't crying, I didn't want Jane to feel bad about going away.

Jane sat down beside me on the bed, and put her arm around me.

'I'll be OK, Mum,' she said gently. 'Try not to worry. You always taught me the first rule of life was that I was to take no shit off anyone, remember?'

'I don't think I put it quite like that.'

'It's what you meant, though. And I don't. We'll all be OK, yeah?'

I gave her a huge hug. 'I love you, darling,' I quavered. 'I'm so proud of you!'

'OK, Mum, I love you too. But can we go so we get there before the others in the flat nab the best rooms and shit, please?'

We went downstairs together, where Simon was standing in the hall (which looked remarkably big without the giant roasting tin and all the bog roll).

'Where have you been?' he complained, huffing out to the car, as I flung sunglasses, tissues, keys and other essentials into my handbag.

He was revving the engine when we went out. 'Bastard,' I hissed.

Several hours later we were in Edinburgh. Simon and I hadn't been back to Edinburgh since we graduated many, many moons ago. Since those days the road layout had changed somewhat, due to a complicated new one-way system, but Simon was insistent that he knew the way, and did not need Google Maps. After we ended up on the bypass for the third time, he reluctantly conceded that he did indeed need Google Maps, while Jane became increasingly agitated in the back, lest all the good rooms be bagsied and all the hot boys taken already (I mean, she didn't actually say that, but that had been Hannah and my fears on the long, slow journey all those years ago. Jane has already been WhatsApping with her flatmates and most of her course – not for them the fear of the unknown, but maybe it's worse if you already know who the hot boys are and fear them being snapped up before you get there).

We finally found the flat and picked up the keys. As far as the eye could see, there were seas of stressed-looking parents unloading overladen cars around offspring taking selfies for Instagram. Jane was no exception, as Simon bellowed, 'For fuck's sake, Jane, what's in this? I think I've given myself a hernia!' as he attempted to hump a huge suitcase up the steps.

'Books,' said Jane innocently. 'Like, could you move, Dad, I'm trying to get Arthur's Seat in the background?'

Eventually it was all in. Jane was the second to arrive, and I hustled her, ninja-style, to the kitchen, to nab the best cupboards, while she protested. The first arrival had obviously had the same idea, as the biggest and most convenient cupboard was already filled with dishes and boxes labelled as belonging to someone called Chloe. Chloe had also labelled the outside of her cupboard, lest there be any confusion that it was Chloe's cupboard. I decided I did not like Chloe, but two could play at that game – I also had a large pack of labels and a Sharpie, and I wrote JANE in big letters for the second-best cupboard. Chloe had omitted to score a drawer, though, so FUCK YOU, CHLOE, I chortled to myself, while Jane took more selfies and Simon panted in the corner, attempting to recover from the exertion.

'NO!' yelped Jane, as I shoved the giant roasting dish in the cupboard.

'YES!' I insisted. 'YES, it's in! Ha! Now, put loo cleaner and bleach in the bathrooms, Jane, and I'll put the bucket under the sink. Remember where it is in emergencies.'

'Muuuum! Enough!' whimpered Jane, as another girl and her parents came into the kitchen also bearing vast quantities of boxes to find homes for.

'Hello!' I beamed. 'I'm Ellen, this is Jane, this is Jane's father, Simon.'

'Hi! I'm Carole, and this is Rachel, and my husband Tony,' said the other lady. 'Isn't this nice? Oh no, Rachel, I never thought to bring labels for cupboards and things.'

'Oh, I have plenty!' I said helpfully. 'Here, take what you need.'

'Thank you,' said Carole. 'Isn't everyone nice, Rachel? I think you're all going to get along *splendidly*.'

Rachel and Jane both looked like they wanted to die, there and then.

'Right!' said Jane, taking matters into her own hands. 'Not room for everyone in here, is there, Mum? Why don't you and Dad go and check into your hotel while I get unpacked, and I'll text you later when I know what's happening?'

'But we were going to take you for dinner,' I said. 'We've booked a table.'

'Oooh, can you suggest anywhere nice?' said Carole. 'We were going to take Rachel out too, but we don't know Edinburgh at all!'

'Oh yes!' I began, while Rachel said, 'MUM! Just use TripAdvisor like a normal person. Why do you have to be so embarrassing?' and Jane bodily propelled me out of the kitchen and towards the front door. A fourth girl and her parents were just coming in, as Jane shoved me through unceremoniously, hissing that she'd text me later. I took some small revenge by crying, 'Bye, bye, sweetie darling, Mummy loves you lots and lots!' which resulted in her giving me the finger as we went down the stairs.

'Well,' said Simon. 'What shall we do now? We could drop our bags at the hotel and go for a quick drink in the Pear Tree, for old time's sake?'

'We could,' I said. 'Yes, maybe that would be nice,' though I did wonder at the wisdom of going for a drink with Simon in the pub where we'd first met. Would it stir up old feelings, old hurts and grudges that were better left undisturbed?

In the event, it did none of those things, because going to the Pear Tree on the first Saturday of Fresher's Week was one of the most spectacularly stupid ideas we'd ever had. We peered through the gate of the courtyard into the packed and seething mass of humanity within, and turned as one and fled. Simon hailed a taxi.

'Come on,' he said. 'That was an awful plan. Rather than trying to relive our lost youth, we should embrace the fact that we're grown-ups and can afford rather better than pishy cider and warm vodka and Coke while being jostled by overexcited freshers. Cocktails at the Balmoral it is!'

That was a far more civilised idea. Over ice-cold vodka martinis (without olives, obviously, for I was not that grown up yet), I confessed to Simon that although I was terribly worried about Jane leaving home, I was also rather envious of her.

'All that potential,' I sighed. 'Her whole life ahead of her, the opportunity to do anything, be anything. All those friends she's going to meet, all the fun she's going to have! It's true what they say, youth is wasted on the young. They don't appreciate what they have.'

'All the hangovers she's going to have, all the worries over exams and boys and finding a job. Honestly, hand on heart, would you rather be sitting here over cocktails, or getting your toes trodden on and chatted up by unsuitable boys in the Pear Tree right now?'

'You were the last unsuitable boy to chat me up in the Pear Tree, actually,' I pointed out.

'I was, wasn't I?'

'Yes, and look how that ended up.'

'It wasn't that bad, was it?'

'Mmmmm. Maybe I *should* go back there, see if I can get myself another husband!'

'Or maybe we should have another martini here.'

'Well, they're nice. And it's nice to be able to afford to come somewhere so nice. We never could back then, could we? Though I did come here once, remember?'

'Did you? When?'

'I must have told you about it?'

'No, I don't recall.'

'Really? It was literally the worst date I'd even been on. How did I not tell you?'

'I don't know, but I'm intrigued now!'

'Well, it started with going out on the lash with Sadie.'

'Sadie with the big tits that fancied me?'

'Yes, only they weren't that big, and she didn't fancy you that much. Anyway, we met these two German guys in a bar. Maybe that's why I never told you. It doesn't sound good, does it? Well, Sadie got totally trolleyed and the German chaps helped me take her home. They were very chivalrous and kind, so I gave one of them my number when he asked. He rang me the next day and asked me to meet him for a drink here in the Balmoral. From what I could recall of him, I didn't much fancy him, but I did quite fancy a drink at the Balmoral. Yeah, this story is sounding worse now I'm saying it out loud. I'm starting to see why I didn't tell you!'

'Well, you've started, so you have to finish now.'

'OK, so I met him, and he hustled me into that little bar by the door and bought me an EYEWATERINGLY expensive vodka and tonic, and told me I had to wait there until they finished dinner and vanished. I'd no idea what was going on, who was having dinner or why I had to wait, but it was a *very* expensive vodka and tonic, so I thought I'd better drink it. He came back and took me through to the *ballroom*, whereupon it turned out he was a German teacher at one of the big private schools in Edinburgh, and this was their summer ball and I *was his date for it*! It was utterly mortifying!'

'What did you do?'

'I didn't know what to do. I mean, I didn't want to be *rude*, but I didn't want to be at a bloody school dance either! I did what was my solution to most awkward situations in those days.'

'Started talking about how otters have opposable thumbs?'

'No, I didn't know that then. No, I tried to have a fag. And of course he got terribly agitated, because no one was allowed to smoke in front of the fucking *children* at the sodding *school dance*, and said I'd have to go through to the little lobby bit outside the ballroom. So I did, and then I just kept walking, faster and faster, until I was out the hotel and *running* down Waverley Steps, IN HEELS, and luckily, of course, in those days the taxis were in the station so I just flung myself into one and shouted "DRIVE!" I'd been expecting to feel a hand on my shoulder at any moment, demanding to know where I was going and dragging me back to the school dance on pain of double detention and five hundred lines of "I must not run away from German teachers who take me unwittingly to school dances!"'

Simon was doubled up laughing. 'Oh God, I can just see you,' he snorted, 'hurtling down the steps like the devil was on your heels. I wish I'd seen your face when you realised you were the teacher's date for the school dance!'

'It wasn't funny!' I said sternly.

'It's quite funny,' insisted Simon, waving at the lovely barman for more cocktails.

'Well, maybe a bit funny,' I admitted.

'What do you think he said, when he found you were missing and people asked where his date was?'

'Do you know, isn't that terrible? I've never even thought about that, poor chap. On the other hand, he did get me there under false pretences, so bugger him, actually. Oh God, maybe it's not so bad not being young again. I think we only remember the good bits and not the shit bits, like my flatmate who used half-eaten Chinese takeaway cartons as ashtrays, or the time we found a mouldy sausage under a table. Maybe I should just be glad I'm a mature, responsible adult!' I said, spilling half my third martini down my chin and into my cleavage as I missed my mouth. 'Ooops!'

My phone pinged with a text from Jane.

Mum, everyone going on a pub crawl tonight, do you mind if I go too, instead of coming for dinner with you and dad? I'll see you tomorrow before you go x

Crafty little witch. The 'do you mind' was obviously a rhetorical question, as she had no intention of coming for dinner, and the 'x' on the end was clearly only put there to mollify me about the fact we were being royally binned off in favour of dubious shots in dive bars.

'Oh God, Simon,' I said. 'I'm sure that isn't a good idea, though. I remember those pub crawls. Hannah and Sadie and I got roped into leading one once. We tried to teach them the words to that "Do You Fuck on First Dates?" song, and when they proved resistant to learning, we got bored with them and abandoned them in some dank pit of a pub on the Cowgate. I'm sure we oughtn't to let her go, it probably isn't *safe*!'

'Ellen, we're going home tomorrow. If you don't let her go

tonight, she'll just go on one tomorrow night. And she'll resent you for spoiling her fun. You need to start taking a step back. I'm going to stop making restaurant reservations for my children, since they invariably seem to have a better offer than a meal with me.'

'Where did you book anyway?'

'Chez Jules,' said Simon, naming an eccentric little French bistro that did the best steaks in Edinburgh for a ridiculous low price, which had been our restaurant of choice more than twenty-five years ago, on the rare occasions that we felt flush enough to go out for a proper sit-down meal. In fact, it was the very first place Simon had ever taken me out for dinner.

'Really? Is it still going?'

'Yep. Looks exactly the same too. Even the menu hasn't changed. Thought we could introduce Jane to it. Sort of like a family tradition.'

'Oh. What if it's shit now?'

'Well, we'll soon find out, won't we? Do you want to go back and change before dinner?'

'I probably should, if only to wash the martini out of my cleavage and sober up a bit. I seem to be a tiny bit sloshed.'

'That mightn't be a terrible idea,' Simon agreed.

Slightly later, slightly soberer (I'd contemplated a cup of tea at the hotel to sober me up, but remembered no, lest there had ever been a Kettle Pants Incident in the room), we walked through the town to the restaurant. There were already several raucous Freshers' Week pub crawls in progress that we passed, though fortunately not the one Jane was on, or she would never have forgiven us for being so mortifying as to exist in public within 500 yards of her.

'God, I'd forgotten how beautiful Edinburgh is,' I sighed, looking up at the castle. 'Sometimes it felt like a dream, when we were living here, it was so heart-stoppingly glorious on a nice day.'

'Mmm,' said Simon. 'Except for Princes Street. It's a bit shit.'

I sighed. He never had been one for poetical outpourings, and just looked like he wanted his dinner.

'Oh, come on then, Grumpy,' I said, 'before you get hangry.'

Chez Jules had not changed at all. The staff were still French, eccentric and rather bad-tempered. It was still dark and lit by candles in wax-encrusted bottles, and was just saved from being actually dingy by a certain amount of Gallic charm.

'Oh, my goodness!' I said. 'It's just like I remember it. I feel about twenty-two again!'

'Do you?' said Simon with a smile. 'What do you want to drink?'

'Oh God, are we actually going to order off the wine list, instead of just getting the house red? I don't even know how that works. We never did that.'

'Same as any other wine list, Ellen. You've been to restaurants before, you know the drill.'

'I know, but it doesn't seem right. Not here. Just get a bottle of the house red.'

'Fine. What about a starter?'

'What? A *starter*? What mad extravagance is this?'

'Adulthood, darling. Adulthood. Every time you feel envious of Jane's freedom and life potential, remember you have the ability to read further than the first line of a wine list, and to order multiple courses.'

'It's scant consolation for saggy tits and the fact that soon I'll have whiskers,' I sighed.

'You'd still be beautiful, even with whiskers.'

'Shut up!' I said.

'It's true,' said Simon earnestly. 'Whiskers would make you a very hot bearded lady. You could probably make a fortune if you joined the circus.'

'Wanker.'

'God, this even tastes just like it used to,' I mumbled later through a mouthful of dauphinoise potatoes. 'Shall we getta nuther bottle?'

After dinner, rather drunk, we stumbled out of the restaurant.

'What do you want to do now?' I slurred.

'I know!' said Simon. 'We should go an' climb Arthur's Seat in the dark. Freshers' Week tradition!'

'Only we aren't freshers, and we're quite pissed,' I pointed out. 'And it's *miles* away. And think how embarrassing it'll be if we get stuck or fall and break our leg and the mountain rescue has to be called and it'll be on the news – "Sad old fuckers balls up trying to recapture lost youth". Jane would *never* forgive us!'

'Oh, come on,' said Simon. 'Where's your sense of adventure? We'll get a taxi to Holyrood Park, then we can walk from there. You said you felt twenty-two again earlier, let's just do it!'

We got into a taxi, me continuing to protest that this was a terrible idea, and tottered out at a side gate into the park – fortunately they still don't lock them.

'Simon, I'm not sure about this,' I insisted, as he turned on the torch on his phone and said, 'Come *on*, Ellen!'

We wandered around the park for quite a while, Arthur's Seat looming above us all the while, pin-pricks of light from other, more intrepid explorers' torches winding their way up the hill, before we admitted defeat and conceded we couldn't find the start of the path. My shoes hurt, and I was starting to sober up.

'Enough!' I protested, pulling my shoes off and throwing myself down on the grass. 'I'm not twenty-two. Have mercy!'

Simon sat down beside me.

'It was fun, though, wasn't it?'

'Yes. It was. I do feel a bit less middle-aged. But also, I'm starting to feel dangerously sober!'

'Oh, well, I can help with that,' said Simon, reaching into his coat and pulling out a bottle of red from the inside pocket.

'Where did you get that?' I said in astonishment.

'The restaurant. I ordered it while you were in the loo, and got them to open it and shove the cork back in. I thought it would be a nice surprise when we got to the top, but we might as well have it now. Lucky it didn't leak, actually,' he said, proffering it to me.

'God, drinking wine straight out the bottle!' I said, taking a swig. 'Now we really are trying to relive our lost youth.' I shivered as I handed the bottle back. 'I'd forgotten how cold Edinburgh is, now we've stopped walking!'

Simon shrugged his coat off and wrapped it round me.

'You can't do that, you'll freeze!' I protested.

'I'm fine,' he insisted. 'You never did wear enough warm, sensible clothes. A nice fleece, that's what you need.'

'Don't start. And give me another drink.'

I shivered again. Simon put his arm round me. It was rather pleasant, actually, and I huddled into him for warmth. We sat for a few minutes, sharing the wine and looking at the stars.

'Ellen?' he said.

'Mmm?'

'This is nice, isn't it?'

'Mmmm.'

'Are you still awake?'

'Mmmhmmm.'

'Ellen, I love you.'

Well, that jolted me out of the pleasant stupor I was slipping into!

'Simon, don't. Don't spoil it.'

'No, please. Hear me out. There's never been anyone but you. There never will be. I've been stupid, I've been so stupid, and I've been an arsehole and I don't deserve you, and I probably never did. I mean stop me anytime, if you want to tell me I'm wrong?'

'No, you're quite right, for once,' I said.

'Fair enough, I do deserve that. I love you so much, I always have. Oh God, I thought if I ever said any of this to you, I'd have this whole impassioned, coherent speech for you, but I'm just rambling. Ellen, I knew there would never be anyone else when I first saw you when I came back from France, after all those months not seeing you, but I didn't think I'd have any chance with you, so I thought I might as well give it a go with Marissa. And then, that day I saw you in your wedding dress, I knew there was no point in it with her. All I could think about was you. How beautiful you looked the day we got married. How much *future* we had ahead of us. Just now, talking about how we felt at twenty-two again. God, we were so happy then. And even when we were married, when things were bad, they were never *that* bad, because I was with you. And then, then I fucked it all up, because I'm an arrogant, thoughtless, stupid *prick.*'

'You really are right about a lot of things tonight,' I put in.

'*You* were right, though. When you said I didn't help enough with the children, with the house, with childcare, when you said I put my career ahead of you and our family, when you said I was selfish.'

'I *think* I said you were a selfish, self-centred, spoilt, pigwanking cockgoblin, actually,' I supplied helpfully.

'Yes, you did, and yes I was. And you were right to call me all those things. And I lost you for being like that, and I haven't been happy – not really happy deep down inside – since you threw me out. Not until the last few months. We've been spending so much time together, we've been getting on so well, I feel like a big lump of misery inside me starts thawing when I'm with you.'

'Like in *The Snow Queen*?'

'What? Isn't that that incredibly warped children's story where a little girl freezes to death in a doorway?'

'No, that's *The Little Match Girl*. In *The Snow Queen* – oh, never mind! Go on.'

'Everything feels better when I'm with you. And you … maybe I'm imagining it, but you've seemed happier too, these last few months. I … we've been talking more than we have in years. About all sorts of stuff. And all the talk of being twenty-two again, I just … I thought maybe I should seize the day. Like I did then. Tell you I love you, only without a pigeon.'

'Thank fuck.'

'And just … see if maybe we could try again? You and me?'

'But, Simon, we're *not* twenty-two. We never will be again. And I'm not that person you fell in love with back then, and I'm not that person you were married to either. We can't go back. And … and I don't actually know *who* I am anymore, that's something I'm trying to find out.'

'I *know*,' he said. 'I know that. But … I'm not that person either. I've changed too. You've become stronger. You were always so strong, but now you can cope with almost anything by yourself. Except maybe pigeons. And I … I know what matters now. And that's you. Supporting you. Being with you. And our children. I don't want us to go back. I want us to go forward. Find out who we are now. Together.'

I was, to be frank, quite discombobulated. I hadn't been expecting this, yet at the same time, hearing him admit all his faults, all the things he'd got wrong, was very cathartic. And the last few months with him *had* been good. He'd become someone I felt I could turn to again. Someone I could rely on. Someone I liked spending time with, and yes, someone I fancied. But did I want *this*? To go back to him? Would it be going back to square one again, and we'd just find ourselves facing all the same problems, all the same arguments? I said this to him (minus the fancying bit, obviously, he didn't need to know that).

'But those were those people's problems,' he said. 'We've both just said, we're different people now. I'm not saying there won't be problems, I'm not saying we won't have arguments. But things will be different. They'll be better. *I'll* make them better. I know now, relationships have to be worked at. They don't just magically float along, everything in the garden rosy; they take work, *hard* work. I think twenty-two-year-old me thought you just say "I love you" and that's that, happy ever after. But that's only the start, and it's the little things – taking the bins out before being asked, for example.'

'What a romantic example to pick!' I said dryly. 'And you've never once taken the bins out without being asked.'

'That's what I'm saying! I *will*. I'll be less of a dick, I'll do my fair share, I'll notice when you're tired and bring you tea or wine or gin, I'll record your favourite programme if you're out.'

'I don't think that's a thing now, with on-demand TV.'

'I'LL BRING YOU ANOTHER FUCKING PIGEON IF THAT'S WHAT IT TAKES!'

'No, please don't. I'm all good for pigeons!'

'Ellen, I'll write poetry and get an albatross to *shower* you with it!'

'I've seen the standard of poetry your family produces, and if an albatross is circling overhead, I fear one would be showered in something other than poetry. You really aren't very good at romance, are you?'

'No, no, I'm not. But I'm *trying*. I'll let you finish this wine! I'll let you finish every bottle of wine we share for the rest of our lives.'

'Better. I just don't know. It seems such a big step.'

'It's not, though. I'm just … asking you to give it a go. Spend more time together. Maybe as friends at first, but maybe with the thought in mind that we might become more than friends. We don't have to jump into it with both feet if you don't want to; we can take it as slowly as you like. Just give me a chance. Please.'

'I'm not marrying you again,' I warned. 'Whatever happens.'

'Oh. About that. You can't actually, as I never sent the papers back. I just couldn't bring myself to, so technically we're still sort of married.'

'Simon! What about the whole moving to Australia mercy dash scenario I explained to you in such detail?'

'I know. But there will never be anyone I want to marry but you. And if you want to marry someone else, I promise I'll do the mercy dashing and save you the trouble.'

'I can't believe you haven't signed them.'

'I mean, I can, if you want? If that's what it takes? If I divorce you, will you be my girlfriend?'

'Well, maybe just leave it for now with the divorce.'

'Does … does that mean that you'll give it a go?'

'I … well …' I knew I should be sensible. I knew this was probably a bad idea. I knew at the very least, I should say nothing more than that I would think about it. I thought about how I definitely didn't *need* Simon in my life, or any man for that matter. I was *fine* without a man, but I thought about life with a Simon-shaped hole in it, and it wasn't a thought that made me happy.

There were a lot of things in my life that technically I didn't *need*, but that it was pleasanter to have than not to have. My Netflix subscription. The SodaStream. All my Jilly Cooper books. No, actually, I did need the Jilly Coopers – they contained a lot of wisdom for life. If you think about it, most things in our lives are not things that we need. They're just things that make life more comfortable, or that we want. And did I *want* Simon? This new, more thoughtful, non-fleece-wearing Simon? I rather thought I might. And just because I *could* manage without a man, was I betraying the sisterhood and giving in to the patriarchy if I wanted one, on my own terms? Surely not. And then, twenty-two-year-old me rose to the surface and I had an 'Oh, fuck it!' moment and threw caution to the winds.

'Sod it. Let's give it a go!'

Simon gave a whoop of joy.

'Really? Oh my God, Ellen! I'm so happy!'

'But now, we should head back to the hotel. It's late, all the wine's finished and the grass is wet and I'm soaked through to my knickers.'

'And you say I'm unromantic,' he said.

'You may buy me a nightcap at the hotel when I've changed into something dry, but nothing more,' I said. 'Single malt, none of your blended nonsense. And you needn't expect there to be any funny business afterwards, either.'

'Whatever you want. I can't believe this is happening, Ellen. God, I love you. I'm going to tell you I love you every single day for the rest of our lives. I'm never taking this for granted again, darling.'

'That might get a bit annoying, actually.'

'All right, what about every second day then?'

'Deal.'

We stood up and started walking back. Simon took my hand in his. It felt very right all of a sudden, like there was nowhere else my hand could possibly be at that moment. Also, my hands were very cold, and his were warm.

DECEMBER

Friday, 13 December

The last three months have flown by, much faster than I ever thought possible. Work has been chaotic, busy and stressful, but ultimately more enjoyable than I ever thought a job could be. I feel stretched and challenged and fulfilled by it all at once, and I'm loving it!

I've been coping rather better with Jane's absence than I thought I would, too. We only had one incident, where she stopped answering my texts and I convinced myself she was dead and stalked her flatmates on Instagram and sent one final text threatening her that I was going to message them and see if she was still alive if she didn't text me back. I got a reply instantly, tersely informing me that she'd been 'busy'. I sent an equally terse text back informing *her* that she was not too busy to text her mother back within twenty-four hours, unless she wanted to suffer social death because I could and I would send her baby photos to her flatmates. The threat (which obviously I wasn't going to carry out) clearly worked, because not only did she reply to texts after that, but she has taken to phoning me about once a week!

The first time she called, I panicked. I snatched up my phone and babbled, 'What's wrong, darling, what is it, what's happened? What do you need, what can I do?'

'Errr, nothing?' said Jane. 'I just, like, thought I'd call you?'

'But why?'

'For, like, a chat?'

'A chat?' I said stupidly. '*You're* calling *me*? On the electric telephone? For a *chat*?'

'Yes. Is that OK?'

'Of course it is, darling, no problem at all, how lovely to hear from you. How are you? Are you eating any fruit and veg?'

She seems happy in Edinburgh, though. Her flatmates all seem nice girls that she gets along with well, she assures me that she occasionally partakes of something nutritious to eat and even went so far as to inform me that she'd made roasted broccoli and why had I never cooked broccoli like that, it was far nicer than how I made broccoli. I was just so relieved to hear that she'd eaten something green, I didn't even take umbrage with her critique of my cooking skills.

It also turns out that Simon and I aren't actually very good at taking things slowly. After a few weeks of Peter going to Simon's when I was away, and Simon spending most of his time at my house when I was at home, Peter sat us both down for a 'A bit of a chat, Mum, because this isn't making any sense.'

Peter pointed out that it seemed ridiculous that he packed up all his stuff, went to stay with Simon for a week and then came home, shortly followed by Simon, who 'I know is staying over, I know what's going on, I'm sixteen and I'm not stupid.' Peter proposed that it would make far more sense if he stayed at home, and Simon came and stayed with him while I was away, reminding me that would also save me having to send the dogs to the dog sitter and pay someone to feed the devil chickens and let them out and shut them up.

'Well, that's fine by me,' said Simon. 'But it's your mother's house, it's really up to her.'

'It would make more sense,' I admitted. 'If you're sure you don't mind, Simon? And you're OK with it, Peter? I'd have thought you'd like being at Dad's flat, with his superfast broadband?'

'Yeah, but it's a pain having to pack up all my computers and then reconnect them all here a week later,' grumbled Peter. 'So if everyone just stayed here while Mum was away, I think that would be much better.'

'And are you OK with the rest of it?' I said awkwardly. 'You know, me and Dad?'

'Why wouldn't I be? Just, you know, I don't want to *hear* anything. And no PDAs, right?'

'OK.'

So that was that. I broached the subject of Simon and me with Jane as well when she rang one night.

'So, darling, the thing is, I'm sort of seeing someone.'

'Is it Dad?'

'Well, yes. How did you guess?'

'Mum, it was pretty obvious that it was on the cards. Also, Peter told me.'

'You talk to Peter?'

'We message sometimes.'

'Oh. So … is that OK?'

'Yeah. Gotta go, I'm meeting some people at 7. Bye, Mum!'

Even Hannah and Sam and Colin were unsurprised. Apparently, the only person who hadn't seen this coming was me! Most remarkably, Sylvia, Simon's mother, rang me to tell me how happy she was, and informed me that Simon was under strict instructions that if he cocked it up again, he'd have his mother to answer to. Since I'd always felt that she thought her darling boy could do no wrong, and any faults in our relationship were entirely my fault, this was very heartening.

And then today, Simon had another proposal. Not an actual down-on-one-knee proposal, obviously. But, he said, it was wasting money, really, paying bills and council tax and insurance on his flat, when he was never there, and maybe we should think about him moving in here properly.

'What about your flat?' I said in a panic. 'What, are you going to sell it? What happens then? Joint mortgage on here? I can't, no, I'm not ready for that, Simon. This is *my* house, I need the security of having my own place still. This is too soon!'

'No!' he said quickly, 'not sell it. Rent it out, though. It's pointless it sitting there just draining money away when I'm pretty much living here. And if I was renting that out, we'd obviously come to some financial arrangement between us about the mortgage here, where I contributed, but as, I don't know, a sort of lodger for now?'

'Cocklodger,' I said, still mildly hysterical.

'Hopefully slightly more than that,' said Simon.

'But you love your flat, it's always been your dream, your perfect white box. Are you sure you want to give that up to move in here, with all my clutter?'

'Well, your dogs and chickens wouldn't exactly fit in my flat, would they? And you love it here. And what makes you happy, makes me happy, so we'll stay here. And also, you have a shed. I've missed having a shed.'

'Oh, I see. You only love me for my shed. Well, if I let you have my shed, you have to promise never to watch *Wheeler* Fucking *Dealers* while I'm in the house.'

'Done.'

'Simon? Do you really mean it about what makes me happy, makes you happy?'

'Yes, of course. Why?'

'Well, I saw this dog …'

'Ellen!'

'No, listen. She's a poor old soul. Another Border Terrier like Judgy. She's fifteen. FIFTEEN, Simon. Poor old girl, she's practically blind and quite deaf, and her owner died and there was no one to take her on. She's in a shelter and she's so lonely and confused, and she needs a home, Simon!'

'But you're away so much!'

'And you work from home a lot more now. Look, Simon!' I brandished my phone at him. 'Look at her little face! She could be here by Christmas, Simon. You couldn't let that poor sweet little thing live out her last years in a shelter, could you? No one else will want her, she's so old. And also I feel very outnumbered if you're moving in properly, with all the maleness between you and Peter and the dogs. I need some female solidarity.'

'You have the chickens for female solidarity.'

I looked at him. He knew where the chickens stood when it came to female solidarity.

'Well, what will Judgy say?' he tried.

'He'll get used to it. He got used to Barry. And Barry won't mind, he loves other dogs. She'll be someone else for him to look after.'

'This isn't actually a discussion, is it? You're merely presenting me with a fait accompli under the guise of pretending to discuss it with me.'

'Yes. But the alternative is I'll cry all over Christmas at the thought of the poor pupper ALL ALONE in the shelter. Is that what you want?'

'No,' Simon sighed.

'And you did say whatever made me happy?'

'Yes, but we were talking about me moving in properly and letting my flat out, and now suddenly we're onto getting another dog!'

'Well, I did warn you that was my plan for old age, and you said you were fine with it!'

'Yes, but I didn't think you'd be starting to execute it *quite* so soon. I think we need to discuss it a little more. Anyway, about the flat. Is that settled then? I'll rent it out, and move in here?'

'Yes, fine, and I'm picking Flora up tomorrow.'

'Flora?'

'The poor old dog. *My* poor old dog.'

'Flora? Why do your dogs have such undoggy names? And it's all arranged, is it? Nothing more to discuss?'

'No, not really. And Flora's a fine name for a dog. It suits her. Look, she looks like a Flora. Are you going to come with me to get her?'

'Oh fine. Fine!'

'You'll love her once she's here.'

Later, I met Hannah for a long overdue #FIAF catch up. Hannah's so much better than she was a few months ago. Edward's in nursery now, and Charlie, who'd assumed since Hannah had never said she wasn't coping, that she was fine, was appalled by how much she was struggling and insisted on getting a cleaner two days a week so Hannah could have some time to herself, and although he still works long hours, when he's at home he really pulls his weight with Edward. And Hannah, who isn't very good at doing nothing, decided that the best use of that time would be to go back to university, so she's a mature student now, doing a maths course of all things, and absolutely loving it.

We finished the second bottle.

'Fuck, I'm sloshed,' slurred Hannah. 'Less do shots!'

'Iss not a good idea!' I mumbled. 'Shots iss alwaysh BAD idea!'

'Noooooo!' giggled Hannah. 'I'm a shtudent! S'practically the law I do shots! TWO TEQUILAS! I luffs shots!'

It was so nice to have Hannah back to herself again that I thought it would be worth whatever hangover the shots brought tomorrow, so we had more shots to celebrate doing shots.

Saturday, 21 December

Jane is home. Flora is here and settling in, and as I predicted, Simon adores her. In fact, Simon has claimed her as *his* dog, and got quite angry with me when poor Flora had a little accident because I'd shut her in the sitting room by mistake, and she couldn't find her way out and got stressed. I couldn't even be annoyed with him for being arsey with me, because it was so amusing to see him so besotted with Flora, just like I told him he would be.

I'd been so excited about Jane coming home, having my family together again and us all being under one roof for the first time in a long time (well, the first time in forever for us with Flora as part of the family). Not only would we all be together, but it was Christmas, so there would also be the Festive Magic and Cheer thrown into the mix to complete the joy.

Things started well when I picked up a clearly very hungover Jane from the train station, complete with giant bags of laundry.

We arrived home, and Judgy and Barry were ecstatic with joy to see her again. Barry was so very ecstatic he peed on the Christmas tree in his excitement and Simon shouted at him, and I yelled at him not to yell at my dog, and he said he wouldn't shout at my dog if he didn't piss everywhere, and I pointed out he hadn't got cross with Flora when SHE weed in the sitting room, and then he shouted that that was MY fault for shutting her in there, and don't bring HIS good dog into it.

'Ah,' said Jane. 'It's nice to be home, parentals. I see nothing has changed!'

We both looked slightly sheepish.

'It wasn't Flora's fault,' said Simon mutinously, scooping her up, as she was nonplussed by the arrival of Jane and all the barking and shouting. 'She's a very good girl, aren't you, darling?'

'It wasn't Barry's fault either,' I said hotly. 'He just gets over-excited, and he's always confused by the Christmas tree!'

Judgy sneezed in furious indignation because no one was paying him any attention at all.

'Like, just chill, parentals? You really need to discuss things like adults and not shout, you know. I've been doing a psychology module, actually. You two would make a fascinating case study.'

'No,' we said instantly, together. 'You're not analysing US, Jane!'

'OK, parentals. I'm just trying to help.'

'Are you going to call us "parentals" all the time you're here?'

'Why?'

'It's quite annoying.'

'Well, what do you want me to call you?'

'Maybe just Mum and Dad, like usual.'

'Interesting,' mused Jane, making a note on her phone. 'Very interesting. The parental unit wants to be seen as individuals and does not want to be treated as a cohesive whole. Hmmmm.'

'Jane!'

'WHAT?'

'Don't you dare use us for your psychology module.'

'Oh chill, Mother. It's only an extra module for one term. But I could definitely give you and Dad some helpful tips on how to communicate more effectively?'

'I don't need tips, thank you, I can communicate with your mother just fine!' said Simon. 'Can't we, Flora darling? Yes, we can! We CAN, bestest girl, can't we?'

Flora snuggled in closer.

'I think she's cold, Ellen. We should get her a little jumper for in the house, and a nice warm coat for when she goes out,' he said anxiously.

Jane looked at Simon. 'I'm not sure your attachment to that dog is entirely healthy,' she announced.

'Don't be silly, Jane,' I said crossly. 'There's nothing at all wrong with a man who loves a dog as much as that!'

Despite her helpful offer of advice for Simon and me, clearly Jane needed to work on her own communications skills, because five minutes later she'd managed to fight with Peter and he'd told her to 'Die in a hole,' which was just the atmosphere I needed for the Festive Magic.

By the time we got to my carefully planned 'Welcome Home, Jane, and Isn't It All Lovely That We Are All Here Together Dinner', no one was speaking to each other. I'd had enough, as Jane wailed that Peter was taking all the gravy and it wasn't fair, and Peter yelled that he had more right to the gravy than her because he lived here all the time, and Simon bellowed that they could both shut up about gravy, this was ridiculous, and that they were scaring Flora (who was sitting happily on Simon's knee, eating his beef, because 'The other two push her out the way and she never gets her share of the treats otherwise, Ellen').

I banged my knife and fork down on the table and roared, 'ENOUGH! ENOUGH! We're all here, we're supposed to be having a lovely meal together, and you're all being arseholes, and you're upsetting ALL the dogs, and just for ONE NIGHT you can all stop it and GET ALONG, or if you can't say anything nice, DON'T SAY ANYTHING AT ALL!'

Everyone looked sheepish.

'Sorry, Mum,' mumbled the children.

'Your mother's right!' said Simon. 'We should listen to her.'

'I almost always am,' I reminded them. 'It's just usually none of you will admit it!'

'Well, I mean, there was that time that you –'

'And you weren't right when you said –'

'You were wrong about –'

'SHUT UP! I'm right, and that's all that matters!'

'Yes, darling,' said Simon.

'All right, Mum,' said Peter.

'Just, like, chill, Mum?' said Jane.

I poured another glass of wine.

ACKNOWLEDGEMENTS

As ever, there are no words to express what a massive team effort creating this book has been – there are so many people who deserve a huge vote of thanks that it would take another book to mention them all.

The wonderful team at HarperCollins all deserve a very special thanks, though. I keep saying this, but it's honestly a privilege to be able to work with such fabulous people – their support, encouragement and help are second to none, and I'm so grateful to all of them. My editor Katya Shipster, in particular, is due a huge thank you, not only for doing a wonderful job as always, but doing so while in lockdown with small children, and keeping me entertained with the tales of their antics, especially The Very Bad Day. Katya, you are a hero, as are so many other women who have worked full-time and home-schooled and kept the wheels on everything this year. Jenny Hutton also deserves a special thanks for all her editorial advice, including the difficult task of stopping me going off on long, rambling tangents, mainly about dogs or, Louisa-style, the Patriarchy. Lucy Brown is one of the best publicists around and an absolute joy to work with, even when she stresses the Very Important Thing I have to mention in a radio interview and then I have to ring her and confess I did not mention the Very Important Thing. She could not be more lovely, so thank you! Thank you too to Hattie Evans and Julie MacBrayne, who are not only fabulous at marketing, but also brilliant laughs. Thank you also to Kate Elton and Oli Malcolm for all your help and support, and of course, as ever, to Oscar.

Claire Ward and Tom Gauld are the utter geniuses behind the cover designs – they get it perfectly spot on every single time and beautifully capture the essence of the book, so thanks a million. I'm always incredibly excited to see your cover designs, because I always love them so much.

Thanks too to Mark Bolland, my patient and long-suffering copy editor, who has to tackle what actually seems to be some sort of addiction I have to using the word 'actually' and ending every sentence with an exclamation mark! Mark also deals with the fact, as did my English teachers long ago, that my spelling and grammar are not nearly as good as I think they are … And hugest, hugest thanks to Tom Dunstan, Alice Gomer and their amazing sales team, who work incredibly hard to get the book on shelves so people can read it. And thank you so much to Marie Goldie and all the team at the warehouse in Glasgow, where they all work so tirelessly getting the books distributed to where they need to be – again, a particularly difficult job this year and one that is very much appreciated. And finally, a massive thank you to Sarah Hammond, who has the task, rather like herding cats, I suspect, of co-ordinating all of us and keeping us on track.

Paul Baker at Headway Talent, my lovely and indulgent agent – thank you very much for putting up with me, and for everything you do for me, and I'm sorry for introducing you to Patrón XO Cafe the night before your children's sports day.

Thank you to everyone who contributed stories of toddler carnage for Edward's rampage, especially to Julia who told me the tale of the pants flushing and to everyone who reminded me of the pure evil that is Sudocrem and carpets. Thank you also to Ross Watson, whom I traumatised with the story of the Little Match Girl, and who then suggested the alternative, more sensible ending.

And to all my friends who kept me sane, provided shoulders to cry on, hugs, Rioja and gin and tea, and who always believe I can do it, even when I don't. I love you all, and there are too many of you to mention, but special thanks to Alison, Eileen, Helen, Katrina, Liz, Mairi and Tanya. And an extra special thanks to Lynn for introducing me to the phrase 'the Fucking Oldness'. Thank you as ever to Linda and Graham for always being there for me, and for everything. And thank you to the Dahlings, past and present. I'm so lucky to have you all in my life.

And finally, my family. Thank you to Buddy and Billy for sitting on me and keeping me warm, despite hot water bottle duties being beneath the dignity of Proud and Noble Border Terriers. To my husband, for making such excellent gin martinis and for putting up with my many and random whims and notions, even though he won't let me get another dog, which is very unfair. Thank you also for letting me borrow your laptop to finish this book after I cunningly hid mine when I was a little tired and emotional after your gin martinis and couldn't find it. And last but not least, my own precious moppets – thank you for being you, for being funny and sarcastic, and for only needing to be asked six times to empty the dishwasher, and for occasionally actually answering my increasingly irate texts.

Now you know Why Mummy's Sloshed...

Discover why she drinks, swears and doesn't give a ****!